THE KILLER OF DEVILS

BOOK 1

CLOWNS

Viktor Bloodstone

FORTRESS PUBLISHING, INC.
WWW.FORTRESSPUBLISHINGINC.COM

This is a work of fiction. All names, characters, places and events are either products of the authors' imaginations, or are used fictitiously. Any resemblance to actual people, events, or locales is purely coincidental.

All rights reserved, including the right to reproduce this book, or portions thereof, except in the case of brief quotations embodied in critical articles or reviews.

The Killer of Devils, Book1: Clowns
© 2023 Fortress Publishing, Inc.
ISBN: 978-1-959797-01-2

Edited by: Catherine Jordan

Cover by: Dave Nestler

This book is available for wholesale through the publisher, Fortress Publishing, Inc.

PUBLISHED BY:
Fortress Publishing, Inc.
1200 Market Street
Unit 17 / Box 137
Lemoyne, PA 17043

WWW.FORTRESSPUBLISHINGINC.COM

May 2, 2002

Bring me blood.

Collin paused. He'd been collecting wood for the campfire, and his arms were full of broken branches. He shook his head at the weird, random thought – bring me blood. The voice didn't sound like his. Did he truly think those words, or had he heard them?

He looked around, listening to the ambient noise from deep in the forest. Tall pines and oaks creaked. Branches snapped. Leaves and acorns dropped. Squirrel nests high up in the branches meant the little critters were scurrying around, and Collin had seen a brown rabbit hopping off in the distance only a few minutes ago. Thankfully, no reports of bears or mountain lions. White-tailed deer roamed around, but what forest in the Northeast didn't have deer?

Plenty of light filtered through the leaves of the dense trees, but the canopy was thick enough to turn twilight into nighttime. And twilight was coming soon. Had the snap of that last branch cued his imagination to run wild in the darkening forest? Could the raspy voice have come from his vivid imagination and nature's sound effects? Taking a quick glance over his shoulder, he grabbed one last easy to reach kindling stick and headed back to camp.

Maybe it was one of his jackass friends messing around and whispering crazy shit, trying to scare him. Definitely something they'd do. He was close to the campsite, after all.

Tromping his way through a patch of ankle-grabbing brush, he heard his wife's laughter. His frown broke into a grin. Dana's distinct laugh started as a rat-a-tat, then ended with a honk-snort. She was aware of its uniqueness and always said her laugh sounded like a clown in a blender. When she really got going, Collin couldn't disagree. But it was *her* laugh, and he loved it.

Not everyone did. Over the years, he had gotten in a few skirmishes with shitheads making disparaging comments about her laugh. A little over six feet tall and supporting enough muscle to win a couple semiprofessional boxing matches, Collin had no issues making those shitheads change their minds and apologize.

Tad, Brin, and Dana were anchoring the tents into the ground while Dean and Sara were digging the firepit. They had selected a spot about two miles from the sanctioned camping sites in a part of the forest with high tree density, and wanted to make sure they had a safe campfire. Nothing could ruin a camping trip faster than being the asshole who burned down the forest.

Collin tossed his branches on the large pile at the edge of the small clearing and joined his wife. Dana dropped her hammer and brushed her hands together, having finished sinking her stake to the ground. Gesturing to her accomplishment, she said, "Hey, handsome. Look what I did."

"Hey, gorgeous. Looks great. And the tent looks nice, too."

A smile and wink, her non-verbal, "Thank you for the compliment."

"How you doing?" Collin asked.

"Good. Still a little nervous, but good."

"Still? I know it's been a while, but we've camped a hundred or so times before."

Dana looked overhead into the darkening sky. "I know, but usually at a camping site, or a cabin. It's been a looooong time since we've camped this deep in the forest. And never in an area clearly marked 'restricted.'"

Collin put his hands on her hips and pulled her close. "Yeah, we haven't hiked like this in a while, since becoming parents. But we already talked about doing more for ourselves. Jacob's seven now. It's time we got back to hiking and camping. It's like riding a bike. Muscle memory will take over."

"It's not that. I'm happy for us, and I love being here with you and our friends. But... I don't like that we ignored the ropes delineating the restricted area."

Collin chuckled. "That was two miles ago. We already checked with the Game Commission about bear and mountain lion activity, and there is none. What else could there be to worry about?"

Dana glared into his eyes. "Terrain pitfalls. Mask-wearing psychos. Stealth bears. Landmines."

They shared a laugh. Collin kissed his wife's forehead as she continued, "I'm being ridiculous, aren't I?"

"Not at all. I mean, I've heard a million stories about this area teeming with landmines."

Dana twisted her mouth into a smirk and punched his shoulder. "Jerk."

Collin took her into his arms again and said, "Don't forget, Brin is an award-winning nature photographer. She hikes literally all the time for her career. She says the government restricts areas because of dumb schmucks who either get lost or make a fucking mess as they go through. No coincidence that she gets her best shots in restricted areas."

"I know, I know. I'm a paranoid mother."

"Nothing wrong with a little paranoia. It keeps us alive."

"Amen to that," Dean said as he strode over, flask in hand. After a swig, he handed it to Collin. He gave Dana a friendly shoulder-slap. "But there's nothing to be paranoid about here."

Collin slugged back a shot and then handed the flask to his wife. "See? Nothing to worry about."

"There better not be," Dana said. She wiped her mouth with the back of her hand after taking a drink. "Or I'm going to be pissed."

Dana went to hand the flask back to Dean, but Collin intercepted it. After another swig, he said, "I'm going to grab one last armload for the fire before it gets too dark. There were a few more good-sized branches. Dead and dry, but not decaying."

"Be safe," Dana said. "And watch out for landmines."

Collin passed the flask to Dean, then gave his wife a lip-smacking kiss. "Always."

His wife's silly clown-laugh followed him, and he smiled as he went on his way with a jaunty clown-tune reserved for circuses stuck in his head.

Their voices faded.

The tree groupings looked familiar, so he was confident he was headed in the right direction. The fallen branches he wanted to collect were just a bit farther ahead and...

He sniffed the air. What was that smell? It was sweet, familiar. But it didn't belong in the forest. His mind struggled with where he knew the scent. Of course – the circus. Or even a carnival. Cotton candy? Yep. That was it. Cotton candy. He stopped and sniffed again, heavily, audibly. Pine trees were known to give off a heady scent, but this was weird. Did they inadvertently camp closer to civilization? Were other people camping nearby? No. He hadn't heard or seen anyone else. And he had personally checked the maps before they set off. Maybe the smell was attached to that smoke.

"Smoke!" Gone for a minute and his friends had set the forest on fire already!

This smoke rolled along the ground, thick and white.

No, not smoke, he realized. Smoke was never this pure white, and it would flow upward on a windless evening. This rolled out in sheets, its purple tips curling like fingers, beckoning him closer. Was it mist? It seemed too thick to be mist and if he remembered the maps correctly, there was no water for a few miles. Did he remember correctly? His mind felt murky, like this mist that enveloped him. His vision blurred. Or did the mist make everything hazy? He couldn't think straight. Why did it smell like cotton candy? And who's this guy who just stepped out from behind a tree? Maybe he would know what's going on, maybe he'd know what to do.

Porcelain white skin, white like the mist. *Am I in the mist?* Cotton candy purple smell, cotton candy purple hair. *Is he in the mist with me?* Big red mouth.

Bring me blood.

"I know that voice." But Collin hadn't recognized his own voice when he spoke. Weird.

Bring me blood.

The Killer of Devils

Of course the man with the talcum powder skin needed blood. Look at those teeth! A man with so many pointed fangs like that needed blood. Blood for those teeth. Blood for that big red mouth. Blood.

Have to find blood and bring it back. Have to find...

"Collin? Collin are you okay?" she asked.

I know her. Dana. Her name's Dana and I'm in some sort of camp site.

"Dude!" Another voice. A Dean-voice. "You're covered in white and purple powder. You look like a clown."

I'm a clown. Dean said that I'm a clown.

"Did you hit your head?" Dana asked. "Let's... let's get you to our tent and I can check you out."

In the tent. Shirt off. With Dana.

"Why are you *covered* in powder? Where the hell were you? What happened? Collin?"

I'm a clown.

"I'm a clown."

"Collin? What are you talking about?"

Knife. Collin had a big hunting knife attached to his belt. No, not on his belt anymore. In between Dana's ribs, in her lung.

Like a deflating balloon, her words squeaked, but Collin didn't understand much of what she said, other than, "Why?"

"Because I'm a clown, and the other clown needs blood."

Chin and lips quivering, she cried. "No... Collin... Why?" Giant tears flowed over paling cheeks. She placed her hands on his face. They felt warm and familiar. But not as warm as the blood flowing over his hand.

He pulled the knife out. She winced in pain, and a look of hope skittered across her face. Collin didn't like that look, so he slid the knife back in, through a different pair of ribs. More tears as she pleaded, "Please... I... love... you..."

He knew the words, but not the meaning, so he stabbed her again. Her legs trembled and she fell to her knees.

"Please..."

He slid the knife under her jaw and up into her head. Then she stopped talking.

"I'm a clown," Collin said. *I'm a clown and I need a smile.*

Collin coated his hands, then wiped her blood over his mouth, outward from each corner of his lips. A smile. A clown's smile.

Sara screamed when Collin exited the tent. So, he made her stop with his knife.

"What the fuck?" Dean yelled.

"No!" Tad yelled, too.

They both roared like lions and charged Collin. He knew them, knew they'd attack him. He was prepared.

Dean got to him first, tackling him around the waist, slamming him to the ground. It hurt, but it didn't stop him from using his knife a third time. In and out of Dean's back, blood arcing through the air like life-giving rainbows splashing onto the dirt. Stab and splash. Stab and splash. Stab and—

Tad grabbed Collin's stabbing hand.

Still on top of Collin, Dean's punches slowed, softened, and then stopped. All done, bye-bye, Dean. Collin grabbed Tad's wrist and pulled himself out from under Dean. Collin was bigger and Tad was never a boxer. Punch, punch, punch the heavy bag filled with sand. Punch, punch, punch the heavy sandbag with a Tad face on it. Punch, punch, punch the heavy sandbag filled with gristle and goo. Punch, punch, punch; splash, splash, splash. Collin laughed at the funny noises, laughed a laugh like Dana's honk-laugh. He hadn't needed to use the knife on Tad.

But Brin?

Brin was smart. She ran. The screaming and crying must have slowed her down, because Collin threw his knife and hit her in the leg with ease. She tumbled to the ground.

Bring me blood.

Brin stood, blubbering as spit and snot flowed over her face. She continued to run. Much slower now, limping. Collin caught her with ease and tackled her. Dragging her by her ankle, he'd bring her to his new master, and come back for the others. He'd deliver blood to his master, and it was fresh.

June 18, 2002

Dank. Moldy. The smell of mildew clung to the walls, an advertisement of what awaited anyone who entered the three-story building. The abandoned edifice once hosted a butcher shop, the tangy scent of long forgotten meat still lingering. Death's perfume, a familiar smell to Calista "Cali" Lindquist.

Even though this part of the city didn't boast anything worth visiting, enough foot traffic along the sidewalk and plenty of cars driving by discouraged Cali from breaking in through the front. That, and the solid gate over the door. She'd have to try her luck with the back of the building.

A security camera also loomed over the metal back door, but it was easily avoidable. She used her mini crowbar to pry enough wood away from the boarded-up window farthest from the camera, and slipped inside.

"Why is it always creepy buildings?" she whispered. "Why can't psychopath sickos hide in luxury condos?"

"The rent would be too high," her mother answered through Cali's earpiece. "And think about all the zoning permits they'd need to file for the torture dungeon in the basement. The condo's committee board would always be up the psychopath's ass about maintenance fees and adhering to the building codes."

Cali chuckled. Gallows humor. Mother and daughter considered it necessary in this line of work. They hunted monsters after all, and one hid in this building.

But the man she and her mother tracked here didn't quite meet the "monster" requirements, despite what his surviving victim had claimed. Cali knew about monsters – she had faced an actual, not-part-of-God's-creation monster once before.

Sarah Wellington was a buxom woman in her twenties with a tiny waist and a flare to her hips – the same description given to the seven other women who went missing over the past four months. In Sarah's statement to the police, she described her kidnapper as a nightmarish figure:

tall, pale, spider-like arms and legs with long fingers and toes, bulbous eyes that never seemed to blink. Her statement also said that she had been held captive with another woman. What caught Cali's and her mother's attention was how Sarah described her kidnapper's actions. Fast. Faster than humanly possible.

The man tortured and raped his victims until they died, blaming women for all the wrongs of his life. He toyed with his prey, allowing them to escape from the room where they were held, only to give chase. He had released Sarah and the other woman, but no matter where Sarah ran, he was always there, ahead of her.

Two things the man hadn't counted on regarding Sarah: One, she hadn't been dead when he disposed of her naked body in the landfill outside the city; two, the surprise state inspection that next morning at the landfill. Though Sarah had been lucky, she couldn't say the same about his other victim, and had no idea what became of her.

Cali and her mother had the technology to hack into cameras around the city, and they didn't have to worry about being ensnared by the red tape the police had to face. Legality be damned when hunting monsters. It took less than a day to find his lair, and now as the sun was setting, Cali crept through the backroom of the building, her Glock 9mm pointed downward. She prayed that the victim Sarah had mentioned was still alive.

"The walk-in freezer will be to your right," Cali's mother said. "And according to the blueprints, there should be a basement door across the room, on your left."

"Got it," Cali whispered. Her view of the world was green from her goggles' night-vision mode, but she was able to see everything quite clearly. "Checking the freezer first."

Cali tightened the grip on her gun as she slipped between the shelves, simple stacks made from cheap metal. The only things they held were rust, dust, and spider webs. Cali shivered every time a stray cobweb brushed her forehead. "Ugh, this is so gross."

"What do you see?"

"Nothing yet, but I keep walking through cobwebs."

"Oh. And how many times have you had other people's blood on your face."

"Can't count that high."

"Yet you think cobwebs are gross."

"Seriously? Blood is ninety percent water. Cobwebs are ninety percent spider ass."

"Okay, Lady Bathory, we'll schedule a spa day to get the cobwebs out of your hair. Are you at the freezer yet?"

Cali slid out from the aisle of shelves, gun aimed and ready to fire. Clear. No reason to use it yet.

"I'm at the freezer. The door is closed. It feels warm against my palm. It's quiet, not even humming. There's no power to it."

"Just because no power is going to it doesn't mean it's not being used."

Clever, Cali thought as she crouched down. The dust around the bottom of the door wasn't as thick as it was elsewhere. "There's a tiny wire connecting the door to the frame. Could be rigged to explode?"

"Careful," her mother said. "Your bodysuit won't protect you. Fire, yes. But an explosion? No way."

Cali brushed a hand against her torso. The black Teflon microfiber weave bodysuit hugged her skin. It was more effective than a bullet proof vest, but it didn't make her invincible. Even if the fridge wasn't rigged to explode, then it was a silent alarm ready to let the bastard know he had company. *Not today, Satan.*

The door across the room was a different story. The door handle was chained to a metal ring on the wall. "This looks new," she said, tugging on the silver, shiny lock and chain. Cali holstered her gun and unsnapped her mini crowbar from her tool belt. "New lock and chain don't mean shit if you attached it to a half-rotted stud." She wedged the ring out of the stud and kissed her tool before snapping it back in place. "You're the best eight inches a girl could ask for."

"Are you talking about your crowbar again?" her mother asked.

"I am. I really am."

"Then you're really doing sex wrong."

"Mom, please. Don't make it weird."

"It just seems like you need help with your dating life."

"Nope. Dating life good, Mom."

"Just saying if you need help, I can help."

"Don't need help, Mom."

"I could tell you stories that would leave you amazed. There was this Afghani prince nicknamed 'Camel,' and not because he had a hump on his back."

"Mom, I swear to God I'm going to pause the mission so I can walk through more cobwebs to help me think about anything other than what you just implied."

Her mother laughed. "Sorry, Sweety, I couldn't help myself. Take a minute to refocus if you need to."

Cali pushed the images of her mother's proclaimed dalliance out of her head and opened the door. She squinted, stunned by the brightly lit basement. She turned off the night vision but left her goggles on for protection, just in case. Gun drawn and pointed downward, as a precautionary, lest the sicko bastard had a hostage for a shield. She descended the stairs as quietly as her thick-soled boots would allow. The only other noise was the thumping of her heart.

Calm down. Deep, cleansing breath; in through her nose, out through her mouth. Her heartbeat receded.

The basement was supposed to be an open design, according to the blueprints on file with the city. However, Cali was greeted by a long wall forming a hallway. The drywall was crooked, with seams and screws exposed. Left or right? A soft moan of old building. Water dripping in some unseen corner. The faint whimper of a girl who had lost all hope. To the right.

"Moving now," Cali whispered. "Staying quiet."

"Confirmed," her mother replied. "We might lose comms. The way these old city buildings are built, the basements are like bunkers."

A string of bare light bulbs dangling from the ceiling led the way, and she kept her back against the wall. Every few steps forward, she checked behind her, the other end of the hallway. Suspicions and theories told her the sicko bastard was human, but it didn't hurt to act as if he wasn't.

Keeping a steady pace, she crept to the first open doorway, and looked inside. Like the wall behind her, the room's walls were unfinished drywall. But they weren't bare. Far from it. Degrading ways to refer to a woman were scrawled all over the walls in pen, marker, and spray paint. A lone bulb from the ceiling shined light on every word and phrase, a few Cali had never heard of before. Dried blood streaked the floor by the doorway. Two dog bowls had been placed in the room's center. This room was used to house women, kept as animals.

Cali moved farther down the hall toward another room, similar to the first. Streaks of dried blood swept from the hallway's floor into the open room. Feces sat in piles in the corners. Cali stifled a cough and a gag.

She doubted that the man in charge of this dungeon was the type of monster she and her mother hunted, but she wanted to kill the sick fuck just the same. Sometimes hunting unnatural monsters meant killing a few human ones as well.

The whimpering noises grew louder as she continued, the hallway opening to a large room, two of the walls lined with old storage cages. Three light bulbs hung from the ceiling, but they didn't give off enough light to illuminate the entire room. Strange shadows ranged from short and dense, to tall and reaching for infinity. Cali found her target. And his latest victim.

Hands over her head and bound together at her wrists, the young woman dangled from chains attached to the ceiling. Blood ran along her naked body. Fresh cuts ran deep red, then flowed pink as they mixed with her sweat before dripping to the floor. Her body hitched with every sob, her head drooping low. Two years ago, Cali was in a similar situation. Naked. Hanging like a slab of beef. Helpless. A toy for a maniac. *No! Not now. Focus.*

The sick fuck danced in front of his victim. He, too, was naked, his gaunt body moving like a pale spider. He held two knives – paring knives a little smaller than the Bowie strapped to Cali's belt, but sturdy enough.

Props for his theater of torture. Cali wanted to shoot him, but at this angle the bullet would pass right through him and hit his captive.

Aiming at his bulbous head, stringy hair hanging from it like curtains of brown moss, Cali made herself known. "Yeah. You're gonna drop the knives and step away from her."

The sick bastard stopped dancing and turned to face her. Lips curling into a sneer, he glared at Cali, not afraid or confused, but more like he was irritated with her interruption.

Cali continued into the room, stepping to the side to get a clearer shot. The woman's eyes went wide as she raised her head, Cali providing the breath of life, of hope. She tried to speak, but the thick wraps of duct tape muffled her voice and reduced her words to vowels. "Eee! Uuh! Ooo! Eee!"

"Yep, I'm here to rescue you," Cali answered. "But first, I need to take care of this piece of shit."

He dropped both knives and took a step away.

"Eee! Eee! Uuh! Ooo! Eee!" the woman tried again, this time fighting her restraints.

The woman was obviously trying to warn Cali of something. And the man wasn't afraid, his smirk telling Cali as much. But before she could react, she needed to time her next move perfectly, needed to listen to the inflection of the woman's screams, needed to watch the man's posture. It would be slight, almost imperceptible. Cali waited… Now!

The man tightened his shoulders, and his bug eyes widened the slightest bit, but it was enough for Cali. She dropped to a crouch. His forehead exploded from the bullet that was meant for her. A quick spin and she was looking at the man's twin, just as spindly and naked, shrieking. Cali and her mother had been suspicious about the sicko's reputation, about why Sarah Wellington thought he was faster than any regular human. He was no superman, that's for sure. He was merely an identical twin. A man, like his brother. That meant he bled and died like a man, like his brother. And because she was now eye level with it, Cali shot him in the dick.

Delivering an ear-piercing screech, the man fell to the floor, his hands doing nothing to stymy the gout of blood spewing from his crotch. Unwilling to tolerate his headache inducing noise any longer, Cali put one final bullet through his right eye.

"Uuh, ooo, eee!" The woman kept twisting her body, shaking the chain holding her. Cali knew from experience the effects of adrenaline in a situation like this.

"It's okay," Cali said as she holstered her gun. Unsheathing her Bowie knife – the best *nine* inches a girl could ask for – she approached the woman. "I'm here to help. I'm going to use this to cut away the duct tape. I know you're scared... trust me, I truly understand... but try not to move too much, and I'll get you out of here."

The woman's eyes remained wide with panic as Cali carefully sliced the duct tape. The moment she pulled it away, the woman yelled, "One, two, three! There are three of them!"

"Fuck!" Cali's instincts took over. A smell. The change in air. A glimpse of something just outside her peripheral vision. The attack came from her right.

She dropped her right shoulder and spun toward the identical triplet. The third sicko was armed with a knife and stabbed downward. Cali twisted away, avoiding a critical injury, but the surprise was too great, her balance askew. He missed her back, but the tip of the blade found the top of her thigh.

Her bodysuit offered some protection. Had the knife sliced, it would have never made it through to her skin. The material couldn't stop a bullet or a stab, but it helped limit penetration and depth. A blast of fire radiated through her thigh, burning her leg from ankle to hip, but Cali stayed focused enough to drop her elbow into his back. He absorbed her strike and rammed his shoulder into her chest. Somewhere within his lanky physique was enough muscle to drive her to the ground, close to the dangling woman.

His impact knocked the wind out of Cali and sent her Bowie skittering from her hand. She couldn't take a breath as the sicko knelt on her, his right hand around her neck, grinding her tonsils against the back of her throat. With his left, he yanked the knife from her thigh and raised it over his head. *Fucking hubris*, she thought, pissed at herself for ending up in this situation. *Just one chance*, she begged whichever higher power was listening. Just one chance to put an end to the gleam of sadistic joy in his eyes, to close his open-mouthed smile, lips slicked from the flowing drool.

He tittered as he tightened his grip on the knife.

Someone answered her prayer.

"No!" the woman screamed as she kicked. Both feet connected with his ribs, hard enough to knock him off Cali.

That was all she needed.

Lungs not yet functioning normally, she inhaled as best she could and threw all her weight into a throat punch. Perfect hit – knuckles smashing his windpipe. His turn to writhe on the ground gasping for air.

It took a few heartbeats, but her lungs began working as they should. It burned to breathe. That'd feel better soon enough, but she didn't have time to wait, and reached for her gun. No, she changed her mind. The mini crowbar.

Dropping a knee on his chest, she slammed the curved metal bar against his head. The satisfying crack of his skull resonated in her ears. Again. And again, each hit faster, harder. Shredding his skin, exposing bone. Again, and again. Globs of goo twirled through the air as arcs of blood painted her face. She finally stopped when the crowbar sent a pink spark off the wet concrete, and she realized that the person screaming was her.

Panting, she stood and returned the mini crowbar to her belt. She spat the bastard's blood from her mouth. This wasn't the first time she tasted someone else's, and the copper tang no longer bothered her. After all, two years ago, she tasted her own father's blood.

Cali retrieved her knife and cut through the cuff binding the woman's hands together. Sobbing, she fell into Cali's arms. "Thank you. Thank you. Thank you…"

"It's okay. We're going to get you out of here."

Cali helped prop the woman into a sitting position on the floor, and then explored the cages. One held a pile of clothes. Grabbing a shirt and a pair of sweatpants from the top of the pile, she helped the woman dress. "Can you walk?"

With Cali's help, the woman took a few limping steps.

"Okay, good. You're doing good." As they shuffled their way out of the room, Cali said, "My name is Cali. What's yours?"

"Everly. Everly Westin."

"Everly, you're doing great."

The closer they came to escape, the faster Everly moved. The stairs were a challenge and by the time they reached the first floor, the pain in Cali's throbbing leg kicked into overdrive, but Everly no longer needed her assistance.

"Mom? Can you hear me?" Cali tapped her earpiece. "We'll need an ambulance."

"The comms went in and out, but I heard enough to get the gist. One is on the way. So are the police."

Once outside, the approaching sirens grew louder.

Cali helped Everly sit on the ground and said, "I have to go, but help is on the way. The police sort of frown on vigilantes using crowbars the way I did."

The woman grabbed Cali's hand and squeezed to the point of potential broken bones. "I don't. Thank you. I can't thank you enough."

Cali did her best to pull her hands away without seeming unsympathetic. "Get well."

Pain stiffening her leg, she pressed her palm against the knife wound and hurried as best she could down one alleyway to another. "Well, I almost fucked up. There were three of them."

"Triplets, not twins?" her mother replied. "Are you okay?"

"Yeah... took a bit of knife to my leg. Gonna need shots. All the shots."

"Confirmed. So... are you *okay*?"

"I'm fine. Just want a spa day. All the spiderwebs, you know?"

"Still with the spiderwebs?"

"Yep."

"Is your face covered in blood?"

"… no…."

"Liar. We can do a spa day tomorrow. And more shots. You need to stop getting other people's blood on your face. Do you want hepatitis? That's how you get hepatitis."

"Blood, spiderwebs, knife wound, whatever, I just need a spa day."

"You sound frustrated."

Cali paused on the dark street. She tore off her goggles and removed her ponytail to relieve the tightness in her forehead. She ran her fingers through her hair. Sweaty. Messy. Sighing, she said, "As much as the piece of shit trio needed to die, they weren't monsters. I know, I know, they *were* monsters, but not the kind I'm looking for. These are numbers eight, nine, and ten. We've killed ten in the past year. But after what I went through two years ago… after what happened to Dad… I want *real* monsters."

"I understand. And I found something we can discuss tomorrow after our spa visit."

"Really? What?"

"How do you feel about clowns?"

June 3, 2002

The models and actresses and athletes and sex symbols were getting younger and younger. Always on display, always telling everyone who looked at them how much they wanted the attention. "Look at me," they'd say. "Look at me. Fantasize about me. Take me, for the right price." So, it wasn't his fault really, the urges. If society didn't want him doing what he did, then they wouldn't advertise what he wanted so much.

Keith Donnevuccio couldn't afford the models and actresses and athletes and sex symbols. But he could afford a white, windowless van and clown makeup. He hated the cliché, but it was effective. He'd seen lots of white windowless vans in the city and suburbs. Witnesses probably couldn't pick out one from another. Hopefully no one could pick out his. Especially since he took pictures of other vans' license plates and printed them off using his home computer. He easily slid a sheet of paper inside the clear plastic cover over his real license plate. Uncle Mick had taught him that trick. Taught him a lot.

Uncle Mick used to rob stores, usually jewelry stores. One time, a new guy had come into town, stealing from the same neighborhoods as Uncle Mick. Instead of taking him out with a bullet or even busting him up with a bat, Uncle Mick acted friendly toward the guy. After a month, Uncle Mick hit a pawn shop, wiping it clean of any valuables. He left the entire haul – except for one pair of diamond earrings – on his own coffee table and anonymously called the cops. The cops went to his place, saw the stash, and picked him up at the neighborhood bar. Uncle Mick said, "You think I'm fucking stupid enough not to hide a stash like that? I was set up." Uncle Mick pointed his finger at the new guy in town. When the cops searched the new guy's place, they found a pair of diamond earrings hidden in his sock drawer.

Criminals don't use their real name, which was why no one would suspect "Keith the Clown" was Keith Donnevuccio. Not at first glance. Of course, Uncle Mick taught him that as well. Taught him *more* than that. Taught him that this country was too uptight. Too many bullshit laws.

Uncle Mick explained that in other countries he could do so much more, explore his primal, God-given instincts, which was why he enlisted before the draft told him to go to 'Nam. He told young Keith stories about saving tiny villages with dirt floor houses. Since the men in the villages were gone or dead, the women thanked their saviors in a variety of ways. That was Uncle Mick – a savior. Because what else do you call someone willing to risk his life in a God forsaken country for a shitty village with dirt floor houses? And as a savior, he wanted to be thanked like one, treated like one. If the villagers didn't want to thank him as such, then he'd make them. Toward the end of America's time over there, Uncle Mick and his friends no longer wanted the women of the villages to thank them. Instead, they wanted the daughters. And they got them. Uncle Mick had the pictures to prove it.

Once Keith hit high school, Uncle Mick decided he was old enough to hear the stories and see the pictures. After all, Uncle Mick was in high school when he enlisted, having been held back twice. Feelings stirred within Keith when he looked at those pictures. Feelings that the laws of this country didn't allow. However, overseas in the name of the same flag that denied his feelings, he could do whatever he wanted, as promised by his Uncles Sam and Mick.

While Keith was getting Middle East sand in his ass crack, Uncle Mick died from that shit America made him breathe in 'Nam. Keith would later hear the big, long, complicated terms and excuses, added by the hospitals saying the condition was accelerated by Uncle Mick's drinking and smoking and eating habits and drugs prescribed by his common sense rather than quack doctors. But Keith knew the cancers were caused by Agent Orange; that was when he learned what a liar Uncle Sam truly was.

The government lied to Uncle Mick about the deadliness of Agent Orange just as it lied to Keith about him going to war. The only time he discharged his weapon over there was for practice and drills. Never mind being the hero in a God forsaken country saving shitty villages with sand floor houses. No opportunity for gratitude from women or girls. And then to come home with his pent-up urges and bullshit laws meant to stop him? Fuck that.

Now he was sitting in his van with his laptop open, the video feed displaying James J. Naperson Elementary School. Little Lily attended this school. Keith met her two months ago at her eighth birthday party, and today he planned to reintroduce himself.

He watched the school from two and a half blocks away. It took time, effort, and money to get this video setup working. The parts went beyond what Radio Shack had to offer, but it was worth it. Checking the time, he shifted in his seat as he watched the school's main exit and cafeteria exit, knowing kids would soon pile out those two doors. Any time now. He cracked his knuckles, needing his fingers nimble to work the radio control system. The camera was strapped to a radio-controlled toy car, ready to roll at a moment's notice. And that moment was now.

The fire alarm went off. His accomplice flashed across the far corner of the laptop screen, running out the back door of the school. Some stupid high school kid Keith found loitering around a convenience store instead of attending classes. Keith promised that a fifth of vodka would be waiting for the kid at the big blue public mailbox on 4th Street if he snuck into Little Lily's elementary school at this exact time, lit a few of those silly little novelty smoke bombs, and pulled the fire alarm. Why this exact time? It was when Little Lily would be ending lunch.

Order and civility accompanied a planned fire drill. An unplanned one? Well, that was when mistakes happened. Any given school in America consisted of too many kids to too few teachers, and lunchtime made that situation worse. Especially since this school's cafeteria was located too close to a side exit, one they weren't supposed to use. While most of the students and teachers spilled out the main exit – the kids all good and riled up from seeing smoke – those in the cafeteria ran out the school's side door. The teacher to student ratio was so bad that more than two dozen kids ran out the door unsupervised. Little Lily being one of them.

A few kids glanced at the radio-controlled car, their faces immature portraits of fear and confusion. Then Little Lily's face appeared, and Keith's breath hitched. She did a double take and stared at the toy car, just like Keith had planned. When he had performed at her birthday party two months ago, he showed up in makeup and wig, but asked to use the bathroom to put on the finishing touches. With everyone out playing in the backyard, he had plenty of time to snoop. Finding her room was easy, and snatching her favorite stuffed animal from her pillow was even easier. That floppy dog fit perfectly on top of the video camera strapped to the remote-controlled car.

Little Lily broke away from the crowd without a second glance. *So far so good.* He cracked a half-smile and guided the car around the corner of the block. He sat straighter, excited that she was following. This part was the trickiest, keeping one full block ahead of her and hoping everyone was too preoccupied to notice a girl chasing a stuffed animal on wheels along the suburban neighborhood sidewalk. Her little legs ran faster than he expected, bringing her closer to her dog, to the car. Sweat percolated along his wig, the elastic digging into his head as she reached out with her greedy little hand, eyes wide with desire. Keith would watch this recorded scene again and again. Later. He turned the remote-controlled car off the beaten path at the next intersection.

Right at the border of middle class and lower income, the car bounced along the uneven sidewalk and stopped in front of an alley that traversed between two rows of small houses. Little Lily turned the corner. She paused to regain sight of her stuffed animal. Her eyes went wide when she saw it. Then her tight mouth broke into a broad smile, and she continued pursuit.

That was when the remote-controlled car zipped into the alley.

Keith had spent a month studying this area. Two houses were empty and up for sale. Two others belonged to people who couldn't afford to miss a day of work. And that knowledge afforded every confidence that no one was around to notice his parked van. Surely nobody saw him slip from the driver's seat to the back and open the door.

He scooped up the car, video camera, and stuffed animal.

Sitting on the cold metal floor of the van, he waited with the back door cracked open no more than an inch.

When Little Lily rounded the corner into the alley, he pushed the door open. She spied him and stopped. Eyes wide, chest rising and falling, breathing fast. This sent Keith's nerves into a frenzy, but he got control of them, reminding himself that no urges could be satisfied if he messed this up.

"Lily? Little Lily? Is that you?" He spoke with the goofy inflection of reading a nursery rhyme, the way people expected clowns to talk, and it seemed to put her at ease. Her posture relaxed, her eyes no longer wide. Sounding too stupid to be threatening, he continued, "Why yes. Yes, it is Little Lily."

Tiny fists clenched, she took a tentative step forward and squinted, the gears behind her eyes grinding along to jump start the motor of recognition. She uncurled her fingers and a sweet smile spread across her face like jelly on bread. Keith the Clown wore a blue wig instead of a red one like he did for her party, but she recognized him. Children always recognized him no matter the wig or face paint or clothes. Adults sucked at recognition. He could run into an adult the day after a party while wearing the exact same getup and they wouldn't know him. But with kids, there was a connection.

"Keith the Clown?" she asked, voice as soft as a makeup brush. She took another hopeful step forward.

Keith jumped from the van, big shoes flopping as he landed, and stretched his arms as wide as Jesus'. "You better believe it's me, Little Lily."

An open-mouth giggle. But she didn't move any closer. Keith looked down at how he was dressed, then looked back up at her with an exaggerated expression of surprise. "Oh me, oh my, I'm a mess. This won't do for my Little Lily." As he fussed with his over-sized tie, a balloon inflated from inside his jacket, the air pump hidden under his overlapping vest. When he finished straightening his tie, the balloon was fully inflated. A quick knot and he offered the pink heart-shaped balloon to Little Lily with a deep-waisted bow.

Another step forward. Only four or five more to go. But she stopped and looked behind her. Keith the Clown knew how children thought, knew she was contemplating the need to let an adult know where she was. "You liked my magic tricks at your birthday party, right?"

Little Lily whipped her head around, and nodded so hard her long, silky hair rippled. She liked Keith the Clown. They all did, even the little shits who thought they were too cool for clowns.

Like many clowns, Keith incorporated magic into his routine, but instead of lame store-bought tricks, he was a master of close-up magic. So adept that even the parents were captivated. One time after a child's birthday party, some asshole paid him a hundred bucks cash to have Keith show him how a "pick-a-card" trick was done. He took the douchebag's money and showed him the trick, not concerned about selling the information. The secret to all magic – the secret that the asshole would never learn – was practice. And when Keith was sitting in a tent, in a desert, not shooting anyone and not being thanked by any local women or girls, he had nothing but time to practice. Something about that asshole, though… Oh, yeah! He was Little Lily's father.

"Well, come on over, Lily, and take the balloon, because I need both hands to show you the new trick I made just for you."

Eyes bright as flashlights, she closed the distance in a run, outstretched hand ready for her prize. She took the foot-long, thin plastic balloon tie and gave it a quizzical look. "This balloon string is weird."

A zip-tie.

"It's a special string just for you. But that's not the magic trick. This is."

With a flourishing wave of his hand, he produced her stuffed dog. Still holding on to the balloon, she snatched the stuffed animal from his hand and hugged it with every ounce of strength in her wispy body. He loved this age; never once questioning how the toy came into his possession, just happy to have it returned.

"Did you like that trick?" Keith the Clown asked.

Nodding with gusto, she squealed, "Yes! Thank you!"

"Would you like to see more amazing tricks from Keith the Clown?"

More vigorous nodding.

Keith the Clown gestured to the opened door of the van. "Step right into my magic emporium and I will show them all to you."

Little Lily climbed up and inside.

Keith followed and shut the door behind them.

June 19, 2002

Philadelphia. *Fucking Philly. Ugh. At least the city understands the concept of brunch.*

A beautiful mid-June day outside *Café Du Fou*, the restaurant had opened their large bay windows to give the illusion that the six tables closest to the wall were enjoying their brunch on the sidewalk. Cali absently chewed the last bite of her eggs benedict while watching city life playout before her. She and her mom could reach out and touch each passerby. Not that they would. Only weirdos touched perfect strangers as they walked by. *Though… it would be kind of funny.*

She shook the thought from her head, unsure if it was hers or the Bloody Mary's. It was her third Bloody, after all, the magic drink-number when Mary usually started talking to her. Cali took another sip and then held it out to a toast. "To spa day."

Mother smiled and gently clinked her flute-filled mimosa against Cali's glass. "To spa day."

"Don't know why we couldn't have stayed in New York for that, but hey."

"Don't be shitty. The wraps, soaks, peels, and massages are just as delightful here."

Despite the latex sleeve around her leg, Cali didn't disagree with her mom. The tight sleeve bandaged yesterday's bloody knife wound to keep it from leaking everywhere, and it itched. But all the aches and pains from the evening before were gone. "I don't mean to be a whiner. I'm just… frustrated."

"That you didn't kill any monsters yesterday?"

Cali looked over both shoulders, wondering how her mother could talk so cavalierly about the topic. *Or are you being paranoid?* Bloody Mary asked.

"Yes," Cali answered her mother. "No. I don't know. I mean, I know what we did yesterday was justified, and yeah, that trio of freaks were certainly monsters in every sense of the word. But... I don't know why it wasn't as satisfying as I feel like it should be."

"Because of your father."

Cali twisted her lips, and then took another sip of her drink. She didn't want to talk about it and Mother knew that, yet she continued. "Your father was taken from you, immediately and violently, right after you learned there was much more to him. Then you killed the... thing... that took him from you before he could answer any of your questions. Your quest for revenge ended before it began. You have a new crusade, but it's not quite the same as revenge, is it?"

"You're a really weird mom."

A smirk played at Mother's lips as she brought her mimosa to her mouth. "Just because I know a little something about killing, death, and revenge?"

Cali tilted her glass at her mom. "Exactly. I know it was Zebadiah Seeley who killed Dad, but I still blame Roger Templeton."

Mother nodded. "I understand. And *you* killed Templeton last year. Again, your quest for revenge was short-lived. By the way, how is Maxwell? You still keeping a good eye on him?"

Right before Cali ended Roger's life, she had promised him that she'd spy on his son, Maxwell, to make sure he didn't follow in his father's nefarious footsteps. Maxwell used to be one of her friends. But now? "He's trying to wrap his arms around his father's assets. So far..." Cali shook the ice in her half-filled glass. "He's behaving himself."

"Good. How about Melody?"

Cali took a noisy slurp, swallowing guilt. She had allowed her best friend, Melody, to think she was dead. "Still with Maxwell."

"You two used to be so close."

"It's a little creepy that you know that."

Mother leaned in closer. "I realize I've been in your life for only two years, but I've been watching you the whole time."

"'I spied on my daughter from afar for twenty years.' You should use that for your mother of the year speech."

She leaned away. "Okay, I admit that didn't come out as I had hoped, but the sentiment is this: you are my daughter, and I love you. I am *all* for this crusade. I just don't want you to define your life by it. You're young. You're a twenty-four-year-old woman in the twenty-first century. You should be socializing with people other than your mother and our informants."

"Ugh. I've made peace with what happened to Tanner, but the last thing I want to think about is dating or socializing or whatever."

"What about Linda?"

Cali shifted in her chair. She pulled at her shirt in a feeble attempt to cover the tattoo over her heart. A single word in delicate script: Linda. She shrugged off her mother's question.

"You had feelings for her?"

No answer.

Mother leaned back in her chair and brought her mimosa along as if getting ready to settle in for the rest of the day. "If you like women as well as men, you can let me know. Hell, if you're completely done with men and only like women... I'd understand."

"I don't want to talk about it."

"Well, then I think you know what I have to do."

"Mom, no."

Mother finished her mimosa and set the empty flute on the table. "You're giving me no choice," she said while rooting through her purse.

"You have a choice. You totally have a choice. Choosing *not* to do what you're about to do is a really *good* choice."

"You're unfocused right now and that creates dangerous situations in the field. I truly believe the best thing is for you to talk about it."

"Jesus, where's the waiter?"

"You're not done with the one in your hand."

"I can finish it reeeeeeeally quickly if you—"

"Found it." Mother placed a card on the table in front of Cali. Cut with dimensions of a standard playing card and coated in a white background, it had only one word in black ink on it. "Sharing." Its glossy surface gleamed in the sunlight.

Cali slouched as she heaved out a sigh, her body deflating along with her will to live. Fight or flight kicked in, but neither option was viable. Though Cali had exceptional defensive skills, Mother surpassed her and would snatch her out of the air if she even tried to leave the table. "God, I hate when you do this."

"It's for your own good," Mother said, her tone sympathetic.

"Mom—"

"If you don't share, I will."

Cali squirmed, the chair suddenly as comfortable as a bush of nettles. "Mom—"

"My first time was 1986. I was in Brazil for The Carnival."

Cali's eyes widened into the realm of eye-popping pain when she realized where her mother was going with this story. "Oh, God, Mom, stop talking."

"She was a dancer in the parade. I don't know how she saw me in the crowd, but when we made eye contact, I just knew we'd end up—"

"I don't know!" The heat of embarrassment flashed across Cali's face and down her neck, never imagining the topic of the day was going to be discussing her sexuality with Mother in the middle of brunch. Cali's unexpected outburst drew curious glances from neighboring patrons. Resting her elbows on the table, she repeated much more quietly, "I don't know. There was an attraction with some feelings. I know that happens to people when they share a traumatic experience, but my attraction to Linda started before that."

"You only knew her for about two days, right?"

Cali exhaled so hard that her cheeks puffed out. Hands in her hair, she dug into her scalp with her fingertips, massaging her brain. If only she could think of a way to escape the "sharing" card on the table in front of her.

It had been almost two years since the events surrounding her and Linda. Those same events took her father from her, but brought her mother into her life. She had shared the bullet point version of what had happened with Mother, keeping the details, and her feelings, sparse. She slurped down enough Bloody for Mary to say, *Fuck it. You may as well "share." Tell her and get it over with.*

"Okay." Deep breath. "A couple months after I graduated, I took a job with Harkins & Powell, an advertising firm in California."

"I know."

Cali rolled her eyes. "Of course, you do, you fucking creeper. But what you don't know is that I was thinking about breaking up with Tanner."

"You're right. I didn't know that."

"I wanted one last, nice week with him, a couple's getaway with Dakota and Jordon, and Melody and Maxwell. I had hoped it would save our relationship. But at the last-minute Maxwell and Melody cancelled even though it was Maxwell's dad's house. God, I should have realized something was up when Maxwell canceled."

Mother took Cali's hand and gave a supportive squeeze. "No, you shouldn't have, sweety. No one could have realized what was going to happen during your trip."

Cali wiped away the stray tear rolling over her cheek with her free hand. "As I told you before, Hook and his girlfriend came along instead."

"Linda Salazar."

"Yes. She and I clicked right away. I mean it was more than just fun and great conversation. Being around her, I was somehow excited and calm at the same time. When she wasn't around, I wanted to find her. Smart, strong, funny, compassionate. All qualities I'd love to find in the right someone. And… and I liked how she made me feel about myself."

"How did you feel when you found out she was a DEA agent?"

"Pissed, obviously. At first, I felt lied to and betrayed. But after I thought about it and realized that of course she couldn't have told me the truth, that she was investigating Hook – and technically Tanner, Jordon, and Maxwell, though we didn't know that at the time – and his involvement in the local drug running scene, I knew she wasn't really lying *to me*."

Mother leaned across the table and took the card. Dropping it inside her purse, she said, "There, don't you feel a little better?"

You do. You should tell her that you do, Bloody Mary said. Cali ignored Mary and went with, "Thank you for the therapy, but let's get down to business. You said there's some kind of… clown? … activity."

Mother dabbed the corners of her mouth with the cloth napkin, and stood from the table. "Your therapy session isn't over yet. You need to remember what talking to other human beings is like without punching them in the face to get information. I'm sure you haven't noticed, but the waiter has been eyefucking you. Hard."

"I'm feeling waaaaaay too misanthropic for this little exercise."

"Just let him say hi and use whatever pickup line he's been working on."

"You're forcing me to talk to another human being *and* making me pay for brunch?"

"Call it my fee for your therapy. And one last thing…" Mother placed another card on the table, same dimensions and style as the one prior, with the word: "Truth."

"Jesus, Mom."

"Please, be true to yourself."

"I have guns, you know. Plenty of them to use on the whackadoodle therapist who gave you these cards."

Mother's cat-at-a-canary-buffet smile made Cali flinch.

She gave Cali a kiss on the cheek, and then whispered in her ear, "Your father gave them to me when he proposed."

"God damn it," Cali mumbled.

"Yep." Then Mother took the card back, turned on her heels, and left the restaurant. She passed in front of the window and waved. "We'll meet up later and talk about why we're in Philly."

Fuck. Cali slouched in her chair and stared into the remnants of her drink. Her mother was trying to force her back into society. *Honestly, you have been a little feral lately*, Bloody Mary said.

"Yeah, you're right," she replied.

For the past two years, Cali did nothing but train, train, train, honing her skills with weapons, fighting, and investigating. Whenever she wasn't practicing with her mother, she was pouring through internet references to monsters. If a story shattered her suspension of disbelief and struck her as unexplainable, she'd investigate. When she uncovered enough evidence, she then brought it to her mother. Most "monsters" were serial brutalizers but hunting them down and ending them was good practice. The trio from yesterday was the closest to what she had faced before, to what had killed her father. But the more she and Mary thought about them, the more she wanted to—

"Ooooh, that's kinda rude."

Cali looked up from her glass, nothing left but flecks of pepper on red streaked ice cubes. The waiter was smiling down at her. Wistful. A bit suggestive. Sympathetic yet confident. Why shouldn't he be confident? Angular face, handsome and devoid of any facial hair, eyes a pleasant shade of blue. Nicely styled light brown hair, tall body covered in lean muscle. Cali became very aware that she was slouched deep in her chair with the glass resting on her chest, celery clinging to her bottom lip. Clearing her throat, she sat up and placed the drained glass on the table. "So… What, in particular, do you consider rude?"

"Your sister. It looks like she left and stuck you with the bill."

Cali chuckled. "No need for platitudes. I think we all know she's my mother."

"Really? Actually, I didn't. She's very pretty."

"If you want, I could give you her number so you can ask her out."

The waiter smirked. "Maybe. Depends on your answer when I ask you for your number."

"That's your line? You had all this time to think of something and that's what you came up with?"

"Actually, no. That's my ad lib, because I wasn't expecting you to offer me a date with your mom. I was debating between asking if it hurt when you fell from Heaven or if your father was the thief who stole the sapphires for your eyes."

My father wasn't a thief. He was a mercenary assassin. Okay, that might not be as flirty as I think it is. "Aaah, the classics."

"I'm nothing if not classic," the waiter said with a deep bow.

Cali hated to admit it, but she was intrigued. "Classics are classic for a reason. I'm Cali."

"Chism."

Cali made a face akin to smelling rotten garbage. "Jesus, that's awful." And immediately hated how snobby she sounded. She blamed her beverages for her lack of social filter.

"I know, right? I'm assuming Cali is short for something. Please tell me your full name is better than mine."

Who is this guy? I openly insulted his name, yet he's still talking to me. "Calista. My name is Calista, but I go by Cali."

"Yes, I would absolutely agree that your name is better than mine. But if not for my awful name, I wouldn't have become a boxer."

"I'm guessing you got beat up a lot in school over your name?"

"Actually, no. A friend of mine was getting beaten up by a couple bullies, and yelled out, 'Chism, help!' I ran over and fought them off. It was really sloppy, so I decided to learn how to fight."

Cali blinked, unsure what else to do while she tried to process this information. Was he serious? "That's… a heck of a story as to why you became a boxer because of your name."

"Yep. Now I'm more focused on mixed martial arts, but that was after my acting stint. Neither have anything to do with my name, rather my love of learning different fighting styles."

"Are you sure you didn't get hit in the head too many times?"

"Nope. I'm pretty good. Wouldn't want to mess up my handsome face."

"Full of yourself, huh?"

Chism shrugged. "Not in the slightest, but that's the conundrum, isn't it? I'm sure you know it too. You're gorgeous. I'm handsome. If we admit that, then we're conceited assholes. If we try to deny it, or downplay it with false humility, then we're a different kind of conceited asshole. And then double bonus, most people only see us as pretty faces, not realizing there's more to us, that we have thoughts and feelings and the ability to make fun of ourselves because one of us is named Chism.

Obviously, there're benefits to being attractive, as you know. I bet you never paid for a drink in your life, right?"

Cali chuckled and shook her head. This was exactly what her mother was talking about, even though it burned to admit that she was right. It was doubtful Mr. Diarrhea-of-the-Mouth could grow into any kind of relationship, but he was entertaining. She'd be stupid to let an opportunity to get to know him better slip by.

She flashed him with a full, genuine smile. "Well, since my mom stuck me with the bill, this'll be my first time paying for my own drinks. And I get what you're saying. About people seeing nothing more than a pretty face."

Chism's smile grew, creating the faintest dimples. "Excellent. We have something in common. Maybe we could have dinner tonight and see what lies beyond the pretty faces?"

"When's your shift over?"

"In a couple hours."

"One thing that my pretty face hides is that I, too, dabble in different fighting styles. So, give me your gym's address and I'll meet you there in three hours. For a little sparring. That is, if you don't mind getting your ass kicked by a girl."

Chism pulled out a pen and napkin. As he wrote, he said, "If I do or if I don't, it will still be the most interesting first date I've ever been on."

After handing the napkin to her, he turned to walk away. Cali almost called out to him that he forgot the check until she read the napkin. Under the address of the gym, he had written, "You still haven't paid for a drink in your life – brunch is on me."

June 14, 2002

Maxwell Templeton leaned his elbows on his desk and placed the half-empty tumbler of Old Rip Van Winkle 10-year bourbon, on the rocks, against his forehead. Cool condensation offered the slightest relief against his hot skin. His fourth pour, but the same ice since his first. For the past half hour, the fiery liquid managed to burn down the emotions threatening to bubble up from his gut. A few sentiments belched past, and into his head, causing trouble. The sting of loss behind his eyes. The tightness of regret at the back of his throat. The punch of anger against his forehead.

The mouse pointer hovered over the video file. He put in long hours today, trying to ignore the date. Trying to occupy his mind. Trying to do anything other than watch this video.

Fuck it. Maxwell double clicked the file name. It was the first anniversary of his father's murder; he was allowed a little self-wallowing.

Technically, today was the first anniversary of his father's "disappearance." Which was why this desk was technically Roger Templeton's. The bourbon. The office. The companies. Everything Maxwell owned, he owned because of his father's disappearance. But Roger, his father, had not disappeared. He was *murdered*. And this video proved it.

Grainy and in black and white, the footage came from an ATM across the street and showed the front of this building. Coincidentally, this building's security system went out for a few hours on that day. A case of bad luck, the police had told him. But it was her, the woman in the video.

Calista Lindquist.

The video proved nothing, according to the police, especially since the image was too blurry to detail any features. But Maxwell knew it was Calista. The shape. The size. The way she moved. The way that blonde ponytail swayed.

They had met as sophomores in college when he first started dating Melody. Calista and Melody were best friends, along with Dakota. They all hung out so often that Maxwell knew Calista and Dakota as well as he knew Melody. And sure as death and taxes, that was Calista-fucking-Lindquist walking into this building, carrying a duffle bag. *Had she carried him out in that?* Maxwell thought. *In pieces?* There was no evidence of her leaving the building.

"Knock, knock!" Melody all but sang as she cracked open the office door, peeking around it. Maxwell's hand went to the top of the screen, ready to shut the laptop, but he stopped himself. This wasn't his mother catching him with porn; this was the woman he would someday propose to. She would be half-owner of this empire that his father built. Plus, he knew the look on his face had given him away.

"Oh, Max." She entered the room, and shut the door behind her. "You're thinking about him, aren't you?"

"It was a year ago today that he was murdered." He was pushing her buttons. He shouldn't have been, but he was upset. Melody never took his side about this, and there was a morose comfort in going through the same argument, like seeing a movie he didn't like, but watching it anyway because the one positive was that he knew what would happen next.

Melody crossed farther into the office, past the shelves of books Maxwell would never read, past the gaudy statue of Zeus that he promised to remove someday soon, past the couch, and stopped right in front of his desk. Her doe eyes seemed extra dark, heavy with sympathy. "I know. I'm sorry."

"So, you've finally come to the same conclusion? You believe he was murdered?"

"I never said I didn't, Max."

"It was her."

"*That* is what I can't believe."

"It was her. We found a hair in here and the DNA testing proved it was hers."

"Max, the reason you had something of hers to compare it against was because you asked me for her hairbrush from my apartment. And I brought it in here. Had I known why... Her hair probably fell all over the floor and the furniture—"

"Melody, please, not that again. It didn't fall from the brush you brought in or fall off one of the many tops you shared with her over the years, or a ball cap, or a hair tie. You hadn't stepped foot in this office well over a year before he disappeared."

"That's true, but it's not like hair dissolves or rots away. It could have been here for years."

"With as many times as this office gets cleaned, there's no way it would still... No. You know this argument and so do I. Why are you defending her?"

"You know why. She's my best friend."

"Same friend who went missing after slaughtering our friends and killing my father."

Swallowing hard, Melody pressed her fist to her lips. Shaking her head in disagreement, her cheeks reddened as she worked her jaw muscles. The one time Maxwell made the mistake of answering, "Yes," to her question, "Do these pants make my ass look fat?" she had responded the exact same way. He hadn't meant to hurt her, but he was only being honest.

She poured herself a glass of bourbon, sat on the couch, and said, "I can't believe it. I won't. I refuse to. She isn't capable of that."

Maxwell wanted to protect Melody. As her boyfriend, it came with the job description. But he also needed to help her come to terms with life's unpleasantries. "We have to see what the evidence shows."

After slugging back the bourbon, she exhaled through pursed lips, then leaned her elbows on her knees and frowned. "I know, I know. It's been almost two years since the lake house burned down and the police found... the police found what they found."

"The decapitated body of a kidnapper, rapist, and murderer named Zebadiah Seeley. And the body of an unidentified man."

"And not us, because we canceled at the last minute."

That stung. He knew Melody didn't mean to be hurtful; she wasn't like that. Her survivor's guilt had reared its blessedly ugly head. True, they were supposed to have been there but at the last minute they couldn't go. It was Maxwell's father's house after all, and Roger demanded he stay at the office and complete the job assignment he'd been given. At the time, he was twenty-two, and not a rebellious teenager.

The trip to the lake house was supposed to be the official start of what he had hoped would be a much more lucrative drug distribution business. He, Tanner, Jordon, and Hook, stupid as they were back then, had come up with the dumbass idea. They had plenty of buyers lined up since they had access to the rich and bored college students of rich and bored parents. Hook had set up a purchase of product and wanted to meet – during the trip to the lake house – with a buyer. But Maxwell couldn't go, held back by his father. At first, Maxwell thought about sneaking there anyway. Then the calls from the police came, and he was happy he hadn't gone. Relieved. Blessed as if touched by divinity. A few months after the incident, suspicion crept into Maxwell's mind – that his father knew what was going to happen at the lake house. When he had asked his father why he really kept Maxwell away, he responded, "Just a hunch."

Maxwell believed him because he wanted to. So, he cast aside his suspicion. Plus, he needed to focus on Melody's well-being. One of her best friends was dead, the other missing. Nightmares plagued her for months. Then Roger was murdered. When Maxwell started to take over the companies, he found a couple of odd transactions: Roger had sold his largest company to the employees and liquidated his second largest, the cash in the company's coffers subsequently disappearing. Try as he might, Maxwell couldn't follow the money. There were too many transfers. It wound up in a holding company in Asia where the funds were withdrawn. Tens of millions of dollars vanished. It was enough for Maxwell to revisit his original suspicion regarding his father's knowledge of that fateful weekend.

"And not us." Maxwell mumbled, repeating what Melody had said.

His face must have been a portrait of guilt. Over the past year, he had gotten better at hiding his emotions from his employees and the different boards of directors, but he could never hide his feelings from Melody.

"I'm sorry," she said. "I... I shouldn't have said that. Today is the anniversary of his death and you don't need me dumping guilt on you."

Maxwell gave her a smile. She always put others' needs in front of her own, and he loved that about her. "No need to apologize. I understand your feelings about what happened. There are a lot of 'what ifs' and even more unanswered questions."

Melody shook her head. "It's been two years and I still can't believe that they're dead. I can't believe we were almost there with them. The authorities said Tanner, Jordon, and Hook had been butchered. I can't…" Her watering eyes turned pink. "I literally can't comprehend. I thank God every day that your father forbade us from going. Like he…" Her voice trailed off as she turned away.

Maxwell finished her sentence. "Like he knew."

Melody turned back to Maxwell.

He should have allowed her to drop the conversation. But he had been thinking the same thing over the last few months.

Maxwell now owned a portfolio of more than a dozen companies, even after the mysterious removal of two of them. After months of fighting with the authorities over whether his father was alive or not, as the only surviving family member, he was finally able to assume control. Learning about the companies took months, and he still wasn't finished.

Most of his holdings were pretty standard – an art gallery, a few apartment buildings, a couple small restaurant chains, a botanical chemical company, one casino, a night club, a gentleman's club, a small investment firm which took the biggest hit when Roger disappeared. Each business was in a different city, but up until last year money flowed from every single one of them – even the art gallery – into the two bigger companies. That stopped once they had been removed from the portfolio.

Maxwell loved his father and looked up to him, had him on a pedestal while growing up. He imagined his father's life as a staged play – the glitz and glamor of a well-acted show for the eyes of the theatre audience. Now he had the opportunity to pull the curtain away and look backstage. He saw the props, the scripts, the actors out of makeup.

As much as it pained him, he had to assume that his father had been involved in activities outside the purview of the law. After all, just minutes ago, he had said to Melody, "We have to see what the evidence is showing us."

"Are you saying...?" Melody lowered her voice, as if anyone else might overhear her scandalous notion.

Maxwell nodded. "My father might have been involved with illicit operations."

Wide-eyed, Melody stood from the couch. She walked to the desk, grabbing her glass along the way. She poured herself another drink, then refilled Maxwell's tumbler. After a swig, she asked, "Find anything else while learning about the companies?"

No need to tell her this is my fifth, Maxwell thought as he matched her swig. The burn in his throat partnered the one behind his eyes. His increasing headache, one of today's many, came from debating what to tell Melody. Should he tell her about the email he had received earlier? He wanted to protect her, but he'd be doing her no favors by keeping her ignorant. "I received an email from a man named Harold Varvaro, claiming that he works for my fath... that he works for me and that he wants to meet."

Melody frowned as she took another drink. "Did he say who he is or what he does? Or why it took so long for him to contact you?"

"No, no, and no. I asked him those and other questions, and he gave me answers so vague that if any form of law enforcement agency were monitoring, they'd observe nothing suspicious. Only one piece of concrete information came out of our discussion: Harold is in Philadelphia. I set up a meeting with him tomorrow at the art gallery."

Melody exhaled slowly, fanning him with spicy bourbon-breath. "That's... that's a lot to absorb."

"This whole process has been a lot to absorb."

"What do we do?"

"Tomorrow, we're going to Philadelphia."

June 19, 2002

A date. Cali couldn't believe she was on a date. It had been two years since she had been on a date. Technically longer, since couples didn't date once they officially began a relationship. Or did they? She heard about married people with kids going on a "date night," but she thought that was just a euphemism to sneak away for a little naughty fun time. There were "double dates," but when she and Tanner went out with Dakota and Jordon and/or Melody and Maxwell, they never called it that. Hanging out, or partying, but never a double date. Maybe she and Tanner were doing it wrong? Probably. God knows so much of what they had done together had been wrong.

Try as she might, Cali couldn't remember how she and Tanner had met. It involved a typical frat party. Booze. Games. Games involving booze. She would love to remember the cheesy line he had used. She assumed he used a line; that's just the way he was. She also imagined they met while playing beer pong. It was his favorite game, and he had pure mastery over it. Cali was the only person who could beat him, and it pissed him off to no end. She remembered waking up next to him the morning after, both of them naked, her bedroom smelling of stale sweat, alcohol, and pot. And she remembered her first words to him – "Nice ink."

"Thanks," he replied, looking down at the thick black curves intersecting on his shoulder, as if he had forgotten they existed. "It's something tribal."

All the dude-bro warning signs were there, but he put Adonis to shame, so she aggressively ignored the flashing red lights and klaxons during their three years together, until...

Get your shit together, Lindquist, she scolded herself as she finished wrestling with the sparring glove. Similar to boxing gloves, which she had plenty of experience with, they were fingerless with padding on the back of the hands. She adjusted her headgear – thick padding across her forehead and her cheeks – and accepted the mouth guard from Chism's coach.

"He telegraphs his left hook," Coach said. "He won't listen to me, so if maybe you could knock some sense into him, I'd consider it a favor."

"I'm standing right here," Chism said from the other side of the mat.

"Which is why I said it loud enough for you to hear!" Coach had the toned physique of an athletic lifetime. His short brown hair sported random grays. His skin hadn't hit the leathery stage yet, but the black of his tattoos had faded to a dull green. Cali was five foot nine, and Coach was short enough to look her directly in the eye when he said, "Kick his ass."

"Still right here, having my emotional needs stepped on."

"You'll live."

Cali chuckled, even though this scenario reminded her of her first date with Tanner.

After morning sex, they had grabbed breakfast at the nearby diner. They talked for two hours, long enough for Cali to think they were heading into a mature relationship. Working out had been a shared interest, and Cali ignorantly assumed he did more than just move steel plates around at the gym. The next day they signed up for a 5k obstacle course, including, but not limited to, carrying forty-pound bags of sand, scaling multiple walls, and marching through a creek of waist-high water. Out of two hundred participants, they finished in the top forty. Cali could have won but held back to stay with Tanner. The next day, Tanner tried to hide his aches and discomfort, but winced every time he moved. At the time, Cali thought it was cute and gave him a blowjob. Today, not so much. She realized she had set a bad precedent. She limited her potential for his benefit, and then rewarded him.

No more. She might have to kick Chism's ass for the betterment of her nineteen-year-old self.

The gloves were weird. She met Chism at the center of the mat, curling and stretching her fingers to get used to the fit. "I never had anyone bring their coach to a first date with me before. Did you think we needed a chaperone?"

Chism laughed. Even with his face distorted by the headgear and his teeth hidden by the black mouth guard, his smile brought a tickle to Cali's spine. "First of all –" She suppressed a giggle; his mouthguard forced his "s" into a slurred lisp. "Let me remind you that you knew I had a coach before you suggested this date activity." He then pointed to the front desk. As one of the owners of the gym specializing in mixed martial arts training, Coach greeted potential customers. He was ignoring every customer while paying extra attention to two perky blondes asking about joining the gym. "Second of all, a porn director would make a better chaperone."

"Jesus, I can actually see the testosterone wafting off him." She turned her attention back to Chism. "Okay, we have the keys to the liquor cabinet and no one is watching, now what?"

Chism took a step back and raised his fists, ready to punch or block. "Now you show me what you got."

Cali raised her fists to her face. "Aren't you gonna take your shirt off?"

Chism pulled the bottom of his shirt down and struck a pose as if trying to keep a billowy dress from blowing up on a blustery day. "Why, Calista!" Still lisping. "I'm not that kind of guy."

For the second time today, he made Cali's jaw drop. Literally, mouth hanging open. Then she laughed. There was no other response her body would allow. In a gym geared toward training people how to beat the crap out of each other, Chism acted as if no one else were around, certainly not the other dozen men and women training. Was this an act? Was he goofing around to lull her into a false sense of security? No, Cali didn't think so. His actions took her by such surprise that all she could muster was a lame, "The matches I've seen, the competitors always have their shirts off."

"Even the women? If so, then you might not be watching sanctioned matches," he said. Even with his headgear on, Cali could tell he was smirking as he raised his gloves. "First of all, this is light practice, not a real match. Second of all, if you really want to see me shirtless, you need to buy me dinner first and tell me I'm pretty."

"Light practice?"

Chism shrugged. "Okay, then, if you want to amp it up a little, let's see what you got."

He brought his hands up closer to his face, his fingers were curled, not into fists but ready to grab. With a slight bend in his knees, he swayed side to side as he stepped forward. Cali was happy that he didn't try any macho nonsense, like standing soldier straight and spurting, "Give me your best shot." That's something Tanner would have done. Chism respected the possibility that she might have something to offer. To reward him, her high kick to his head was at half speed.

Chism blocked it, but he was sloppy. Reflex, not training. "Whoa! Hell of a kick! Speed, power, poise. Were you fibbing to me about your skill level?"

Cali raised her hands to her face and matched Chism's step as they danced in a circle around an invisible point. "I never mentioned my skill level. I think you made assumptions."

"Nope, no assumptions made." He punctuated his statement by advancing and throwing a few right jabs followed by a left hook. Every strike was easy to block. And Coach was right – she saw his left hook coming a mile away. She tagged him with a couple jabs to his face and followed up with a light kick to his side.

Chism stepped back and continued his circular path. There was a glimmer in his eye, one of admiration, not resentment. Tanner would have left the mat and tossed his gloves in the nearest trash can. Not Chism. He actually smiled as he came in again. This time, faster.

A few of his strikes connected, but they weren't hard. She allowed the weaker hits so she could block the stronger strikes, and then hit back. He took a step back. She advanced.

Heart rate increasing, Cali threw a few more punches. A few more pops from her padded gloves to his padded headgear. Heat flowed up her spine turning to fire in her arms with every hit, and getting hotter. The white of his headgear blurred, his eyes and mouth smudged. His face disappeared, replaced with one of the triplets from yesterday. Cali hit harder, faster. Her opponent blocked and backed up, circled around her to get a better vantage point for a counterattack. Circling. Striking. A fist. A kick. A tingle ran up Cali's back, a burst of adrenaline's cold fire raged through her veins. The white face blurred again within her tunnel vision. It darkened as brown fur sprouted from a growing snout. Black nose, rounded ears atop its head, dead black eyes. A bear's head.

Every motor in Cali's body revved, anger gunning the engine of hatred. The beast was bigger, but she had to bring it down, get it to the floor. Three steps back, then two forward, followed by a jump, driving both knees into the bear's shoulders. She was only one hundred sixty pounds, but she had enough force to knock it down. Momentum pushed her forward once they both hit the ground – she wasn't going to let it win. Hands out, she pushed against the mat and thrust herself backward. Her knees pinned the bear's shoulders down. She released her fury. Fist to face, hitting faster and faster.

Hands grabbed her, so many hands. Four? No, six. Three men pulled her off the bear… no, not a bear… Chism!

"Whoa! Easy, there," Coach said, one of the men pulling her away from her date. "I told you to kick his ass, not pulverize his face."

Other people's blood had covered her hands many times before, and she checked her knuckles out of reflex. Red streaked the back of her left hand. She killed him. She killed her date.

The horrid thought disappeared when the men released her. She looked down at Chism. A splash of blood on his head gear, from his nose.

Coach helped him to his feet and said, "Got yourself a fiery one."

Cali didn't know if he responded or not, because she had turned and walked toward the exit. This date was a mistake. This was too much, too soon. Her mother had implied she'd gone feral, and this only proved it. The only words she heard in between the raging river of her pulse was from one of the girls Coach had been flirting with: "Sign me up for whatever training package she has."

No, you really don't want that, Cali thought, pushing back tears. She wriggled out of her gloves and removed her headgear, dropping them on her way to her gym bag, close to the door. Before she could leave, a tap on her shoulder stopped her. Had she been thinking straight, she would have kept going, maybe even sprinted, but she was wound too tightly and spun around.

Chism. Head gear and gloves off, nose bleeding. "Where you going?"

"Are you fucking serious?" Cali asked in an angry tone to keep her voice from warbling into a cry.

With a wide-eyed frown, he nonchalantly wiped the back of his hand under his nose. "Umm… yeah?"

"I almost killed you and you're stopping me from leaving."

"This?" he asked, pointing to his leaking nose. "I get nose bleeds all the time. If I sneeze too hard, nosebleed. I chew too hard, nosebleed. I think your definition of attempted murder is a bit overblown. I mean, you thoroughly kicked my ass and I might die of verbal harassment from all those who witnessed it. You hit hard, really hard, but I'm fine."

"Oh my God, Chism, I'm a sociopath. Can't you see that?"

"Actually, a sociopath is a person who doesn't get upset about hurting other people after using fake charm to reel them in. You're the exact opposite."

"You should totally run away screaming from me."

"Look, it's obvious that some of your wires got crossed for a few seconds, but the fact that you're mad at yourself means you're a good person. You are absolutely like no other woman I have ever met before, and I'd really like to learn more about you."

Dashing to the front desk, Chism grabbed a flyer advertising the gym and a pen. He ran back to her while scribbling on the pamphlet. "But I'm going to leave it up to you. Here's my home number and cell phone number. If you'd like to see me again, call. If not, then I'll respect that decision and leave you alone. I just want to make sure you know without a doubt that whopping me in my own gym has not made me change my mind about wanting to see you again."

Cali should crumble up the paper and throw it away, or drop it on the ground, or chew it up and swallow it. But she put it in her pocket before she walked out the door.

June 16, 2002

Chet cracked open a Goose Island IPA and flopped onto his couch, a smile on his face from ear to ear. The television was all his. So was the couch and remote. And the leftover pizza in the fridge.

One of his wife's friends invited her to a spiritual hippie-shit cleansing retreat. Looking like the supportive husband, Chet insisted that Trina go. Points scored for him in the marriage ledger, and he had the house to himself for the next three days. Finally!

Chugging half the beer, he flipped through the channels until he found MLB. Being able to watch baseball in peace, didn't care which game, was all he needed at the moment. Trina certainly had her good qualities, but God damn, her nonstop sermons about how modern sports debase civilization's psyche drove him up a friggin' wall. And her eyeroll every time he cracked a cold one was a mood killer.

Chet took another swig, swished it around his mouth, gargled for a second, and then swallowed. Then ripped an earthshattering belch. Laughing, he felt like an idiot, but he couldn't stop himself from enjoying the moment. How come no one ever told him marriage was such a drag? Well, plenty of people told him, but he never *believed* it. Jesus, he wasn't even thirty yet, and he felt like one half of a ninety-year-old couple.

IPA finished and can crushed, he propped his feet on the coffee table and settled into the cushions. He thought about taking his clothes off to really assert his dominion by marking his territory with his primal funk. Nah. It'd be weird watching baseball with his junk hanging out. He wanted another beer, but was too comfortable.

Sitting back even further, he glanced at two photos hanging on the wall, on either side of the television. The massive black and white photos in three-foot by four-foot frames were taken by Trina's sister, Brin, while on an assignment. Close ups of wolves, one in each photo, their upper lips curled into snarls, shimmering teeth bared. When Trina first hung them on the wall, Chet loved the beasts' "in-your-face" awesomeness. However, over the past couple of years, they reminded him of Trina and her sister; teeth always gnashing, nagging. The wolf on the left yelled at him in Trina's voice, "Get your feet off the table! Stop drinking beer! Turn off that trash!"

Fuck it. Chet got himself another beer.

But just as he sat down, his phone buzzed. A call from "Chuck."

"Yeah?" Chet answered.

"I'm bored," a woman's voice said with a sigh.

"Sorry to hear that."

"Come over. I know Trina's out of town."

"Kimberly, I—"

"I'll let you do the porn stuff."

Chet took a gulp from his beer. The universal debate – a night of drinking, watching baseball, and letting his mind blissfully drift away, or a night of kinky sex. "I'll be right over."

Beer number two chugged, television off, Chet put on shoes and grabbed his keys.

When he got to the door to the garage, he paused. Something wasn't right. A familiar noise from behind the door. "What the hell?"

Pssssssssst. Pssssssssst.

Soft, almost like a forced hiss. Like air let out of a tire.

Pssssssssst. Pssssssssst.

Or a spray from an aerosol can. Yeah, that was it.

Pssssssssst. Pssssssssst.

Someone was in his garage! Chet ran to the kitchen and grabbed the biggest knife in the block, then hurried back to the door. Arm raised, blade out and ready to stab, he puffed a few times and then held his breath as he whipped open the door...

The sight was so surreal, so incomprehensible, that he dropped the knife, shuffling farther into the garage. Three clowns stood swaying before him as if moving to the same tune in their heads.

"What... the... Hey! Trina? Is that you?"

Trina was home, which was surprising in itself, but...

At a petite four foot ten with big, green eyes, she had a child-like look to her, which was why she got so teeth-gnashingly argumentative when asserting how serious she should be taken. Now she stood before Chet with cans of spray paint – he'd set them aside for a custom hotrod paint job on his '69 Camaro – rolling around by her feet. Her face, neck, and the top of her chest had been sprayed white. Silver plus signs were painted over her eyes, her teeth and her smile painted gold. She posed like a car show model. "Hi, dear! I'm a hotrod! Vroom vroom!"

And was that Brin... in clown makeup? Yes, Trina's sister stood in between her and some guy who was also clowned up. *Do I know him? Yes*. Chet couldn't recall the dude's real name, but he went by Collin. They had met a couple times. A work-friend of Brin's, Collin and Brin were the only survivors of a bear attack a month ago. Chet's mind swirled in a whirlpool of confusion, too disoriented to form any meaningful words, to ask why they looked like clowns.

Brin's long hair was bright green. Known for altering her hair color and style every few months, Chet had no idea if it was a wig or a recent dye job. A purple square over her left eye, a triangle over her right, and a jagged yellow smile went from ear to ear. Collin had a base of white face paint as well as big blue circles over his eyes. His smile was red, overdrawn, and dramatic. However, his light brown hair seemed untouched.

"Trina... What the Hell...?" Chet started, his own voice unfamiliar, but trailed away when he saw what had been spray-painted on the wall behind the trio: FUCK YOU CHET!

"Vroom vroom!" The mocking sound of a speeding car came from his wife. The childish noise grew louder. Faster. Inhuman.

The flash of a hammer was the last thing Chet saw.

*

Collin and Brin laughed as Trina cracked her husband's skull open, dropping him to the floor. She stood over his body, each slopping hammer-crack accompanied by, "Vroom, vroom!"

Collin screwed the top back onto a thermos. He'd need to fill it again soon enough. It was the perfect vehicle for transporting Master Poppie's gift, the white mist. There was no predicting what would happen to people exposed to the white mist, but it brought Trina into the fold. Even though she was now... different.

"Race car!" Trina cried out. "Vroom vroom!"

"Yes, you are sweetest, sweet sister," Brin said, clapping with encouragement.

"Success," Collin said. "Though your sister may have mush brain."

"We got the purple mist, she got the white mist like Master Poppie instructed. She's joined the party, and that's all that matters. That and getting Master Poppie food."

Trina released the hammer, the metal banging against the cement floor. The smell of wet, warm copper mixed with the spray paint fumes. Trina dropped to her knees on Chet's chest. Her fingers dug into what was left of his head, slorping and squishing.

"After we feed him Chet, Master Poppie will be strong enough to get his own food," Collin said. "Allowing us to focus on the bigger picture."

"Making more clowns."

"That's right, Brin. Making a few more clowns like us, and *a lot* more like Trina."

"This neighborhood is perfect for that."

Collin nodded. "This one and the other one."

A thick forest ran between the two neighborhoods. The forest was where Master Poppie lived now, a better place to find food than the forest where Collin and Brin had found him last month. Yes, the police would be involved eventually, but Master Poppie will tell Collin what to do, how to handle them. By then, Master Poppie's plan would be coming to fruition, and it'd be too late for police.

Trina stood, dragging her goopy fingers through her long, once-blonde hair, now stained red as Chet's blood with pink bits of brain clung to the strands. "I'm a race car!"

Brin cackled and bent over to hug her sister.

Yes, Master Poppie's plan was going to work. Start small to build big. And the next piece in the puzzle was small, but very, very big – Collin's son.

June 3, 2002

Keith slouched in his basement's office chair, spent, almost sliding off the cracked leather. Sweat smeared his clown paint, streaking it along his neck, shoulders, and chest. He smiled, satisfied for the third time in the last two hours, this time finishing in one of his wigs. The video was magical. But it wasn't enough.

He huffed as he shifted, his muscles sore. Keith reached for the mouse and clicked off the video, the fifth in his special folder, and his favorite so far. But it was the shortest. He got too excited while making it. Little Lily was special, too special and Keith had rushed the process. Too excited. Now he was angry with himself.

He tossed his sticky wig into the trash can by his desk. The wig was old and he had dozens more on Styrofoam head-forms. They were next to a rack of costumes and half a dozen oversized shoes. The pride of his studio, though, was the trunks. Two wooden trunks, edged in brass like pirate chests, were stuffed with tricks he performed on a regular basis, and they sat on the floor under a long white folding table. The new tricks sat on top of the table; the old ones he no longer used were immortalized behind glass in tall, museum quality wooden display cases. Too bad no other eyes would see this room.

His studio, as he thought of it, was his basement. The cliché was distasteful, especially since he lived by himself in a two-story rowhouse. He could do whatever he wanted whenever he wanted wherever he wanted. The basement offered plenty of room for his needs as Keith the Clown. Those needs required a lot of radio controls and wireless technology and gear that wasn't cheap or easy to acquire. Luckily, he still had contacts from his time in the Army.

His desk was nothing more than sheets of plywood on sawhorses, sturdy enough to hold his computers and recording devices. He positioned his set up close to the furnace, rigged to blow and look like an accident. Always have contingencies. That included backing up his material onto an external hard drive that he kept in a bank's security deposit box.

He'd visit the bank tomorrow to make sure his time with Little Lily would be forever saved.

Five videos. He needed more. He always needed more, but he had to wait. He'd made video one before he was a clown, of a princess named Elisa. Video number two was his first as a clown; that was with Superstar Shae. Then came video three with Wee Wanda. He was cautious, though. No police visited him yet, but there was always the chance they'd connect the dots. When he met Beautiful Becca, he decided to wait six months before making video four, and he used that time to create evidence that would guide police down a different path. Video four immortalized Beautiful Becca, and it worked out perfectly. After viewing Little Lily's video, he knew he couldn't ever wait six months again. The urgency was painfully strong. And frustrating.

Too irritable to think straight, he answered the annoying phone the second it rang.

"Hello?"

"Hi! I'm looking for Keith the Clown." A woman's voice sing-songed against his eardrum. The same sounding voice of Little Lily's mother. But no way was this her on the phone.

"Speaking."

"My name is Madison Holcomb and my daughter, Marissa, will be turning eight later this month, and I heard great things about your performance."

Something about her voice made him hate her immediately, like she was doing him a favor. Like he owed her.

Answering had been a mistake; he wasn't clear headed yet. He always, always, always let the calls go to voicemail. This was a moment of weakness, but he could get out of it. *Tell her you're booked, or going on vacation.* "Thank you for the kind words. Just send me an email with the pertinent information. Do you have my email address?"

"I do! I will send that immediately, and you can get ready to give your best performance yet for my Marissa."

She followed up her statement with a whimsical chuckle. Keith didn't think her words should be taken at face value, but said, "I have no doubt that it will be my best performance."

Suddenly, Madison's tone switched to all business. Melodic, but with a hint of sharpness. "Okay, email sent. Could you confirm that you received it?"

He was still at his computer, still naked. Sure enough, there was an email from *futurestarmommy*. Keith opened it.

"Did you get it?" Madison asked.

"I did." The words fell out of his mouth in an automated response.

"I included a few pictures of my Marissa hoping you'll be inspired to tailor your performance around her, so you can make it more special. She saw you at Lily Pennington's party, and said she wanted you at hers. I assume your performance will be different than Lily's."

His breath hitched. He remembered Marissa. She had caught his eye, but it was Little Lily's party, and it wouldn't have been right if he had shown Marissa too much attention. But now, she looked like a tiny little model. A shrunken, fragile adult. An offering to the demented gods of beauty and fame, willingly sacrificed by her parents, the very people who should be protecting her from those deities. If she grew up following the path her parents put her on, then the congregation who worshipped those disgusting gods would ruin her. Keith couldn't allow that. Wouldn't. He'd immortalize her, just the way she was.

"My routine for Marissa will be better than Lily's. I promise."

"Wonderful! I included my home phone number and my cell phone number. I can be reached at either, so don't hesitate to call should you need anything."

"Thank you. You have a nice day. Bye."

He turned off his computer monitor. He had work to do, needed to prepare. And he had to hurry.

Shower. Shave. Clean clothes – simple jeans, tee shirt, sneakers. He was average height for a man, but wider at the shoulder, thanks to Army training, with the start of roundness to his belly, thanks to cheap beer. He kept his hair buzzed, and no facial hair. Should he be seen when he didn't want to be, then he'd be described as "nothing noticeable, bigger than average, maybe."

Latex gloves on, he grabbed Little Lily's stuffed dog on his way out. He wanted to save it as a souvenir, but now it had to be used for something else. He felt fifty-fifty about this plan's success rate, but since he was going to make a new video so soon after his last one, he needed to execute. If not for Marissa, he'd have let Little Lily be, let the missing person's search find the body and simply wait for the hoopla to die down before hunting again. Not now. Not with Marissa's birthday coming up. Now he needed to guide the police down a different path.

Little Lily lived in a neighborhood just nice enough for the residents to call themselves upper-middle class, even though a better neighborhood was on the other side of a dense forest.

Eight hours since she'd gone missing from school. Friends and family had been called and places she loved to frequent had been visited. The police had responded. The dogs were next, probably soon.

Venturing inside the forest where he had laid Little Lily to rest, he scurried to her shallow grave at the base of a big pine tree. The surrounding area remained completely undisturbed. Good. He was able to dig her up easily and clip a couple of her fingernails.

Almost two football fields of a walk to the edge of the forest, he saw that a few neighbors had gathered with Little Lily's parents in front of their house. No one was out back. No one was watching. A short run from the forest to the side door of the garage and he made quick work of the lock with his fancy motorized lock pick – another benefit of having special friends.

Crouching low, he duck-walked to the Lexus, an older model. Using his tool again, he popped the trunk. He had brought a plastic hand with him, one stolen from a child-sized mannequin at a Carter's Store and raked the fingers across the trunk's carpeted interior. Satisfied he had collected enough grime, he dropped fragments of Little Lily's clipped fingernails inside the trunk. One last touch. The ear from the stuffed dog came off with ease and he tucked it in the corner of the space. Trunk closed. Garage door closed and locked. Little Lily's ignorant parents and their stupid friends too myopic to notice anything beyond their own short-sightedness.

Keith ran back to Little Lily's grave. With a gloved hand, he smeared the grime from the mannequin hand over Little Lily's fingers, under her fingernails. He tucked her stuffed dog under her arm and covered her back up with the loose dirt. She'd be found soon enough, most likely tomorrow morning. Satisfied, he started to hurry away, but suddenly froze. Nervous, like ants were scurrying up and down his spine, he turned.

He wasn't alone.

Holding his breath, he listened to the forest while eyeing every tree. Nothing but the thud, thud, thud of his own heartbeat between his ears. There was someone... no, that wasn't right. Not a person. A presence. There was a presence with him in the woods. But... it felt kindred, like his thoughts had been turned into a living thing. It owned the forest, but it liked him enough to allow him to leave.

Not wanting to tempt it, Keith left the forest, running.

June 19, 2002

Cali's mother's eyes widened, her smile more of a smirk. "You're going to call him, right?"

"Mom! Stop!" Cali rubbed her temples, elbows on the small hotel room table. This was the third time she had asked since Cali stepped through the door two minutes ago. It had been an hour since her date, and she still wasn't sure if she was calling it that. Twenty minutes to get back to her hotel room – a different floor than her mother's room, because sharing a room with Mom was... eww – thirty minutes in the shower to wash away her anger issues, ten minutes to be mentally prepared for the interrogation.

"It's a perfectly reasonable question."

"Wine."

"Cali—"

"Wine, please."

Mother sighed and went to the kitchenette. Two wine glasses from the cabinet and a bottle of Chardonnay from the refrigerator. She sat at the table with Cali and poured. "We might need to discuss your dependence on alcohol when dealing with difficult topics."

"My dating life isn't difficult. I don't want one. I don't think this is the right time to look for a man—"

"Or a woman."

"—or a woman to spend the rest of my life with."

Cali grabbed her glass and turned away. Mother sat with her legs crossed, left hand resting on her lap, eyes peering over the top of her glass as she drank. Like a therapist. Cali didn't want her mother studying her like that.

"You're putting way too much meaning behind the word 'dating.' You don't need to find a soulmate or life partner or husband or wife. You *do* need to connect with people."

"I do connect with people," Cali mumbled. It was a trivial attempt at an argument, but she said it anyway.

"I'm not talking about meaningless sex."

Cali gulped a swig of wine so she could blame the alcohol for the sudden flare-up within her cheeks, even though she had nothing to be embarrassed about. She got laid when she wanted, and on her terms, so what could be more empowering than that? Sure, her encounters were nothing more than one-night stands, most of the men looking like Tanner. And yes, just last month, she walked into a bar, went up to a guy and asked, "Wanna fuck?" Replaying that scene, Cali realized that his response, "Hell yeah," was the entirety of their conversation. Okay, so maybe Mother had a point.

"Fine, I'll call him. But I'm not going to call him right now with you staring at me like a rabid hyena."

Mother laughed and got up from the table. "That's fine. I'm just happy that you actually interacted with another human being."

"You have a warped sense of the word 'interacted' considering I kicked his ass."

"The fact that he still wants to associate with you after you did that means he may be more than a pretty face." Mother ventured across the room to a leather attaché. "But we can change the topic," she said. She slapped five manilla folders filled with papers and pictures, onto the table, and sat back down.

"Maybe he has mental issues. Or maybe he –" Cali opened the top folder. "Oh my God!"

As Cali flipped through the pictures of the folder labeled "Lily," Mother opened three of the other folders and spread them across the table. "Oh my God is right. I have three more files of kids like that one, and one on the potential suspect."

Disgust swirled within Cali and formed a lump in the back of her throat. She wanted to cry or throw up, or both. Picture after picture of Lily made the lump grow, burn. The bruises over her pale skin, still dirty from her shallow grave, were the worst. On her thighs and around her neck. Cali knew what happened to poor Lily. She had so many questions, but when she tried to speak, her voice cracked before she could form a single word.

"Police dogs found her buried in the woods behind her neighborhood. They also found her scent in the trunk of her father's Lexus," Mother said.

Cali nodded as she moved past the pictures. The information her mother shared was in the police reports and newspaper clippings Cali sifted through.

Mother reached across the table and touched Cali's hand. "If this is too much, we can put the folders away and I'll just tell you the info."

Cali drained the remainder of the wine and pushed the glass to the far end of the table, almost dropping it to the floor. She closed Lily's folder, wiped away a stray tear, and gestured for her mother to hand her the next one. "No. If this is the work of a monster, then I want to do this."

"This is probably not the kind of monster you're looking for."

"It is now."

Mother nodded and slid the next file to her, one labeled, "Becca." Similar situation. A girl too young to speculate about such horrors, let alone experience them. Ghastly pallid body, lifeless and naked in the dirt. The same pattern of bruising.

Stomach roiling, Cali grabbed the other two folders. Similar pictures. Similar police reports. "These girls were killed the same way, but by four different sickos."

Hand on the last folder, Mother said, "That's the theory. An uncle killed the one girl. One case went unsolved. A neighbor was blamed for one girl and the father was arrested for Lily."

"Then why are we looking at these poor girls? Most of these cases have been closed."

"Think, Cali."

Cali clenched her fists and closed her eyes. Her temper held her back, obscuring what was right in front of her. How could she not get mad about young lives snuffed out so violently? Why would her mother show her these files, these pictures, to wind her up to exact justice when it had already been served? The police had investigated, found their evidence, and made their arrests. *Wait... Police investigate until they find enough evidence to make an arrest.* Once the arrest was made, they moved onto the next case. Convicting a father, an uncle, and a neighbor meant they'd never look for more evidence or any other way to connect the cases, because they already found enough for an arrest. And evidence could be faked.

Anger aside, Cali thought about what she had read in Lily's file, taking apart the puzzle that had been assembled and turning the pieces of evidence around to see if they fit another picture. The trunk of the car. That piece didn't fit at all.

Cali opened her eyes. "Wait! You said that the dogs picked up Lily's scent in the trunk of the car?"

"I did."

Rifling through the folder, Cali grabbed the police report. "Why the fuck would he put her in the trunk? They found scape marks, a couple broken fingernails, and a small piece of her stuffed animal in the trunk. The rest of the stuffed animal was found buried with her. There was car grime found under her fingernails."

"Correct."

"The report said that she went missing when a fire alarm went off at her school, the alarm pulled by an older kid. A few students said they saw Lily outside. If her father was going to abduct her, it'd be easier to say, 'Hi, Honey, get in the car, we're going for a ride,' than to stage a false alarm."

"Very well done!"

"How did the police fuck this up?"

Mother stopped spinning the last folder and placed it on top of the other folders. "They didn't. They found what they were looking for, which was evidence pointing them toward an answer. They aren't looking for what we're looking for."

Cali opened the folder and almost jumped out of her chair. "The fuck?" An eight by ten color photo of a clown's face. "You could have warned me."

"Sorry. Didn't want to ruin the surprise. Or your epiphany."

"Ha, ha. So, you're thinking this clown is involved."

"I'm thinking he's the killer of all four of those little girls."

Cali flipped the picture over. Blank. She flipped it back and studied his white face-grease, thick to hide wrinkles, blemishes, distinguishing features. Red circles on his cheeks, wide enough to create an optical illusion through facial contour. Bulbous orange nose, foam hiding the flesh and cartilage beneath. Wig of puffy red curls. "Well, he does look like a creeper."

"His name is Keith the Clown."

"Seriously?"

"Seriously, and that's his only picture on his website. There's no address and he doesn't list his real name. Accepts cash only and lists a phone number to call to leave a message. One email address."

"Jesus that's suspicious. Are you going by your gut on this creepy guy, or do you have evidence?"

Mother leaned back in her chair, getting comfortable. "I wrote a program to comb through news articles relating to disappearances and deaths, flagging any that seem suspicious. Lily's caught my attention, because I, too, thought it odd for her father to put her in the trunk of his car. I was scanning the browser history of Lily's parents – they had visited Keith the Clown's website. I hacked into their phone records, and sure enough, they called his number. By narrowing the parameters of my search for children who were… abused in the same fashion as Lily before being murdered within a two-hundred-mile radius, the other three victims popped up. When I checked browser histories and phone logs of the victims' parents, guess what?"

"Fuck you, Keith."

"Exactly."

"Did you trace his phone number and email address?"

"Tried, and his website, too, but he uses an impressively sophisticated rerouting sequencer. It showed a different location around the world each time I searched."

"Double fuck you, Keith."

"Exactly."

Cali leaned back and stared at the ceiling, combing her fingers through her hair. "Okay, so how do we track him down? Should I call and leave a message? Come up with a story about wanting to use his services for my kid's birthday party?"

"No. He might have a vetting process, and he goes months between attacks. I think we should take a different route. At least three of the families went directly to his website. That means they didn't find him through an internet search. Someone recommended him."

"You're saying it might be better to contact Lily's mother and find out who referred her, and if she had referred him to anyone else."

Mother shrugged. "It's a long shot, but whatever we do next is a long shot."

"Okay. A bad plan is better than no plan." Cali went back to Lily's folder. "In the meantime, I want to learn all there is to know about these victims."

"You sure?"

"I'll call Chism later, Mom. I promise."

"Okay. Want more wine?"

"No thanks. I want to be clear-headed for this."

Mom smiled softly but didn't say anything else. She wanted to, Cali read it all over her. Though her mother had been in her life behind the scenes, parenting by observation from the shadows, she had been an absent mother, out of Cali's perspective from age two to twenty-two. Cali knew her mother wished to impart her wisdom and care all at once, but Cali wasn't in a good space for that right now. She had a monster to hunt.

June 15, 2002

Maxwell entered the 8th Street Gallery, surprised his father would own a place like this. The store front was nothing striking, mostly windows with a few abstract paintings on easels. It was one of three spaces in a big block of a building across the street from a pay parking lot. Inside, the artwork hung on moveable walls within the room, creatively accessible and intriguing even to the unattuned eye. Sculptures occupied any accommodating spaces in non-aggressive ways. A few glass cases of handcrafted jewelry, other trinkets, and the cash register lined the wall closest to the door. The prices for the merchandise ranged from affordable to students from the nearby college, to shut-the-gallery-down-early-for-the-weekend ludicrously expensive. Maxwell wasn't sure why his father would invest in this location.

Roger Templeton wasn't narrow minded, but his train sped along on only one track, never switching until his destination was reached. Growing up with every need and want met, Maxwell wasn't curious about what his father did for a living. He knew he owned businesses and spent too much time in the office, according to his mother who left before he hit his teenage years. As long as he got good grades and kept his football, baseball, and track coaches happy, Maxwell never experienced his father's wrath. He rarely experienced any form of warmth either, but he knew his father loved him. There were ballgames and the occasional fishing trip, mixed with advice on how to command respect and what girls liked. His father's wisdom on those topics didn't quite translate to modern times, but Maxwell got enough out of the talks. How to garner respect and what girls liked seemed to boil down to the same thing – money. Maxwell had it and learned how to use it wisely.

He didn't need money with Melody, but he did with her friends.

Melody, Dakota, and Calista had been friends since grade school, following each other to Bucknell. Maxwell had met Melody in Accounting, a class he needed for the degree he pursued to appease his father. After a few tutoring sessions, he and Melody became an item.

Unlike other women, she was genuine, and he could be himself around her. Not so with Dakota, the vapid daughter of a B-movie star actress, or Calista, the sarcastic blonde with the better-than-everyone attitude. Their boyfriends, Jordon and Tanner, both small in mind yet large in bank account, were likeable, once Maxwell passed their net-worth test.

He grew to like them well enough to finance a business with a mutual friend, Hook. Maxwell wasn't thrilled about distributing recreational substances, but they had enough connections in the college party scene to make it worthwhile. It all came crashing down two years ago; Dakota, Jordon, Tanner, and Hook were found dead. Calista missing.

Maxwell didn't know how or why, but Calista was involved with the deaths of his friends. It became obvious after she murdered his father a year later. "Bitch."

"Hmm? Did you say something?" Melody asked, distracted by the plethora of artwork.

Maxwell hadn't realized the word escaped his mouth, but thankfully he hadn't said it too loudly. He gestured to a nearby painting with an orange background and bright yellow vertical lines running through the center. It reminded him of an abstract cityscape. "Rich. This piece. The colors are rich, aren't they?"

"Oh! Yes, they are." Melody glided closer to the artwork, eyeing it as if measuring the living room of their house to figure out which wall it might go on. Did *he* own all the artwork in here? Could he simply pluck it off the wall? He couldn't do that with any of the other companies, so he doubted he could with this one.

"It is a lovely piece, isn't it?" a young man said. As if he were a magician, he had appeared out of nowhere and handed a glass of wine to Melody. His short hair was found in most modern men's style magazines, and his smart blue blazer fit his thin frame perfectly, the color going nicely with his light blue shirt and khaki slacks. A thin black scarf ran to his knees as more of an accent than a form of warmth. His smile was sharp enough to cut the diamonds in his earrings. "You two looking to revamp your entire living space, or just one room? Either way, I can help create the perfect atmosphere for you."

Maxwell stepped forward and said, "Actually, we're looking for the gallery manager, Justin."

The young man did a half-bow, the tone of his voice implying flattery. "Well, I'm Justin. Who might be looking for me?"

Maxwell held out his hand. "Maxwell Templeton. Roger was my father, and I've recently acquired all his holdings. I wanted to meet you, to learn more about the gallery."

The handshake was unenthusiastic, and Justin's smile lost most of its luster. He looked like a kid who learned his parents would be coming home sooner than expected. Not because he was up to no good, but because he had been enjoying the freedom. Maxwell didn't know how hands-on his father was with the gallery, but he assumed that Justin enjoyed having full autonomy for the past year. "I'm sorry to hear about your father, but it's very nice to meet you, Mr. Templeton."

"Maxwell, please. And this is my girlfriend, Melody."

"Pleased to meet you," Justin said.

They made small talk, until a trio of men walked through the front door. A sour burst of acid gurgled up from Maxwell's stomach and splashed the back of his throat. As much as he wanted nothing to do with these men, he suspected that one of them was Harold Varvaro, probably the one leading the way. He wore a simple black overcoat atop a gray suit, nicely fitted for a man with a prosperous midsection, and had the face of a 1940s movie mobster. Maxwell was genuinely surprised that no fedora adorned his salt and pepper hair. It was the man's eyes that unnerved Maxwell – lids half shut in a calm manner, but with sinister intelligence. A shark conserving its energy, floating with the current until it was time to strike.

The two men standing behind him were just as suspicious; one overweight, the only care in his eyes was for the cannoli he was eating, the other man short and thin, his bulbous eyes adding another level of intensity to his frown. They, too, wore suits, but not as tailored. No, Maxwell did not like the look of this trio at all.

Justin broke away from the conversation with Melody to address the bigger man. "Excuse me, you know very well there is no outside food allowed in the gallery."

Defiantly, the bigger man took another bite while staring at Justin, bits of shell crumbling to the floor.

It was obvious Justin would prefer to continue running the gallery without oversight, but this was Maxwell's gallery now, and he was going to act like it. Taking a step closer to the three men, he addressed the cannoli. "I believe the manager of *my* gallery said there was no outside food."

The bigger man paused his chewing and looked at the leader. As raspy as Maxwell expected, the man with the air of local royalty said, "You know the rules, Mikey. Take that outside. Big, you go with him. I have a feeling Mr. Templeton would like to discuss business without you two fogging up his glasses."

There was such an authority to the man that Maxwell had an urge to kiss his ring. Mikey shrugged and did as instructed, chewing away. Big followed Mikey, but not before shooting a backward glare at Maxwell.

The man stepped forward and extended his hand. "I apologize for the behavior of my associates. They know better and I'll make sure it doesn't happen again. My name is Harold Varvaro."

The handshake was like getting caught in a machine press, but Maxwell refused to show any intimidation. In fact, he attempted to take control of the conversation with a pleasant smile. "Call me Maxwell, please. This is my girlfriend, Melody. It seems you already know Justin?"

"I do." Without so much as a glance to Justin, Harold gestured to the back of the gallery and said, "May I suggest you and I adjourn to the gallery office?"

"Certainly. However, Melody will be joining us."

"You sure?" Harold looked bored enough to fall asleep, but Maxwell didn't like the defiance in the man's eyes. Maxwell was Harold's boss, he just didn't know in what capacity. "I'm sure."

The bright office had potted plants on two metal filing cabinets, a two-drawer wooden desk free of stray papers, and a small decorative table in the corner of the room. A dozen unframed paintings leaned against one wall. Three photos of Justin and another young man, his significant other, judging from their smiles and closeness.

Maxwell sat in the chair behind the desk. A simple, low-end model with arm rests, found on sale in any office supply store, nothing like the leather-covered throne in his main office. Melody grabbed a chair and dragged it next to Maxwell. With no less lethargy than previously displayed, Harold took the chair in front of the desk, his posture relaxed, hands folded together and resting on his lap.

Maxwell put his elbows on the desk, to make sure everyone in the room knew that as the boss, and he had the right to be at ease. "Thank you for contacting me, Mr. Varvaro, but I think the first question I have is this: What did you do for my father?"

Harold raised the corner of his upper lip and tilted his head, as if saying, "Meh," when asked for his feelings toward a mediocre meal. He followed up his expression by saying, "My position in your father's organization didn't have a title. If pressed, I believe he would say, 'supplemental sales and opportunities,' or something like that."

Melody inhaled sharply, almost a gasp. Maxwell couldn't blame her; he didn't like the inference. He kept the tone of his voice polite. "Mr. Varvaro, I'm not entirely sure what you're implying."

Harold smirked. "You've been getting a handle on the businesses, the ones he has left. The puzzle is missing pieces. *I'm* those missing pieces."

Maxwell sat straighter, Harold's words like electrical shocks down his spine. "Mr. Varvaro, I highly doubt my father was involved with anything illegal, let alone the malfeasance you're hinting at."

A chuckle. "Very few multimillionaires are, according to their P.R. department and lawyers, that is."

"If what you're saying is true, and I don't believe that it is, then your final duty as my father's employee is to dissolve whatever off-the-books 'supplemental sales and opportunities' nonsense there is."

Harold stared at Maxwell for what seemed like an eternity, those sleepy eyes hiding their darkness. He smiled softly, accepting his loss and graciously congratulating his opponent, then spread his hands as he

The Killer of Devils

stood. "Very well. I will let those who need to know, know. My condolences to you for the loss of your father."

"Thank you," Maxwell said, unable to muster more than a whisper as he tried to process his father's involvement in illegal activities. It didn't make sense. No – it didn't make sense to the naïve, youthful ideals regarding the man he remembered as a child. But it made sense to the adult who had spent the last many months going over the books. His father had been wealthy, and from what Maxwell had discovered through his research, there was no way he could have reached that level of success without "help." But the companies in the current portfolio weren't all the companies he had owned. Even Harold had referred to the missing companies. "Wait!"

Hand on the doorknob, Harold paused. He cocked his head, the extent of his acknowledgement.

"You said, 'the ones he has left' when referring to his businesses. What did you mean by that?"

Harold sighed and turned around, putting his hands in his pockets, and striking a relaxed posture. "I'm sure you know by now."

Maxwell did, but Harold was still a stranger who Maxwell didn't trust, yet. As a test, he asked, "What are the names of the two companies we're about to talk about?"

"Maxwell?" Melody whispered, her voice shaking.

"It's okay," Maxwell said. "I want to hear Harold's answer."

For the first time since stepping into the gallery, Harold's expression changed. No longer bored, now angry. The look in his eye made Maxwell think that Harold wasn't angry at him, rather angry for him. "Forward Technologies and Albathia Pharmaceuticals."

"What happened to them?"

"Albathia was liquidated, and the proceeds disappeared. Tens of millions of dollars gone without a trace. Stolen. Forward Technologies was sold to the employees of the company. All of it. Both things happened right before your father was murdered."

Murdered. The magic word that changed everything. Mere minutes ago, Maxwell had wanted this man to leave his sight, but now? Now he wanted to hear everything Harold had to say. "The police said he disappeared."

Harold jutted his jaw and shook his head, looking away. After a few seconds of staring at something only he could see, he turned his attention back to Maxwell. "I ain't saying your old man and I were the best of friends, but I knew him. He was not the kind of person to disappear, especially when things were going as well as they were."

"But murdered?"

"In the weeks leading up to his 'disappearance,' his closest accountants and lawyers wound up dead or disappeared. Right when me and my associates started to investigate, he vanished."

Maxwell had seen evidence regarding the transactions Harold was talking about, but zero reason as to why either company had been removed from the portfolio. He had no access to either company's books. Albathia's history had been wiped clean, as if it never existed, and he was denied access to Forward Technologies' numbers since everything had been transferred out of his father's name. Harold was right – he was a missing puzzle piece.

Gesturing to the empty chair, Maxwell said, "I apologize for my curt tone, Mr. Varvaro. I had to realize fully what you were saying. Please, let's continue our discussion."

Harold looked at Melody. "Are you sure?"

Wide-eyed, Melody turned to Maxwell. He didn't need to say anything. She took a deep breath, turned back to Harold, and said, "Yes. We need to hear what you have to say."

Harold nodded and sat back down.

June 19, 2002

Collin laughed along with Brin as Trina played with her balloon animals. They squeaked as she twisted them into knots, struggling to keep them from slipping out of her hands. Blood dripping down her arms, she presented a twisted mess to her audience. "A doggie! Woof! Woof!"

"Yes, it is!" Brin squealed as she clapped her hands.

Collin didn't see a dog at all, but he remained encouraging. "Nicely done, Trina."

"See?" Delvin yelled to the dead dog on the ground. "That one is a good doggie." Unlike the balloon animal, the dog at his feet had once been a living animal. Until Delvin crushed its skull with one stomp of his big black buckled boot. A yippy-yappy thing with long white fur, little teeth, and big wishes, barking and barking until it got stepped on. Delvin told the dog he was going to turn it into a purse. "No yap, yap, yap from that doggie!" he shouted at the fur corpse. Collin saw no reason why Delvin couldn't keep it, since it wasn't big enough to be a morsel for Master Poppie. The two people the dog kept as pets, on the other hand…

Yesterday, Collin, Brin, and Trina met Delvin – a tall homeless man with a big, bulbous, bobblehead head. At first, he was going to be food, but Collin had a thermos of the white mist with him and offered it to Delvin. Inhaling the white mist, Delvin became their new friend.

Immediately afterward, he had used a full pack of cigarettes to burn his skin from his temples to his cheeks, searing his flesh in the form of a big X over each eye. Now, he wore white makeup like everyone else, but blue covered the burned skin, the same shade of blue as his newly dyed hair. His red painted clown smile, like Collin's, accentuated the real smile held in place by fishing hooks which pulled the corners of his mouth up and under his ears.

Today, Collin and friends brought Delvin into the forest to meet Master Poppie. The yippy yappy dog's owners, Man and Woman, had been walking the dog in the forest. The same forest where Master Poppie now lived. They got lucky when Man and Woman appeared with their dog, and now Collin and friends could offer them as food to Master Poppie. But there was no reason not to play with the food first.

"What animal should I do next?" Trina asked.

Man was tied to a tall oak tree and crying. Since he didn't respond, Delvin pried Man's mouth open and closed, answering for him as if he were a ventriloquist. "I'd like to see a bunny rabbit next!"

"Okay!" Trina said. She reached down and shoved both hands into the opened belly of Woman who was lying on the ground, and pulled out slimy lengths of gray and pink rope. As with her other balloon animal, Trina struggled to shape the tubes as a maroon curtain of ooze draped from the shimmering intestines. It was slippery, but she prevailed by pressing one section into another and twisting a knot at the fold. The slorping made Collin hungry for macaroni and cheese with tomato sauce.

Woman moaned and squirmed on the ground, but still reached for the greasy cords trailing out of her belly. Trina kicked her hand away and held up the massive ball of entrails. "A bunny!"

Man wailed, screaming and blubbering so hard that his spit and snot ran over Delvin's hands. Those wordless noises were calls to Master Poppie, a prayer to summon a god. A hungry one.

The milky mist started with wisps of white crawling over the forest's carpet of leaves and decay, thickening with every beat of Collin's heart. Or was it Master Poppie's heart making the ground beat? No matter. The mist had thickened, now accompanied by the smell of cotton candy. Master Poppie was here!

Collin and Brin dropped to their knees. Delvin followed and so did Trina – after she dropped the gooey parts of Woman.

The mist was dense, gauzy, making it hard to see. And then Master Poppie stepped out from behind a tree and approached his meal.

Blood! Collin clearly heard Master Poppie's divine message as a thought inside his head.

Woman whimpered while Man screamed and thrashed against the binding ropes. Man's shoulder popped from his efforts. That must have hurt.

Blood!

Master Poppie's bright red smile split his white face like summertime clouds, and his teeth glistened wetly through the thick mist. He reached for his food, arms extending farther and farther. Wriggling fingers found Man and Woman, wrapping around and around and around them.

Master Poppie yanked Woman away, then Man. The tree Man had been tied to snapped, and it leaned toward Trina. She squealed with delight and clapped when it fell beside her with a bone-rattling thud, missing her by inches. Stray branches and leaves flew through the air.

Master Poppie disappeared into the depths of the forest, taking his food with him. By the time the debris settled to the ground, the white mist was gone. The afternoon sun no longer needed to hide.

"I need to wash," Collin said to Brin as he helped her to her feet. She still had a limp from when he'd thrown a knife into her leg last month, and they headed back to Trina's house.

"Shall we search for more recruits, or more food?" Brin asked.

"There's a special recruit Master Poppie wants me to contact on Saturday. He's like us, but not quite. I need to plan, so I'll be mundane for the rest of the day."

"Okay. The three of us can stay inside for the day as well."

Collin looked behind them as Trina skipped along while singing songs about balloon animals. Delvin stroked the dog corpse he carried. "We'll need more, though, even after the special one joins us."

"Understood."

After they arrived at Trina's house, Collin showered and changed into mundane clothing, camouflage for the uneducated. Trina occupied herself with spray paint in her garage while Delvin sat at the dining room table with the dog and a sewing kit he found in a closet. Brin turned on the television, the radio, and her computer, all to news outlets. Couldn't be too careful.

Collin made it back to his own house in perfect time. As soon as he shut the door, the school bus pulled up to the curb. His son, Jacob, was the second kid off the bus.

Both hands gripping his backpack straps, Jacob walked toward his dad with a spring in his step. Well, more of a spring than he'd had over the past month and a half, ever since his mother died. The school had been doing a great job helping Jacob cope with his mother's death after getting mauled by a wild animal. From her remains, the police suspected a grizzly bear, despite the wilderness not having a sighting in over three decades. Collin thought about getting the word "grizzly" tattooed on his chest and started to laugh.

"Hi, Daddy," Jacob said as he approached. "What're you laughing about?"

"Nothing really, son. Just a thought I had about something I saw earlier."

"It was a weird laugh," Jacob said. He dropped his backpack on the foyer floor, and worked on removing his boots.

"Weird? Weird how?"

"I dunno. Silly. Like a weird clown, weird. Silly."

Jacob's vocabulary was limited to the parameters within his seven-year-old mind, but Collin understood that he needed to be more careful with what he did and said. Even though it became easier to slip from real-self to mundane-world self, he still needed to be wary of his behavior. Jacob wasn't ready to learn the truth, not yet. Collin had a plan to help Master Poppie fix everything, and Jacob was an important part of that plan. "Huh. Silly like a clown? Well, that is weird."

Collin grabbed the backpack and escorted Jacob into the dining room, the table where homework was done. Master Poppie was going to change the world, but until then, homework must be completed. "How was school today?"

"Good."

"How was your time with Miss Mary?"

"Good. We talked more about Mommy. Miss Mary says I'm making progress."

Collin joined his son at the table. He opened the bag and disbursed the textbooks. "That's wonderful news," Collin said with a smile. "I know a great way to celebrate."

Eyes wide with anticipation, Jacob cocked his head. "How?"

"Your friend Marissa Holcomb is having her birthday party on Saturday. I think it'd be a great idea if we attended."

The enthusiasm left Jacob, deflating him like a balloon. "I really don't know her."

"You're in the same class, right?"

"Well, yeah, but we're not *friends*."

"That's okay, Jakey! I talked to Miss Mary today." Collin lied. "She said it'd be a great idea."

Jacob twisted his face in something akin to a pout, while seemingly deep in thought. He then sat up straight and shrugged his shoulders. "Okay."

Ahhh, the fleeting feelings of children. He mussed Jacob's hair. "Attaboy! Need help with your homework?"

"Nah, I'm good."

"Okay. Holler if you need me."

Collin headed to his bedroom. The closet. He unlocked it – because Jacob was only seven, he might one day find it acceptable to break the "stay out of Daddy's closet" rule – and turned on the light. He grinned wide, admiring twenty boxes of face paint that occupied the space where Dana's clothes used to be. He missed her, but ultimately, he knew he did the right thing. Master Poppie had been hungry, and Collin couldn't imagine her joining him on this mission. He also desperately wanted to paint his face. Maybe tomorrow he'd hire a babysitter and set out to find another recruit or two. Trina had plenty of space for more recruits at her house.

Collin shut and locked the bedroom door. Time to plan for Marissa's birthday party.

June 21, 2002

The hole at the base of the massive pine tree was no longer a grave, not as far as Cali was concerned, but a void. Just another divot in the forest floor. Cali heard Lily's parents' wailing as if they were right next to her, watching the police dig up the earth to reveal their missing daughter.

"Find anything?" Mother asked, her electronic voice tickling the inside of Cali's ear.

"No."

"What were you hoping to find?"

The motivation to do what she needed to do, to get into the character she needed to become. "I don't know. Something the police missed? Clown makeup? A big red foam nose? Keith the Clown's business card?"

"We've been over this already. It sounds like you're stalling."

She was. Cali leaned with her hand against the tree marking where Lily had been buried, the bark rough and cool through her latex glove. "Just being thorough."

"It's not too late to swap places. I can talk to Bethany Pennington and you can listen from the black SUV down the street."

Cali pushed herself away from the tree and started toward Lily's house. Gloves off. Long hair down to cover the earpiece. This was something she had to do. "No, I got this. We determined that it'd be more realistic to have the young hottie pose as the insurance woman."

"And how many times do I get mistaken for your sister?"

"Yeah, my much older sister."

"You tend to lash out when faced with uncomfortable roles. We need to work on your misplaced aggression."

But you don't understand. Sure, Mother had lost friends and her husband, sort of, but that was due to private wars carried out as mercenaries.

This was different. There was a connection between Cali and Lily's mother, even if she didn't know what. Bethany had lost her daughter and husband because of a monster; Cali had lost her father, boyfriend, and a lifelong friend to a different monster. Cali had killed hers; Bethany's was still at large. "Sorry. I still think I should pose as a cop."

"Negative," Mother snapped with a "do as you're told" tone. "If you pretend to be a detective of any sort, she'll have questions. That, and you'll have her thinking that the police reopened their investigation. I know our idea is far-fetched, but I believe *you* can sell it."

Leave it to Mother to make me feel good and bad at the same time.

Cali left the forest and strode across the overgrown back lawn of the Pennington house. She circled around the side and cut through the knee-high hedges lining the slate-paved walkway to the front door. The quintessential shrine to upper middle class, a McMansion; not big enough to qualify as a mansion, but bigger than three people needed, and enough to rub their status in the noses of those who saw it. Cali assumed that in a few months, Bethany would have to start selling things to afford the mortgage, and then eventually lose it to foreclosure.

She rang the doorbell and adjusted her black blazer over top of her white turtleneck. Jeans and plain black wedge booties completed the outfit. No jewelry – too much potential to trigger a grieving woman. She whispered, "Here we go."

Facing armed lunatics was a piece of cake compared to waiting for the figure behind the curtains to lurch to the door. A latch clicked, a lock turned, and a puffy-eyed Bethany answered the door in a flimsy robe over her tee shirt and sweatpants. "Yeah?"

"Hi. Mrs. Bethany Pennington?"

She held a coffee mug, the whiskey smell wafting toward Cali a split second before the hygiene funk. "Yeah."

"My name is Dakota Hadden, I'm from Tripoli Insurance." Cali held out her counterfeit identification card.

"Have I mentioned yet how weird it is that you use your best friend's name for these situations?" Mother asked in her earpiece.

It's to honor her by making her a part of my life, and to remember that a monster took her.

Bethany frowned, her jaw muscles rippling. Her pasty lips made a noise when she opened her mouth. "Are you here to fuck me over like everyone else?"

"Neither confirm nor deny," Mother instructed.

Cali cleared her throat. "Mrs. Pennington, I assure you this has nothing to do with your policy. I'm an investigative actuary sent here to ask you a few questions."

"An investigative actuary?"

"Yes, ma'am. One of the few that gets out from behind the desk to see what the sun looks like."

"A few of my friends are actuaries. You don't seem to have their personality."

"Well, you know what they say – the best form of contraception for an actuary is their personality."

"Cali! Jesus!" Mom yelled into her ear.

Bethany chuckled, then reared back as if surprised. Eyes pink, she sniffled and shook her head, ultimately looking into her mug. "The first time I laughed in weeks. Forgot what it even sounded like."

Cali took two small steps away from the front door. "I know it hasn't been that long since your tragedy and I told those assholes in Corporate that it was too soon, but they about pushed me out the door. I apologize. I'm gonna go back and spend the rest of the day yelling at them. My mother taught me a few things about soul-crushing guilt."

"You're a real piece of work yourself, Sweety," Mother grumbled.

Bethany looked up, a new sorrow behind her eyes. "No. No, that's okay. Come on in. It's been... I don't know. Come in. Ask what you need to ask."

Cali followed Bethany into the living room; it reeked of cigarette smoke. To get rid of the smell, Bethany would have to wash the walls and repaint, throw out the cream-colored carpets and chenille drapes, and have the furniture professionally cleaned. Pity – the deep blue of the couch, love seat, and armchair went nicely with the carpet and white walls. Too bad about the obvious red wine stains on the couch and coffee table.

Bethany flopped onto the couch and a dollop of coffee splashed her wrist. After setting the mug on the coffee table, one among half a dozen, she wiped the back of her hand on her sweatpants. "Can I offer you something to drink?"

Cali sat in the armchair, close enough to the coffee table where she leaned over and grabbed one of the empty mugs. A quick peek inside to check for mold. It was clean enough. "I'll have what you're having."

"Coffee?"

Cali cocked her head, flattened her brow, and drew her lips tight, giving Bethany a look that said, "I know exactly what you're drinking, lady."

Bethany snickered with a hint of sad loneliness. A field of used tissues occupied the cushion next to her. She grunted and swept them on the floor. "Sorry. I fired the house cleaning service."

"Actually, that's why I'm here."

Bethany fished between the cushions and behind the decorative throw pillow until she found the small bottle of Jack Daniels. She added a splash into her mug and a three count pour into Cali's. "You want to talk about my cleaning service?"

"Not just them, but all the services you use."

Bethany took a swig from her mug, and blinked the burn away. "Why?"

Here we go, Cali thought as she took a hit of whiskey. "When tragedy occurs, such as what you lived through, we collect as much data as possible for the potential to adjust our numbers moving forward. I assure you, no one is in trouble, and we're not looking for causation. We're just curious about correlation."

"Correlation? You can't be serious."

Cali took a bigger gulp this time. "Mrs. Pennington, I'm not going to insult you by asking if you remember the Twin Towers falling nine months ago. Of course, you do. *Everyone* remembers. And *everyone* is still afraid. Hell, I *still* drink plenty of this special blend of 'coffee' to calm my nerves. Corporations are afraid as well, especially insurance companies. Security and safety have rocketed up everyone's priority list, and dangers linger all around us. New ones, technological ones. Cell phone usage has gone up and up as well as eCommerce. There is a lot of data flying around. Sensitive data. There's a reason why it's called the world wide *web*. All the data is connected, like a spider web. Every service you use, including the paper boy and pizza delivery guy, has collected data about you. So, companies like mine are sending out people like me to see which parts of the web are touching other parts." Cali set the mug down and reached inside her blazer for a pen and small note pad. Flipping it open, she concluded, "All I want to do is write down the names of the services you use and how you communicate with them."

"Nicely done," Mother whispered into her ear.

Bethany frowned and looked away, twisting her lips. After a swig from her mug, she looked back and nodded. "Yeah, I guess that makes sense. What do you need to know?"

Cali started with the cleaning service, then the places Bethany ordered pizza, and asked if she had her newspaper delivered. Laundry and dry-cleaning services. Accountant. Lawyer. Bethany answered every question with the monotone of reading a report, and Cali scribbled notes for authenticity. Finally, she asked, "Regarding your daughter… Any extra services? Babysitter? Nanny?"

Bethany drew in on herself. Leaning forward, elbows on her knees, she wrapped her hands around her mug. A hard swallow. "No."

"Did I read that she had a birthday recently?"

Bethany tightened her grip and gave a quick head nod.

"Did you do anything special for her birthday?"

Head shake. Not good.

"No? No birthday party, or anything like that?"

Bethany shook her head. She then leaned back, eyes wide as if suddenly remembering. "Yeah. Yes, we threw her a birthday party."

"Any entertainment? Magician?"

"Clown."

Eureka. "Okay. How did you hear about him?"

"My daughter saw him at another birthday party and liked him. The party was for some other kid from her school, can't remember who."

"Tell me about the clown."

Bethany shrugged. "Keith the Clown. Good show. The kids loved him."

"Does he have a website? Is that how you set up an appointment?"

"He does, but there's not much to it. You call a number and leave a message."

"Did you recommend him to the parents of any of your daughter's friends?"

"I don't know. Maybe?"

Shit. "Please try to remember, Mrs. Pennington."

"I think one of the moms came up to me after the party asking questions."

"Yeah? Okay. Which mom asked you about Keith the Clown?"

"Madison. Madison Holcomb asked me." Bethany leaned forward and squinted. For the first time since Cali arrived, Bethany looked dubious. "You said you were looking for how I communicate with my different services. Why do you need Madison's name?"

"Don't answer that question," Mother said, tension high in her voice. "Just get out of there."

Cali stood and aimed for the front door. "Just wanted to follow the trail of communication."

Bethany jumped up from the couch and gave chase. "Do you really work for my insurance company? Who do you *really* work for?"

"Don't answer her, Cali," Mother said. "No matter what answer you give, it will only lead to more questions."

When Cali opened the door, Bethany grabbed her by the elbow. "What are you looking for?"

"The truth."

Bethany squeezed. "The truth? The truth is, my daughter is dead and my husband has been falsely accused! He's in jail and he didn't do it!"

Shit! Mother was right. Why the hell couldn't I keep my mouth shut? Cali yanked her arm away with such force that Bethany almost fell over. As Bethany regained her balance, Cali backed away, out the door.

"He didn't do it!" Bethany yelled.

Cali wanted to comfort the grieving woman. She hunted monsters to prevent people like her from falling victim, and to exact vengeance. She wanted to offer Bethany hope, but…

Bethany's nose, cheeks, and chin reddened as her lips quivered. "He didn't do it."

"I know."

Bethany's legs buckled and she crashed to her knees. Slouching as if her bones had turned to jelly, her body hitched with every spastic breath. "He didn't do it. He didn't do it."

Cali turned and hurried away, Bethany's pitiable words lashing her like a whip.

June 21, 2002

Shouldering past the hotel room's heavy door, Cali aimed for the refrigerator. Only wine could stop the tremble in her hands, and rectifying the situation was top priority.

Her phone buzzed – a text from Mother: `Got lucky. Bethany's info paid off. Let me know when you get back.`

The first glass of Chardonnay steadied her hands, each gulp helping her decompress. She repeated to herself, *Adding salt to a grieving woman's wounds would be worth it.*

A second glass later, she called Mother – she had tracked down Madison Holcomb's phone number and address.

Cali accepted the information but rejected her offer for company. Not at that moment, at least. The third glass of wine put her into character. Clearing her throat, she dialed Madison's home phone number.

"Hello?"

"Madison? This is Brittany's mother?" Cali added a fraction of breath to each vowel, and an upswing at the end of each sentence to make them sound like questions.

"Which Brittany?"

Cali picked the name Brittany, because there was *always* a Brittany. Apparently, there were so many that she had to feign offense from the question. "Oh, Madison, don't be such a kidder."

Yep, just as Cali assumed – Madison staved off perceived embarrassment by pretending she knew who she was talking to. "Oh, hi! I didn't recognize your voice."

Cali thought about blowing kisses through the phone but decided against it. She gave an over the top, empowering, "There you go! Now you got it. Anyway, I was calling about Marissa's birthday party. I *compleeeetely* lost the invitation. I remember seeing it while in a session of Mommy-juice therapy prescribed to me by Dr. Xanax, if you know what I mean, but with schedules the way they are, and one thing led to another thing, and now I don't know where the darn thing got to. Would you give me the date and time again?"

"Oh, I know what you mean, girlfriend. I threw out a credit card bill once during my time with the same doctor." They paused the conversation to share a laugh, loud and shrill. Cali was getting a headache. "Anyway, you're lucky you called. The party is tomorrow, ten a.m."

"Perfect! Just perfect! Brittany will be excited to know that she hasn't missed it. It's not often Mommy gets to be the savior, know what I mean?"

"Oh, I do! I soooooooo do! Anyway, we need to get together for Mommy-juice therapy."

Cali rolled her eyes. Either the invitation was an empty gesture, or she didn't care which Brittany-mom she wanted to escape suburban existential ennui with. Yet, Cali played along. "Definitely! We can make plans at the party."

After the goodbyes, a tickle of emotion hit Cali right behind her chest. She suddenly felt herself missing Dakota and Melody. The countless hours they had spent together, gabbing about everything and nothing. The ability to let her guard down. The warmth that came with connecting with other people, friends. That tickle made her feel lost, and it made her dial Chism's phone number against her will.

"God damn it," came out of her mouth right when Chism picked up.

"Oh, bullshit," he said in response. "I don't know if these new salutations are going to replace 'hi' and 'hello,' but they're kind of fun. Great way to throw off telemarketers."

Cali chuckled and shook her head, a wasted gesture since there was no one else around to see it. But that was how Chism made her feel, free to be herself, and who cares if he wasn't here to see her uninhibited reaction. "Sorry. I... I stubbed my toe."

"Yeah, sounds like a 'God damn it' reason to me. So... What's up?"

"Just wanted to see if you'd take my call after I kicked your ass the other day."

"Well, it'd be difficult to set up another date with you if I didn't pick up."

"Another date? How do you know I'm not a headcase?"

"No better way to find out than a second date. And since you've repeatedly stated that you're a headcase, and since I still want a second date, then logic dictates that I, too, am a headcase, so, you know, that's something we have in common."

Cali bit her bottom lip. She shouldn't do this to the poor guy, not with her line of work, not when she was following a similar path as her father. He, too, eschewed relationships. She had never known why, always assuming he was such a great guy that no one else was good enough for him. That was back when she thought he had some boring desk job. Now that she knew he had been an assassin, it was obvious why he kept his relationships as casual "flings." She should tell Chism to forget about her and hang up, but… her father never seemed happy. No, not the right word. He had always *seemed* happy. He never seemed *complete*. "All right, buddy, you can't say I didn't warn you. Second date might leave you crying. Well, crying more than our first date."

"I wasn't crying, I just had something in my eye."

"Yeah, my fist."

He laughed. Genuine, rich laughter from the other end of the phone. *God damn it*, she thought as she smiled. She was on her third wine. *Actually, I'm your fourth*, the wine said when Cali glanced at the empty bottle. "How about tomorrow night?"

"Can't. I'm going to a birthday party," he said.

"Heh. What a coincidence, I'm going to one tomorrow morning."

"Early start. I like it."

"It's a kid's birthday party. You don't have any kids, do you?"

A pause. "I… umm… I actually do."

Well, I'm an asshole. "Oh! Then I'm really sorry. Not sorry that you have a kid, but sorry that I phrased it the way I did. That's cool. That's awesome. That's really good. And now I'm sorry I can't stop making this whole thing awkward."

Chism laughed. Not at her, though, rather with her, a future her who would one day reflect upon this conversation and find it hysterical. Cali blushed. "No need to be awkward," Chism explained. "His mother and I were in high school, met at Spring Break. She and my son are living great lives with her parents in Cali." Another short pause. "Heh. I'm going to start calling you California."

"You absolutely will not do that."

"I absolutely will not do that then. But… if that means you would prefer no date number two, I'd understand."

"I'm a headcase, not shallow. Date number two is still good to go. Night after tomorrow?"

"Works for me. Do you like danger and do you like Chinese food?"

"Umm… Sure."

"Okay, dinner at The Dragon's Blessing."

"Where's the danger in eating at a Chinese restaurant? Did they fail health inspections?"

"No, they're clean. But rumor has it that they're owned by the Chinese mafia. Very dangerous."

"What the hell is wrong with you?"

"Well, I'm dating you and I get hit in the head for fun and profit, so there's two things. I'll text you the address."

"Sounds like a plan. Bye."

Cali needed that. Just like she needed a second bottle of liquid courage to take to her mom's room and confess that she was right.

June 22, 2002

God, Keith hated these kinds of developments.

Another God damned middle-class development pretending to be upper class. Blocky, two-story houses were more important to the owners than the land they were on. More than a few houses were crammed so close together that it'd take only two passes of a push mower to trim the grass between them. Two garage doors fit four cars for a family of three, the vehicles costing about half what they paid for these McMansions.

A community of lies. Big smiles painted on their faces thicker than the one Keith painted on his face this morning. He lived in a shithole in a bad part of town, but at least it was honest. The killers and thieves lived in the open, almost proud of who they were.

Here, the McMansion killers and thieves went to corporate offices every day, hiding behind laws, selling death and misery to make a quick buck, destroying the planet in the name of the Almighty Dollar, never once giving a shit about their legacy, what they were leaving behind. Openly hurting the children and then shrugging their shoulders when asked why the kids were in pain. Fuckers. All of them.

"We're the ecru house, between the taupe house and the beige house." The exact quote Madison Holcomb gave to help Keith find her house. He found it not by the color, but by the actual street address.

Keith guided his van to the curb and stopped behind a Lexus SUV. The Holcomb's house had more space between their neighbors: six mower lengths on the one side, eight on the other. As soon as he got out of the van – one he found after midnight at a 24-hour Walmart, license plate swapped with five other vehicles – he heard the squeals of small children and assumed they came from the back yard. At least these ridiculous plots of land offered backyards.

The only thing Keith put in the back of the van was the three-by-two-foot trunk of props he took from gig to gig. It had a secret compartment in the lid big enough to hide a trophy, a stuffed animal like the dog Little Lily had. The compartment was empty, at the moment.

The doorbell rang with a standard "ding-dong." At least it wasn't a chiming version of some classical piece of music. Keith hated that. Big smile accompanied the painted one when Madison Holcomb opened the door.

Canary yellow scoop neck top and a white pleated tennis skirt to show off this cesspool-neighborhood's definition of a toned body. Unnaturally tanned crepe paper covered the two cantaloupes attached to sticks and twigs. She was late thirties but looked mid-fifties trying to impersonate early-twenties. What disgusted him the most was his certainty that she spent three figures every month on a stylist to make sure her hair was shoulder length and straight. Gobs of money to look like she didn't spend any at all. When she smiled, Keith heard the sounds of balloons inflating right to the point of rupture, and wondered how many cows how to die to make the collogen that plumped her balloon-lips. "Hi! You must be Keith! Well, if you're not, then you're the most creative mail man I've ever seen!"

Her laugh was hollow and soulless.

Keith had a big ol' Bowie hunting knife strapped to his right thigh and hidden under his clown outfit – oversized jeans held up by rainbow suspenders, stuffed with padding along with multiple layers of flannel shirts. A blend of the classic hobo and a rodeo clown. He wanted nothing more than to pull out the knife and saw her head off with its serrated edge. "Sorry, not the mail man, but I do want to deliver happiness and memories."

"Oh, aren't you adorable. I hope your show is just as good. Come in, but please wipe your feet first."

Wearing size eighteen shoes on his size eleven feet – another classic clown look – he wiped his feet with exaggerated swipes even though Madison had already retreated into her house.

An open floor plan, lots of half walls and shelves with no backing, furniture scattered about in whatever pattern an overpriced decorator had dictated. Madison stood next to an island with a granite countertop in her kitchen, the birthday cake taking center stage. Keith assumed the granite was fake, just like Madison and her tits and lips. "So, how does this work? Are you going to perform now?"

The Killer of Devils

Tone soft, yet professional, Keith continued his act. "Actually, could I use your bathroom to put on the finishing touches? It'll take about ten to fifteen minutes and then I'll head right outside and start the show."

"Sure! There's one right past the kitchen."

Marissa's room wouldn't be on the first floor. Keith nodded toward the stairs. "Mind if I use the one upstairs? If one of the kiddos sees me coming out of the bathroom by the kitchen, it might take away some of the magic."

Madison twisted her balloon lips in thought, looking up as if using x-ray vision to see through the ceiling. After a few seconds of examining whatever she saw, she moved farther into the kitchen and opened the refrigerator. "Okay, but I can't guarantee its cleanliness, so if it's a mess, promise me you won't tell anyone."

Keith smiled and offered a slight bow. "I promise. Thank you."

Madison bobbed her way outside with a bottle of designer water, all the permission Keith needed to head upstairs.

He noted three bedrooms and a bathroom. Keith set his trunk down in the hall and hurried down its long end.

Door one was closed. He peeked inside. A home office.

Door two was open. Marissa's room!

Her name was on the inside of her door, a different color for each blocky letter. Keith took a deep breath and held it. This was her, more than what would be found if he could visit her soul. This was where she dreamed. Fantasized. Cried. Laughed. Created. Dealt with whatever new problem the world threw at her in her young life. But this was also her gilded cage.

Undoubtedly, the poor girl would become another plastic suburbanite. The highlight of her life would be hosting successful dinner parties and mixing perfect mojitos, brainwashed into this by her suffocating mother and one-dimensional father. She'd be a nobody, lying to herself and desperate to show the world that she was a somebody. That fate was not fit for anyone, let alone a little goddess like Marissa. Keith intended to rescue her and release her from this caricature of life. If he did nothing, she'd wind up a meaningless speck of sand in a desert, eventually blown away by the wind and not remembered by anybody. Instead, he'd make her immortal, her images forever captured and added to his collection where she'd be worshiped like the tiny goddess she was.

Inside her room, Keith exhaled, closed his eyes, then took a deep breath through his nose until his lungs pulled in every bit of Tiny Goddess Marissa's essence. An aroma of fake cherry. Her lip gloss, maybe? The faintest hint of powder. Did her shit-heel parents allow her to wear makeup already? The subtle freshness of dryer sheets. Her bedding must have been laundered recently.

A tickle in his nose, and he opened his eyes. He smiled at the thought of possibly ingesting a stray piece of glitter, Tiny Goddess Marissa's favorite crafting medium, judging by its proliferation in her artwork. White walls held framed photographs of her and her parents in exotic locations. An off-centered stripe of pink streaked the wall behind her headboard, hers to do with as she pleased, a way to truly express herself. The pink stripe was filled with handmade artwork, mostly glitter framed photos of Tiny Goddess Marissa and her friends matted on construction paper of various colors. Oh, how Keith wished to take one or two or all the photos, but they would be missed, obviously stolen. No, he needed something that would be missed but *assumed* to be misplaced.

Her desk was clean and organized, ready for homework. A small, framed picture of her mother hugging her from behind, resting her chin on Tiny Goddess Marissa's shoulder. How could that witch not see the look of desperation and discomfort in her own daughter's eyes? Next to the picture was a round foam piggy, the perfect size to fit into Tiny Goddess Marissa's hand, begging to be squeezed for stress relief. Tiny Goddess Marissa wouldn't care about anything on this desk.

A shelf on the wall held a half-dozen stuffed animals and a few dollies. Shelves were for displaying trophies, and stuffed animals were for hugging. The plushies were so indistinguishable from one another that Keith doubted she'd notice if he took half of them.

The bed? Three stuffed animals sat atop her pillows, including a foot tall Hello Kitty. Perfect size for cuddling, but it wore a Philadelphia Eagles jersey. A gift from her father, most likely, since it was the only

The Killer of Devils

reference to any sports team. It was flanked by two other Hello Kitties, but they were too small to hug, just decorative minions. If he took the bigger one, she'd notice, but probably not care.

Another step into her room. He debated looking through her closet, but then he saw it. A rocking chair in the corner by her bed, too small for her to sit in, but the perfect size for her best friend. A stuffed rabbit.

It had light blue matted fur and massive feet, thick floppy ears hanging from head to chair. The right arm had been reattached with sloppy crisscross stitching. Yes, this was the one Tiny Goddess Marissa loved.

Once he grabbed the rabbit, his internal alarm clock went off. Two minutes. He had been in her room for two minutes, but his flight sense made it feel like hours. Adrenaline flooded his system, and his heart revved. Only eight paces to cross her room and get into the bathroom. He had done this charade before and he'd do it again, but the anxiety never lessened.

He shoved the rabbit inside his bulky shirt.

Out the door.

WHAM!

Keith ran smack into a man.

The rabbit fell out of his shirt and onto the floor.

He had smacked chest to chest into who he assumed was Tiny Goddess Marissa's father. "Sorry. I just wanted to peek inside her room to get better sense of who she was and see if there was anything unique about her that I could work into my act." He had practiced that excuse many times, but never needed to use it until now. He didn't like how hurried it came out. Guilty people hurried their words.

Keith didn't like the way the man smiled at him. Whenever Keith was bored and feeling introspective, he'd wonder if he was crazy. His answer was always no. But this man? Judging from this man's smile, his answer was a resounding yes.

His angular face, one that most women would find handsome, was devoid of any facial hair. He was tall and lean, muscular, like an athlete or a boxer, the former version of Keith when he was in the army. But this man's hypnotic blue eyes, like swirling spiral discs, made Keith think of old *Twilight Zone* episodes. It had been a long time since Keith felt threatened, and he instinctually wanted to jam his hidden knife into the man's jugular and jump out the window.

"No worries," the man said, holding Keith's gaze past the point of discomfort. He crouched down and picked up the stuffed rabbit. Keith prepared himself to put this man in a chokehold as soon as he turned around. Jumping out the window was still an option. But Keith wasn't prepared for the man to hand over the rabbit. "I understand. You and I have the same calling. We'll be in touch later."

Couldn't be Tiny Goddess Marissa's father. One of the other kid's parents?

The man turned and walked away, descending the stairs.

Stunned, Keith stood holding the rabbit by its scraggy neck, wondering, *What the fuck was that about?*

June 22, 2002

A suburban development of middle class trying to be upper class. Back when she was in high school, Cali and Dakota referred to these blocky, two-story neighborhoods as less fortunate. But never in front of Melody since she had grown up in a neighborhood just like this one.

Melody shared stories about her parents arguing all the time, the stress of her father spending all his time in the office to afford the mortgage, luxury cars, extravagant vacations, all while her mother remained a housewife. Melody would say that this development was trying too hard, its inhabitants living unhappy lives to show how happy they were.

The house Cali grew up in was twice as large as any of these houses and included a well-maintained inground pool with an acre of perfectly manicured lawn between homes. Her father also had an equally massive house tucked away in the forest where she liked to spend time during her precollege years. Thanks to her inheritance, she not only owned those two houses, but three others she had never known existed. Over the past two years, she'd been to the forest getaway a few times but hadn't spent a night in any of the houses yet, either staying with her mother or spending her nights in various hotel rooms. Too many ghosts haunted those houses. Too many ghosts haunted Cali and she didn't want to deal with whatever the hell stage of grief she was in regarding the loss of her father.

Instead, she threw herself into monster-hunting duties, like sitting in her rented Ford Explorer and staking out an upper-middle-class house to wait for a deranged clown.

"This is promising," Mother said into her ear. "Classic white, windowless van pulled into the development."

Cali slouched in her seat and pulled out her binoculars. "I got eyes on him."

A glimpse of red curly hair. A face as white as bleached hotel sheets. Cali swore she saw a red nose. "It's him. It's our guy."

The van pulled up to the curb in front of the Holcomb house. Sure enough, a clown got out.

"Yeah, he's our guy. I can feel it," Cali said. "Do you want to put a tracker on his van?"

"Affirmative."

After a few minutes, Mother came into view, walking along the development's sidewalk. Just a late morning stroll for fresh air and exercise. Her sleight of hand would rival any street magician's as she slipped a tracking device inside the rear wheel well. She continued walking the curve of the road, then disappeared out of sight.

A few minutes later, she was back in Cali's ear. "Tracker placed. I got his license plate and I'm running it now... Interesting."

"What's up?"

"The plate belongs to a Toyota Camry."

"He switched plates with another car?"

"Looks that way, if that's even his van. Hold on a second... Five Chevy Expresses have been reported stolen this past week."

"So, he steals a van and replaces the license plate. Any report of a Camry owner claiming they have the wrong license plate?"

"Nope. But there is one from a Jeep owner. Our target must have switched plates a few times."

"Come on, people. How could you not know your license plate isn't right?"

"What's your license plate number?"

Cali knew that question was coming as soon as the words left her mouth. She barely knew she was sitting in a black Ford Explorer. "It's a rental."

"Even more reason to know it. We're going to add more mental exercises to your workout routines."

Cali rolled her eyes.

"I heard that eyeroll," Mother said.

"Okay, let's reduce the amount of chatter on the line, keep it open for emergencies."

An hour later, the clown left the house with little fanfare, escorted by a smiling, stick-thin woman, who continually thanked him for his services. If she only knew. How would she react knowing this man might be stalking her daughter? Her little girl, at an age somewhere between learning how to walk and puberty, the age where she was learning that the world was a bigger place, even though she was still so tender and helpless. Madison would wind up as broken and hollow as Bethany, every bit of love and hope scooped out and thrown away, leaving nothing but alcohol-soaked skin.

Once Keith tossed his case in the back of the van, he drove off. Cali put the Explorer in drive and pursued. The van made a right out of the development and so did she. Five minutes turned into ten, which slipped into fifteen.

Mother chirped into Cali's ear, "Where are you?"

"I'm following this son of a bitch."

"Negative. Do not pursue. This is not a part of the plan."

"It is now."

"Cali, we have a tracker on him and it's working perfectly."

"But what if it stops? What if he has a bug sweeper? If he's smart enough to steal a van and swap plates, then it's not beyond the realm of possibility that he sweeps for trackers. Hell, since he stole the van, then there is a good possibility that he's not even going to his house."

"If either of those scenarios happen, we can at least narrow down where to look for him."

"Not good enough, Mom."

Keith was heading back into the city. Cali stayed at least five car lengths behind. Traffic was lighter than usual, but every now and again a car or two swerved in between them. Whenever he hit the gas, so did she; when he braked, she braked. Natural, just as natural as any other car on the road.

"There's a chance he could make you. We know nothing about him, other than he's smart."

"That's a chance I'm willing to take. We can't lose him."

The names of the cross-streets were numbers, decreasing as they drove along, and now she was only three car lengths behind him, trying to remain inconspicuous. As fast as the lights would allow, they moved from the twenties into the teens.

"Cali, this isn't—"

"You didn't see the empty shell that Bethany was, Mom!" Cali snapped. She forced herself not to cry, tears would blur her vision. "You didn't see. The fucker in that van took everything from her. Her family, her soul, her life. I honestly wanted to pull out my gun and put her out of her misery. And I think she would have thanked me for it. The look in her eyes… if she knew I had a gun, she would have asked me to use it. I know she would. And this… this… monster that I'm following did that. I'm not letting him out of my sight."

Silence for another two blocks.

"I'm following the tracker, so I'll rendezvous with you at some point. Please be careful and please do not engage until I'm there."

"Confirmed."

"Okay, don't forget your training. Tell me what you see."

"Cars, people, cars, buildings, a metric shit ton of city. Wait… He's turning into a parking lot. A regular pay lot."

"Drive past the lot and—"

"Sorry, Mom, but no. If he's ditching the van, I don't want to lose him."

Keith pulled into the parking lot and barely waited for the bar to lift before turning right. Cali followed suit, grabbed a ticket, and drove forward once the bar lifted. The van's brake lights popped on.

Reverse lights.

"Fuck!"

Cali's whole body jerked when the van's rearend slammed into the passenger side of the Explorer.

June 22, 2002

Keith noticed the black Ford Explorer right away. It didn't seem like it belonged in that development; not showy enough. The only Fords in those garages were Mustangs.

The Explorer was following him.

Obeying all rules of the road, but keeping an eye on the SUV, Keith continued on his way home. The driver was shrewd enough to stay a few vehicle lengths behind him, but when she got close enough for him to see her in both of his side mirrors, he knew she was tailing him. Her mirrored aviators stared at him, only him. She looked like trouble; he could feel it, as tangible as hands around his throat. Who was she and what did she know?

Keith crossed the Schuylkill and kept heading northeast. Every turn he made, she made. Yep, he had zero doubts that she was following him. The determination in her scowl let him know he wasn't going to shake her, not in a stolen van that he knew nothing about. He saw a parking lot coming up on his left, and quickly devised a plan. It was risky, but a weak plan was better than no plan.

She was no cop. The Explorer didn't seem official, and there was a certain recklessness etched on her face. Maybe one of the families connected the dots back to him and hired someone to track him? Was this woman a private investigator? Or something worse? Yes, he decided that he needed to try his plan, take the risk. It was going to be loud, and he'd have to give up his hopes of immortalizing Tiny Goddess Marissa, but he needed to take care of his pursuer.

Ticket taken, stick-like bar up, Keith gunned it into the parking lot. Right turn. Fifty feet and then he put the van in reverse and waited. *I got you now, bitch!*

Direct hit to the Explorer's passenger side. The crunch of plastic and metal, the explosion of glass, all satisfying noises.

No time to celebrate.

Knife in hand, Keith hurried out of the van and ran around the front of the Explorer, through the acrid odor of burning oil and the tangy smell of antifreeze. The SUV's door flung open with enough force that if he hadn't been primed to jump back, he would have ended up on his ass.

The woman behind the wheel shot out like a blonde bullet, fist glancing off Keith's cheek. Arms up, he blocked a second punch and a quick kick. He jabbed at her with a couple knife slashes. They were sloppy, but effective enough for her to jump back, giving him a second to assess.

The frown on her face looked permanent, and she was surprisingly pretty. He thought about telling her she needed to smile but didn't want to give her extra emotional incentive; she was angry enough as is. About five-nine, a buck sixty, maybe more, judging from the taut muscle rippling underneath the black turtleneck. Black cargo pants and boots as well. Fists up, glasses off, she had the look of hot murder in her blue eyes. She was ready for this. She planned this. Damn it, that meant she *knew*.

Keith mimicked her boxer's stance, knife in his right fist, blade pointing down. A few jabs from her that didn't land, followed by another kick. Fast. Keith knew she was just testing him, though, trying to figure out his strengths and weaknesses. *Let's find yours.*

A right hook, which she dodged with ease. Okay fine – his backswing would be deadly, the knife tip aiming for her neck.

She stopped it, grabbing his wrist with both hands. As fast as blinking, she brought her right knee to his ribs three times.

His outfit was the furthest thing from tactical, but the padding offered a lot of protection, downgrading her strikes from rib-cracking to bruising. While she had his right arm immobilized, he reached under with his left and delivered an upper cut. Not a lot of power behind it, but the pop to her chin was enough to make her release his arm and back away. But not enough to keep her away.

She had training, good training. Keith had training, too, from the United States government. It had been years since he needed to use it, though. Thank God for muscle memory.

She came at him with jabs to the face, but he blocked them and then slashed at her with his knife. She dodged it, but that allowed him to land a punch to her cheek. Unfazed, she spun and smashed her elbow into the side of his neck.

That hurt, but Keith threw a few jabs, backing her toward the Explorer. He wanted to pin her against it and use his size advantage.

She advanced again with a few more jabs then followed with a knee to his padded ribs.

He punched and missed, slashed with his knife…

Which she blocked. A chop to his wrist.

A river of pain rushed up his arm from his hand, but he didn't let go of the knife.

She shifted and kicked his knee.

He got lucky, turned just in time to bend his leg with her kick.

More punches to his face. Too fast!

Pulse ramping up, he pushed her back.

Backing away, she rolled her neck and cracked her knuckles. "Not bad, you sick fuck," she said. "But it's obvious you're a weak little bitch boy since you need to attack little girls."

Keith wasn't weak! Who was this bitch to talk shit about him? She was close enough to the Explorer for him to slam her into it. He charged, knife up. Too late he realized that she had set him up, flinging open the driver's side door. He slammed into it, his wrist hitting the frame hard enough to make his hand numb. The knife clattered against the pavement. Stunned, he couldn't react when she reached through the window and grabbed the back of his head. Forehead to door. Stars burst through his vision, their explosions reverberated through his head, neck, and upper back. The world went uneven and he fell backward, his wig softening the blow as he hit the pavement, splashing in fluids.

Wig.

Fluids.

Keith ripped the wig from his head and swiped it through the pool. His vison was still blurry, but the blonde had come around the door and was close enough that he couldn't miss when he threw the soppy mess at her face.

"Fuck!" she yelled.

That was all Keith needed to hear to know he had blinded her. At least temporarily, so he had to move. Fast.

On his feet. No knife and too wobbly to attack, running was his only option. The parking lot was too open. Across the street. A small building with a few store fronts.

Cars had stopped on the street, the few onlookers close by. No crowds yet.

The more steps he took, the sturdier he became. A full, clear-headed sprint by the time he got to the first store front. An art gallery.

He flung open the door and ran inside. A lone brunette stood close to the door, screaming. Take her as a hostage? No. Too involved and that'd create a situation where he had no control. He pushed her out of the way and kept running.

There had to be a back exit. Every store had a back exit.

A man ran out of a back office, and yelled, "Hey!"

Wearing khakis and a blue Polo, the dumbass swung at Keith. Putz missed. If you're wearing dorky clothes, that means you can't fight.

A punch to the gut doubled the guy over. To Keith's surprise, after he turned, the guy lunged, slamming Keith's chest into a wall. *I don't have time for this!* Keith threw himself back, slamming the guy into the opposite wall. Keith's fists itched with the desire to beat the crap out of him, but the blonde could burst into the gallery at any moment.

Keith yelled, "If you try to follow me, I'll come back and kill you and your bitch," and then pushed through the exit door.

Keep running, no time to stop. An alley across the street. Perfect. The other end would offer an escape.

Once he got home, he could gauge his potential for getting caught, maybe even figure out who that bitch was and eliminate her. He'd have to delay his next immortalization video, but there'd be another opportunity, and after he figured out the flaws, then he'd—

A weight hit the back of his legs and he fell face first onto the pavement. His arms protected his face, the outfit's padding protecting everything else. That bitch had tackled him! Kicking and bucking, he got to his side, to see where to aim his next few kicks. Chest, shoulder, shoulder, and she let him go. He scrambled to his feet just as she did.

Like in the parking lot, she came at him with fire and fury.

Jab. Jab. Jab. He missed twice and connected weakly to her shoulder. She had learned his moves. Three jabs of her own, all hitting his cheek. A spinning kick to his chest was punishment for being sloppy.

Keith had been in fights before, real ones with men who had been trained to deliver organ-shifting punches. Her hits were up there with the best of them. He wasn't one for male ego and didn't take a macho view of the world, but he never thought he'd lose a fight to a woman, especially one that looked like a model. Wouldn't be long before a kick would hit a sweet spot and ruin his ribs.

But he could learn, too.

This woman's attacks were high, probably trained into her by sparring with men. As uncomfortable as it was for Keith, he crouched down and went low. Punch. Punch. Right to her ribs, getting a grunt out of her with each hit. Keith twisted and put his hands on the ground for support to deliver a donkey kick. Bang. Right to her hip, hard enough to knock her off balance. Now to take advantage of the size difference.

Jacked up like a fighter, she was still lighter than him by a good fifty pounds or so. Keith charged and wrapped his arms around her. Damn it, he pinned only one of her arms.

Crack. Crack. Her free elbow was a bony club against his skull.

Keith planted his feet and shifted enough to grab a fistful of her pants and her free arm at her shoulder. With a roar, he engaged dormant core muscles and lifted her over his head.

Too much adrenaline. Had he been thinking straight, he would have dropped her on his knee to break her back. But he wanted to throw her. Throw her out of this alley. Throw her across the city. Throw her into a fucking volcano. Another roar and he threw her against the nearest dumpster.

"Fuck!" she yelled over the clank of her back slamming into the dumpster, the metal ramming against the side of the building.

She swore a lot, mouth like the garbage found in this alley. Well, trash belongs with trash and that was where Keith was going to put her, permanently. She got to her hands and knees and Keith geared up to kick her in the gut. He swung his leg and – the bitch was fast! The dumpster rang out again, this time from Keith's foot striking it.

"Asshole!" the woman yelled, now standing next to him. She grabbed the back of his neck and slammed his chest against the side of the dumpster. His head snapped forward, and she slammed the lid.

His shoulders took the brunt. Panic kicked in and he shoved himself out from under the lid just as she jumped on top of it. Not far enough away. She crouched, smashing the sole of her boot into his cheek and nose. He stumbled backward and fell.

Electricity radiated along the side of his face, activating a familiar sting of tears behind his eyes. This wasn't the first time his nose had been broken, but if he didn't want this to be his last, he needed to get to his feet. He pulled himself along the ground toward the other building's wall, where muck and dirt and gravel had collected. A handful of it went at her face.

She was prepared this time, blocking the mess with her arm, but it was enough of a distraction for Keith to clamber to his feet. Not enough to slow her down, though.

This time, she was the one who roared as she leapt up and grabbed the base of a fire escape. Adding momentum to her kick, she planted both feet into Keith's chest, sending him flying backward and slamming to the ground. Padding or not, his everything hurt. Head. Shoulders. Ribs. Arms. And for the love of God his chest hurt! Keith wanted to rip off his outfit and open his rib cage like a set of closet doors to relieve the crushing pressure.

No. Don't give in. Push past the pain. *If I give in, I'm dead!*

Keith grabbed a nearby dumpster and climbed to his feet. Using the building wall for assistance, he stumbled toward the end of the alley. It wasn't freedom, but he wanted out of the alley.

"You're not getting out of here, fucker," she said, her bootsteps echoing off the building walls. "I'm going to make you pay."

Keith didn't look back, didn't need to. She beat the crap out of him; he knew it and knew she wanted to do more. This crazy bitch was going to catch him and possibly kill him, but he was going to make her do it out in the open, in front of pedestrians and drivers.

Then a black van screeched to a halt at the end of the alley. The side door slid open to reveal...

Clowns.

Two men and a woman in full clown makeup waved for Keith to join them, cheering him on. A weird, miraculous situation, but he wasn't about to ask questions. The promise of deliverance invigorated him, and he sprinted the last ten feet, diving into the van to a flurry of hands pulling him and slapping him in congratulations. One of the men said, "Welcome, brother! We'll take you to salvation."

Keith didn't know who these people were or what kind of salvation they were talking about, but he was happy to get away from that crazy blonde bitch. But first...

He struggled to turn over, to face the alley while he reached into his pants pocket. "Wait!"

About twenty feet into the alley, the crazy bitch stood with her mouth open. A quick shake of her head, frown returning, she clenched her fists and started running toward the van.

Keith held a remote trigger, and he pushed the button, detonating the C4 in his props trunk. The explosion wasn't large, doubtful it would create any kind of crater, but it was loud enough to make the blonde flinch and stop in her tracks.

The van would burn. Keith hated to destroy his props and the trophy he earned from Tiny Goddess Marissa, but he needed to destroy as much evidence as possible. Should he activate his contingency plan and detonate the bombs in his home? Maybe.

First, he needed to wrap his head around the situation he found himself in. And figure out who this woman was. He had never seen her before, but he would never forget the glare of pure hatred in her eyes as he and his new friends sped away.

June 22, 2002

Melody couldn't believe her ears. What she was hearing couldn't be real. Sitting in the 8th Street Art Gallery's back office, she listened to Harold Varvaro, a stranger they had met a week ago, discuss Roger Templeton's illicit business dealings with her boyfriend. And Maxwell sat there lapping up the information like a thirsty dog with a bowl of water. He wasn't asking Varvaro the right questions, wasn't asking for proof to back up his ludicrous statements. His questions were all future focused on what to do next. However, Melody had plenty of business experience throughout her young life. She knew how to read financial statements, how to reconcile numbers, how to draw logical conclusions from a limited set of facts. She was weighing the evidence to justify Harold's claims.

What he was saying made sense.

For the past year, she helped Maxwell make heads or tails out of his father's businesses. A few heads were easy to comprehend, some tails had straightforward business plans with numbers matching the predicted expectations. At times, the numbers were like a jigsaw puzzle's box displaying a Renoir image, but all the pieces forming a Picasso. Then Harold came along and supplied different pieces. Everything he said fit perfectly. A set of customers didn't seem real? That's because they weren't. A set of numbers missing? They were hidden in those accounts over there. Where were research and development expenses? Disguised as equity in an off-the-books company.

This was their third meeting and it put the final touches on the painting regarding Maxwell's new portfolio. He clicked his pen closed and set it on top of the notepad, half the sheets filled with new info gathered from the meetings. Hands folded together, Maxwell leaned back in his chair and tapped a finger against his lips a few times. Melody hated when he did that, creating an intolerable silence as he tried to formulate the perfect plan or question. Finally, he said, "Tell me about Forward Technologies."

Harold always started these meetings sitting soldier straight in the chair in front of Maxwell's desk, but he'd relax after the first hour.

Around hour two he'd lean back and slouch. This was hour three. As if melting from boredom, his shoulders slumped below the top of the chair back. "What'd you want to know?"

"You had mentioned that right before my father was murdered, all their shares were transferred to the employees. What did the company do?"

Harold sat up, grunting. "Forward Technologies was his pet company. Technically, advanced weapons and vehicles, but it was more of a hobby than anything else. He made expensive toys, just to see if he could. He secured a few high-tech security contracts to keep it legit, but for the most part, it was his way of goofing around. There was a serious part to it, though. He planned to expand his reach overseas. He still had a few connections from his days as a mercenary, and he was going to leverage them with the weapons and vehicles made at Forward Technologies."

Melody wasn't sure what she had a harder time believing – that Roger Templeton used his company portfolio to assist his organized crime empire or that he was a member of a mercenary team. From what Harold had shared during their last meeting, Roger had gone by "Hawke," his father's last name. Templeton was his mother's maiden name. Roger changed it when he returned to the States after a botched mission in Afghanistan. He was left for dead and decided to perpetuate the ruse so he could create a new life for himself, and a better one for Maxwell.

"You said he had a few contracts. Were they enough to keep Forward Technologies profitable?"

Harold chuckled. "Not even close. If you had access to their books, you'd see that their money came from intercompany loans from Albathia Pharmaceuticals."

"The company that was liquidated. All the funds disappeared into the ether."

"That's one way to put it. Another way to put it – the money was stolen. I ain't a smart man, Max, but I'd bet my left foot that whoever murdered him took the money."

The jaw muscles around Maxwell's cheeks rippled. Melody could tell he wanted to share his theory about Calista being the murderer. He wanted to show Harold the footage of the blonde woman entering the building the day his father disappeared. But that would shift the purpose of the meeting. Another time, not now.

"I'd be inclined to agree with that theory," Maxwell said. "But Albathia...?"

"Yeah, that was the paper and bullshit company. We – his street level employees – sold drugs through that company. All cash."

"Did it... you know... make any product?" Maxwell asked.

"Just the normal stuff. High quality, but nothing out of the ordinary. He had employees on the books listed as 'market researchers' who ran the labs outta abandoned buildings. The raw ingredients came from Zeus Chemical."

Maxwell raised a brow. "Zeus Chemical? But they seem like one of more legit companies in the portfolio, manufacturing botanical products from fertilizers to pesticides."

"Are you an expert on chemicals? You know what goes into what to make what?"

"No, but..." Maxwell's voice faded. He probably inferred the same message Melody did. Zeus Chemical had a massive research expense and Melody assumed that they could legally get all kinds of chemicals and then write them off as a loss for failed experiments that never happened.

A warmth bloomed behind her cheeks, embarrassed that she hadn't connected the dots until now.

Harold stood. "I'm gonna head out and leave you to your thoughts. Let me know what you'd like me to do when you figure it out."

Maxwell needed time to process what he had just learned; it was written all over his face.

"Yeah," Maxwell muttered. He cleared his throat and sat straighter in his chair. "Yes. I definitely will. Thank you, Harold."

After Harold closed the door behind him, Melody whispered, "Jesus."

"Yeah," Maxwell leaned back in his chair and stared at the ceiling as if asking the heavens for clarity. "It's one thing to learn that he sold weapons and drugs on the side, but to learn that it wasn't just on the side, but it was most of his business and he was manufacturing them, planning on going global because of his mercenary connections, which we just learned about a couple days ago. Christ, Dad, what the fuck?"

Melody reached over and put her hand on his. She loved that he had no issues sharing with her what was on his mind. "What are you going to do?"

Maxwell squeezed her hand and gave her a look she had never seen before. Fear. Ever since she had known him, he had radiated confidence. Not all his decisions were great, but he moved through life with his head held high and surety to his step. Even during this past year while struggling to understand his father's portfolio of companies. He had no issues asking for help, and he had faith that he'd learn what he needed to know. But not now. He looked like a child who just found a loaded gun – he knew he had a dangerous power, but no idea what to do with it. "I... I don't know."

Liquidate everything and move on. Melody wanted to be supportive, so she softened her thought and said, "This could be an opportunity for a clean start. Each company you now own is viable as a legitimate profit maker."

He nodded. "Yeah, but my father's businesses were built upon working outside the realms of legitimacy. I mean, he was building an empire. I don't want to tear down everything he built without at least understanding it better."

Melody's fake smile started to hurt – she heard him but disagreed. "I find it hard to believe that this lovely art gallery is a part of your father's criminal empire."

Maxwell returned her smile. "I know. You're probably right. I should cut out all the illegal shit going on. Let Zeus Chemical research legitimate botanical products. Hand the gallery over to Justin. Give Harold a golden parachute. Make sure the other companies are on the up-and-up. I'm sure I'll get to reconciling it all in my heart, but I need to process what we learned and try to understand why my father did what he did."

That was the man she loved. Rational. Reasonable. Logical. Yes, she'd still love him if he decided to pick up his father's saber and charge forth into the criminal underbelly, but him not doing so made her more comfortable. She stood up and kissed him. "Okay. Take all the time you need, and I'll offer you any help I can. In the meantime, since Justin isn't scheduled to come in for a couple more hours, I'm going to open this lovely, non-criminal art gallery."

"You're the best."

"Yes I am."

Not once in the past week did he bring up Calista, and Melody couldn't have been happier about that. Sure, it took sorting through his father's financial malfeasance to distract him, but she hoped he'd move on from that, and allow himself to heal. Once he started to clean up the companies, he could get back to a better life.

She turned on the main room's lights while making her way toward the front door, unlocking it.

A crunching metallic boom. She jumped. "Holy… what the hell was that?"

A car accident in the parking lot across the street. A white van and a black SUV. Judging from the damage, someone had to have been driving pretty damn fast in a parking lot. When Melody saw the driver of the van – a clown – she wasn't sure if she should laugh.

In white face paint and red wig, a clown in an oversized hobo costume hurried from the driver seat toward the SUV. Melody expected big, floppy shoes, but realized it'd be impossible to drive in shoes like that. She wondered how many more clowns were going to file out of the van, until the driver of the SUV threw open her door.

A young blonde. She almost whacked him with the door! Was that on purpose? Probably, because the two of them were going at it like mortal enemies. Melody wondered if this was an elaborate circus marketing stunt, but who wrecks a car for marketing purposes? The blonde and the clown were… The blonde…

The blonde…

"No… Impossible. Calista?"

Melody's breath abandoned her, eyes unable to blink. Feet planted firmly to the floor, her body refused to move, offering her only a slight tremble as she watched her best friend punch and kick a clown across the street.

When she finally blinked, her eyes watered from staring too long. *Breathe!* A deep breath, loud and desperate. *Couldn't be Cali.* Could it? Impossible. That could *not* be Calista. Even if she didn't look exactly how Melody remembered her, she moved like Cali. The closest she had ever seen Cali fight was when they took an occasional kickboxing class, and that was exactly how Cali moved. How she punched. How she kicked. *How is this happening? Why?* Those questions fell out of Melody's mind when the clown threw his wig at Cali, scrambled to his feet, and ran.

Toward the gallery.

Melody remained frozen. *What's happening? This can't be real. This can't be happening. Move!*

Right as the door flung open, she jumped back.

The clown paused and looked her over. Streaks of sweat cut lines through his face paint. He paused long enough, looking her up and down as if studying her, calculating unfathomable formulas. Dissatisfied with the results, he shoved her out of the way and ran toward the back of the gallery.

Maxwell exited the office and yelled, "Hey!"

The clown punched Maxwell in the gut, but Maxwell grunted and fought back, grabbing the clown from behind. After slamming Maxwell against the wall, the clown darted to the door. "If you try to follow me, I'll come back and kill you and your bitch!"

Staggering, Maxwell got to his feet and ran into the gallery's main room, to Melody. "Are you okay? Are you hurt?"

Melody wiggled her fingers and toes. Nothing hurt. "No. No, I'm fine."

Eyes big as the moon, Maxwell gently touched her face, her shoulders, her arms. "Are you sure? You screamed. You sure you're okay?"

"I'm sure. Just startled, that's all."

Hands trembling, Maxwell's Adam's apple bobbed with his swallowing. He had faced too much loss a year ago and it was obvious that he thought he might have lost her. "What happened?"

"I unlocked the gallery doors and heard a crash. There was an accident in the parking lot and…" Melody turned and pointed out the window. Calista was gone. "And that clown got out of the van and ran through the gallery."

"What? Why?"

"I don't know. He didn't say anything."

"Was there anyone in the car he hit? Was he being chased?"

If she told him what she had seen, he'd lose his mind, she was sure of it. "I… I don't know."

Maxwell hugged her, a squeeze so hard she thought she might end up in the ER anyway. "Thank God you're okay. Don't know what I'd do."

"I'm okay, I swear," Melody squeaked.

Maxwell released her and looked toward the back exit as if he had forgotten that the man had punched him as he barreled past. "Come with me." He took Melody by the hand and they hurried to the back. The door remained open, providing a view of the alley across the street.

"What the fuck?" Maxwell said in an exhale as they both caught sight of the clown staggering. He hadn't seen them, yet.

She grabbed Maxwell's arm and backed away from the door, pulling on him.

The clown looked even more beat up. Melody assumed Cali had something to do with that. She squeezed Maxwell's hand, worried that their fight wasn't over and that Cali would pop into view at any moment. No one else lingered nearby, at least not as far as she could tell from her vantage point. She secretly hoped it stayed that way.

But then a black van came zooming out of nowhere and screeched to a halt in front of the beat-up clown. And as the joke goes, the van was filled with more clowns. Whooping and hollering, they collected their comrade from the alley. Right before they sped away, a deafening explosion shook the building. Art pieces fell off the walls, a few of the frames cracking. The glass in the windows rattled. It felt like an earthquake had rumbled through. Maybe. But Melody smelled burning rubber and knew better.

The Killer of Devils

Maxwell and Melody ran to the gallery's front door. The two vehicles involved in the crash were now engulfed in black smoke and random licks of orange flames. She could practically taste burnt tires and gasoline.

"What the fuck is going on?" Maxwell asked.

"I honestly don't know."

"A car accident. The driver, a man dressed as clown, runs into our gallery and attacks us. Then a van full of *more* clowns picks him up. Then these cars explode. A bomb. It had to be a bomb, right? One of those vehicles had a bomb in it, probably the clown's van."

"A bomb? That sounds crazy."

"Crazier than a clown running into our gallery and attacking you? And then him being rescued by more clowns?"

"The accident in the parking lot… There must have been all kinds of gas spilling everywhere. Maybe something ignited and caused the explosion."

Jaw set, Maxwell shook his head. "It's been a few minutes since the crash. All that spilled gas would go up in a whooshing flash. Even if one of the gas tanks blew, it wouldn't have been big enough to rattle the building. I'll confer with Harold to get his opinion."

Chunks of ice dropped into her gut from a cold truth she didn't want to swallow. "Confer with Harold?"

Maxwell turned to face Melody. "Yes. I figured out what I want to do with my father's legacy."

June 22, 2002

Keith snapped awake. It felt like an ice pick was sliding through his skull. Cold and wet, he was sitting in a comfortable armchair, a shade of light blue that would be perfect in any living room, yet he was in a garage... with five people dressed as clowns. The one standing closest to him – light brown hair, white face paint, perfectly symmetrical blue circles over his eyes, sloppy red smile – held a bucket, water dripping from its lip. By the casual loose way he held it, Keith guessed it was empty, the reason why he was now cold and wet.

The dude's real smile was almost as wide as his painted one. "Hello, brother."

Still a bit groggy from being knocked out – he had his ass handed to him from some blonde, and then got sucker punched in the cheek once the van door closed – Keith mumbled, "Not your brother. Got no siblings."

The five clowns laughed with different intensities, speeds, and pitches. A weird strobing effect of noise. Made his head hurt. The lead clown crouched down, elbow on the chair's armrest, head resting in his hand. "Oh, Keith, we're brothers of a different kind. A more special kind. I'm Collin, by the way. We met at Marissa's party."

Keith tilted his head. "Oh yeah. You're the guy I ran into outside of Marissa's room?" Yep, he recognized him through all that face paint – he'd never forget those laser intense eyes. And he was about the right height and size. "Heh. All right."

Collin waved to the woman with long, green hair and white base paint. A purple square over her left eye, a purple triangle over her right, and a jagged yellow smile, like lightning arcing from ear to ear. "Brin, he sounds like he could use water. To drink. From a bottle, not a bucket."

Keith took the water bottle from her and gulped down half. He didn't thank her; manners didn't seem to apply here. Intelligence sparkled in her eyes. Same with Collin. Not the other three, though. Since Keith had already made the decision to skip common courtesy, he stared directly at the three of them. They looked like idiots.

"Those three?" Collin said, gesturing toward the dazed clowns. "They're our friends as well. Delvin and Trina and Sally. Sally's the newest. We found him yesterday."

Sally was shaped like Keith but surpassed him by about thirty pounds worth of beer and tacos. He'd look perfectly normal behind the wheel of an eighteen-wheeler, or on a barstool, or in a recliner watching television. Right now, he was licking the front fender of the black van.

Pausing mid-lick, Sally stood at attention, his fat, pink tongue hanging from his mouth like an uncooked piece of ham. Bright yellow grease paint coated his face with a thick black line across his mouth. Red paint covered his eyes, rough ideas of circles with streaks, like blood frozen mid-drip. Keith wouldn't have been surprised if it was blood. Sally spoke a few words – unintelligible from his tongue lolling outside his mouth – then went back to licking the van.

Delvin was no less unsettling. Standing soldier straight by a set of metal shelves, he stared at Keith while petting a dog's dirty white pelt of curls. Or was that a purse? Upon further inspection, Keith was right on both counts. Brown leather cords formed the purse strap, attached to each of the dog's feet. Upside down, its tongue hung from its head, neck limp. The insides must have been gone, because three cans of spray paint and a small bottle of lighter fluid stuck out from its belly.

Tall dude with a big ol' head, Delvin's face was somehow creepier than Sally's – painted white with blue Xs over his eyes, but the skin under the blue rippled like burn scars. What gave Keith phantom mouth pains, though, was his big red smile, held into place by fishhooks.

The other girl-clown started off promising. A tiny wisp of a woman. Thin. Not even a full foot taller than Little Lily or Tiny Goddess Marissa. But there was a level of crazy in her bright green eyes that made Keith's nut-sack shrivel. At first. Until he got a real good look at her as she approached in jerky motions like a marionette pulled along by a drunken puppet-master. She was small enough to kneel on the chair's armrest. She climbed on to it, and then inched her crazy closer to him until their noses almost touched. He had the weirdest boner of his life.

"He's not like us." Trina's breath was too warm on his cheek, like a hair dryer had replaced her lungs. Acetone fumes reached into his nose and dared him to sneeze. Keith was confused by the smell, but now that she was this close, he saw the dried lakebed of cracks in the white parts of her face. The silver over her eyes and the gold on her mouth had the sparkle of paint. Spray paint, he assumed. She ran a finger from his forehead to his chin, and examined the runny white makeup on her fingertip. Her wide eyes held the curiosity of an innocent child along with horror, an expression formed after learning that monsters are real. "There's a skin under his skin."

"He is like me and Brin," Collin said, grabbing Brin's hip and pulling her close. His eyes made something squirm inside Keith – he knew horrible secrets Keith didn't. Collin then ran a finger over Brin's cheek; her eyelids fluttered with ecstasy. White paint on his fingertip, he said, "He wears his real face over his fake face. The three of us use our fake face to interact with the outside world."

"Fake face? Fake world?" Keith asked, looking for any God damned scrap of sanity.

"Your skin is fake. You don't know that, or you'd wear your real skin, like we do," Trina said, heated breath blasting Keith's face. She turned to Collin. "We're going to change the world, right? Make it real, right? Right real?"

"Yes," Collin replied. "We'll make it right real."

Trina looked back at Keith with the fire of a burning church in her eyes. She made "bat-shit crazy" seem like stoicism. She cocked her head and said, "Are you right real?"

Keith had no idea what she was talking about, but when it came to crazy chicks, he knew it was best to agree with them. "You bet your sweet ass I am."

Her crazy eyes shifted from lost to excited as she hopped off the chair's arms. On her toes, she looked over her shoulder and spun in

The Killer of Devils

circles like a music box ballerina, trying to look at her own backside. "He said I have a sweet ass. He said I had a sweet ass. He said—"

Snap.

The sudden snap of a rat trap interrupted her. Keith had heard plenty of those things go off in his lifetime. He was thankful for the distraction, the clacking and the squeaking that followed. Not many chicks could make him uncomfortable, but Trina was one of them. Though he quickly learned that she gave varying levels of discomfort.

The gleam in her eyes burned brighter than the gold paint, and she turned to Delvin and Sally. Clapping her hands together, she squealed. "Did you guys hear that? You know what that sound means, right?"

All three smiling faces took a deep breath, and then exclaimed in unison, "Furry pizza!"

Like kindergarteners running to the ice cream man, they charged through the garage to a space between two sets of metal shelves, Delvin's purse dog flopping against his hip. They held hands and giggled at whatever was clacking against the cement floor. The squeaking ended quickly.

Collin and Brin watched with the delighted pride of entitled parents, as if Trina dangling a dead rat from her hand was perfectly normal. She tore the front legs away in bone crunching bites, then passed it to Delvin who bit off the head. Clapping his hands, Sally accepted the rest of the torso, legs, and tail.

Collin looked down at Keith and gestured for him to stand and follow. "Come on. Let me show you around the house."

Keith wasn't sure he wanted to see it, but he definitely wanted out of the garage. So, he hurriedly pushed himself out of the armchair, and followed.

The house was a lot nicer than he imagined after seeing the post-apocalyptic design scheme of the garage. It reminded him of the 3,500 square-foot museums of excess in the suburbia neighborhoods of Tiny Goddess Marissa and Little Lily. Everything was modern, new, and stylish, grays and whites with strategic pops of colors. The poster-sized photos of the wolves were pretty cool, though. Keith was entranced; he didn't hear Brin creep up beside him, her mouth inches from his ear. "I took those myself," she said.

"The pictures?"

"Yep. I was in Alaska where the wildlife is still wild. I was roughing it for an assignment, hiking and camping around. One day, right around twilight, when ghosts get restless and the sun spirits tell the Earth to fuck off, this lone wolf came skulking around my camping area. It was just me and my camera. It growled and barked, posturing, making threats. I took these pictures, then growled and barked back at the wolf."

"Did you run?"

"No. I took a chunk of beef jerky and threw it over the wolf's head. As it scampered away from my tent to go get it, I grabbed my gun. As soon as it finished, I shot the ground next to it, and it ran off. Then I pissed all over my campsite to claim it as my own."

Keith turned to look Brin in the eyes. This level of crazy mirrored the others in the garage, but with different intensity. Like she was just sane enough to know she was nuts. And there was a hunger in her eyes. Keith wondered if she was holding back details of the story, because her ravenous eyes told him she could have easily killed and eaten that wolf. "Yeah?"

"Yeah. Have we mentioned yet that this is Trina's house? Have we mentioned yet that Trina's my sister?"

Makes sense now. Crazy runs in the family.

Keith grunted. He thought about puffing out his chest and scowling but remembered that posturing would do no good. "Good to know."

"Okay, Brin, back off," Collin said, his cheeriness sticky as warm syrup. "I'm sure he has a lot of questions."

Keith wanted out of this nuthouse and back in his own, to see if anything that happened today would lead authorities back to him. Not only had the psycho blonde found him, so had these guys. How? Okay, if this Collin guy was at Tiny Goddess Marissa's party, then it stood to reason that he could have followed Keith.

The red digital time displayed on cable box by the television let him know he'd been unconscious for about an hour.

The Killer of Devils

"Why did you rescue me?" Keith asked.

When Collin stretched out his arms as a gesture of brotherly acceptance, his dark blue golf shirt and jeans made him look like a twisted minister of a new age church. "Because you're one of us."

"One of you guys. Riiiiiight. Okay. So, how'd you find me?"

"Why, Master Poppie, of course."

Jesus, even the normal one is a bag of squirrels. Keith was losing patience. "What the fuck is a master poppie?"

Collin's intense eyes got wider, more insane. "Master Poppie is the one who will free the world from the madness of limitations. This world hates you, Keith. Not only does this world disapprove of *what* you love, it hinders you from *doing* what you love. It threatens to imprison you. Imagine a world where your only limitation is your imagination. Imagine a world where you could have anything you can imagine, or desire, at any time. If you follow Master Poppie, he will lead you there."

Well, damn. Master Poppie might be a cult leader, because Collin sounded like one of those ministers yapping away about a great fairytale offering everything Keith ever wanted. Sure, he'd love to live in a world where he could immortalize the majestic girls through video, but it'd be insane to think it could possibly happen. "Look, that's a nice fantasy and all, but there's no way your leader could pull this off."

"I respectfully disagree, Keith. We already have plans in motion. Plans that will benefit Master Poppie, benefit us. All of us."

Plans. Yep, Keith started formulating his plan to escape. Sure, Collin was bigger and younger and healthier, and Brin was batshit crazy, but the element of surprise was in his favor.

He assumed this house was in a fancy suburban neighborhood. Once Keith got a chance to run out the main door, they'd be foolish to follow. Even if they did, he could yell for help, yell that they kidnapped him and dressed him like a clown, tried to make him look like them. Stupid plan, but it was better than none. Just needed a peek out a window to see if he could figure out where he was for sure.

Jutting his jaw and nodding in contemplation, Keith strolled farther into the living room – drapes pulled shut – then toward the kitchen entrance. Looking around as if measuring and weighing his options, judging the suitability of this lair, he said, "Plans, huh? What kinds of plans?"

"We can't go into detail with you yet. We'd like you to join us in our campaigns for chaos and power, Keith. We need to add to our numbers. We need more soldiers like the ones you've met in our garage, but soldiers need generals. Thinkers like you."

Keith strolled into the kitchen, examining it. He went to the sink and looked out the open, uncovered window. The forest behind the house sent his guts squirming, like getting three gulps into a glass of milk before noticing it's spoiled. Something about it woods seemed familiar, though. "Where are we?"

"You feel that don't you?" Collin asked, joy in his voice. "That's the presence of Master Poppie. He lives in that forest. It runs between two developments."

Forest between two developments. This feeling of ants skittering under his skin, the exact feeling of being watched when he buried Little Lily. Her house was nearby, either in this neighborhood or in the one on the other side of the woods.

"This is why Trina's house is our operation base," Collin said. "These two neighborhoods will give us everything we need to build an army and keep Master Poppie nourished. The authorities don't know of our existence yet, but when they find us, it will be too late."

Army against the establishment? Keith liked what was being sold, liked the idea of being a general in an army, but he didn't believe the salesman could deliver. Despite the twisting in his belly, he had more questions. If he didn't like the answers, he'd go back to his original plan of plowing over Collin and Brin to get out the front door. But when he turned to address them, he got a face full of purple smoke. "What the fuck?"

More to it than smoke. It flowed across his face, over his skin. A sweet odor, like cotton candy. At first, it was so thick he couldn't see through it, but it quickly dissipated into his nose and mouth, leaving a chalky residue on his shirt. "What the fuck was that?"

"The madness mist. It frees your mind, allowing you to become a disciple of Master Poppie." Collin replaced the top back onto a plain, metal thermos. After a few seconds of staring like a lunatic, he said, "See, Brin? I told you he was a general like us."

Instead of punching Collin, Keith snorted and blew a plume of purple powder from his nostrils. At first, he thought they had drugged him, but he felt no effects. No numbness, tingling, or blurred vision. But... What did Collin just say? Keith asked, "Madness mist?"

"Master Poppie provides it, to convert others. It helps release the inner us, tapping into our repressed yet natural insanity. We repress natural insanity in order live in a world of *manufactured* insanity."

"So... the three in the garage all got a snort of this?"

Eyes gleefully wide, both Collin and Brin nodded. "White mist. Not purple. White makes soldiers, who are willing to do anything we generals tell them to do in the name of Master Poppie. Brin and I inhaled the purple, which makes generals. And now you're a general, too."

Keith wasn't sure about this Master Poppie nonsense, but he liked the idea of being a general in an army. Liked the idea of people doing whatever he told them to do. Liked the idea of whatever the hell this madness mist was. Oh, yeah, he needed to get his hands on more of that. "Cool. Let's fuck some shit up. What's next?"

Collin said, "I have to remove my real face and wear my fake face, then get rid of the van. It's Sally's. He was a delivery driver. After we converted him, we gave the van a quick paint job. We needed it to rescue you, and now that you're part of the family, I'm going to dispose of it before Sally's ex-employers send anyone to investigate. And I have to pick my son up from Marissa's party. In the meantime, make yourself at home. Get acclimated to your new life."

Yeah, Keith could get into this lifestyle. He looked at the closed garage door and thought about Crazy Trina.

He felt Brin's hateful stare. Something needed to be done about that.

June 22, 2002

The alley wasn't as disgusting as other alleys Cali had investigated. It lacked the tang of stale vomit and hint of ammonia that came with homelessness, drunkards, or those needing a urinal. It should bother her that she had visited enough alleys to compare and contrast. A mere two years ago, alleys were on the peripheral of her life, places she passed by on her way from trendy new restaurants to banging hot nightclubs whenever she found herself in a city worthy of her presence. Now she spent an inordinate amount of time in dark, fetid areas. Creeping through long abandoned buildings, skulking through basements that created underground labyrinths, frequenting alleyways like this one to meet informants, chase suspects, and fight clowns. *What a glamourous life.*

Twilight was about to begin its shift and she checked her watch to see how long she had been at this. Too long. Five hours since her skirmish with "Keith the Clown" in this alley.

Mother argued against returning, but Cali wanted to rummage around to see if she could find anything of interest. They split the difference and decided she'd come back once the police presence was minimized. The CSIs came and went while the uniforms asked the bystanders questions. The flatbeds were in the parking lot now, getting ready to remove the burned out remains of the vehicles – thank God she used an untraceable fake name for the rental; she'd already brought too much attention to herself.

Not a single police officer remained in the alley.

Cali wanted to investigate their fight arena before the natural light disappeared. It'd be too difficult to find anything with a flashlight. When she lifted the dumpster lid and got punched with the sour stench of rotting trash, she was inclined to agree with her mother – there was no point to this.

But her gut told her there had to be *something* here. Maybe he dropped his wallet or cellphone or business card or balloon animal. Hell, she'd even take a few stray hairs or scraps of skin or blood or red sponge nose for DNA analysis. She knew DNA analysis only worked if he was already in the system. The way he fought? He had been trained, possibly military. He'd be in the system somewhere. She doubted his name was really Keith.

As much as it pained her to admit, she should have listened when Mother told her to back off and let the tracker do its job. If she hadn't followed, then Keith wouldn't have noticed her and engaged. If she had listened to her mother, the bastard wouldn't have gotten away. *God damn it! Mother can't be right twice in one day.*

God bless Mother, though, because when she picked Cali up after the mystery van full of clowns rescued Keith from the scene, she never once said, "I told you so." Never yelled at her.

The ride back to the hotel had been quiet, allowing Cali to stew in her own mental and emotional filth. They cleaned up, ordered a pizza, and proposed a few plans, none that needed immediate action.

But her critical error burned like acid and the corrosion kept spreading through her chest. She needed to clean up this mess and fix her mistake. Her mother had voiced her opinion – that Cali wouldn't find anything meaningful – but Cali would rather fail at trying than succeed at nothing. Now, here she was in an alley, peering under a dumpster lid to find…

"Oh my God," Cali whispered.

"What?" Mother asked through the earpiece. "Did you find something?"

"Yeah. There are like fifty empty microwave meal trays in here."

Mother sighed. "Cali…"

"I mean, it's quasi-terrifying to think about. Who goes through this many microwave meals in less than a week? There's an overpriced Italian restaurant in one of these buildings. Are *they* charging twenty-five bucks for a three-dollar chicken parm? I don't know what's sadder: these coming from a swindling restaurant or a single person eating all these by themselves."

"There is an old adage about tossing rocks while residing in glass houses, you know."

"Oh, I've eaten my fair share of microwavable meals, but I don't think I've had as many in my lifetime as I'm looking at in this dumpster."

"That may be true, but when was the last time you had a home-cooked meal?"

"I don't know. When was the last time we were at your place?"

"Have I made my point, or do I need to keep going?"

Cali examined the lid for blood or hair. Nothing. When she released the dumpster lid, its echoing clang rang through the alley. She strolled to where Keith had landed after she kicked him in the chest.

"What point?" Cali legitimately didn't know what *point* her mother was talking about. "We've been on the road a lot."

"And when we're not, you've been staying with me."

"We've been training and hunting these past two years. Don't you like my company?" Cali hated that her voice tilted toward whiny, but she wasn't expecting a deep life conversation while sifting through back-alley trash.

"I love your company, but you have five houses. Have you spent one night in any of them since your father died?"

Cali paused to think about the question. "Ummm…?"

"That's what I thought. Any particular reason?"

"Ummm…?"

"That's also what I thought. This is another part of your myopia that we need to work on."

"Another part of my—? Are you serious?"

"Yes, Sweety, I am."

"We're in the middle of a hunt."

"That may be, but we're also in a position to rest, take a breath, recharge. Take a moment to live life."

"I'm going on a date with Chism tomorrow night. Between now and then, we need to find this Keith the Clown freak."

"He's on the run and the authorities are looking for him."

Mother made sure of that. As soon as Keith rammed his van into Cali's rental, Mother tapped into the parking lot's security cameras. When the authorities asked the lot for the footage, the footage strategically cut in

The Killer of Devils

and out. The only useful images remaining for the cops were of a clown getting out of a van and running from the scene. Mother didn't stop there, though. She put together a nice little montage of clear shots of Keith, as well as the image taken from his website for comparative purposes, and anonymously sent the package to local news stations. As a cherry on top, she included the fact that he was the birthday entertainment of four missing girls, including Lily Pennington. Each station reported, but the police reserved comment as to what it all meant. That wasn't good enough for Cali. He needed to die. "You worked your techie wizard voodoo magic and made his situation bad. But he could easily disappear. We don't know who he is – who he truly is – and don't know who's helping him."

"I used my techie wizard voodoo magic to give us a break. You wanted to tell Bethany what we were doing, I could hear it in your voice, but we didn't have any evidence. But now we've connected enough dots for the police to get involved, to give Bethany the hope you wanted her to have. Let's take a break, regroup, refresh, recharge."

Cali crouched down near the wall Keith's body had hit. Running her hand over the bricks, she hoped to find the exact spot. No blood streaks. No clumps of hair. Her finger hovered over a streak of white that could be anything from his makeup to bird shit. She didn't bother trying to collect it. "I still—"

"Which one is your favorite?"

"Wait... What?"

"Which of your new houses is your favorite?"

"I've only been to two of them. Well, technically three. I didn't know he owned the one in Florida. I thought it was a timeshare."

"Okay. Which of those three is your favorite?"

Cali pinched the bridge of her nose. Having her mother speak directly into her brain regarding a topic she didn't want to think about, let alone talk about, was distracting her and it gave her a headache. It'd be so easy to pull the earpiece out and turn it off, but the earful she'd get back at the hotel room was too steep a price to pay. "The upstate New York one, the one in the woods."

"Why?"

"Because I didn't have to pretend there. No thinking about how I needed to act. No trying to be the perfect girlfriend, or the greatest friend, or the best student possible. I could take my 'Cali-persona' mask off."

"So, it's a place for you to take a break, regroup, refresh, recharge."

"Maybe."

"Why don't you do that. Let's call it a night and go to dinner. We'll have another spa day tomorrow and you can go on your date with Chism. The day after, go to your house in the woods, even if it's just for a couple days."

Huffing, Cali stood. She turned toward the alley opening. "I don't think—"

WHAM!

Someone had stepped into the alley and walked right into Cali. Too wired to think like a rational human being, she pushed herself away, punched the person in the cheek, and jumped back. Knees bent, fists clenched, she held her breath.

The person was a… very handsome man.

"Oh, wow," Cali whispered. She then cleared her throat. "Sorry about that. You okay?"

"Cali? What's happening? Who are you apologizing to?" Mother asked.

Rubbing his cheek, the very handsome man smiled.

"Damn," she whispered, in awe. Maybe she had been missing Tanner more than she wanted to admit, but this guy had similar features that enticed her. Over six feet tall, the chiseled face of a mythological hero, and a tight tee shirt over tighter muscles.

"It's been a while since I got popped like that," he said. *God, he has voice similar to Tanner's.*

"You punched someone?" Mother asked. "Can you not go half a day without punching someone?"

"You get punched in the face a lot?" Cali asked him.

"I used to. Once upon a time, I was a boxer."

"What the hell is with you and boxers lately?" Mother mumbled into Cali's ear. "Wait… Did you just meet a hot guy while digging through trash in an alley?"

Cali wanted yell, "Shut up, Mom," but that would convey a really weird message to this guy. Of course, it would convey an accurate message – that she was crazy – but she wanted to let him figure that out on his own, after she snuck out of his bedroom tomorrow morning. The first chance she got, she'd yank out the earpiece, but until then she had to endure Mother's unwelcome commentary.

His intense eyes ensnared her. So hypnotic, she didn't want to break eye contact. "If you're not a boxer anymore, then what are you?"

The man shrugged and gave the same smirk Tanner gave when he was about to say something clever. "Male. Human. Mammal."

"Ha, ha, funny guy. What do you do for a living now?"

"You wouldn't believe me if I told you."

"Try me, funny guy."

"I'm a professional poker player."

"Huh," Cali grunted as if she just found out the best chicken parm she had ever eaten was a microwave meal.

"Knew you wouldn't believe me. As a professional poker player, I'm trained to read people and make certain assessments."

"You're a dude skulking through an alley. No one would believe you're a professional poker player."

He laughed and put his hands in his pockets, his stance relaxed. Did he do that to show Cali he wasn't a threat, or that he didn't believe she was one? "Despite the fact that you look like you're going to throat punch me any second, I need to point out that you are the one skulking around the alley. I was cutting through, taking a shortcut."

Cali glanced at her own fists as if they were disobeying a direct "down, girls" order. She then looked into his inescapable eyes. "Throat punching is still on the table. What's your name?"

"D.C."

"Nope."

He winced. "Nope? As in that's not my name?"

"Nope as in I'm not calling you that. It sounds like a dude-bro name that your dude-bro frat brothers used to call you." To emphasize her point, she dropped her voice in mocking manner. "Yo, D.C., wanna get wasted and crush beer cans off our heads, D.C., before we go out and roofie some sorority chicks, D.C.?"

"Jesus Christ, Cali!" Mother cackled. "This is you flirting? Oh my God, how the hell did you ever get a date with Chism?"

Chism. Fuck. Forgot about him. Wait, that's tomorrow night. All good. Wait… Not only does hot alley guy look like Tanner, but he looks like Chism, too. Jesus, I have a type!

D.C. shook his head and regarded Cali with the wariness of a mouse looking at a piece of cheese on a set trap. *Good. About time.* "I wish I could say that was an inaccurate impression of my old fraternity brothers, but there were way too many like that, which is the main reason I don't speak to many of them anymore."

"Seems like a sound decision. What does the 'D' stand for?"

"Dallas."

"Ugh. How about the 'C?'"

"Trust me, it's worse."

"Fair enough."

"What's your name?"

"Cali."

"California?"

Cali relaxed her attack stance, her hands on cocked hip. "Why in God's name would you think my parents named me after a state?"

"It's a pretty state," Mother said.

Dallas shrugged. "My parents named me after a city. I keep lying to myself and saying it's their favorite vacation spot and not because I was conceived there."

"Right. My name's Calista."

"So, Calista, Great Sentry of the Alleyway, may I pass? Or should I go back the way I came and leave you talking to yourself?"

She should deny him access. She should tell him to turn around and not look back. She should tell him that he reminds her too much of an ex-boyfriend. She should... Wait. "You heard me talking to myself?"

"Yeah, you seemed pretty angry."

"Oh. Well... I had a few too many last night and stumbled around. Lost my phone. I know I cut through here, thought maybe I dropped it."

Dallas walked farther into the alley. "That sucks. I'll help you look."

"Umm..." Tanner would never be this nice. "Okaaaay..." Cali couldn't hide the dubiousness in her tone. But she recognized this as an opportunity to ditch Mother. "I'll check over there, behind that other dumpster."

Cali hustled to the other end of the alley and ducked behind the dumpster. Whispering, she spoke quickly. "All right, Mom, I'm hanging up now."

"You are something else."

"Hey, you told me I need to socialize more."

"I said make a connection to people, not hook up with a random alley stranger."

"I'm not— He's not— Okay, this is exactly why I'm hanging up. Bye."

She dug the communicator from her ear, but not before her mom shouted, "Okay, but make sure he wears a cond—"

Cali stood and shivered with a "walked-through-a-spiderweb" dance, as she often did whenever her mother directly commented on her sex life.

"Everything okay?" Dallas called out from two dumpsters over.

Cali snarled as she walked out from behind the dumpster. "Yeah, just a dead rat that maggots got to. You know what? I don't feel like looking for my phone anymore. Thanks for helping, though."

Dallas shrugged. "Alright. Hey, um, how about I take you out for a drink to ease the pain?"

"You don't have to do that. I had zero attachment to that thing."

"Okay. How I about I take you out for a drink because I think you're interesting?"

Cali wondered how good of a poker player he was because she could see through his intense eyes, directly into his brain. He wanted the evening to end in the bedroom, just like she did. *Or might I be projecting my libido onto him? Okay, buddy, I'll give you one chance to run away. If you don't take it, then by tomorrow morning you'll either need medical assistance or therapy.* "I punched you, insulted you, grilled you, and refuse to call you by the name you used to introduce yourself."

"That makes you more interesting than all three of the last women I went on a date with, combined. And you're not wearing a pair of Uggs, so bonus points for you."

"Furry boots in the middle of June? Fuck that."

"My thought exactly, but when I asked, every one of those dates said the boots weren't as hot as they looked." With a smile that made Cali's toes curl, he gestured to the other end of the alley. "If you're interested, I know a great bar this way."

"Oh, I'm interested," she said, looking forward to tomorrow's hangover.

June 23, 2002

A stray thought passed through Maxwell's head: *I need to redecorate.* As much time as he spent in the back office of 8th Street Gallery, he should invest in making it comfortable. Right now, three people sat awkwardly at the cheap wooden desk, barely big enough for one person. His laptop was positioned where everyone could see the screen.

Melody sat in what passed as an executive chair while Harold Varvaro sat in the uncomfortable thrift-store chair. Maxwell sat between them, but behind them, to study their reactions as they watched the videos. He had seen the videos plenty of times, no need to watch again.

Maxwell's heart broke as Melody sat rigid, unblinking, petrified. Anger pulsed in his heart as well, directed at that freaking clown for intruding upon their lives, and angry at himself for not being able to stop him. Angry that, apparently, there were more of them. He needed to show Melody that he could protect her. Which is why he asked Harold to his office, to watch the videos, in hopes that he'd assist.

Harold's expression was completely indifferent. Calm and stoic to the point of eerie. Unfazed by the black and white security camera footage from the parking lot across the street, showing a white van slamming into a black SUV. He didn't even flinch when a man dressed as a clown exited the van and ran to the SUV. The footage became jittery and cut in and out, clearing up when the clown ran from the scene of the crash. The footage changed, flipping to a different security camera recording from behind the building. The clown ran into an alley. After a few minutes, a black van pulled up and the clown jumped in. The only time Harold's face changed was when the open van door revealed more clowns. He made more of a sour expression, like an old man offended by someone with a blue mohawk and facial piercings.

The video ended and Maxwell asked Harold, "What do you think?"

"I think this world is full of fuckin' weirdos. I saw the parking lot scene on the news last night. They said the guy's name is Keith the Clown, and the piece of shit is wanted for the kidnapping and murder of little girls. They don't know his real name. The news didn't show this van full of clowns, though. I didn't know he got help escaping. Where'd you get *that* footage?"

"Believe it or not, this footage came from the gallery's security camera."

Harold grunted and nodded. "The one over the back door? Yeah, I sometimes turn that one when your old man didn't want any evidence of me entering the gallery, know what I mean? I guess I forgot to turn it back. You got lucky with that." He turned to face Maxwell and shifted to a reclined posture. Hands folded together with his usual apathetic look in his half-closed eyes, he said, "I'm assuming you'd like me to do something?"

This was it, the opportunity to show Melody that he could keep her safe, he could remove anything that would harm her. "Yes. Help me find them and eliminate them."

Melody gasped and Harold arched his eyebrows in surprise.

"Yeah?" Harold asked, a bit of bemusement in his voice. "Are you talkin' about finding these clowns and tossing their asses at the police, or are you talkin' about something a little more permanent?"

Maxwell shrugged. "I think we start the process and see where it takes us."

"What are you saying, Maxwell?" Melody whispered.

"I'm saying we have the resources to protect ourselves and others. I trust that Mr. Varvaro is excellent at what he does, or my father wouldn't have him on the payroll for such a sensitive position."

Harold smirked and tipped an invisible hat. "Appreciate it."

"So... Where should we start?"

"I'll have my boys ask questions on the street level. See if anyone knows anything."

"What about the person he hit? Melody and I hung around outside while the police investigated. I heard one of them say the SUV was a rental. I could probably get the license plate. Would that help?"

"Nah. Unless you can hack into the rental agency's computer system. The cops might have a name, but that does us no good unless you know a cop or two willing to share, because I don't."

"No? So... My father didn't... have...?" Maxwell felt too ashamed to finish the sentence, so he hinted just enough for Harold to pick up on it.

"Did your old man have cops on his payroll? No. He always believed that would cause more problems than it was worth. A dirty cop ain't easy to find, and if you do find one, they have more power over you than you'd think. They can get their department involved and drop a ten-ton hammer on your head. The law moves real fast when it wants to."

A sense of relief swept through Maxwell like a wave. His father had been involved in illicit operations, but not dirty cops, which in Maxwell's book meant that he wasn't one hundred percent evil. "Okay. Should we try to find the person the clown hit? It looked intentional."

Harold sat straighter and rubbed his chin while deep in thought. "Did you actually see who it was?"

Lips drawn tight, Melody shook her head.

"We didn't see anything," Maxwell said. "But we overheard the police interviewing witnesses. What a mess. The bystanders that said the driver was a woman all varied in description from tall to short with every possible hair color, ranging from long to short. One person thought it was a man with long hair, and two people said she was black, even though everyone else said she was white."

Harold snickered. "Yeah, that sounds about right. Do we know if Keith interacted with the driver after he hit them?"

"Witness testimony was just as muddled about that. Some people say he got out and ran. A couple people said the driver tried to interact with him, but he pushed them and ran. A few people actually said they got into a fight before he ran."

"I can't think of any good reason to waste our time asking about the random unidentifiable person. It'd be easier to ask about a bunch of clowns. Right?"

Maxwell nodded. "Right. What do you think, Melody?"

*

Melody jerked when she heard her name. Her eyes had drifted to the black and white image of the escape van and paused on the computer monitor. She was relieved that the video footage only captured the man getting into the van full of clowns, and nothing from within the alley itself. She wanted to watch the footage again, scrutinize it for evidence of Calista. But as far as she was able to tell from just one viewing, she didn't see anything, and Maxwell hadn't brought her name up once.

"Melody?" Maxwell asked again.

She turned to him and fake-smiled, but she doubted he bought her attempt at confidence. "I don't think we need to waste our time with that."

Maxwell reached out and squeezed her hand. It was obvious that he thought she feared this Keith the Clown and his cadre. As terrifying as a clown kidnapping little girls was, Maxwell scared her more. How would he react if he knew Cali was alive? What would he do? Send Harold to hunt her down? Probably.

Melody didn't like Harold. At all. He scared her, too. Who wouldn't be frightened sitting in the same room with a criminal who used phrases like "my boys" and "street level?" If that wasn't upsetting enough, it seemed like Maxwell wanted to follow in his father's footsteps. She didn't know what to do about that. Hopefully, he'd just use Harold's services to find the clowns and be done with him and "his boys." She couldn't worry about that now, though. She needed to find Cali.

And it was Cali. There was no evidence of her on either security camera, but Melody had seen Cali. It had been two years, and she looked a little different – bigger, angrier – but it was without a doubt her. What was she doing in Philadelphia? How did she learn to fight like that? Wait… She fought him hard enough to make him run, like she was ready for him. Did she know the clown did horrible things to little girls?

"Sounds like we have a plan," Maxwell said.

Harold stood and replied with a smirk, "That we do. I'll keep you posted about what I find."

That smirk made Melody's skin crawl. Smarmy. Devious. He enjoyed the idea of hunting other human beings. It excited him. Unfortunately, it seemed to be rubbing off on Maxwell.

Harold left and even after the door shut, Maxwell's smile remained, as if pleased with himself.

"Well, if we have to use him, then at least it's for something like this," Melody said.

Keeping her hand in his, Maxwell pulled his chair closer and stroked her arm. His eyes held pain and hope, like someone ready to begin the healing process. "Yes, we'll use him for this. I have faith in him, that he'll find Keith and those assholes. When he does, you… *we* can feel safe again."

She forced a smile, a better, more practiced one this time. "I know."

But she didn't feel safe, didn't like that Maxwell intended to fight fire with fire by using a frightening man to hunt down frightening men. She wanted to tell him that, wanted to share her true opinions about the situation. Instead, she started to devise ways to track down Cali.

June 23, 2002

Cali's date with Dallas last night was half a beer and a taxi ride back to her room. She had been too busy exploring his mouth with hers to remember the ride, but she recalled the tip was more than twice the cab fare.

His performance was everything she had hoped for. After two rounds of using him for the desired release of her pent-up feelings, she decided to shift her attention and break out a few moves she hadn't tried since her relationship with Tanner.

When she woke up this morning, her hotel room looked like an 80s metal band had stayed there. Not a single item was in the same place from the day before. The desk had been shifted ninety degrees, to make room for a new position Dallas read about in a magazine and wanted to try; lamps had fallen while moving the nightstands to make room for a position Cali read about in a magazine; the armchair laid on its back because of a position they had both read about in some other magazine. The position itself failed after the armchair toppled over, but she didn't care. After a few laughs, they just tried something else.

She and Dallas had their fun and stayed in sync while going at it like rabid beasts and stayed in sync while lying on tussled sheets chatting about whatever came to mind. Actual pillow talk. Pillow talk with Tanner had been weird and meaningless dude-bro haiku: "Hitting the gym next/ Need to work my pecs and glutes/Wanna fuck again?" With Dallas, it ranged from comparing the size of their hands to skin and hair care products. Their favorite animals. Books, movies, live theater. Nothing too deep or complex, just talking for the sake of having voices fill the void. Still infinitely better than what Tanner ever produced. And there'd been zero pillow talk with any guy since Tanner, because Cali always left after getting what she wanted.

What made this morning unique was that Dallas was still there. And that made her smile.

Like two mature adults, they strolled to a café around the corner for breakfast. Their discussion went only a modicum deeper from last night, ranging from favorite bands to who could eat more pancakes. The date ended with a sweet kiss, and Dallas entering his number into her phone.

By the time she made it back home, Chism texted. His plans changed, so he couldn't do dinner, but he could meet in an hour. After a brief exchange and a long shower, Cali found herself in a newly rented Explorer – a different fake, untraceable name than the last one – heading north of the city. She followed the GPS instructions and wondered why she didn't cancel the date with Chism, considering that her date with Dallas had only been mere hours ago. But… Why? *It's 2002 for fuck's sake. I promised monogamy to no one, and guys do this shit to women all the time. You know what? I might fuck Chism tonight in the name of womanhood.*

"Where the fuck is he taking me?" Cali mumbled to herself, half disappointed no one answered her. She was so used to her mother yammering away in her ear or some form of alcoholic beverage whispering bad advice. It's not like she expected answers from the monitor of the portable GPS resting on her lap.

The computer's synthesized-voice said, "Turn right."

Country road, lots of trees, random house. She was thankful that there was still signage but confused at how quickly the landscape had changed from city to country. Another turn, more trees, now a small town. About a mile to go. Pennsylvania was a strange state.

She made what became one last right turn, and followed the long driveway into a parking lot. Chism was leaning against his Jeep Wrangler. His *Dragon Ball Z* tee shirt was two sizes too small over his toned muscles, while his jeans perfectly fit everything they needed to fit. Then he smiled as she got out of her car.

Damn, that boy looks good. Similar features to both Dallas and Tanner and Cali's insides melted. Yep, she had "a type" all right. "Hey. I see you let your inner ten-year-old dress you today."

"I did. And he told me to tell you that hay is for horses," Chism replied.

"Is that what we're doing out here? Going for a horseback ride? Please tell me it's not. I am sooooo not a fan of horses."

Fidgeting, Chism looked around, eyes wide as he stammered, "Ummm...? No... Yeah, no, totally not. No horses." He pulled out his phone, his thumbs bounding over the buttons.

Cali thought she'd screwed up a romantic gesture until he mumbled, "Dear Mr. Horse Man, cancel the horse ride, the horse drawn carriage, the horse balloons, and horse shaped cake. Thank you."

She chuckled and swatted his shoulder. "You're such an ass."

Chism shrugged. "Gotta play to my strengths."

"So, if this isn't some form of horsetopia, then where are we and why are we here?"

Chism stepped away from his car and gestured with both hands to the "Welcome" building at the end of the parking lot. "Morris Arboretum."

"You're taking me to an arboretum for our date?"

"Yep."

"Interesting choice."

"Well, the way you kicked my ass on our last date, I figured that there was a little *something* else behind the ass-kicking. I know it wasn't something I did, because we all know I'm delightful, but it was *something*. Maybe a kind of PTSD, or stress, or perhaps you got a dent in your car or a rip in your favorite jeans, but it's not my place to ask. A date like sky-diving, rock climbing, or bull riding might be fun and exciting, but that might only add to your... *something*. There is no *something* involved while looking at flowers and trees in an arboretum."

Okay, the sentiment was sweet. So, why not?

Comparatively, this date wasn't as hot and heavy as last night's date with Dallas, but the conversation was riveting. As they strolled along, they talked about everything. And Chism listened, he really listened. There were other people around, but Cali felt like she and Chism were the only two people in the world.

This wasn't good. She didn't want to like him.

Dallas was what she wanted if she was looking for that human connection her mother kept harping about. But Chism? He was more.

Other than an awful name, he was boyfriend material. Observant, since he deduced that she was damaged. Of course, kneeling on his chest and repeatedly pummeling his face might have been a pretty obvious clue, but he never once made her feel bad, and he didn't badger her about it. He had given her space and allowed her to express herself when ready.

After an hour or so, she gave in a little, and told him that her father went on "missions," and had died on one a couple years ago. She told Chism that his death had been difficult to process, but it allowed her an opportunity to reconnect with her mother. Before he had a chance to ask questions, she changed the subject, "So what's with the love of trees and flowers?"

They stopped under the shade of a tall, mature weeping willow. "What do you mean?"

She rolled up the brochure she'd been referring to every now and again, and stuffed it in her back pocket. "You've schooled me on most of the trees we've seen. You know more than this brochure."

He took a few willow branches in his hand and petted them. "You act like it's weird."

Cali laughed. Damn it, it felt good. Laughter was freedom. A few seconds of bearing no yoke, confined by no shackles. This was what she had always wanted but couldn't have.

Chism regarded the tree and let the wispy strands fall gracefully from his fingers. "Nature is pretty fascinating. So are animals like lions and tigers and ligers, but plants are pretty crazy. And they can be just as nasty. There's a tree called the *manichell* with a milky, toxic sap that can burn a person's skin, even cause blisters. The poisonous fruit has the adorable name *manzanilla de la Muerte*, which means 'little apple of death.' Then there's a vine found in Central America called the *boquila*. It's a tasty vine for herbivores, so it likes to attach itself to non-tasty plants and mimic whatever it's attached to. And don't forget about the carnivorous plants. I'm not talking about little Venus flytraps; I'm talking about ones like the *nepenthes rajah*. It's a big ol' canister plant capable of holding a half gallon of the digestive liquids needed to eat small mammals."

He had a brain. It was strange and random, but he had a brain. Cali liked that… and it made her want to run. "Wow. That's… really amazing, and terrifying."

"Well, apparently that's what I like." Chism stepped close enough to put one hand on her waist, his other on her cheek.

Ohhhhh no. He's coming in for a kiss. Maybe it'll suck. It'll be awful and I can end the date without any reservations and…

Damn it.

The way he held her, the way his hand felt on her cheek, the way their mouths and tongues moved together – it was everything she liked about kissing. She thought about jumping him under the curtain-like canopy of the willow but decided that getting arrested for educating children in more than botany was too great a risk. She settled for the tingle behind her chest.

For the rest of the tour, they held hands. Whenever he talked, she heard the smile in his voice. She heard it in hers as well, no matter how hard she tried to hide it. All the way back to their cars.

"So…" she started.

"So, this has been great. Fucking amazing, actually. I know this sounds cheesy, but I've never brought a woman here before. Not many I know would find any of this interesting." He sighed happily. "I'd really like to see you again. But I'll leave that up to you. Call me. Only if you're interested."

He ended the date with one more kiss. Shorter than their first one, but nice. Cali wanted more, so much more, and when they finished, she said, "I will. I'll call you tomorrow."

"Perfect."

Cali sat in her rental and watched Chism drive away. Her heart fluttered – the euphoric feeling reserved for preteens sharing the school lunch table with a puppy-love crush. Then her pulse revved full speed into anxiety territory. This feeling wasn't for her, not anymore. Not with the path in life she had chosen to travel. There could be no relationships in this way of living. No boyfriends, fiancés, husbands. God, it'd be so easy to call Chism right now and continue the date. Set up the next date. Exchange keys and pick out curtains.

No! Stop it. There could be no exchanging of keys. He lives in Philly, and she lives... Where? She had five houses but lived in none of them. Hell, she barely stepped foot in the one and ignored the other four. *See? I'm too damaged for a relationship. And the world I live in is pain.*

Pain. She had witnessed too much pain. Yet, like a junkie craving a fix, she pulled out her cell phone and dialed Madison Holcomb's number.

"Hello?"

"Hello? Madison?" Cali slipped into her entitled soccer mom obsessed with hot yoga and cold appletinis voice. "This is Brittany's mother."

Instead of asking which Brittany, Madison rolled with it and said "Oh, heyyyyy! How are you?"

"Blessed. I was calling to see how you're doing with... Well, you know."

With the start of a slur, she replied, "Oh sweety, I'm fully stocked with little tablets of happiness."

Cali softened her ruse, shifting to her usual voice. "No, Madison. I mean how do you *really* feel?"

"Oh, sweety, I..." She started with her fake chirpy happiness, but her voice cracked. "I..." She stopped talking. A few seconds of silence and then a sob. Whimpering, she continued, "He was in my house. That... *monster*... was in *my house*! He performed at my daughter's birthday party. He was close to *my daughter*! If anything happened to her... If anything... Oh, God!"

Madison cried loud and hard, the only way she could verbalize her fear and pain. Cali assumed that no one in her life had asked for her feelings, other than out of perfunctory politeness. Probably not even her husband. "Let it out, Madison. Let it out."

Cali sat in a parking lot and stayed on the phone with a crying stranger for about an hour, but she wasn't entirely sure why she had called in the first place. Was it to make herself feel better? Or worse?

June 24, 2002

At the desk in his bedroom, Collin finished his journal entry right as Jacob yelled from the living room. "Dad! Marcy's here!"

"That's great, buddy! Be right out," Collin replied. He closed the leather-bound journal and hugged it close to his chest while humming a jaunty ditty, one he made up. Every thought, every reason, every secret that had entered his mind since meeting Master Poppie flowed through his hand into this journal. This journal was his legacy to his son. Jacob was too young to understand, too young to accept the word of Master Poppie. Collin wanted his son to follow in his footsteps – the same hope as every father across the world – when he was ready. Just not yet. There was still much work to do.

Dancing a jiggy-jig to accompany his jaunty ditty – a new one; the one at the desk got too old – he made his way to his closet. He gasped with a flush of ecstasy – his face burned, his chest, his loins – when he opened the bifold doors. More of the real him was inside here: the face paints, the wigs, the clothes. The only way to extinguish the fire under his skin was to snuff it under a liberal application of white face paint. But that had to wait.

He placed his journal on a shelf and reached for one of the paint containers, then stopped short – now was not the time for his real skin. He had to focus and stay on task and only choose his immediate needs from the plethora of offerings. Dozens of seven-ounce white face paint containers in organized stacks; six went into an empty duffle bag. A blue wig, and a purple one. A thin yellow scarf, spotted with brown stains of dried blood. It was whimsical and he could wear it as an ascot, so in the bag it went. Closet closed. Closet locked. Closet sanctified. Next step of his plan...

Collin pulled out his cellphone and called the number he'd swindled from Madison Holcomb. It had taken half an hour of smooth talking and pretending to care about her inanities. So painful when all he wanted to do was feed her to Master Poppie, which also fell under the "now was not the time" category.

After a few rings, a female voice full of professional poise answered. "Senator Manchester Albright's phone."

"Hello, my name is Collin McGovern, and I'd like to speak with Manchester Albright, please."

"I'm sorry, but Senator Albright is busy at the moment. If you'd like, I could take—"

"My son and his son were at Marissa Holcomb's birthday party. The one with Keith the Clown. I was calling to see how his son, Preston, was doing."

The young woman gasped softly. "Oh, okay. One moment, please."

After Manchester Albright's divorce, he became a very hands-on father, winning custody of Preston. He showed up to every function involving his son, no matter what, when, or where. Collin had interacted with Manchester at every one of those functions over the past couple years, ever since their sons started kindergarten together.

"Hello, this is Manchester Albright." His voice was bold and affirming. A fake one ready to placate a fussy constituent.

"Hi, Manchester, this is Collin McGovern, Jacob's dad. I was calling to see how Preston is doing."

"Preston?"

"Yes. As much as I tried to keep Jacob away from the news about the whole Keith the Clown incident, he still heard... Well, you know. Kids are smarter than we think, right? And they talk. Now, almost every kid who was at Marissa's party is a little freaked out. I was wondering how Preston was handling it all."

"He's... Well, thank you for asking, Collin. He's doing okay. Like you said, a little freaked out, but okay."

"Glad to hear. I was talking to Jacob about it, and he suggested that the four of us meet up at Jackson Park, the one with the fun fort. Maybe tomorrow?"

"That sounds like a great idea. I'll double-check my schedule, but Preston could use a friend right now... I tell you what, even if I have something else, I'll move it. Would right after the boys get done with school work?"

"Absolutely. If you can't make it, you can call me back at this number."

After a few final pleasantries, they hung up. The plan was going smoothly. Time to head out.

"Dad, you got that weird smile again," Jacob said as Collin entered the living room. Marcy, the sixteen-year-old babysitter from down the street, smirked and shook her head, then went back to spreading peanut butter on Jacob's PBJ sandwich.

"Well, buddy, I just got off the phone with Preston's dad. He suggested that you and I meet up with him and Preston tomorrow at Jackson Park."

Jacob crinkled his nose and looked away. "Do we have to?"

"I can't see any reason not to. Can you?"

"Preston is so... I don't know. Stuffy? Snooty? Kinda weird?"

Collin chuckled as he crouched down to address his son eye-to-eye. "Maybe that's because he thinks he has to act that way. Our society has so many rules... too many rules... and some people feel like they have to follow them all. They start acting stuffy because they don't know that they get caught up in all the rules. Let's help Preston by giving him time to relax and escape the rules."

Jacob sighed so deeply that it left him slump-shouldered. Eyes facing the ground, he mumbled, "I guess."

Collin mussed his son's hair. "It'll be fun. In the meantime, you and Marcy have a great time!"

Collin rushed out the door with his duffle bag. He didn't want Marcy to see him wipe his mouth; he was salivating while thinking about how tasty Master Poppie would find her.

During his drive to Trina's, Collin wondered if Marcy would be better served as food, or as a soldier? Was she old enough to be a soldier? She was practically a kid, and Collin debated about subjecting her to the mist. Doing so with someone her age would be a good learning experience. Oh yes, what a lovely thought! But his grin fell away when he turned into Trina's neighborhood.

Police.

At Trina's house.

He guided his car to the curb and watched from afar. Just one officer. Alone. No flashing lights. Would Brin try to use the mist on him? It would certainly benefit them to induct a cop! But their interaction was brief; the officer nodded and then walked back to his car.

Collin made sure the police cruiser left the neighborhood before he parked in Trina's driveway; he dared not open the garage door.

As he made his way to the front door, he nonchalantly glanced around the property. Trees separated the neighboring yards, but the houses were visible between the gaps. No movements at the windows, no curtains fluttering, no looky-loos. Good. It wasn't time to take their houses yet.

Collin dropped his duffle bag on the coffee table. Brin was in the kitchen, smearing a glob of white face paint from her forehead to her chin. Her eyes rolled back into her head as she moaned. "Feels soooo gooooood. It soothes the burn."

An itchy tingle flowed through Collin's cheeks, desperate to join in. Even his scalp tingled. He couldn't, not yet, but he knew how Brin felt. "My fake skin burns sometimes, too."

"Yesssss. My real skin is in the jars."

Keith poked his head in from the garage. "Cop's gone, right?"

"Yep," Collin said.

Keith grunted and entered the living room. The other three followed. Giggling Trina skipped over to her sister. Snarling Delvin scurried to the kitchen. Sulking Sally shuffled up and down the hallway, licking the walls.

Collin unzipped his duffle bag and set the grease paint containers on the coffee table. "Is the cop something we have to worry about?"

Trina giggled as she helped her sister with the face paint, smoothing it, sliding away clumps.

"No," Brin answered. "He asked about Sally. This was the last address where he was seen alive."

"That was it?"

Brin shrugged. "He asked if I saw anything suspicious, and I told him that I didn't."

"That's because there's nothing suspicious happening here," Delvin said as he slammed the refrigerator door shut. He fed a baby carrot to his purse dog.

Trina's vision drifted for a moment, and then her eyes lit up. "The police officer cop man had the perfect shaped head for a cereal bowl. And he was fat, too. A lot of balloons for balloon animals in there, I bet."

Collin laughed. "Oh, I bet you're right, Trina."

Keith flopped down on the couch. "He wasn't a problem, but that doesn't mean more cops won't soon follow."

Trina looked at the white goop coating her hands, then raced to the couch. Squealing, she pounced, almost landing on Keith's lap. Kneeling next to him, she spread the paint across his face. He tensed, looking uncomfortable. Collin wasn't sure if it was from someone touching his face or from Brin glaring at him with her death laser-beam kill-eyes.

"As long as we're careful, we'll be fine," Brin snapped.

"That works for the six of us," Keith said, slouching on the couch, seemingly more relaxed about Trina's hands running over his face. "But how many more can we fit into this place until we need to take over other houses? You told me you wanted an army, that Master Poppie wanted an army. It's hard to be careful and make an army."

"As long as we're careful, we can carefully make an army," Brin said.

Keith shook his head. "Not a sustainable plan. If we take over the neighboring houses, then friends and families will get suspicious. Even if we add them to our forces, it wouldn't be long until someone calls the cops."

"Having a few police officers join us would be beneficial," Collin said.

Trina was still working the white over Keith's face. "Yeah, no shit, but you'd better be prepared to turn the whole fucking department pretty quickly. Once they realize that their men don't come back, or that they come back with someone's pet as a handbag…"

Delvin covered his purse-dog's ears. "Fifi can hear you, you know!"

Collin smirked at Delvin. Then to Keith, he said, "I see your point. I assume you have suggestions?"

"Whenever I look for a beautiful girl to immortalize, I never, ever, choose one close to where I live, no matter how pretty she is."

Collin nodded. "You want us to hunt for generals and soldiers and Master Poppie's food farther away from here."

"That, and we need a big distraction. My face and name are on the news and there's footage of you guys rescuing me. People know we exist. Let's go to the other end of the city, or even outside the city. We'll attract a lot of attention, take containers of the white mist and go fucking crazy. If we get more soldiers, then good for us. If not, we don't lose anything. But the point is, the police will investigate *there* and not here."

Making him a general was a great idea, and Collin was proud of himself. Keith was smart, despite the way Brin continued to glare at him, and he made a good point. Something big. Something distracting. "Keith, I have an idea where we can make some noise. Tomorrow, you'll take Trina and Delvin and canisters of mist to have some fun."

"You're not gonna come along?"

"No. Tomorrow, there's something else I need to do…"

June 25, 2002

Melody reached for the bedroom phone, but stopped herself, fingers an inch away, hand trembling as if the phone might suddenly grow teeth and bite. She wasn't ready for this. But if not now, when? Since Maxwell was in the other room, what Melody called "The War Room," talking on the phone with Harold, now was a perfect opportunity.

The War Room was the second bedroom of the two-bedroom apartment, designated as more of an office space – desk, computer, a filing cabinet, a small table, and a few chairs. She rarely entered. Anytime Maxwell was in there, he was researching the strange clown incident near the gallery or searching for Keith the Clown. She wouldn't be surprised to one day find a map of Philadelphia on the entire wall with annotated locations connected by pins and strings.

Melody laid back onto the bed and watched the slowly spinning ceiling fan. Even as a little girl, she'd spend a hot summer afternoon content to lie on her living room floor and let her thoughts drift away with the blades. "It blows away my worries," she'd say anytime her parents asked her why she liked it. Maxwell's house in New York didn't have a fan. He'd install one if she wanted, but she felt weird about such a request. It wasn't her house. It wasn't her *home*.

Over the past year, she had joined Maxwell on his travels from city to city while he sought to learn more about his father's companies. He loved and appreciated her enough to include her in the learning process and solicit her advice. They weren't even engaged yet, but it certainly felt like they were married. He trusted her and treated her like a partner in life.

His father owned an apartment in every city where he owned a business, even in Philadelphia where the business was a small art gallery. Just like all the others, this apartment's brochure used the word "luxury" to describe the space. Two large bedrooms, amazing living room, full kitchen, well maintained grounds. Melody scored with it being a ten-minute drive to the King of Prussia Mall, depending on the traffic lights.

But none of the apartments felt comfortable enough to call her own, especially not this one.

Melody had a difficult time figuring out why, and who or what she blamed. Certainly, Maxwell's father for heading a criminal organization, and his underling Harold Varvaro for continually offering Maxwell more details about his father's dealings.

And now those fucking clowns dominated Maxwell's attention.

All that mattered to Maxwell was this new, weird crusade to find the clowns who came into their lives. His obsession wasn't isolated to The War Room. On the nightstand by his side of the bed sat a police scanner instead of an alarm clock.

And let's not forget to throw some blame on Cali.

A cold chuckle escaped when Melody realized that she had taken over Maxwell's discarded obsession, proudly waving the I-must-find-Cali flag. Whenever Maxwell watched the security video of the blonde woman leaving his father's office building, he saw Cali, and only Cali. Melody saw a young, blonde woman who could be Cali, if she were still alive. Melody apologized to Maxwell in the privacy of her mind for not believing him. She had seen Cali in a parking lot fighting Keith the Clown. There was no one else it could have been. Which made this phone call all the more difficult. Like ripping off a bandage, Melody hurriedly picked up the phone and dialed.

After two rings she wanted to hang up. Three rings. *Should I leave a message if I get her voice mail? No. I wouldn't even know what to—*

"Hello?"

"Oh… Hi!" she squeaked. *Get a grip, woman!* "Hi, sorry. Is this… Is this Brenda Haddon?"

"Yes, this is Brett Haddon." Brenda "Brett" Haddon, Dakota's mother. Referring to herself as Brett instead of Brenda meant she was acting again. Or at least trying to get back into acting. Melody wasn't sure where she stood with her career after the divorce. After all, Joel Haddon was her agent. "With whom do I have the pleasure of speaking?"

"Hi, Brett, this is Melody Havenbrook."

"Oh! My! God! Melody? Is that really you? It's so good to hear your voice!"

A little louder than necessary, and overly enthusiastic. During her high school years, Melody had been around Brenda enough to know this was stage one of a drunk day. "Thank you. You, too."

"So, Ms. Havenbrook, I hope you're calling to tell me you'll soon be Mrs. Templeton."

Melody gave a fake, socially appropriate chuckle. "No, not quite yet."

Brenda sucked her teeth and huffed. "I don't know what that boy is waiting for. He better get a move on before some other handsome millionaire snatches you up."

"He doesn't have to worry about that. Plus, this past year has been busy for him."

"How busy must he be if he can't find time to—" Brenda stopped herself. "Oh. I... I almost forgot. I'm so sorry Melody. It's been about a year, hasn't it? Since his father...."

"Yes, a year. I've been thinking about that and... well, a lot of things, including you. I just wanted to call to see how you're doing."

"About as well as I can. Better than expected, considering..." Brenda sighed.

Two years ago, Brenda lost Dakota, her daughter. Six months after that, she lost her husband. Melody wasn't sure how to maneuver the conversation without upsetting her. But Brenda continued. "I don't know if I'll ever forget what we went through together, because of what happened at Roger's lake house. Oh my God, Melody, I haven't seen you since Dakota's funeral! And I wasn't in the right frame of mind to ask about you and Max. You two must have experienced such horrible survivor's guilt!"

Melody remembered Dakota's funeral very well. "We did." Yes, she suffered from crushing guilt, the brutal pain clawing behind her ribs. Brenda had been so medicated that she was in a wheelchair for the entire event.

"But you must have also felt so blessed not to have gone on that trip with them," Brenda said.

Melody had come down with a summer cold. That was the excuse she and Maxwell had used for not joining the others at the lake house. She had seen Maxwell cry only twice in their time together. Once at Dakota's funeral, and the next day when he broke down from crushing guilt. That's when he confessed that the trip was supposed to be the startup for a drug distribution business with their friend Hook.

"Despite all that, I'm happy you two were at the funeral. Unlike that bitch Calista Lindquist."

There it was! The opening Melody wanted, and the real reason for her phone call. "Do you think Cali's still alive?"

"Oh, I know she is."

"Has she contacted you?"

"That bitch knows better."

"Have... have you seen her?"

"No, and she better thank her lucky stars."

"So, you don't believe she... umm... she died that night?"

Brenda snorted. "They found everyone else's body. Tanner's. Jordon's. And my Dakota. The guys were mutilated in some old house in the woods. Did you know that?"

"I did," Melody whispered, choking back tears, and guilt.

"*Mutilated*. And Dakota's body... my *daughter's* body... burned in front of a barn. Did you know that barn was being used to manufacture drugs? A drug barn! Why the hell was my daughter – dead and burned – in front of a drug barn? And the decapitated body of a murderer named Zebadiah Seeley was inside the burned down lake house? So many questions, Melody. So many questions. The one person who can answer them has been missing for two years. She was involved somehow. I know that bitch was involved. I know it!"

Melody swallowed the lump in her throat. "I'm... I'm so sorry, Brett. I didn't... I didn't mean to..."

After a few agonizing soft sobs, Brenda cleared her throat. "That's okay, Melody. I know you didn't mean to. I have to go. Thank you for calling, but I have to go."

The call ended in silence.

Melody wiped away her tears. Her guts twisted while replaying Brenda's words, "I know you didn't mean to…" She actually *did* mean to drudge up unpleasant memories and pick at wounds. She had to know if Cali had reached out to anyone. She was surprised that Brenda and Maxwell had similar theories, believing that not only was Cali alive, but directly involved with the death of loved ones.

Melody went to the wall mirror to make sure she didn't look like she had been crying. As she tested the puffiness under her eyes, the police scanner crackled to life with a request for all available cars near the King of Prussia Mall to investigate several reports of violence involving clowns.

Wait. Had she heard that right? And then the voice repeated the message. If clowns were involved, then maybe Cali would be there, too. It was a longshot, but if nothing came from the trip, it'd at least get her out of the apartment.

Shoes on, purse in hand, Melody hurried to The War Room and poked her head in. Maxwell was at his desk taking notes, still on the phone with Harold. Smiling, she waved to get his attention.

Hand over the receiver, Maxwell said, "Harold is gathering info from his men. They might have found where Keith the Clown lives."

"Oh, that's great. I hope they do. I just wanted to let you know that I'm going shopping. Need anything while I'm out?"

"No, thanks. Have fun."

Fun wasn't the word she'd choose, but she kept smiling for appearance's sake. They blew kisses to each other.

Once she left the apartment, she ran to her car.

June 25, 2002

Cali sat in her hotel room, staring at Chism's number queued up on her cell phone. Her thumb glided over the green "send" button. She shouldn't do it. Dallas was on his way over and would show up at any minute.

"I'm young, I'm single, I don't owe anyone anything, and a group of murder clowns could kill me at any minute. Fuck it."

Chism picked up after two rings. "Do you like Turkish?" he asked.

Cali laughed and shook her head. "You're like a Magic 8-Ball. You know that, right?"

"Reply hazy, try again."

"I think I'd rather date a Ouija board."

"I'm certainly not going to tell you who you can and cannot date, but a Magic 8-Ball takes way less effort than an Ouija Board's all-powerful Elder Gods from realms beyond the comprehension of our measly mortal minds."

"Oh, Jesus, I'm dealing with a Cthulhu nerd."

"You caught the reference, so you're just as nerdy as I am. Nerd."

There was a difference between knowing a topic and liking a topic. Her father wanted to make sure she was well-read. Not just the common literary classics, but also popular science fiction, fantasy, and horror. She knew the spice must flow, that hobbits sat around getting stoned all day, and never read from the Necronomicon. Alas, she didn't revel in those stories, but now wasn't the time to share that with Chism. "Yeah. *I'm* the nerd."

"Do not make me turn to the timeless and infallible I'm-rubber-and-you're-glue defense."

"Okay, okay. I surrender, I surrender. The last time I went up against that defense was kindergarten. I lost to it then and I don't believe I can defeat it now."

"I don't blame you. It was my exclusive argument in 1982, so, you know, I've mastered the shit out of it."

Cali laughed again. She hated to admit it, even in the privacy of her own mind; her mother was right about it being too long since she felt this way. "So, I heard talk about Turkish."

"Oh, yes, almost forgot about that since you nerded out about Cthulhu. You like Turkish food?"

"Not certain if I've ever had Turkish food."

"I found a restaurant and wondered if you'd like to try it tomorrow night."

A knock came at her door. "I have to go, but tomorrow sounds great. Text me the address."

"Will do. Bye."

Dallas was at the door. Looking good as always. Her conversation with Chism was amusing, but the only words of his she heard right now were, "I'm certainly not going to tell you who you can and cannot date."

"Hey," Dallas said, turning a single word into a lusty invitation. Intense eyes and a wicked smile helped.

"Hey, yourself. Come in." She sauntered to the small table and sat on one of the two chairs. On the table was a chessboard, set up and ready for use.

Dallas sat across from Cali, studying the game board between them. "Interesting."

"Do you play?"

"I dabble."

His eyes darted from piece to piece, an entire game taking place in his head before the first pawn was moved. He smiled like a hungry wolf ready to eat his first meal of the day. *Dabble? Yeah, I call bullshit.* "Cool. I want to see how well you do. And we're going to make it a little more interesting. Pawns are worthless, but an article of clothing comes off whenever other pieces get captured. Winner gets to choose the sex position. Well, the first position."

Dallas pulled his hungry eyes away from the board and they latched onto hers. "Strip chess?"

Cali couldn't stop a smirk from spreading across her face. "Why not?"

"Love the idea. But let's raise the stakes."

Cali peaked an eyebrow. "Oh? What are you proposing?"

"Well, seeing as how we're only wearing three articles of clothing—"

"You're not counting socks and shoes?"

"I'm not twelve."

Cali laughed. "Go on."

"There are eight major pieces. How about whoever captures a piece gets to decide if the other player loses a piece of clothing or shares a personal detail."

Personal detail? Cali didn't like the sound of that. Sure, they shared some great conversations, but it stemmed from blissful stream of consciousness, the way precocious college kids might explore the world from the comfort of someone's couch. She savored not knowing anything about him, not even his last name. On the other hand, she felt guilty that she was getting closer to Chism but hadn't slept with him yet. Wasn't this a similar, yet opposite, situation? This was the opportunity to learn more about Dallas. Or scare him away. "Deal. If you notice, you're white."

Dallas moved first and Cali followed as soon as his finger left his pawn. He wasted no time on his next move, and neither did she. The next two moves were both made before she had a chance to blink. The most difficult part of the game was fighting the urge to tap a chess clock, the way she always had when playing against her father.

Dallas put some thought into his next play; his cocky smile betraying that he thought it was a good one. Cali's turn, but she was already three moves ahead. She'd sacrifice a bishop, grabbing his in return, setting herself up nicely. But first… "Pawn takes knight. Shirt off, buddy."

As he freed his biceps and abs from the tyranny of cotton, he chuckled. "No personal question? No interest in my inner workings?"

"Not yet. I'm more interested in your outer workings."

As predicted, he took her bishop. "Well, it's only fair that I'm not the only one sitting here shirtless."

Tee shirt off; she wasn't wearing a bra. Dallas maintained eye contact and shifted his smile, a sly one, implying self-control. He knew very well what was going to happen later, so he didn't need to be a pig about the situation.

No matter. Cali took his bishop. The game was going to end in her victory, so she said, "All right. Let me have a personal detail. Better be something interesting."

Leaning back, he crossed his arms over his chest and chewed his bottom lip. It still seemed like he was smiling, and clearly debating what to tell her. "I have a son. Is that a deal breaker?"

Holy shit. Chism and Dallas both have a son? Cali's default setting was to respond as glibly as possible and deal with feelings later. "Not for the next seven to ten hours at least."

He turned his attention back to the board.

Maybe this was what her mother was trying to discuss with her? Maybe she was trying to get Cali to think before she spoke, to acknowledge her own feelings as well as take other people into consideration instead of being so dismissive? *Ugh, why are you thinking about Mother right before impending sexy time with the hot guy?*

Cali left her knight wide open, too enticing not to take.

Dallas leaned back in his chair again. "Okay, your turn to give an interesting tidbit."

Cali's first instinct was to hiss and scream, "It burns! Emotional intimacy burns!" However, she took a breath and went with, "I have a marketing degree from Bucknell."

"Interesting. Is that what you do here in Philly?"

Cali chuckled and shook her head. "No. I had a job in California lined up shortly after graduation."

"Obviously to live in the birthplace of your birth name."

"Don't start with that crap." She paused, and wondered if he knew her first name was Calista. *Yes, he does.* Did he know her last name? *Yeah, probably not.* "My name is Lindquist. Calista Lindquist."

"Well, Lindquist Calista Lindquist, what happened to that job?"

"I never took it."

"Any reason why?"

The Killer of Devils

Cali stared absently at one of the white pawns she had captured, her index finger on top of it while she used her other fingers to spin it. "My priorities got reorganized after a sudden and turbulent shift in perspective."

"That cryptic and vague answer means I should stop prying."

Cali continued to play with the pawn. Instead of studying the board or Dallas' bare chest, she saw flickers of flame and splashes of blood. "A week or so before I was going to start, I set up a couple's vacation with my closest friends. I was going to tell them about my job and... and I was going to evaluate the relationship I was in."

"That sounds pretty heavy for a vacation. I'm guessing that's the reason you no longer have a boyfriend."

"It is. He died during that trip."

"Whoa. I'm... I'm really sorry."

"My best friend and her boyfriend died, too. And so did a mutual acquaintance and his girlfriend."

Dallas shifted in his chair. "Shit. What happened?"

Cali wanted to stop talking but didn't know how. This was either catharsis or self-sabotage. "A monster. An escaped convict named Zebadiah Seeley. He... um... well, he's why I have dead friends. And a dead dad. My dad, of all people, was there and... he died too."

Mother would be furious if she knew the level of detail Cali just shared. Well, too bad! She was the one always harping on Cali to open up, to share her feelings, to connect with people. Hadn't she literally played that card? And so what if Dallas decided to research the events? The only thing he'd discover would be a snippet of factoids about Zebadiah's decapitated body being found in the summer home of Roger Templeton. Nothing else. Calista Lindquist barely existed on paper or online, and *no one* would find anything about her parents.

Shaking her head to knock away the daydream, she sat up straight and wiped away the tears sliding down her cheeks. She chuckled as she captured another one of his pawns. "Sorry. I was thinking strip chess would be sexier."

Dallas shook his head and quickly took his turn. "No need to apologize. I kept pushing and prying and asking questions I shouldn't have been asking."

Cali moved her queen and grinned. "Well, one good thing came out of it. Checkmate."

His omnipresent smile widened. "Nicely done Lindquist Calista Lindquist. But... Do you want to talk about...? Anything?"

"Nah. I said enough. I want to focus on the future, not the past—"

The ringtone from Cali's phone interrupted her. "Nor my mother." She hit the red "end" button. "Now, as undisputed chess champion of the world, I think it's time I collect my winn—" Her phone buzzed from a text, and then the ringtone started up again. Her impatience waned when she saw the one-word text: clowns.

She turned away from Dallas and answered her phone. "What's going on."

"The King of Prussia Mall," Mother said. "The police scanner is going nuts with calls coming in about hostile clowns. Be ready in five minutes."

"On it." Cali hung up and jumped out of her chair. "Sorry to completely ruin this date, but I need to head out."

Dallas stood and put on his shirt. "Nothing to be sorry about. We can do this another time. If this is an emergency, is there anything I can do to help?"

Cali guided him to the door. "That's sweet, thank you, but no. I'll call you later. Bye."

She heard a muffled, "Okay. Bye," from behind the closed door. She'd make it up to him later. Right now, she had clowns to kill.

June 25, 2002

Keith watched the children play, specifically the tiny goddesses. Most of the mall-shoppers were faceless and soulless, just plastic people no better than the ridiculously posed mannequins trapped within the various stores observing nothing outside of their own myopic little world. A few people glared at the three clowns with duffle bags strolling through the mall. A few of them smiled, probably thinking this was some form of publicity stunt, others cringed and sneered and gave Keith and his companions a wide berth. He ignored those who couldn't ignore him.

The King of Prussia mall had recently added a store where children created their own teddy bears, and Keith took a moment to window shop. He had broken away from Delvin and Trina, sidetracked by the little fingers bringing new best friends to life. Some added the stuffing with the precision of a surgeon, others jamming the fluff inside like a machine piston. Keith liked to watch those little fingers.

This store wasn't the mission, though.

He had no idea how the little goddesses would react to – how did Collin put it? Oh yes – Master Poppie's gift. Too young, Collin said, so Keith was relegated to watching and dreaming.

Having seen enough to run a few fantasies, he was ready to move on, until one tiny princess looked up at him. At first, she jerked her head back as if startled, but then she smiled and waved. He wasn't dressed as Keith the Clown with his usual face and outfit, not since it was all over the news. He wore his standard white face paint, but his mouth was far more vicious – a dark brown, jagged smile reached beyond his lips and crept up his face, almost to the top of his head, and then took a sharp cut downward over his eyes. His wig was a style he'd never tried before, with shimmering strips of purple foil flowing down to his shoulders. It looked like a cheerleader's pompom had died on his head. Again, thanks to his picture on the news, he couldn't wear any of his curly haired wigs for a while. He thought this look would be too intense for children, but the little goddess kneeling on the ground in her white stockings and sparkly pink shoes, waved at him. After all, a clown was still a clown.

Trina skipped over to Keith and tugged on his duffle bag. "Come on, come on, come on." She was dressed outlandishly in a green girl's youth skirt and vest, green sash crossing from shoulder to waist. Gold spray paint coated the right side of her body and silver covered her left.

"Oooooh, I know what Keith wants." Holding her own duffle bag with both hands, Trina twirled, her short skirt flipping up, briefly showing the world her secrets, the metallic colors meeting in the middle of her naked cleft. She giggled her wide-eyed maniacal giggle. "I wore this for you!" She skipped away, repeating, "Come on, come on, come on…"

Keith followed, suddenly aware of his erection. And the onlookers.

Trina skipped and laughed, her skirt flouncing.

Delvin had the hurried step of an earnest businessman late for a meeting, mumbling to his dog purse as he petted it.

A passerby gaped open-mouthed at the tall clown with blue hair and fishhooks in his face.

More people started to notice. Security wouldn't be too far behind. Good.

They arrived at their destination: Catlin's Clothier, Sports City, and Magic R You. They were here to add numbers to their army, and no clown would be complete without a painted face, their true face as Collin and his followers had put it. Trina danced her way into the woman's store, while Delvin stormed into the sports memorabilia place. Keith took the magic shop.

Five customers milled through the magic shop, two staff members assisting as best they could. They were all about to be part of something bigger.

Keith opened his duffle bag, heading to the back of the store, and pulled out a thermos. Top off, he opened the door reserved for employees, and tossed the thermos into the backroom. The mist plumed, followed by swearing and then coughing. Sauntering toward the front of the store, he paused right in the middle and dropped a second open canister. The fog was thick enough to obscure everyone from his view. But he heard the screaming. Their throaty howls quickly turned to shrieking laughter. At the opening into the mall, he dropped the last container, the white cloud engulfing the store's entrance, including a wide-eyed idiot too shocked or too stupid to run.

Music. That was how Keith heard the sounds of chaos, as a musical score set to the world falling apart. Laughter as the new soldiers destroyed half the store, clamoring to get their fingers on the containers of face paint. The howls of glee as they smeared white grease to expose their new, true faces. Streaks of whatever colors they could grab added the details. Red was from blood as some of the new recruits had difficulty containing the excitement within, often slamming themselves into shelves and racks of products.

They ran into the mall to spread the word of Master Poppie.

Keith inhaled deeply. He wasn't sure what they experienced with the mist, but his first-time partaking hadn't been as transformative. It smelled like cotton candy, but his current thoughts hadn't differed from what they had always been. He certainly had no desire to tackle a man and gnaw on his face like that clown over there by the giant potted palm tree. Nor did he want to tear off his clothes and bang on a trash can, like the woman by the mall's placard map. And there was no appeal to jumping in the fountain and drowning someone, like that clown was now doing. But he absolutely loved the chaos.

Foggy wisps escaped the two store fronts next to the magic shop. The new recruits rushed out from the neighboring stores, whooping and hollering like berserker Viking warriors hellbent on pillaging.

Women sprinted from Caitlin's Clothier, most of their faces covered in layers of makeup, smeared in bright blue and green and purple eyeshadows, their mouths widened and colored by different shades of rouge or lipstick. One woman painted her forehead and cheeks a bright pink hue, her smile wide and powdery and blue. Light brown plus signs over her eyes. She cackled as she flew from the store and jumped an old man, too slow for his own good. Armed with metal display hooks, she stabbed him with a great flourish, his blood squirting up into the air. It rained down, splashing her and the floor. The new soldiers dashing out of the women's store brandished similar weapons and used them enthusiastically.

The recruits from the sports memorabilia store were just as entertaining. Faces colored with standard face paints for various sports teams. Lightning bolts and slashes, angular and aggressive, had been drawn over their eyes. Their smiles were jagged lines and curves. A big dude with a smear of black over his mouth and chin donned an Eagles helmet with a player's signature on the front. But when the new soldier grabbed ahold of a younger kid, his violent headbutt cracked the kid's head open. Nothing bleeds like a headwound. After another twenty or thirty headbutts to the kid's face, dripping red obscured the signature.

The recruits delighted Keith with their wicked choice of accessories. Baseball bats, hockey sticks, golf clubs, ice skate blades. One freak had white face paint with red handprints over his eyes, his weapon of choice was a fishing rod.

Keith grinned as the soldiers tore into the fabric of society, this fat and bloated civilization that worshiped excess and gluttony. No one was willing to help, or aid others. Never in his life did Keith experience a fraction of the wealth these shoppers had. Who knows? If he had the means that these worshippers of commercialism flaunted, then maybe he'd be like one of them. He only knew what he knew, and he knew that this society needed to have its insides pulled out. And that was what most of the new recruits were doing – pulling out the insides of anyone they got their hands on.

Keith cackled.

He hadn't been entirely sure what to expect from this outing, but it surpassed his wildest fantasy. What kind of power did he have over these people? Could he control it? Collin kept referring to him as a general, so he might as well try acting like one. "To the food court!"

Dancing, skipping, jumping, running; their laughs and gleeful screams echoed along the hall. One woman spun and twirled, and one dude marched along while dragging a dead body with him. But they all followed Keith.

The Killer of Devils

Delvin stomped alongside Keith, his grumpy mumblings to his purse dog belying his smile. Even though it was held into place by fishhooks through his cheeks, Keith expected him to be in a better mood, like Trina. *Okay,* he admitted to himself, *no one could be in a better mood than Trina.*

Draped in a loop of someone's intestines as if it were a feather boa, she sashayed beside Keith and used a severed finger as a pretend cigar. "I thought we were going to take them home with us?" she said, drawing out the syllables in a mock rich-person-at-the-country-club dialect.

"No," Keith said, not sure if her gore fascination was turning him on or off. "This is a distraction, remember?"

"I'll say!" Delvin snapped. "Fifi doesn't know what's going on or who to bite."

By the time they reached the second-floor food court, it was pure bedlam. Keith hadn't felt this whimsical since he got his first BB gun on his sixth birthday. Dozens of people were crashing into each other; those running from clowns crashed into the ignorant fools still chewing their burgers and pizza. Chairs went flying as tables toppled over. This was how society worked – trampling each other for selfish needs and desires. Not a single soul tried to protect anyone else. They just wanted to flee, run away no matter who got hurt, as long as it wasn't themselves. People stepped on people. Children ended up on the ground, under the feet of adults, as they so often did. In a display of "might makes right" only the strongest and the fastest made it out of the food court alive. The elderly and the infirm didn't stand a chance. Keith considered their deaths a mercy. At least it was fast, unlike what society had been doing.

Screams of terror echoed down from the third floor. People stood above the food court looking over the railings, away from the attacks, yet they endangered others while trying to avoid the chaos. Guns drawn, two police officers on the third floor aimed at the madness below, shouting stupidities like, "Stop! Hands where I can see them! Drop your weapons!"

Amid the peril and the screams from the food court, Keith heard the buzz of an unspooling fishing line. The soldier with the red handprint eyes had cast the reel. Perfect aim – the weight and hook latched inside the mouth of a cop. The clown pulled. As the cop tumbled over the third-floor railing, screaming and holding onto his cheek, three laughing clowns descended upon him when he hit the ground with a thud.

Five other clowns raced up the closest set of stairs to get to another cop. He fired at them, taking down two clowns, but those remaining grabbed the officer and sent him over the stair-railing, crashing onto a table.

The pandemonium subsided in the food court area. Those who could have escaped were gone, those who couldn't were being defiled. Keith took a moment and counted twenty-six remaining clowns. Twenty-six rained destruction on people, furniture, mini-restaurants, kiosks, garbage cans, and plants.

"Would you like fries with that?" Trina asked, holding out two handfuls of French fries. Keith knew very well that wasn't ketchup.

"No."

"Is it time to go yet?" Delvin asked. "Fifi needs to tinkle."

"She can piss in the potted plants. The cops know we're here, so we need to wait for them and get situated before we make our move."

Delvin shrugged and took his purse dog to the nearest potted plant. Trina giggled as she smashed the fries against her face. Neither of them were aware of Keith's secret anticipation. That blonde bitch.

He was definitely on her radar, and if she had found him in a suburban neighborhood, she'd certainly find him here.

Her arrival would come as no surprise.

June 25, 2002

The King of Prussia mall parking lot was the picture-perfect representation of insanity. Lines of cars pressed against each other to exit onto Dekalb Pike. Horns blared. People shouted profanities. Many people didn't bother with their cars and opted to run on foot, worsening the mass exodus. Police cruisers were scattered haphazardly at every exit with officers whistling and waving their arms, attempting to keep traffic moving. A majority of the police presence formed at Macy's hub, dashing here and there, barking orders into their cell phone and walkie talkies.

Cali's mother hopped a curb against the flow of traffic to get into the lot. She slipped past burgeoning barricades with no resistance; the police had their hands full elsewhere to be overly concerned about people trying to enter.

After the initial 911 calls, the police had yet to secure the mall. It was too large and information was lacking. The first responders stormed through Macy's with their guns drawn, heading to the food court. Cali and her mother had heard the screams over the police scanner.

"Entering through Macy's is out, so you'll have to enter through the east side," Cali's mother said as they drove up the ramp of the parking deck. "Assume it's just as dangerous."

"Understood," Cali said from the back seat. Hair pulled back, protective goggles over her eyes, two loaded Glock 9mms strapped to her thighs, a few extra magazines and her favorite Bowie knife attached to her belt.

Mother gestured to the laptop on the passenger seat. "I already hacked into the mall's surveillance cameras, keeping our anonymity, and I'll start checking for stolen vehicles. I'm assuming a cargo van like last time. Now that we know about their license plate swapping trick, I'll cross-reference any reports that might have come in. Hopefully, we'll get lucky."

A tremor rippled through Cali's fingers, and she squeezed her hands into fists. "We sure could use a little luck." Her pulse throbbed at the back of her skull and beat against her eardrums. *This is no different than the other times,* she told herself. Was this what her parents felt when they went on missions? Did these feelings ever get better? Or worse? *No time for introspection. Time to go!*

"Make your own luck," her mother said. "Keep the comms open. Be careful. I love you."

"Love you, too."

Cali practically rolled out of the SUV the second her mother screeched to a halt. She hurried to the mall's glass doors, eyes scanning for potential traps or trip wires.

"What do you see?" Mother asked in her ear.

"Nothing yet."

"Proceed with extreme caution. Don't forget, this mall is like a fucking Escher painting. You can go from first floor to third floor and get turned around without realizing it."

"Confirmed." Cali pulled the door open a crack. No explosions, gunshots, or alarms. A little more of a pull. Still nothing. She opened the door just enough to slip inside.

The mall was post-apocalyptic still, and "The Girl from Ipanema" played overhead. Drawing one of her Glocks, she crept to the closest map to get her bearings. Food court located.

Both hands on her weapon, pointing it downward, she hurried along the third-floor concourse. Head on a swivel. Eyes alert for anything. Ears ignoring the catchy tune and concentrating on anything out of the ordinary. She heard a screech and ducked into the nearest store. A clothing store. She stood shoulder to shoulder with a mannequin, gun raised.

The screech, muted by distance, could have come from anywhere. It could have been anything. She counted to sixty, and all remained eerily still.

She exited the store and continued along the concourse. Another shriek from the same direction – it sounded human. Laughter followed. "What the hell," Cali whispered.

With every store she passed, the noise pitched louder. Howling laughter. Maniacal cackling. Shrill bursts of joy. Cali squeezed the gun grip so tightly she'd leave indents in the metal. *What am I walking into?*

Giggling. From behind!

Cali whipped around and raised her gun, but the full weight of a body slammed her to the ground hard enough to send the gun clattering across the floor. Her ponytail knot absorbed the blow, but her vision flickered. With no time to react, a pair of hands circled her throat. When she saw the face, she knew what her nightmares were going to be tonight.

A woman's eyes, impossibly wide and mouth stretched into a rictus, reflected a maniacal zeal. Bright pink covered her whole face while pluses in a shade of light brown were over her eyes. Powdery blue created a thick smile from ear to ear. *What the fuck?*

The woman's arms were locked, and she put her full weight into her hands, so when Cali hit the insides of her elbows, she came down hard. Cali dipped her chin and lifted her head as best she could. The result was as she had hoped – she smashed the woman's nose against her forehead.

Cali outweighed her assailant by about thirty pounds of muscle. As the woman reeled back, Cali delivered a punch to her cheek and then pushed her off. Scurrying across the floor, Cali went for her gun. Got it! But she still didn't have a chance to shoot.

With a hyena's laugh, the woman tackled Cali again like an untrained maniac. Cali twisted and stayed on her feet, trying to push the woman away. The psycho grabbed Cali's arm and held on as momentum sent them over the railing.

Fuck! was Cali's only thought as she fell into the pagoda of upscale, overpriced sunglasses. She landed on her back, the impact knocking the wind out of her. Her shoulders and right thigh screamed in pain, but she told them to shut up as she focused on catching her breath. Flailing, she kicked away the cheap display stands and pushed her way through the sunglasses.

Breathe! Her lungs cooperated as she tossed away a wire rack. Pulling in big gulps of air, Cali aimed her gun at the woman in the pagoda debris, her aim off as she fought to regain control of her frenzied body. The freak lay on her back, unmoving, chest rising and falling, her breath labored and gurgling. Broken from Cali landing on her.

Both hands gripping her weapon, Cali stepped through the debris, plastic crunching and snapping underneath as she approached. The woman suddenly coughed. Blood bubbled out of her mouth and trickled down her lipstick-coated face. Still smiling though, and with her last breath, she said, "Feed me to Master Poppie."

Cali holstered her gun and stumbled to the nearest bench to catch her breath. What would drive that woman to paint her face and act like a homicidal lunatic? Like a deranged... *Wait, the police reports mentioned clowns.* Was she one of them? How many more of them are there?

Judging from the screeches and laughter floating toward her from the food court, a lot.

And what the hell was a Master Poppie?

Breathing controlled, Cali drew her gun again and rolled her shoulders. Pushing through the aches in her leg, she got moving. Toward the laughter. And the voices. And the coppery smell of blood, the acrid odor of urine, the foulness of shit.

Cali took cover at every potted tree, signage, and kiosk – until she saw the food court and its semicircle of fast-food eateries. It looked like an abattoir in the middle of an active war zone.

Crazy people running. Jumping. Dancing. All with bizarre and twisted clown faces drawn on in different colors.

A few ran in circles around the dining area. Table and chairs had been broken and gathered into piles, with more than a few pieces scattered across the open area. Lights flickered throughout the restaurants; smoke and the smell of burnt food wisped from the kitchens, but apparently not enough of a fire hazard to set off alarms or sprinklers. Blood streaked the walls. Smeared handprints on the floor. Bodies scattered. Organs strewn about. Limbs tossed onto the piles of tables and chairs. Intestines running from one decorative potted plant to the next like a slimy pink garland.

Crazies were behind the counters, gleefully destroying the kitchens. At least two men were naked, one masturbating in front of a trash can. A woman juggled severed hands. A man with a fishing rod – *where'd he even get that?* – threw his line at the pile of organs, hooking a set of lungs. A tiny woman twisted a strand of guts, like she was making balloon animals.

"Cali?" Mother's voice broke her out of her traumatic stare. "You there? I found their van. I'm looking inside of it. The seats are sliced to pieces, and I see jars of white face grease."

"Mom?" Cali whispered with the frightened timbre of a child. "I found monsters."

"You found them?"

"Yes. In the food court."

"How many?"

"Hard to tell… They're fucking crazy, jumping around like animals. I count … maybe two dozen? Thirty?"

"Thirty? Cali, get out of there. We'll regroup, but get out of—"

Too mesmerized by the circus of carnage, Cali hadn't seen a clown sprinting toward her until he collided with her. Had he been professionally trained, Cali would have been dead. Luckily, he just knocked her off her feet. She hit the floor hard and slid over the tiles away from the gore with a tight grip on her gun.

BLAM! BLAM! BLAM!

Three shots tore the top off his head. Yet the sick smile remained as his body collapsed.

She was on her feet in time to target two more shrieking clowns as they rushed her. Two bullets, two headshots. A third clown leapt from the top of the mall directory. Spotting him just in time, Cali dove out of the way and took great satisfaction when he crashed into a table and chairs, breaking more than just wood. But she was now closer to the food court.

Clowns skipped, scrambled on all fours, and cartwheeled toward her from every direction. A few clawed their way over the blood covered furniture piles.

Second gun out, she blasted the closest nutjob. Two. Three. Four. Streamers of red unfurled from the back of their skulls. Laughing. All of them whooping as if this was a sporting event. Another direct hit to a clown's face. And another. The one with the fishing rod cast his line with precision, the hook sinking into Cali's left shoulder. He yanked hard enough to send a fire blazing through her arm, disrupting her aim.

BLAM! BLAM!

She dropped one, but then her gun clicked. "Fuuuuuck!" Out of ammo, so she smashed the steel against a smiling cheek and then threw it at the clown behind him. It took a painful second to yank the hook from her shoulder, but that was all the time needed for the three psychos to converge on her.

Two clowns reached for her. Three more. And more! Too many bodies pressed against her, pinning her arm upward, unable to swing but able to jam her thumb into someone's eye. Hands in her face, and she crunched down on fingers with her teeth, careful not to swallow the gushing blood. She thrashed and screamed as she kicked and stomped with her steel-tipped boots. No use. She would die here, pressed to death, suffocating.

"Stop!"

The mass of bodies relaxed against her as the lunatics turned to face the commanding voice. Six clowns – three on the left, three on the right – held her arms.

She stopped struggling to conserve energy.

Walking toward her was a man dressed as a more traditional clown. The man's dark brown jagged smile menacingly reached up to his forehead then angled down over his eyes. His wig was made of shiny strips of purple cellophane. Flanking him was a tall man with blue hair and fishhooks in his face. He was petting a dead dog cradled in his arms. A short woman with a gold and silver face – were those intestines wrapped around her shoulders? The purple-haired man in the middle... he looked familiar...

"You!" Cali yelled.

Stopping mere feet from Cali, he reached into an oversized pocket of his oversized pants and pulled out a thermos. Grinning, he said, "Yeah, me."

The short clown slapped Keith's arm with the length of pink tubing. "Keithy! You know this skank?"

Keith chuckled, a grumbling phlegmy noise. "Trust me, Trina, this bitch ain't my type."

"Ha!" Trina slapped the cord of intestine across Cali's face.

Cali's stomach lurched and she fought the urge to retch. "Fuck you."

Trina gasped, her eyes wide with indignation. For a split second, she looked like a rational, sane human being. But then it was gone. The wide, toothy smile of a maniac returned as she cackled, "Mist her, Keithy! Mist her so she can be my new friend-toy!"

Keith's smile oozed along his face like a diseased slug. He held the thermos in front of Cali's face and unscrewed the lid.

June 25, 2002

Collin guided his car into a spot in the parking area at the park, which was only minutes from his house. A beautiful day usually beckoned people to the open areas for picnics, tennis, basketball, dog walks, and kids running around on the playground, but there were less people here than usual. Perfect. Few distractions.

"Daddy?"

"Yes, Jacob?"

"You're smiling that weird smile again."

It was difficult not to. His plan was timed impeccably to the minute. He'd had to race from his prior engagement to pick up Jacob, but they arrived here in time. "Am I? I'm just happy to spend time with you and our new friends on such a beautiful day. Aren't you?"

"Well, yeah, but... It's your *weird* smile. It might weird out our new friends."

"Sorry about that, buddy. I'll be sure to keep it under control."

"And you keep checking your watch. You and Mommy always told me that checking your watch too many times was rude."

Collin couldn't help himself. Keith and the others were engaged at the mall. Collin couldn't wait to see what kinds of chaos they would cause, but his son was right – he needed to focus on the here and now, wear the face paint of the faceless, the colors of the colorless. "Look, I think I see them by the playground."

Collin got out of the car and guided Jacob toward the bench closest to the swing set. A young woman with stern eyebrows and pointed lips sat with Senator Manchester Albright. He wore a white golf shirt and dark khaki pants, relaxed yet presentable, his attention on the file of papers in the woman's hands. The Senator's kid, Preston, sat between the adults. Preston's face paint was duller than a dullard's, a doll's doldrums doled out to the boy. His mussed hair shared the same shade of yellow as a pool of urine, and he was dressed like his father. Such lost and empty eyes. A

The Killer of Devils

shame that he was too young for the mist; he was all but begging to follow Master Poppie.

Game face, game face, game face. Dull, drab, dreary, dreck colors.

Collin approached with a smile, under the suspicious eyes of Preston.

Manchester paused from talking to the woman. "Collin McGovern. Great to see you again. You, too, Jacob."

"Hi, sir," Jacob said, trying to sound mature, yet standing with his shoulder pressed against his father's leg.

"I'm happy that you could join us. One second, though…" Manchester turned to the woman and said, "Thank you, Rachel. I'll look at the rest tomorrow."

Her sharp lips smiled to kill and to lie. "No problem, Mr. Albright. See you in the office tomorrow. Have fun today."

As she left, she waved to Preston. His dull face remained dull.

Manchester stood and extended his hand to Collin. "The weather couldn't have been more perfect for a day in the park."

Collin stepped forward, a lacquered smile for show, and shook Manchester's hand. "I couldn't agree with you more, Senator."

"Please, call me Manchester."

The senator gestured for Preston to step closer and shake Jacob's hand. The result was clumsy and awkward.

"I believe you know Preston," Manchester said.

Jacob nodded with vigor. "Yes sir, we do." He then pointed to the playground. "Let's go to the playground."

"I don't know any games," Preston replied, his voice as sad and desperate as the look on his face.

"I know plenty." Jacob pointed both thumbs at himself. "Just stick with me and everything will be great."

"Okay!"

The two ran toward the swings.

Collin and Manchester took their seats on the bench. Collin didn't have a good plan for tricking him. In coming here to meet the Senator, his best idea had been to punch him out cold when the kids weren't looking and drag him to the car. Okay, that was Delvin's idea, and it wasn't very good, but it was the only one he had. He began with the dreaded small talk.

"Senator, I hope your meeting me here didn't take you away from your work.

"Manchester, please."

"Right, Manchester. I wasn't sure if your title was your job or your way of life."

"Believe me, being a senator on the state level is no way of life. Plenty of state level politicians eat up what they read in the papers or internet and choke on their own self-importance. But plenty of us have offices in strip malls with common lives outside the capitol. Either way, it's nothing but paperwork and complaints."

"You get a lot of complaints?"

"Everything from potholes and stop signs to disputes with neighbors to alien invasions."

"Alien invasions? You get that complaint a lot?"

"Yes and no. Only one person complains about it, but I hear it a lot. *A lot.* And now this Keith the Clown thing."

Obviously, Manchester didn't know what was happening at the mall right now, but he would soon enough. Collin needed to make the most of his time. "The local media is saying the authorities still haven't found him."

"That is correct. He used a P.O. Box for his business address. His website is a dead end. Somehow, he routed his phone number through Guam. How does one even do that?"

Collin shrugged and bowed his head, shaking it with pretend incredulousness.

"Sometimes I feel like this world is a swirling vortex of crazy," Manchester said.

"Or not enough crazy."

Manchester replied with a hearty laugh, and Collin joined in, reminding himself not to display his "weird smile."

"That is certainly one way to look at it," Manchester said, gazing mournfully at the playground. "I feel like I have to lie to Preston at least once a day. You ever feel like that? Like you have to lie to protect Jacob?"

"All the damn time."

"It's gotten to the point where I'm not even sure what the truth is anymore," Manchester said. "Like I have to wear a mask. Many masks. Just to get through the day."

"Or clown makeup."

Manchester regarded Collin with a sideways glance and a frown, searching Collin's face for an answer to a question he was afraid to ask.

Shit. He'd said something stupid, maybe incriminated himself.

Manchester then smirked and nodded. "Clown makeup. That, my friend, is a great analogy for a local politician. A circus clown. Never allowed to take the makeup off."

There it was, a tone of longing, helplessness. Collin figured out Manchester's secret, figured out how to add him to the fold.

Collin leaned forward and put his elbows on his knees while keeping an eye on the children. They flew around the jungle gym, chirping and trilling like baby birds. When he sat back, he had scooched a couple inches closer to Manchester and looked him in the eyes.

"Is that why you're divorced."

Manchester frowned.

Play the part, play the part, wear a different face. Collin moved an inch closer and arched his eyebrows in sympathy.

Manchester's expression softened. "Something like that. I was no longer the man she married all those years ago out of college. I had… changed."

"Have you allowed yourself to be that changed man?"

"I can't."

"It's the twenty-first century."

"Not if you're Republican."

"Funny. How about dinner tomorrow night? No kids."

"I… I don't… I—" Manchester's cell phone chimed, cutting him off. He apologized and answered it. After a brow-knitting conversation, he hung up and said, "I'm sorry, but Preston and I have to go. Something is happening at the King of Prussia Mall and the phone is ringing off the hook, so I'm going to go back into the office."

The men stood up at the same time, but Collin grabbed Manchester's forearm. With words as soft as cotton, he said, "Dinner. Tomorrow night. Just you and me. At the very least, it's drinks and meal with a new friend."

Manchester's brow wrinkled as scenarios and calculations crashed into each other in his head; Collin could practically hear the screeching wreckage. Finally, Manchester nodded and whispered, "Okay. Yes. Dinner tomorrow night."

Keep the face as is, don't change it.

Collin waved Jacob over as Manchester told Preston they had to leave. "Aw, man!" both children exclaimed.

The Albrights got in their car and left.

"Daddy?"

"Yes, Jacob?"

"You're doing the weird smile again."

"I know, buddy. I know."

June 25, 2002

Flickering lights from the food court restaurants created long, wavy shadows, all moving quickly and chaotically, not with purpose. Inhuman voices echoed through the space as they swirled with the moving figures.

Cali, restrained by strong pairs of hands in the open eating area, held her breath when Keith pulled the top off his thermos, releasing a white cloud. Eyes brimming with anger, Keith grabbed her cheeks and squeezed. "Breathe it in, bitch!"

Too much cackling and screeching and laughing from behind him drowned out the clanking of metal as three, four, five cannisters hit the floor. Smoke grenades. A gray miasma quickly ensconced the food court, and Cali took advantage of the distraction, wrenching herself free from the clowns' hold. It felt so good to jam the base of her palm against Keith's chin.

"Fuck!" Keith yelled. "Damn you, you bitch!" He and Trina hurried backwards, disappearing into the smoke.

Dropping to the floor, Cali kept her face close to the ground where the smoke was thinnest, and cupped her hands over her mouth and nose. She exhaled through a small gap between her fingers. With fingers closed tight, she inhaled. Her method wasn't perfect – she smelled cotton candy and fireworks – but at least she got enough of a breath to get her bearings.

Gunfire and muzzle flashes at the far end of the food court.

"Mother!" Cali unsheathed her knife and commando-crawled under the smoke toward the one-woman calvary. The grenades spent; the smoke lingered. A screech sounded from Cali's left.

Springing to her feet, Cali thrust her knife toward the noise. Perfect timing – the blade slid into the clown's eye all the way to the hilt. Raw egg goo spattered Cali's hand as she twisted the blade for good measure, before extracting her knife from his skull.

Wavy shadows coalesced around yellow flashes of light and gunfire, as if devils were being summoned from the pit by witches of folklore. A flicker of light, a crack of bullet-thunder, and a shadow fell. Bullets exorcised the demons, but more arose and continued the march of the damned.

As Cali hurried closer, the center of the storm grew clearer – her mother with a bowie knife in one hand, a Glock in the other. Her mother shot a nearby clown, and a red spray of cranial fluids spotted Mother's shirt.

A woman was creeping up behind Mother. Her exaggerated movements lacked stealth, but the nearby clowns had caused a distraction, making her mother an easy target. Her curled fingers reached for Mother.

Not today. Cali dashed through the dissipating smoke and yanked the woman back by a fistful of greasy hair. Snarling and spitting, the clown shrieked and gnashed her teeth, her fingers clawing at Cali.

Cali searched for a spark of humanity in the woman's eyes, a glimmer of logic or cognition. Nothing remotely recognizable. With a quick slice across the throat, Cali put the creature out of the world's misery.

Mother and daughter stood back-to-back, in the center of an ever-growing pile of corpses. Cali resorted to fists and steel to fend off the monsters. Faces distended in open-mouthed howls. Wide eyes circled in blues or reds or greens were windows into twisted souls, and targets for Cali's knife. Vocal cords rippled as she plunged her blade, her hand vibrating with their screams as arterial spray painted her face.

Her mother grunted as she stabbed and slashed in between firing rounds at their attackers. Three. Five. Eight bodies by their feet before the madness slowed, the smoke from the grenades long gone.

"Eleven left, including that fucking Keith. I think he's their leader," Cali said, sucking wind.

"I'm out of ammo," Mother whispered.

Cali tightened the grip on her knife. "Well, fuck."

"Yep."

Keith, Trina, the one with the fishhook smile, the one with red handprints over his eyes, and the one wearing a football helmet huddled together, inching away from the others toward a side exit.

A group of three other clowns slowly moved a different direction and out of the food court.

The Killer of Devils

The remaining three grabbed chairs as weapons. And attacked.

Cali dropped to a crouch, her hands on the floor for support, and drove her boot heel into a clown's left knee. He screamed, but it didn't stop him from slamming the chair down on her. Arm up to protect her head, her forearm took the brunt. Fighting through the fire of pain running up her arm, she stood and yanked the chair from his hands. More fire as she hurled the chair at one of the other clowns and then twisted to drive her knife into her attacker's ribs, neck, belly, thigh, neck. She spat on him as he crumpled to the floor.

Mother had forced a clown to his knees – the other clown held his neck, gurgling as blood flowed between his fingers – as he struggled to get out of her headlock. She tossed a set of keys to Cali. "I parked in the southeast corner, close to where we came in. Go after Keith; I'll take care of this one and do a sweep."

Keith and the other four were easy to follow – no clearer path than their bloody footprints and crimson splashes.

Sunlight stung her eyes when she burst outside. Four police officers lay on the ground, bleeding and moaning as they rolled around holding their faces. Still too busy and confused trying to coordinate the front of the mall, there wasn't much of a police presence here. These officers certainly hadn't been prepared for five homicidal clowns to bash in their faces.

No time to stop and help, Cali yelled, "Sorry!" as she sprinted past them toward the SUV's general direction.

An engine roared to life. A black van smashed into neighboring cars as it pulled out of its parking spot.

Cali wasn't too far behind – she jumped into the Explorer by the time the van reached the end of the row.

They blew through the sawhorse barricades, running down a traffic cop.

Cali followed, again yelling, "Sorry!" as she sped past.

Once on I-76, the van wasn't as wild. Cali assumed Keith was driving because he was smart enough not to do anything reckless like sideswipe vehicles or make erratic lane changes. Red and blue lights flashed in her mirrors. They were distant, but they and the accompanying sirens grew closer.

A neck snaping jolt almost sent her SUV out of control, and she gripped the steering wheel tight. In her rearview mirror, a red pickup truck with three painted faces, open-mouthed smiles, and evil eyes had appeared out of nowhere. The pickup had smacked into the back of her Explorer. Absorbing the hit, she stomped the accelerator and pulled away. Gripping the wheel tighter, she swerved through traffic as the clowns maneuvered through the cars to catch up, close enough behind her to see their ugly faces again.

Sirens and flashing lights had also caught up with them; two cruisers in pursuit.

"No fuckin way!" Cali exclaimed as the red truck sideswiped the closest cruiser, then sideswiped the other cruiser, sending all three into tire-screeching tailspins and culminated in reverberating crashes. Cali assumed those freaks sacrificed themselves to help Keith escape, so she refocused on making sure that didn't happen. *Calm down. Resist the urge to run him off the fucking road.*

Horns blared and brakes screeched, cars sped up and switched lanes to get out of the way.

Keith swerved, exiting onto 202 North. Cali followed, making no subtleties about her intent. Nerves vibrating, she pursued him through lights, intersections, turns, and stop signs, tooling along the streets of a suburban neighborhood. One that looked familiar. Finally, the road dead-ended alongside a patch of woods.

The van screeched to a halt and all five passengers scampered free and into the woods, howling like rabid banshees.

The Explorer lurched as Cali threw it into park. Her shoulder stung from where the fishhook had snagged her, her hip throbbed from the third floor fall, and her arm burned from the chair hit. The pain fueled her, adrenaline propelling her into the forest.

She caught up with them quickly, but the helmet-clown split away from the pack. After a few more yards so did the one with the red handprints over his eyes. Cali didn't care; her focus stayed on Keith.

The weirdo with the dead dog disappeared in the trees, and eventually so did tiny Trina.

It was down to Keith, and there was no way in hell she was letting him go.

Laughter swirled through the forest, echoing off the trees. Louder than her footfalls, louder than her ragged breathing, even louder than her heartbeat and her pulse thumping between her ears.

She was gaining on him, her long legs outpacing his.

With her roar rising above the laughter, she jumped and tackled him to the ground.

Full weight in her hands, she pushed on the back of his head, grinding his face into the forest floor. He twisted and flailed, his elbow finding her ribs. Cali yelped as he turned under her and found enough leverage to push her and shimmy out from underneath.

As he got to his feet, Cali unloaded a series of jabs to Keith's knees and he fell face forward, a satisfying crunch of bone when he faceplanted into a jagged tree stump.

Rolling over onto his back, he covered his face with both arms. "Bitch!"

"Yep!" Cali yelled, standing, driving her boot into his gut. Curled up, his head was an easy target for her next kick – her sole to his skull.

She withdrew her knife, then heard something whizz through the air. A fist-sized rock careened off a tree and into her temple. After a few blinks and headshakes, she managed to steady her vision enough to see who threw it.

Twenty feet away, the freak with the fishhook smile pointed to his purse dog and cried, "It wasn't me! It was Fifi! Not me!"

Pain exploded between her shoulders as something cracked across her back, knocking her knife from her hand.

Cali caught her breath, and saw Trina a couple feet from her, holding a broken branch.

Helmet-clown lowered his head and charged. The detritus of the forest floor prevented him from gaining too much speed, allowing Cali time to spin out of the way, but she turned into a right hook from Red Handprints. That dropped her.

Soon as she hit the ground, she told herself to get back up, but they were on her like piranhas. A kick to the gut. A stomp on her hand.

A foot to the hip flipped her over. As she got to her hands and knees, another tree branch broke over her shoulder. A shin to her cheek brought colorful explosions of light. The world moved without her, dropping a few feet, then resetting only to drop again, like a failing horizontal hold on a broken television. *Arms over head*! shot through her mind as she curled into a fetal position and squinted through half-shut eyes, desperately looking for her knife.

BLAM!

Helmet-clown cried out and pressed his hands over a free-flowing bloody hole in his leg.

Their assault on Cali stopped.

"Back away!" a voice said. A woman's voice. Mother? No. Didn't sound like her. "I said back away!"

It hurt to breathe. It hurt to move. It just hurt to *be*. Cali clawed a few feet away from her attackers, toward the voice. She coughed and painted the forest floor red. That cough hurt, too.

She looked up at Bethany Pennington, Lily's mother.

With a gun.

Aiming at Helmet-clown. "I'll kill him," she said.

"You think we care about him?" Keith asked.

"Okay," Bethany said, her voice shaking, but her hands steady. She swung her arms, switching target. "How about her?"

"No!" Keith snapped, jumping in front of Trina.

Trina squealed and clapped.

"I have five bullets left," Bethany said. "That's enough for you all."

"My leg," Helmet-clown whined. "My leg is raining from the inside."

Keith glowered, his cheeks puffing with every angry exhale. He backed away, beckoning the clowns to follow him.

Once they were out of sight, and satisfied with their retreat, Cali fell into the beckoning embrace of darkness.

June 25, 2002

Breath coming in raspy gulps and shaky exhales, Melody guided her navy-blue Mustang through traffic, ignoring the speed limit. She had no fear of being pulled over. The police had their hands full with more important matters than a car speeding along the streets of Philadelphia. The real fear was catching the person she was chasing.

As soon as she had heard about the King of Prussia Mall on the police scanner, she jumped in her car and headed toward the madness. By the time she arrived at the mall, the police were doing their best to contain the situation. They had no idea what the situation was, but they were diverting traffic and had set up roadblocks. Melody drove as close to the mall as she could.

According to the scanner, the back of the mall was the weak point – the police were in the early stages of getting that area under control. Melody slowly guided her car to avoid drawing too much attention to herself, and then she saw the second most unbelievable thing she had ever seen in her life – a group of clowns running from the back exit of the mall. They were whooping and hollering as if celebrating. Then she saw *the* most unbelievable thing she had ever seen in her life – Calista Lindquist running after them.

She tried convincing herself that it wasn't really her. She saw Cali only because she had been thinking about her lately. But the blonde who jumped into a black SUV and drove after the van full of clowns was Cali, no doubt in Melody's mind or heart. Then a red pickup tore out of the parking lot after Cali, and ran through the barricade with a couple police cruisers in pursuit.

"This is stupid, this is stupid, this is stupid," Melody whispered to herself as she got on the highway and followed. Sixty mph. Seventy. Eighty. Ninety. One hundred was easy to achieve in a Mustang, the responsiveness quick enough for her to slip in and out of the smallest gaps among cars, before a horn blared or a middle finger raised.

Pushing way beyond her comfort level, she kept her pace, until the red pickup truck swerved into police cars, causing a crash.

Reflexively, Melody swung onto the shoulder to avoid getting caught up in the mess and thanked God she didn't hit anyone in the process.

Damn! Lost her. "Where are you?"

She wasn't about to give up that easily. Up ahead, the traffic seemed to jam right at the 202 exit. On a hunch, she took the exit north.

Neck muscles so tight they burned, she zipped through a neighborhood at twice the posted speed. Nothing seemed amiss. Did she lose them? Had she chosen the wrong direction? They *had* to be ahead of her.

"There!" A black Explorer jerked into the right lane, following a black van. Melody pressed the gas pedal. "Got you!"

Careful not to get too close, she followed with ease. "Where the heck are you going?"

Into a suburban neighborhood, the van kept driving and the SUV followed. Finally, the road curved in front of a wooded area and the van screeched to a halt. All the doors flew open, and the clowns fled into the forest. The Explorer jerked to a standstill, but only one door flew open. Only one person jumped out.

Cali.

Melody gasped and hit the brakes. She suddenly realized she had remained in denial, that subconsciously she had continued thinking she was wrong about Cali, that it couldn't be her. She had thought she was hallucinating when she spotted Cali in the parking lot by the art gallery. She hoped she was hallucinating when she saw Cali at the mall. No hallucinating now. No tricks of the mind or the eye. That was Cali, her friend who had disappeared two years ago.

Melody debated about what to do next. Follow? No. The clowns were dangerous, and Cali was dressed in black combat gear, ready for a fight. The last thing Melody wanted was to put herself in danger and possibly put Cali in jeopardy by surprising her.

"I'll wait," she told herself, engine off, slouching down in the seat. "Just wait."

Not five minutes later, she heard a pop. "Shit." A gunshot?

The Killer of Devils

A few more minutes went by and the clowns exited the woods.

Melody slid all the way down, her chin pressed against the bottom of the steering wheel. She held her breath, tears rolling over her cheeks as her lungs burned. She didn't want to breathe, didn't want to draw any unwanted attention. She needed to do a few Kegels to keep from peeing herself as she peeked over the dashboard.

One injured clown limped along, laughing. They all were laughing. Except for the one getting in van's driver's side. Something was familiar about him. Was he the one who burst into the gallery? She wanted to go back in time and tell herself not to chase the police. She wanted to go back in time and tell her friends not to go to Max's father's lake house. But she couldn't go back. Only forward.

After she was certain the van had driven away, she exhaled and pushed herself up off the floor. She couldn't go back in time to talk to Cali, but maybe she could talk to her now. Assuming Cali would be coming out of the forest soon, assuming she hadn't been overtaken by the gang of clowns. Melody would confront her, ask every one of the hundred questions she had.

Minutes. Ten. Fifteen. A half hour. Something was wrong. Hating to do it, Melody got out of her car, closing the door with a quiet click. She had calmed herself from the excitement of the chase and threat from the clowns, but as she walked into the woods, every bit of stress came rushing back. Shaking. Sweating. Rapid breathing. But she had to press on, had to see if Cali was in trouble.

Nature was nice to look at, but rarely did she want to be a part of it. She hated camping. Didn't like hikes. Mosquitoes, flies, humidity. And peeing behind a tree or bush? No. So, her experience with the woods was marginal at best. But even without practical experience, she recognized a trodden path when she saw one.

And then she saw a drop of red. Blood. Small splashes of blood splattered the ground. The one clown had been hobbling, his leg wounded. Maybe this blood was his? Maybe he had been shot? Melody shook her head. She was not a detective and had no idea what she was looking for. Cold sweat trickled down her spine, followed by the creepy sensation of being watched. She ran back the way she came, all the way to her car.

Her breathing was out of control when she started the Mustang and put it into gear. The Explorer. She couldn't take her eyes off its open driver's side door. Had she come this far only to leave defeated? Had she seen Cali only to let her disappear again?

She put her car into park, and pulled out her cell phone. One text from Maxwell stating that he had an errand to run. A lump of either stupidity or guilt stuck in her throat – she should've sent Maxwell a text letting him know where she was and what was happening. What could she possibly tell him? Nothing, yet. In fact, what she was about to do would help her deal with telling him nothing.

She ran to the Explorer. Melody opened the rear door and shoved her cellphone in between the backseat padding. She and Maxwell had tracking devices on their cell phones. If he pressed her later about not responding, she'd say she had lost it earlier that day. She hoped Cali was okay, wherever she was, but she couldn't wait around any longer. She had to go back to the apartment for a shower and a stiff drink or two.

*

"I don't think this is a good idea," Harold said.

Maxwell watched the mall's parking lot from the safety of the passenger seat of Harold's Cadillac. The activity was highlighted by the asynchronous strobes of red and blue lights. "I can't disagree with you, but I really wanted to see firsthand what's going on."

It had been two hours since the first reports, vague and sketchy at best. As soon as Maxwell heard the word "clowns," he called Harold to pick him up and bring a certain item that he needed.

"I get that, boss," Harold grumbled as he changed lanes. "There's a good chance you'll get busted and there's only so much I can do."

"You mentioned that, and I understand. Drop me off over there, it looks like a good spot."

Harold guided the car to a tree-lined spot with an unobstructed path to the parking lot at the back of the mall.

Maxwell opened the door and held up the dark blue windbreaker with "CSI" printed in big, yellow letters on the back. Harold had gotten it for him on incredibly short notice. He was a miracle worker. No wonder he was on his father's payroll. "Thanks for this. I owe you."

"You owe me a thousand bucks."

"I'll double it if I find anything."

"Counting on it, boss," Harold said as he pulled away.

Donning the windbreaker, Maxwell jogged through the trees and over the manicured grass to the parking lot. Once he stepped onto the macadam, he thought he was in the clear, but a man in wire rim glasses popped up from behind a car.

Accusatory, he asked, "Did you just come from those trees?"

"Yeah, sorry," Maxwell said. *Smile, be confident.* "This is only my second assignment. My bladder got the better of me. Didn't want to disturb what's going on inside the mall, you know?"

The man sneered. "New guy. You from downtown?"

"Yeah. Name's Johnson."

"So new you forgot shoe covers. Where's your gloves?"

Maxwell looked at his hands and shook his head. "Yeah. This has been... Well, you know... Crazy. Just crazy. I was told even though resources are thin, they didn't want a new guy like me inside. Have you been inside?"

The CSI officer's expression softened as he handed Maxwell a set of clear plastic booties and pair of blue latex gloves. "No, not yet. Heard it was... I heard there were entrails spread around like Christmas decorations. I mean, this is Philly and all, but who does that?"

"That's what we're trying to find out, right? Find anything interesting?"

"Nothing. I just got here, though. I hit this section and that one."

Maxwell pointed in the opposite direction and said, "I'll start over there."

With a grunt, the CSI officer ducked back down behind the cars, aiming a small flashlight around and underneath them.

Section by section, Maxwell focused his search on the line of cars leading closer to the mall's entrance. The vehicles were parked haphazardly, abandoned and doors open, but he'd follow them to the mall and see if he could figure out a way in. He fooled a frustrated and distracted CSI investigator, but would he be slick enough to get past a group of them? Or the swarm of police officers and other detectives? Maxwell needed to come up with a better plan than, "Johnson from downtown."

The lot was less than a quarter full, leaving plenty of gaps among the cars. While traversing an empty space between one car and the next, Maxwell observed the activity by the mall. He kept his peripheral vision on the CSI officer he had interacted with, to make sure he wasn't caught eyeballing the main action. Didn't want anyone suspicious of his true intentions.

At the back of the mall, the police activity was nowhere near as bustling as the front. A detective and a couple more CSI officers busied themselves with their Nikons, adjusting their lenses and snapping close-ups of the crimson-stained sidewalk and walls by the entrance. Maxwell searched around the cars as near to the scene as he could. He hoped to overhear their conversation and the clips of voices over their radios, but not attract attention. He'd hate to be called over to help.

From what he gathered, a small group of clowns in a van had fled via this exit, chased by... a woman? Interesting. The clowns assaulted four officers on the way out.

The CSI team moved from the mall's entrance toward the cars in the parking lot. Maxwell hurried along to keep his distance, trying not to look suspicious. They pointed to bloodied footprints and took more pictures. Maxwell kept moving from car to car, farther away from where the officers were investigating.

This was a bad idea. Crazy. Stupid. He let his ambition and anger get the better of him. He needed to contact Harold and get out of here. He needed...

Something caught his eye. The waning sun glinted off metal on the ground by a car tire. As nonchalantly as possible, he wandered over. A canister lay on its side against the tire. After a quick glance over his shoulder to make sure no one was watching, he crouched down.

A thermos. A plain, silver thermos, no markings, or logos.

Hand shaking, Maxwell touched it and pulled back as if shocked. Feeling stupid for being so frightened by a plain metal thermos, he picked it up. Maybe it had nothing to do with anything. Maybe it belonged to a mall employee, or a mall security guard, and fell out of a car or a lunchbox. But maybe…?

The thermos was missing its top, and the opening held a white haze. No drops of liquid on the ground or near the tire. A quick swipe along the rim yielded a white coating on Maxwell's gloved index finger. Powdery. He sniffed it and fought back a sneeze as the faint aroma of cotton candy made it into his nose. Liquids were found in thermoses, not powders. *This has to be something, right*? he thought as he slid the thermos inside his jacket.

Maxwell peeked over his shoulder to see if anyone was looking his way. Everyone was too engrossed with what they were doing to care about him, so he made his way across the parking lot, away from the police presence, and slipped off his windbreaker. He texted Harold to pick him up and wrote that he had two thousand dollars coming his way.

Maxwell couldn't stop smiling… as if something was tickling his brain.

June 25, 2002

Darkness. The darkness laughed and swirled until shapes and colors formed. Greasy milk white skin. Slimy blood red lips. Glistening teeth. Gnashing and chomping, biting their way toward her.

Cali awoke with a start, jolting upright, and was rewarded with an explosion in her ribs. Her breath left her, taking with it a moaned, "Fuck."

"Yeah, it seemed like you got the shit kicked out of you," a familiar voice said. A woman's voice. Friendly, but the last time she had heard it, the woman was drained, weary.

Bethany Pennington.

"You wouldn't believe me if I told you," Cali whispered.

"I think it was by a group of murderous clowns."

Cali was sitting on the couch in Bethany's living room. Leaning forward from a matching armchair, Bethany's eyebrows knitted with worry. Cali moaned, "That's a helluva great guess."

Bethany shook her head in quick, jerky motions. "Not a guess. I watched it happen. Well, part of it, at least. I'm assuming you were also involved with the massacre at the mall?"

The pain subsiding, Cali shifted and looked herself over. Her pants were still on, but she was barefoot and in her sports bra. A dull ache thumped to the beat of her heart from the bloom of a purple bruise on her side. Small bruises speckled the rest of her visible skin. She poked at the bandage on her shoulder, the spot where a fishing hook had torn through her skin. "Define 'involved with.'"

Bethany's posture relaxed. "The news reports are non-stop and vague, but it seems like a group of individuals dressed as clowns went on a killing spree at the King of Prussia mall five hours ago. A few witnesses said they saw a blonde woman dressed like she was on a black-ops mission chase after a group of clowns as they fled."

"Heh. They always say, 'blonde woman.' If I were a man, they'd probably use the words 'brave' and 'heroic.' When a badass boss bitch risks her life, I'm reduced to hair color. Nice patch job, by the way."

The Killer of Devils

"I'm guessing you're okay? Well, at least not dying. Do you want me to take you to a hospital?"

Cali shook her head, despite the ache, and reached for her phone only to find an empty pocket. "No hospital. Feel like I'm dying, but nothing a gallon of booze can't cure. You didn't happen to see my phone, did you?"

Bethany looked at her coffee table and Cali followed her gaze. The last time Cali was here the table was covered with crumbled tissues and empty coffee mugs with whiskey odor. Now, Cali's stuff littered it, displayed neatly. Magazines for her Glocks, knife, utility belt, phone. She tried to lean forward, but the bruise on her side punched her, eliciting a grimace and forcing her to sit back. Bethany moved from her armchair to bring Cali's phone to her, and then took a seat on the couch.

"Thank you," Cali said. She quickly scrolled through the dozen text messages from her mother.

She typed, `Sorry for the silence got banged up but im good. Be back to the hotel in a little.`

"So... How did I get here?" she asked Bethany.

"I..." Bethany paused and looked away, eyes welling.

Cali thought about her last visit, how Bethany lived on the precipice of a breakdown. The anguish was a whole separate person, an uninvited guest who refused to leave, and Cali felt terrible that her presence had brought that all back. And as Bethany fought back tears, Cali feared that her being here again would tear Bethany apart.

Until... Bethany smiled? Eyes shimmered as she wiped away tears. "The Keith the Clown thing... How the police got information about him and what he has done... Was that you as well?"

Cali's phone dinged with a text from her mother: `Thank God! I was getting worried. Where r u?`

`Im at a friends place.`

`Friend?? You don't have any friends. Who do you know in Philly?`

`You know me mom. Im a people person.`

`Ha ha. Happy youre safe.`

Cali set her phone aside and offered a coy shoulder shrug. "Maybe."

"Well, then maybe I owe you a big thank you. My lawyers were fighting hard to get my husband out of jail, but now that Keith has been added to the mix, it's making their jobs a lot easier."

"That's..." A surprise emotion slipped behind Cali's chest. A good one, the residue of altruism. Her crusade was to rid the world of monsters. She was self-aware enough to know it was born from her own anger, frustration, and fear, but it satisfied her to know that killing monsters meant saving people before they became victims. It wasn't often she interacted with someone whose life she had affected. "That's really great to hear. But... That doesn't explain why your couch is now a triage."

A tear rolled down Bethany's cheek, an ocean's worth of emotions in a single drop of water. "I had just gotten off the phone with one of my lawyers. He told me his plan and that my husband – Justin, my husband's name is Justin – should be out within a week or two. I was so happy that I needed to get out of the house, needed to tell Lily her father was coming home. It's weird, I know, that her body... *she*... she is buried in our family plot in a nearby cemetery, but I visit the tree where the police found her to talk to her. Like I said, weird."

Cali knew loss. Not of a child, but of close friends. And her father had been literally torn apart right in front of her. She knew the stray thoughts she had in public, the voices she heard when she was alone, the murky dreams slogged down in Freudian quagmire when she slept. "Not weird, Bethany. Not weird at all."

Bethany smiled and wiped away another tear. "Well, I was by the tree... talking to Lily when I heard a commotion. Running. Laughing. Voices. Obviously, more curious than smart, I went to see what was going on. That's when I saw the woman who had visited my house with a bullshit cover story about being an insurance investigator."

Cali closed her eyes, recalling what she could. The mall. The car chase. The clowns. They had her, but... "You shot one of them, right?"

"I did. I thought I was being paranoid to bring my gun with me. It's just the forest behind my house, right? I'm so scared all the time now."

Cali opened her eyes and had to bury the fear of losing the fight, almost dying, or else she'd curl up in a fetal position and cry the rest of the week away. "Thank you. After what you've been through, it's perfectly fine to be scared and paranoid. And I needed a bullshit cover story. I didn't want to tell you I was investigating Keith and give you false hope, in case things didn't work out as I planned."

Bethany pursed her lips, then nodded. "Yeah, I understand now."

Cali took a deep breath but stopped when her ribs ached. "You wouldn't happen to have any medicine, would you? Like eighty proof or higher?"

"Sorry. I emptied every bottle I had down the drain. I'll never get Lily back, and I'll never heal from that, but I'm getting Justin back. He lost his daughter too, and he has the extra pain of being blamed for it. I needed to clean myself up."

Cali nodded. "Good for you, Bethany."

"Thank you, Dakota. I couldn't have done it without you."

Cali leaned back against the plush cushioning of the couch and slouched down. "Sorry, but my name's Cali. Dakota is an alias."

"A bullshit cover name to go with your bullshit cover story?"

"Heh. Not quite. I use the name Dakota as a remembrance." Cali tensed after she realized what she said. She had just shared too much info. In too much pain, the words had unwittingly slipped out of her mouth.

"Sister? Ex? Daughter?"

"Friend. Lifelong, best friend who I considered a sister."

"What happened?"

Einstein's theory of relativity suddenly resonated with Cali. It had been two years ago, but it simultaneously felt as far away as two decades and as close as two days. The sudden flashes of Dakota's platinum blonde hair and baby doll face weakened Cali's spine, and she shrank further in the couch. She didn't like to share, but what the hell... "She was killed by a monster. So was my boyfriend and a few other friends. And my father."

"Oh my God! I... I... My God, sorry doesn't even begin to cover it."

"It brought my mother and me closer. She and I hunt monsters now."

Saying the words out loud sounded stupid, like announcing that she was a princess who rode unicorns, but Bethany didn't flinch or smirk. Instead, she asked, "Is that why you were at the mall?"

"Yep. Heard something was up and went to investigate."

"What happened?"

She closed her eyes for a moment, to reflect, but that made the memories play out like a movie she couldn't turn away from. The madness. The way the clowns moved, laughed, looked. They were beyond crazy. She opened her eyes. "Just like the news said. A group of people dressed like clowns went on a killing spree."

"And you followed some of them to the woods."

"Yep."

"Why'd they come here? To this set of woods?"

Cali sat up, hating herself for grunting as she did so. "That's a great question. They pulled over and ran into the forest. I chased them and then they surrounded me."

"But why come *here*? I mean, the mall is like fifteen miles away. They could have pulled over in any neighborhood or raced to Jersey. And they surrounded you. Almost like… like…"

"Like they knew the area, knew that part of the woods."

"Oh God." Bethany's eyes darted back and forth. She leapt from the couch and hurried across the living room to close the curtains. "They live around here."

Bethany was right, but Cali couldn't have her spin out of control. She stood up with a wince and a groan, her body playing a painful game of guess-which-internal-organ-is-ruptured. Cali didn't know exactly where her spleen was or how it could hurt, but she felt like that was the winner as she hobbled over to Bethany. She wanted to put a sympathetic hand on her shoulder, but her own shoulder hurt too damn much. "They went back the way they came, right? We can assume they got back in the van and left." It was a huge leap in logic, but Cali was willing to do anything to help calm the woman who saved her life. "The police interviewed your neighbors when your daughter went missing, so they would have noticed a bunch of clowns in a house. I'm sure someone would have noticed a van full of clowns pulling in and out. They probably live in an abandoned warehouse nearby. It's always an abandoned warehouse."

Bethany exhaled, long and shaky, her arms wrapped around her own waist, staring out the window as if she could see miles away. "Yeah, I guess you're right. It's just... God, those... monsters. I feel like they're right outside my house."

"I understand."

She turned to Cali. "Stay the night. Please. You're pretty banged up and the rest will do you good. And I don't want to be in an empty house right now."

"Bethany—"

"Just tonight, I promise. Tomorrow I'll call a locksmith and security company."

You feel like shit. Just go pass out on the couch. "Okay."

A shaky smile of relief skittered briefly across Bethany's face. "Thank you. I really appreciate everything you've done for me."

Cali trundled back to the couch and grabbed her cellphone. Change of plans Im staying here for the night. Be back at the hotel tomorrow AM.

K. It's good to get some after a mission.

Its not like that. A woman I helped and shes scared to stay alone.

A woman? Glad to see you're exploring your options.

MOM OMG!

Now that I know you're safe I might look for some action tonight. Adrenaline is still running high.

Ok we're done now C U tomorrow.

Cali tossed her phone aside and flopped on the couch. The stiffness in her joints made the effort graceless.

"Everything okay?" Bethany asked.

"Yeah, just coming to the realization that my mom might be cooler than me."

Bethany raised a brow and offered a half smile. "Well, since you two are monster hunters, there's high potential that she's going to be cool."

"Ugh." Cali moaned as she slouched down, allowing the softness of the couch to ease her aches. "Don't take her side."

"No sides taken. I've been living on premade meals, so I have a ton in the freezer. I'll go microwave a couple."

"Sounds great. Thank you."

Cali closed her eyes while she waited, but sleep pulled her into its hard embrace.

June 26, 2002

Cali winced as her mother applied the salve. The bruise on her ribs was a majestic purple rimmed by a jaundiced crown. A medal of honor if it didn't hurt so badly. "Your fingers are freezing, Mom. You could have run your hands under warm water first."

Sitting on the hotel room's couch beside Cali, her mother held up the unlabeled jar of goop. "My hands are warm enough. It's the salve."

The miracle cream had always reduced Cali's healing time by half, but her mother lacked a "motherly touch." Another bolt of pain blasted through her gut when her mother rubbed a circle over her fourth and fifth ribs. "Ow. You don't have to be so rough."

"You didn't have to be a dumbass and chase after your target into unknown terrain while heavily outnumbered. You should have waited for me. At the very least, you should have let me know where you were. Dumbass."

"If I'd waited, they'd be long gone."

"You didn't wait, and they're still long gone. And you got your ass kicked. And you're lucky to be alive. Have I called you a dumbass yet?"

Cali curled her fingers into fists, priming them to punch the next clown she saw. "I had them right there in front of me. I couldn't let them go. I couldn't let the monsters win."

Cali's mom wiped her hands on a towel, put the lid back on the jar, and set it on the coffee table next to a half-dozen unlabeled jars. Fingers wiggling in deliberation, she grabbed the green one and handed it to Cali. "This is for the cut on your shoulder." She then got up and crossed the room to the nightstand.

"No," Cali said as her mom picked a card off the nightstand. "C'mon, Mom. Why?"

Mother held a playing card an inch from Cali's face. The word on it was "Temperance."

Cali dragged two fingers through the sludge in the jar and applied it to the gouge on her shoulder, wincing. Her whole arm burned, but this glop worked better on open wounds than the other glop did on bruises. There'd still be a scar, but the cut would heal in less than three days. The knife wound in her thigh she had received in New York was already gone. "Temperance? Really, Mother?"

"It means 'restraint.'"

"I know what it means, but it's more applicable to my drinking problem, or partying."

"It applies to your anger, too. You use it as a crutch, and it results in stupid decisions."

"Fine. I'll show more temperance."

"These are talking cards, Cali. Someone plays a card, and the other person talks."

"Hardly seems fair since I have no access to the cards."

"No shit, Sherlock. Now talk."

"You want me to talk about my anger? Fine. I'm fucking angry. I'm angry that my father kept massive secrets from me. I'm angry that he was taken from me by a monster. I'm angry that my mother has been absent from my life for twenty fucking years. I'm angry that all of the above has derailed my life. I'm angry at myself for being so angry at everything. I'm angry that I took a fishhook to the arm from a fucking clown."

Mother tossed the card onto the coffee table and placed her hands on Cali's cheek. Cali was wrong – her mother did have a motherly touch. "Anger is like fire – a powerful tool that can help build a society, but dangerous enough to burn it all down."

"God, that was such a shit analogy."

"Yeah. I've been a hands-off mother for two decades."

Cali averted her eyes, and mumbled, "Sorry I said that."

Mother's thumbs stroked Cali's cheeks. "Hey. Look at me. Don't be sorry. Your father and I made some not-so-great choices. We were both too addicted to adventure and danger to be good parents. The mission that went wrong in Afghanistan opened my eyes, made me realize I needed to reprioritize. Your father, too. Yes, he used his skills to become an assassin, but he was smart and did his best to avoid face-to-face com-

The Killer of Devils

bat. As his secret behind the scenes broker, I kept an eye on you both and always planned to step in if anything happened to him."

"Why'd you wait so long? Why not come back into the picture when I was, like, sixteen? Eighteen? Twenty?"

"If I had showed up earlier, your father might have retired then, but he'd be resentful of me, and then maybe of you."

Cali understood resentment. "I get it."

"Yeah? You sure?"

"Yes, but I'm still angry. I'm happy you came back into my life, but God, I wish you had come back sooner."

"Do you hate me? Or your father?"

"No."

Mother leaned forward and kissed Cali's forehead. "Good. That's all that matters."

"Okay, now take your damn card back."

Mother laughed. "Fine."

Cali wiped her goopy fingers on a towel. "This stuff is really amazing, but my whole arm is kind of numb."

"I learned all these salve recipes from an unnamed tribe along the Amazon. The shaman who taught me was quite handsome."

Cali rolled her eyes. "Ugh! Don't tell me – he taught you how to make these salves because you had sex with him."

"Cali! That's so crass. I was on a mission to drive away poachers from the area. He taught me how to make the salves because a five-year-old boy from the tribe fell into the river after a particularly nasty storm passed through and the waters were rougher than usual. I jumped in and rescued him."

Right when Cali started to feel bad about being too quick to judge, her mother finished her story. "The sex was just a bonus."

"Okay, we're done here." Cali put her tee shirt back on. "I'm going to get brunch. I think I need a few hours to scrub all the nasty images from my brain."

Cali's mother laughed. "You are such a prude."

"Nope."

Mother laughed even harder. "Okay, okay. Have a good brunch. I'm going digital snooping, to see what the police have. Love you."

"Bye, love you, too."

Cali headed to the elevator. There was a restaurant next to the hotel, a nice place to drown her temperance with late morning Bloody Marys.

When she got to the lobby, she froze in her tracks.

Melody.

First thought – jump behind the potted trees in the corner. But it was too late for that.

Melody looked right at her.

Second thought – throw a smoke grenade for distraction. But she was sadly bereft of the necessary tool.

Third thought – Fuck.

Cali almost died yesterday at the hands of murder-clowns. Two years ago, she ended an unkillable creature. She'd been face-to-face with a dozen killers between then and now. But never in her life had she been as scared as she was with one of her oldest friends walking toward her.

With every step Melody took, protective muscles tensed in Cal's arms. A punch was coming from Melody, she knew it, and Cali tightened her stance. She instinctually readied herself to block or roll with the punch. It'd be easy since she knew Melody was right-handed. When the punch came, she'd take it. She deserved it.

By the time Melody stood within a few feet, Cali saw the tears streaming over her cheeks, dripping to the floor as she walked closer. With a chin-quivering sob, Melody hugged Cali.

It took a few seconds to register that she hadn't been hit, and then Cali returned the tight embrace. And the tears. This felt right, yet wrong. Home, yet foreign. Their hug lasted longer than the creation and destruction of an entire universe, only ending when Melody whispered, "Where have you been?"

Cali pulled away and wiped her eyes and nose with the back of her hand. "I... Oh, God, Mel... So much has happened. I... don't even—"

Melody squeezed Cali's hand. "I'm not letting go until you tell me everything. I mean everything."

Cali saw relief in Melody's eyes, but her voice was edged with an impending anger if her demands weren't met.

"I'll tell you what I can. There's a place around the corner that has the best Bloody Marys. And brunch. And Bloody Marys."

Melody had been serious about not letting go. Holding hands, the obvious desperation of trying to save a friendship that started in elementary school, they grabbed a table at the restaurant next to the hotel.

After ordering two drinks, Cali started talking. "How did you find me?"

"I snuck my phone in your SUV and tracked it."

Cali smirked. "Nicely done." The Bloody Marys arrived and Cali chugged half of hers right down, ignoring the straw. Swiping her bottom lip with her thumb, she said, "Sorry that I disappeared, Mel. I truly, truly am. I want to tell you everything, but there are things that I really, really can't."

"Did you kill Maxwell's father?"

The world stopped spinning. Everything beyond Cali's peripheral vision shattered, leaving only Melody in front of her.

Leaning forward, Melody said, "I know about Maxwell's father. I know what kind of man he was, and I know the 'kind of business' he operated. Maxwell knows, too." She glanced down at the table, and then looked back up to lock eyes with Cali. "He's convinced you killed his father."

Every logic center within Cali's brain told her to lie, flip the table, and run away. But God damn it, she was sitting across the table from a best friend that she hadn't seen for two years. "Please don't tell Maxwell."

"I won't if you tell me why you did it."

"Revenge."

"Revenge? For what?"

"Roger Templeton killed my father."

It was Melody's turn to go wide-eyed. "What? How?"

Round two of drinks, and Cali drained hers in two gulps. "Okay. Okay, so I guess I'm telling you everything. There are things you might not believe, but I promise you – everything I'm about to say is true. Two years ago, we were supposed to have a couples' weekend at Roger's lake house…"

Cali spoke for the next hour, recounting her personal history of the past two years. An unkillable beast named Zebadiah Seeley had donned a bear's head and slaughtered their mutual lifelong friend, Dakota, and her boyfriend. He also killed Cali's boyfriend, Tanner, and their party friend, Hook, and his girlfriend, Linda. Cali even shared that Linda was an undercover DEA agent investigating Hook, even though Linda's name stirred up feelings she kept trying to suppress. Cali talked about her father, that he made his living as an assassin. Even though he died by Zebadiah's hands, Roger Templeton had orchestrated the situation to put Zebadiah in her father's path.

Cali was on her third Bloody and halfway through an order of eggs benedict.

Melody took a few deep breaths. "I thought Maxwell was losing his shit because he couldn't deal with the death of his father. Roger went 'missing,' but Maxwell knew he was dead, felt it in his bones." Melody's eyes were bloodshot from tears and alcohol. "He has you on a security camera video – he's convinced it was you entering his father's office building the day he disappeared. Nothing more than a ten second clip of a blonde with a ponytail, but he's watched that video a thousand times."

"Video?" Cali mumbled, more to herself. "I thought Mom got them all."

"Mom?" Melody wrinkled her brow. "Your mom is working with you?"

"Long, complicated story, but she was my dad's assassin-broker. He never knew it was her, but she's back in my life. She and I have dedicated ourselves to hunting monsters like Zebadiah."

"Like the clowns? From the parking lot the other day and from the mall yesterday. That's why you're in town, isn't it?"

"Yes."

Like tectonic plates, Melody's emotions crashed into each other – pinched-brow anger morphed into wide-eyed confusion, then eroded into slack-jaw weariness. "Jesus, Cali… This is too much."

Cali wanted to tell her to run away, leave the restaurant and not look back. It'd be the safest and sanest thing to do. She loved Melody too much to expose her to the world she now lived in. Unfortunately, it was that same love, the yearning to reconnect with a friend of almost two decades, which caused her to lean forward and put her hand on top of Melody's. "I'm sorry for everything. For disappearing. For not being able to save Dakota. For what happened to... what I did to Maxwell's father. For the past two years being... weird."

"It's more than that, Cali. You put me in limbo. Yes, Maxwell's father started the mess, and he was involved in some illegal shit, but you took away Maxwell's closure, and his ability to find answers. You took away the answers to what happened to *our* friends. You took away *my* closure. I knew Dakota just as long as you did, just as long as we've known each other, but you kept what happened all to yourself. You hid yourself from me, Cali." Melody's face was stern, her words terse. She squeezed Cali's hand.

"Everything you said is true and I can't put into words how awful I feel to have done that to you."

"I don't understand. I mean, I get your *reasoning*, but I think it's flawed. You could have trusted me with this."

"It's not about trust. It's about... I don't know... protection. I can barely wrap my head around what's going on ninety percent of the time, and I didn't want to dump my burden on you. Especially after what I learned about Maxwell's father. It wouldn't have been fair of me."

Melody kept Cali's hand within hers, and Cali could almost see the inner workings of her friend's mind, slogging through the information, compartmentalizing her feelings. Weighing Cali's explanations and determining if they were good enough. The tears came again as she whispered, "It's a lot. There's just so much."

"I know."

Melody squeezed Cali's hand one last time, and then stood. "I need to go. I love you and I'm ecstatic that you're alive, but... This is a lot to process."

She started to leave, but paused when Cali asked, "What are you going to tell Max?"

Melody shrugged and sighed. "I don't know."

Cali couldn't think of anything else to say as Melody left. All of her aches came back, bringing a few more with them, so she ordered another drink.

June 28, 2002

"Eat my cookies!" Trina screamed, rubbing crumbled thin, mint cookies over Keith's face. It was weird, but Keith didn't care; they were in bed and she was riding his dick like a blender full of rocks.

At four foot ten, she was taller than he liked, but she had a child-like thin frame and tiny tits. And the green girl's outfit helped. It helped a lot. The next time Keith immortalized a perfect princess, he'd dress her in an outfit just like that. He had no idea where Trina got the outfit or the cookies, and he didn't care.

Keith hadn't searched the house yet. He'd do that tomorrow if Collin didn't come up with a solid plan by tonight. They'd been here for only a day, having taken it over yesterday. Even though the mall trip didn't increase their ranks by big numbers, they still needed more space than what Trina's house provided, so they had taken over her neighbor's house. It was owned by a couple in their late fifties. They fed the husband to Master Poppie and converted the wife, Judith. They learned her name before making her breathe the white mist. The first thing she did was gut her pet cat. Now she and Delvin had similar handbags.

Trina's box of cookies completed her look. The gold and silver paint on her round cheeks and wide eyes made her look like a porcelain doll decorated by a precocious toddler. Her closed lips were pursed rose-petals, unless she was smiling, then she had a shark's mouth. Or unless she was coming and screaming, "Eat my cookies!"

As she came, she ran her hands over his face. He enjoyed the feeling of her little fingers kneading his cheeks, chin, and forehead, and it made him come too.

Laughing like a hyena, Trina collapsed, her head on his chest. She blew raspberries against his skin and nuzzled his chest-hair. "I'm a race car. Vroom, vroom! I'm shiny and fast. A fast, shiny race car!"

"Yes, you are," Keith said, patting her head. Even though his dick was still in her, he couldn't stop his thoughts from wondering about the mall mission. Master Poppie's white mist set three dozen mall shoppers free. It might have exposed the militia of clowns to the world, but it distracted the authorities – the police spent the last few days canvassing the King of Prussia area looking for leads. That was only a partial success in Keith's mind. The two additional recruits? Two out of almost forty was not a good percentage. And then there was the blonde bitch.

Attacking the mall had successfully flushed out the blonde bitch. And they almost had her – Keith had her right where he wanted her. Until that other blonde bitch arrived. The two blondes looked alike. Mother and daughter? They were a team, obviously. Keith chuckled. *Mother-daughter clown killers. Wouldn't that be somethin'?*

The women had been prepared. They were armed and trained. The daughter – assuming that's what she was – gave chase. Keith lured her into the woods and got the jump on her again. And again, she was rescued. From a random woman strolling around the woods with a gun. *Who does that, strolls the woods armed?* But she looked familiar, like he had met her before.

For three days now Keith's mind couldn't raise any more information about the forest woman with a gun, no matter how hard he dug. It irritated him like a piece of popcorn stuck in his back teeth. And then…

"Fuck! I remember who she is."

"No!" Trina yelled. "Get whoever she is out of your head!"

"It's okay, sweety. She's the mother of an immortal goddess."

"Do you like her?"

"No. Not at all."

"Yaay!" Trina pushed up and smiled. "Can we visit her? I want to have a balloon animal party."

Keith chuckled. "Yeah, we can visit her some time, and you can have a balloon party."

"You're the best boyfriend ever. Vroom, vroom!"

Keith liked the sound of that. Trina was batshit crazy, but that's what made her special. Whenever the time was right, he was confident that she'd support his desire to immortalize his perfect princesses. Hell, she'd probably even help. He rubbed his chest, wondering if they kept following Collin, would that time ever come.

The Killer of Devils

Keith slid Trina off him and got out of bed. Donning a pair of boxers, he said, "Gotta take a leak."

"Leak, leak, splash, drip, drizzle, leak, leak," Trina replied.

Keith laughed all the way to the bathroom. When finished, he went to check on the new recruits, make sure they knew who the boss was.

"What's up?" Keith asked Red and Helmet when he entered the garage.

Judith's garage was bigger than both floors of his rowhouse combined. It could easily fit three cars, but only a Mercedes S-Class and a golf cart were parked inside. Simple observation told Keith that the car rarely saw any action. A work bench occupied a wall. The other pegboard wall displayed hanging tools and small equipment for lawn maintenance. The golf cart really stuck in Keith's craw. Decent sized and gas-powered, it looked like it cost more than his van. Fucking rich pricks.

"My helmet is a helmet," Helmet said while whacking a screwdriver against his helmeted head.

"I'm as right as red rain," Red replied. He wore a black trench coat while tinkering at the workbench. He worked on a metal framework with pivot points and springs. Something useful? Or was he just an idiot like Helmet?

Since Red and Helmet were converted at the mall, they spent most of their time together. Though Red seemed to have more of his marbles, they both spoke in half-crazy sentences, like Trina and Delvin. And neither of them knew their own names. Whenever asked, Red went off on some weird poetry about, "Red is my eyes, how I see the world. Red is inside me, how the world sees me." He had a grease white base and red handprints over his eyes. In the mall, the color came from blood, but now he used red paint.

Helmet would just say things like, "I am helmet. I have a helmet. See my helmet? I'm a helmet." He never took the thing off, opting for two colors on his face – green for the top half, black for the bottom half. His bullet wound was healing nicely.

Though they were both banana-shit-crazy, Keith needed them in case he decided to move against Collin. He had nothing personal against the guy, but he didn't believe in his leadership. Collin kept referring to Keith as a general, but he hardly listened to him and kept him in the dark about plans. When Keith had suggested another attack, Collin said it wasn't time. Keith tried explaining that it'd been three days since the attack on the mall, and now was the time to keep pushing, to make more recruits, to make the world burn with chaos. But Collin wanted to lay low until the dust settled. Fuck that.

Collin would be coming back soon from his date with some guy. Keith didn't know why that dude was important, only that he could help Master Poppie. He didn't care that Collin was on a date with a man. Back in his army days, he acted like that mattered only because everyone else made a fuss about it. But Keith's dick was his own business, and no one could tell him where to put it, so he extended the same curtesy.

"Where'd you get the coat?" Keith asked Red.

"Closet. The closet was full of closet clothes."

"Good to know. So, you two, who's your boss?"

"You are," Red and Helmet replied.

"Good answer. I'll leave you to whatever the fuck it is you're doing."

"Helmet!" was the last thing he heard as he shut the door behind him.

In the hallway, Sally sat against the wall, licking his armpit. Keith walked by him and asked, "Who's your boss?"

In between slurps, Sally replied, "You."

"Good answer."

In the kitchen, Judith and Delvin sat at the table with their purses, making the dead dog and cat carcasses touch noses. Keith wasn't sure about Delvin, and Judith might be too new to reach. Her hair was a frizzy mess, half matted with her husband's dried blood, the other half like rotting hay. No grease paint, but she had drawn giant red circles around her eyes, and painted her mouth and chin blue.

Brin sat on the couch in the living room, her eyes lost in space. As second in command, she hung on to Collin's every word. And she didn't like Keith fucking her sister.

The Killer of Devils

When Keith walked by, Brin's face cranked into a scowl so hard that her jagged yellow smile turned into a frown. "Where's Trina?"

"Bedroom." Keith wanted to give more detail, but egging her on would serve no purpose.

"Tell her to come out. Collin will be here any second. And put clothes on!"

Keith gave her a mock salute and turned on his heels. He marched out of the living room, back to the bedroom.

Trina was kneeling on the bed and pulverizing chocolate covered cookies between her hands. "Vroom, vroom, Keithy! Want more cookies?"

"Your sister's boyfriend is coming home soon, and she wants us in the living room."

Trina stuck out her bottom lip and wiped her hands on the sheets. "Boooo! Collin ruins the cookie fun!"

"You got that right. Get dressed."

Keith escorted Trina to the living room and as she walked past Brin, she wagged her index finger at her sister. "No cookies for you!" Arms crossed, she flopped down on the couch. Brin frowned at Keith again, and he gave her a lethargic shrug. *Let Collin's bitch be pissed off.*

"Just because you're a general, doesn't mean you can do whatever you want," Brin said.

"I thought that was the whole purpose of our mission," Keith replied. "Chaos. Do whatever we want, whenever we want. Or does that no longer fit into Collin's big plan?"

"Collin's plan benefits Master Poppie. Master Poppie benefits us all."

"Then tell me Collin's plan. Don't you think a general should know?" The purple shapes over her eyes were fresh and dark, but Keith saw the slightest shift from anger to doubt. "Maybe you don't know the plan either."

Brin snarled. "He's going to tell us the plan when he gets back from his date."

"And you believe that?"

Brin stood. "I have faith in him and Master Poppie. Keep an eye on Delvin and Judith while I get the others."

As Brin stormed down the hallway toward the garage, Keith looked back into the kitchen.

"Meow," Judith said.

"Woof," Delvin replied through his fish-hooked mouth.

The front door opened, and Collin entered with a man, his date.

Collin smiled. "Senator Manchester Albright, this is half of everyone. Half of everyone, this is Senator Manchester Albright."

Manchester's eyes widened, and his face paled. "What's going on? Why are they wearing clown make…? Wait… Are they *the* clowns? The ones from the mall?"

"Oh, they absolutely are," Collin replied.

Manchester turned and reached for the doorknob, but Collin blocked him.

"Let me go! Let me out of here!"

"Nope."

Collin was larger, but Keith could almost smell Manchester's fear-sweat, the panic coursing through his veins. Manchester pressed his hands against Collin's chin and face, yelling as he tried to push his way past. Collin struggled but continued to block the escape route. Keith thought about helping but wanted to see how their leader handled this. After all, the great chosen one should be able to handle a politician.

"Brin, hurry up!" Collin cried.

Running down the hallway with a canister in her hand, Brin shoved Sally out of the way and then tossed it to Collin. With a grunt, he pushed Manchester back and caught the cannister, opening it right as Manchester grabbed the doorknob. Purple mist plumed forth, enveloping the panicked senator. After a few seconds, Manchester stopped struggling and slumped to the floor, muttering, "I hear him… Master Poppie… He whispers to me…"

Brin snarled at Keith, "You could have helped."

"Nah. Collin had it. Right, boss?"

Half of his face coated with purple powder, Collin smiled like a wicked child ready to rip the wings from a fly. "Yes, Keith, of course I did."

The senator curled on the floor and stroked his own face.

The Killer of Devils

Keith pointed at Manchester. "He's worse than Sally or Helmet. You sure he's gonna do whatever it is you have planned?"

"He won't be like that for long. He said he heard Master Poppie. He'll be like us soon enough."

Keith grunted. He hadn't heard Master Poppie's voice when he got a face full of purple. Should he be relieved or disappointed? "What is it you want from that guy?"

"Didn't you hear that he's a Pennsylvania senator?"

"So? There are two senators for every state." Keith didn't do well in school, but he knew the basics. "How'd you get to him anyway? I thought a senator would have a shit-ton of security."

"That's the U.S. Senate, the federal level. Manchester is a senator for the *state* senate. There are fifty of those."

Keith started to piece together Collin's puzzle. Maybe it wasn't such a bad idea. "Just wish you'd share your plans with me."

Wide-eyed and maniacal, Collin gestured to Manchester. "I just did!"

"Yeah? What about the blonde bitch? You have a plan to deal with her?"

Collin's smile stretched so wide that it looked like his mouth was trying to pull the skin off his face. "The blonde bitch? Yeah, I do. Her name is Calista. And I'm dating her."

June 30, 2002

Maxwell's brain tickled. The odd sensation lasted only a few seconds. But it occurred frequently, a few times a day, and he had to stifle a giggle each time. Now was not the time for random chuckling. Or maybe it was? In this neighborhood, acting a little off might be an asset.

This area of Philadelphia needed hospice. Discolored and flaking away, the outsides of the rowhomes looked like withered skin. Chunks of cement were missing from uneven sidewalks and only three quarters of the streetlights blinked on when the sun went down. Never once had he thought his crusade would lead him here. But when Harold told him that Fat Mikey and Little Big found someone who knew where Keith lived, Maxwell insisted on coming along. If he had known the informant was a homeless man with a flea problem, then he might have reconsidered.

"Are we sure about this?" Maxwell asked Harold as they exited the car.

"Sure, about what, exactly?" Harold asked.

"About trusting a homeless man for information."

Hands in his pockets, Harold looked Maxwell in the eye. "Homelessness isn't a disease, so don't worry, you won't catch it."

Maxwell was stunned by the bluntness of his employee. But Harold wasn't a normal employee, and he had a point. "Didn't mean for my comments to sound elitist or disparaging. I just meant that he's scratching nonstop, looking all around, walking in a circle, and talking to himself. I don't think he'd intentionally lie to us, but what if he tells us a story about aliens or how the government implanted chips in his brain."

Maxwell wondered how Harold was at poker because there was no hiding the disappointment on his face. "Not all homeless people are crazy. Yeah, a few of them are. But think about their situation, what got them here. It ain't easy for them, so quite a few talk to their shoes and see goblins in the shadows. But Mikey and Big have talked to enough to figure out who's telling narratives and who's telling fairy tales."

The Killer of Devils

Maxwell ran his hand through his hair and looked around. This wasn't his kind of neighborhood, and he would never visit it otherwise. Harold had. So had Fat Mikey and Little Big. He paid these men well, so he might as well trust them to do their jobs. "You're right. I'm just... I'm still shook up about the incident at the mall. It's been almost a week since I sent the sample to my—" The ringtone from his cellphone cut him off. "Huh. Speak of the devil. If you don't mind, Harold, I need to take this."

Harold grunted and wandered closer to Fat Mikey, Little Big, and the homeless man.

Maxwell drifted closer to Harold's Cadillac to answer his phone. "Yes?"

"Mr. Templeton? This is Dr. Laura Covington from Zeus Chemical."

"Is this regarding the sample I sent to you?"

"It is."

"Are you able to tell me anything about it?"

Not that it should have surprised him, but Maxwell had been taken aback last year when he discovered a biochemical company, Zeus Chemical, among his father's portfolios. It was the first one he visited after taking over his father's holdings. He wanted to understand what they did, and set up a meeting with Dr. Covington, but the science far exceeded his comprehension. He was satisfied with the soundbite, "We make fertilizers and pesticides." They also made a profit, so he was happy to look at the books every month with a smile. After finding the canister in the mall parking lot with remnants of a mysterious powder, he sent it to Zeus Chemical. He knew they dealt with one area of chemistry and figured there'd be zero chance they'd be able to analyze what he had sent, but he was hoping they could at least give him something to go on.

He was surprised when Dr. Covington said, "The sample you sent came from a plant."

"What kind of plant?"

"There are over 300,000 species of plants with thousands more being discovered each year. Trying to identify the plant sample, especially since Zeus Chemical is not designed to do that, is nearly impossible. What I *can* tell you is, this sample didn't come from an average plant."

"How so?"

"The high levels of psilocybin and the alkaloids."

Maxwell closed his eyes and pinched the bridge of his nose to stave off the headache from her yammering and need for big words. He swore she was making them up to see if he'd know any different. He had no patience but kept his tone appreciative. "Doctor, I'm a little crunched for time and unable to digest the science behind your discovery. Is there simpler terminology?"

"The sample is a lot like opium."

"Opium?"

"On steroids. And aggressive. There seems to be an inhibitor, meaning that the effects don't wear off, or if they do, it won't be for a very long time."

"Sounds like it might make a person go insane."

"Hypothetically, yes, but I can say there's no *compounded* effect on the insane."

"What do you mean?"

She sighed, sounding as impatient and irritated as he felt. "Mental illness is usually caused by a chemical imbalance in the brain. Certain mental illness like psychosis or schizophrenia are caused by chem—"

"Please keep it simple, Doctor."

"The chemicals that cause hallucinations are included in the sample you supplied. And, as I mentioned earlier, an inhibitor to make the effects last longer. It could make a person unstable, unless they're already unstable."

"So, it makes a person crazy unless they're already crazy."

"I, personally, wouldn't phrase it like that, but yes."

That explained the lunacy at the mall. Obviously, Keith the Clown concocted a canister – or canisters? – of the craziness powder and exposed it to people at the mall. As Dr. Covington put it, "Opium on steroids." As terrifying as that sounded, Maxwell's gut twisted as he wondered about Keith's ultimate goal, assuming he had one. "Do you have any of the sample left?"

"We barely had any to begin with."

"Thanks for the information, Doctor."

"You're welcome." Click.

There had to be employees at Zeus Chemical who were involved in his father's illegal drug trade. By the tone in her voice, he could tell that Dr. Covington didn't like him. But could he trust her to help him find out who those complicit employees might be? He'd have to speculate about that later. He pocketed his phone as he joined his less than law-abiding employees.

His back to the others, Harold asked in a low voice, "That call shake you up? You look spooked."

Maxwell now doubted his own poker face. A quick headshake to snap himself to attention and a big smile for everyone to see. "I'll tell you all about it, depending on what our new friend has to say, Mr...?"

The homeless man had a forward slouch and kept his hands close to his chest while looking skyward over his shoulder, but didn't reply.

Fat Mikey cleared his throat. "Bert. Our friend here goes by Bert."

Upon hearing his name, Bert snapped around, eyes wide as if he had forgotten where he was and how he got there. After staring at each man for a minute, his demeaner calmed, but he kept a suspicious eye on Maxwell. "Yeahp. Bert. That's me. Your friend, Bert."

Fat Mikey moved a bit closer to Bert and gestured to Maxwell. "Okay, Bert, this is our buddy, Max, who we been telling you about. He's very interested to hear what you told us."

"Told you?"

"Yeah, Bert. About the clown."

"The clown. Yeahp, I know about the clown."

"You do?" Maxwell asked, softening his voice to make himself less threatening, but it came across as demeaning, like he was talking to a kindergartener. A quick throat clear and he asked, "What do you know?"

"He lives there. Yeahp, there."

Bert pointed at a rowhome with cheap green siding, faded and stained.

"Really?" Maxwell asked. "Ever been inside?"

Bert laughed, not a single tooth in his mouth, and shuffled his feet. "No, nope, no. Ain't never."

Harold lowered his voice and directed it toward Maxwell. "According to Mikey and Big, Bert pointed out that same house the two times they talked to him earlier. I did some research before we got here. It's owned by a guy named Keith Donnevuccio."

"Wait. Keith the Clown is really a guy named Keith?"

Harold shrugged. "Hiding in plain sight."

"Have you seen him recently?" Maxwell asked Bert.

Bert grabbed the back of his own neck and looked skyward again. After gumming his lips for a moment, he looked back at the rowhomes and shook his head. "No. Nope. Saw him about a week ago in a van I ain't seen him in before. He sometimes does that. Yeahp. Comes and goes in his van and comes and goes in vans I ain't never seen him in before."

Harold nodded. "Police say that Keith the Clown steals vans and swaps license plates. Gotta be him, gotta be his place."

Maxwell's father had been intelligent, but not an expert. His wisdom was found in trusting the experts, trusting those who knew more about the products than he did. Harold and his crew knew how to find things, people, information. If Harold thought this was where Keith lived, then Maxwell had no reason not to believe him. "Let's compensate our new friend and figure out the next step."

As Fat Mikey peeled off a few twenties from a thick wad to give to Bert, Harold leaned in close to Maxwell and said, "I think the next step is, we go in."

"Right now?" Maxwell hated that his voice almost squeaked.

Blunt Harold was professional enough to ignore Maxwell's moment of weakness. "Look around, Boss. It's nighttime. No one's gonna say shit about shit. Bert said Keith hasn't been here for a week, so his place should be empty."

The streets were devoid of any other people and Bert scampered to an alley two blocks away. Shadows were the denizens, and none of them spoke. Every cliché and idiom about opportunity passed through Maxwell's head. Hell, even if the police found their way to this neighborhood

– and Maxwell sincerely felt like they wouldn't – then Fat Mikey could use the rest of the twenties in his pocket to get them to look the other way. "You're right. Let's go in."

Little Big took less than five minutes to pick the lock. Maxwell winced and asked, "Shouldn't we have checked for trip wires or booby traps? From how the police profiled him, he seems like that kind of guy."

Harold nodded. "No sign of electronics, so a booby trap would be mechanical. Only two doors to the place, front and back, and according to Bert, this is the door Keith uses regularly. Too hard to rig and disarm every time. His back door might be rigged to napalm the place, but not the front door."

"I'll stand watch," Fat Mikey said as he assumed sentry on the small porch.

The interior was as small and grimy as expected, a simple living room with a door at the other end leading to the kitchen. A door with small curtains covering a tiny window led from the kitchen to the backyard. Maxwell made a conscious note not to touch that door.

He wondered if anyone brought a flashlight, but his concern was moot when Harold turned on the living room light.

"We need to be careful," Maxwell said. The looks on Harold's and Little Big's faces told him they thought he was overreacting, so he clarified. "Keith is making drugs. Not normal street drugs, but some really messed up stuff. The incident at the mall? Where regular people started killing other people? That's the drug he makes. It literally makes people go violently insane."

Harold nodded and then pointed at Little Big. "Don't touch nuthin'! I don't need you knocking shit around and making me go nuts."

Little Big smirked and raised his hands. "No worries. I ain't touchin' nuthin'."

"Good. Check around upstairs. Mr. Templeton and I will look around in the basement."

Little Big started up the staircase. "Basement's always where the creepy shit is anyway,"

The basement door was next to a small closet in the kitchen. And Little Big's sentiment about the basement had been understated.

A single overhead light bulb was enough to illuminate the entire basement. Every step Maxwell took farther into the room offered a new chill along his spine. Flimsy racks full of outfits lined the one wall while a few trunks labeled "magic tricks" were scattered about. A glass cabinet showcased a bunch of props. A small bureau in the corner had a lighted mirror and shelves of makeup.

Maxwell tried to avoid the shelves of creepy wigs. Each wig rested on a Styrofoam head, white with facial expressions drawn on in black marker. A dozen angered and crazed faces stared at Maxwell, made more off-putting by the rainbow of curly hairstyles adorning them.

A computer was on an ersatz desk made from plywood, and Maxwell sat in the accompanying chair. Anything to keep the collection of severed foam-heads from staring at him.

"I'm able to get in," Maxwell said to his own surprise. Either the system was so old that it predated login passwords or Keith was so confident that he never felt the need to create one.

Harold mumbled about the place being a freak show and ambled over to the desk. "Yeah? Anything interesting?"

"Don't know yet." Maxwell found the main directory and clicked random folders until he found one labeled, "Immortality." That folder led to a five more, each with a woman's name. He clicked on "Lily" and quickly learned that they weren't names of women. His throat constricted and he mouthed, "Oh my God."

Something ticked from the back of the basement, but Maxwell was too disgusted by what he was looking at to react.

Harold yelled, "Run!"

Maxwell turned to Harold, now looking at a box attached to the furnace with a red flashing light. Harold grabbed the back of Maxwell's jacket and yanked him to his feet. "Run, now!"

Flashing red light. Furnace. It took a heartbeat for Maxwell to realize what that meant. *Wait! Not yet!* One more heartbeat and Maxwell lunged toward the desk and the CPU tower.

The Killer of Devils

Harold took off up the stairs, yelling, "Run! Get outta the house! Now!"

Cables flying, Maxwell yanked the CPU free and ran. Faster. Faster! Two steps at a time, tripping, banging the CPU off the step, righting himself fast enough to catch up to Harold in the kitchen.

Little Big was halfway down the second floor when the first explosion rattled the house, enough for Maxwell to stumble and almost drop the machine. The second explosion was bigger; the conflagration of heat slapped Maxwell's back as he was launched out the front door, landing hard on the sidewalk.

"Car!" He heard Harold yell, but it sounded like he was underwater.

Get up, Maxwell, get up! Shoulder throbbing, he got to his knees and almost collapsed again from the wind getting knocked out of him. The CPU – had it broken? He sat up, dazed, but cognizant enough to reach out toward the machine. It lay beside him in one piece. He hoped its insides weren't damaged.

Every dog in the neighborhood was barking. People were coming out of their houses. Sirens would be any second.

Fat Mikey and Little Big were already in the car's backseat. Maxwell climbed to his feet and ran as if the townhouse reached for him with giant flaming fingers.

Hopping in the passenger seat, Maxwell hugged the CPU and slammed the door as Harold pulled away from the curb, tires squealing. He watched Keith's neighbors, standing and gaping at the burning home and wondered how he could compensate them while remaining anonymous. Breaking and entering. Searching for a killer clown. Causing a fire. Almost dying. Too much. It was all too much. His brain started to tickle again.

June 30, 2002

A few days of bedrest – imposed by Mother – were followed by a few nights of impotent "patrol," which meant driving around the city and looking for anything suspicious. Nothing more suspicious than a twenty-four-year-old blonde driving a black Explorer through unsavory neighborhoods.

Frustrated, Cali's mind wandered down alleys darker than the ones she drove through. Last night's "patrol" yielded a foot cramp and a wasted half tank of gas. Tonight was no different and she somehow found herself in front of Dallas' apartment building. *Oh, that's right, I sent him a booty-call text and he sent me his address.* He was out, but asked her to wait.

Twenty minutes later, he arrived with dinner. Sex first, then dinner, sex, live band at the local bar, more sex after they got back to his place. It was nice to lay next to someone. That was what she needed. A "normal" night, a night like she used to have before she made it her mission to keep monsters from turning other people's worlds upside down like they had done to her. A mission she had been failing, as evidenced by last week's clusterfuck in King of Prussia.

"Your head seems to be crushing your heart," Dallas said, lying naked next to her.

"You talk weird."

Dallas chuckled and tucked a lock of her sweat-clumped hair behind her ear. "Sorry. You seem like you have a lot on your mind. I'm right here for pillow talk if you care to share."

Cali stared at the ceiling, her mind creating swirls and eddies in shapes that didn't exist. "I feel guilty."

"For the sex?"

"Yeah. Well, I feel guilty for having fun while letting other people down."

"Nothing wrong with recharging your batteries. You can't help anyone if you're drained emotionally. And spiritually. And physically. It's like what airline attendants say right before takeoff – in case of emergency, put on your own oxygen mask first before helping others."

Cali turned to look into his eyes. Intense, earnest. Truthful. Enlightened. "In case of emergency, huh? You believe I needed an emergency recharge?"

"I do."

It wasn't just the strangers at the mall who she had let down. It was also people she knew and had been ignoring this past week. Melody. Chism. Bethany. She felt too inadequate to associate with them, but – *God damn it* – that meant she was making decisions for them without their input or knowledge. She sighed and rolled over to grab her cell phone from the nightstand. "Mind if I send a few texts and then pass out?"

He kissed her softly between her shoulder blades. "Course not. Like I said, you need to heal yourself before you can heal others."

"You were the frat house shaman, weren't you?"

Dallas rubbed his finger up and down her arm and gave her rhythmic kisses along her back while she sent and received texts.

Cali fell asleep and then woke, phone still in her hand, before 9:00 a.m. Refreshed from a night of dreamless sleep.

The shower felt great. Nothing special about the showerhead or the water pressure, and the soap was a mass-produced bar. It just felt good to let the warm water wash away her mild hangover, the lingering aromas from the concert venue, and the dried sweat from last night's sex.

Fully dressed, she entered the living room. Dallas was cooking, shirtless of course. "Wanna stay for breakfast?"

"Can't. Meeting one of the friends I've been letting down for brunch. Don't worry, I'm going with fully charged batteries."

"Good to know. *Namaste.*"

"Fuckin' weirdo," Cali said, enjoying his laughter as the door shut behind her.

Butterflies flitted through her stomach while on her way to see Melody at the same restaurant where they had last met. Odd that she was eager to face down murderous psychopaths who dressed like clowns but uneasy about meeting an old friend. *That's because I know where I stand with psychopathic murder clowns.*

Melody was sitting at a table for two when Cali entered the restaurant. She made no effort to stand as Cali approached. She looked away while taking a sip of her Bloody Mary, using the celery stalk as a stirring stick.

Cali waved to a waiter and pointed to Melody's drink.

She cleared her throat. "Hi, Mel."

Melody took a bite of her celery, crunching noisily. "This is exactly the kind of place you, me, and Dakota would have loved. I feel like I'm looking into the past while trying to get a glimpse of our future."

"Nothing wrong with nostalgia."

"That's just it, isn't it? Nostalgia implies that things will never go back to the way they once were."

"Nothing wrong with that either. You can't grow by moving backward." Cali stifled a smirk – she had heard those words in Dallas' voice.

"Growth? Is that what we're calling this?"

"We've grown, Mel."

"But you've grown into a murderer."

"That's a bit reductive considering your boyfriend's father started me down this path when he killed my father. And don't forget, Roger Templeton is also the reason Dakota will never be able to meet us at this restaurant."

The pink hue of emotion colored Melody's cheeks. She took another sip of her drink and another chomp of celery. Her hand was shaking. Her eyes were as pink as her cheeks and filled with tears. Every celery crunch irritated Cali, and she wondered if Melody was intentionally trying to provoke her. Probably, but every one of Melody's tears calmed that irritation. She had a vision of her mother holding up a card that read, "Tact."

Cali took a deep breath. "I didn't mean to be so blunt. There are reasons why I am the way I am. They're complicated, to say the least."

Melody dabbed at the tears on her cheeks as she regarded Cali. Her eyes reflected the flicker of something burning within. "Last time we met you said you hunt monsters."

"I do."

"When was the last time you killed one?"

"A week ago, at the mall. And then a week prior in New York. A set of triplets. Tall, lanky, pale. They kidnapped and tortured young women. I killed all three of them and helped one of their victims escape."

Melody's high horse bucked her, kicking away her righteous indignation. "Oh my God. You're serious, aren't you."

The waiter dropped off a Bloody Mary and moved on. After a large, gulping swig, Cali wiped her mouth with the back of her hand. "As serious as the liver disease this drink is giving me."

"I thought... I just..."

Cali knew what Melody thought, that she had killed Maxwell's father and justified it by playing pretend. Melody chewed her celery like it was a bitter pill of realization. Cali reached across the table and grabbed her hand. "It's okay. Not sure I'd believe me either if I hadn't been living it for the past couple of years."

"So, you are really hunting the clowns?"

"I am."

Melody shifted in her seat and uncomfortably glanced around the restaurant.

Cali squeezed her hand. "What's on your mind?"

"Maxwell... Well, he discovered something."

"About the clowns?"

"Yes. He's been obsessed with them. I didn't discourage him, because this is the first time in a year he hasn't been obsessed with his father's death or believing you're still alive. I didn't know he'd do this, but he went to the mall right after the incident and snooped around. He said he found an open canister, like a thermos, with a bit of powdery-type residue in it."

Cali went rigid. An image of Keith coming at her with an open canister flashed through her mind. "That fucker."

Melody cocked her head and raised her brow.

Cali explained. "At the mall, I was... in a bad tactical position and one of the clowns opened a canister in front of me."

"How'd you get out?"

"Mom. A few well-placed smoke grenades and even better placed bullets. I'm assuming the powder is dangerous."

"It is. He said there was enough to send to his lab."

"Max has a lab?"

"One of the companies he now owns is a biochemical company. They make fertilizers and plant food. They told him the powder is plant-based."

"That's... interesting."

Melody shook the ice in her empty glass. "It's similar to opium, but more extreme. It can literally make people go insane."

Cali pulled out her phone. "Might explain why people are going on crazy murder sprees." She texted Melody's information to her mom. She then looked up to Melody – the little girl she had known for decades, yet a complete stranger. "So... Now what?"

Melody stared at her for a moment, as if seeing Cali the same way. After a quick head shake like she was snapping out of a daydream, she grabbed the menu from the table. "I say we do what Dakota would have done."

Cali picked up a menu as well. "Eat and drink the afternoon away in blissful ignorance?"

"You got it."

The women ordered food and more drinks while coping with post-tragedy. They shared memories about Dakota, Tanner, and Jordon: laughing along with a joyful story from the past and then succumbing to melancholy, knowing there'd be no such stories for the future. Five hours and a healthy buzz later, the women settled their tab. A long embrace expressed the sorrows and joys of forgiveness.

Just like their last meeting, Cali asked, "You gonna tell Max about me?"

"I still don't know."

"Fair enough. Please stay away from this clown thing, Mel, and try to keep Max away from it, too."

Melody offered a sad smile. "I'll try, but you know Maxwell."

"I do," Cali whispered as they parted ways.

Her alcohol-clouded brain wanted to go back to the hotel room and pass out, but during her texting spree last night she had made a date with Chism. She was tempted to cancel – they hadn't made firm plans regarding when or where – but she'd do the decent thing and meet him. If she were still feeling squishy and sour, then she'd be adult enough to cancel while face-to-face, especially since his last text stated, Meet me at my place and we'll figure it out from there.

She had never been to his place. For the entire drive, she kept asking herself, *What am I doing?* Dallas was fun and interesting, but he could easily become "A guy I know in Philly." Chism? He was different. Boyfriend material. One day the clown situation would end, and then what? She'd move to Philly? *Not happening!* Chism move to…? *Ugh, I don't even have a permanent residence.* A normal dating life was impossible.

She knocked on his door, still with no decision made. Breaking up was the logical choice, the best choice for everyone.

He answered the door wearing a bright yellow Pikachu tee shirt two sizes too small and jeans that flattered everything jeans should flatter. Maybe it was because she had been thinking about Dallas mere minutes ago, but it disturbed her how similar they were. They looked alike and were the same size and build. *Shut up*, Bloody Mary said, *and enjoy the moment!*

"Hey, welcome to Castle Chism," he said with a smile that made Cali melt. "Come in."

The apartment was bland. Spacious living room, dining nook, kitchenette, bathroom, bedroom. Cali didn't care about his lack of décor, too enamored by the way his muscles moved under the flimsy material of the tee shirt. "Hey, yourself. And please never say the words, 'Castle Chism' ever again."

He broke into a wide smile. "They have been stricken from my vocabulary." He walked over to an end table and picked up a handful of brochures. "Here. I know it's a little lame to flip through brochures, but I don't want to make assumptions. You seem involved with… stuff… so I wanted you to pick something that matches your mood."

Skydiving. Indoor rock climbing. 8th Street Art Gallery. Philadelphia Zoo. Nope. Cali didn't want to do any of those things. She wanted to…

"Do you have any beer in the fridge?"

"Let me check."

Cali followed his ass to the kitchen and stopped at the doorway. As he checked the contents of his fridge, she took off her top.

"I have a six-pack," he said, head deep in the fridge. "No wait, two six-packs."

Cali shimmied out of her pants. "You got a favorite pizza shop nearby that delivers?"

"I do. It's just down—" Chism turned just in time to see Cali's bra hit the floor.

"I hope it's okay that I want to do something that's not in the brochures."

"Very okay. Encouraged even."

"Good. Now, show me where your bedroom is."

*

Cali's phone vibrated loud enough to wake her. 9:51. It was dark in Chism's bedroom, so she assumed 9:51 p.m. Bethany Pennington's name glowed on her cell phone display. Too groggy to speak coherently, she croaked, "Hello?"

"Uhh, hi, Cali. It's… It's Bethany. Did I wake you?"

Cali sat up and rubbed her eyes. Chism, naked, lay next to her asleep. Four hours of nonstop sex must have worn him out as well. "Nah. All good. What's up?"

"Well, you told me to call if anything out of the ordinary happened." There was a hitch in Bethany's breathing, clearly thinking the offer had been nothing more than politeness.

"I told you to call anytime, Bethany."

"Thank you. I was talking with a friend of mine. She reached out to me once she heard about the police investigating Keith for… what happened to Lily, and we got to talking. Her husband is a Pennsylvania senator – state level, not federal – and she said that one of the other senators – I think his name is Albright or something – called an emergency meeting at the Monticello Theatre for the day after tomorrow. I don't know if that has anything to do with anything, but I thought it sounded kind of weird, right?"

"The Monticello Theatre, not Harrisburg? And so close to the holiday? Yeah, I agree. Very weird. Weird enough for me look into it. So, is Justin back home?"

"Not yet, but the lawyer is hopeful, maybe next week. Thank you for everything you've done." Bethany sounded like she was on the verge of tears.

"You thanked me plenty. I'd love to hear more about Justin coming home, but I gotta go. And remember, call me anytime, okay? Anytime. I mean that. Talk to you later?"

"Okay. Thank you. Bye."

Cali dropped her phone back on the nightstand and laid back down. Chism rolled to face her and propped his head on his hand. "Everything okay?"

"Yep. Nothing to worry about."

"Emergency at the Monticello Theatre?"

Cali smirked. "You going to focus your energies on stupid questions or on trying to get me naked again?"

Chism worked up a cocky grin and pulled the covers off her. "Ta-da! Now you're naked again."

Cali jumped on top of him. "Good choice," she said, hoping he'd forget all about whatever he might have overheard.

July 1, 2002

It had been a week of not wreaking havoc on the world and Trina was the only thing that dulled Keith's anger. And *that* was only when she was jumping on his dick while feeding him cookies. Lying in bed, he licked stray crumbs from his mouth. *Where the hell does she keep getting cookies?*

Next to him, Trina leaned in close to his head. "I'm looking into your ear," she said. "Hello Keith's brain? What are those thoughts you think you're thinking?"

"I'm still thinking about my house."

She sat up. "Your house? Other than this one and my house next door?"

"Yeah. Where I kept my supplies and my trophies. News said it burned down last night. I'm upset about my trophies. And my videos."

Trina smacked his chest hard enough for him to wince. "Poop! I never got to visit your house. Or see your trophies. Or watch the videos of the goddesses you immortalized."

Keith had always wondered how Trina felt about his view of the world. Hypocritical society wanted to immortalize little goddesses on television, yet frowned upon the way he did it. "You'd want to see how I immortalize little goddesses?"

Trina gasped, then giggled. "I want to help you immortalize the little goddesses! I'm a racecar and racecars go fast!"

"You are and yes you do." He never thought he'd meet a woman he liked for longer than an hour. Never thought he'd meet a woman outside of a cheap motel room, let alone find a woman who viewed the world the way he did. Okay, maybe Trina's view of the world was crazy-bananas, but there were enough similarities between their visions. She supported him and wanted to participate in his ventures. And that felt good.

Keith wanted anarchy, chaos, destabilization. He wanted society's rules to crumble and burn. Collin and his beloved Master Poppie proclaimed that was their intent, though there hadn't been much movement in that direction. Tomorrow would be the deciding factor. If Collin could convert all those senators over to their crusade, then there was hope for a world Keith always dreamt about. If Collin failed, then Keith would take over. He'd kill Collin and Brin, take some canisters of white mist to a Phillies game and have some real fun. The others would follow him. It all hinged on tomorrow.

"Keithy!" Trina said as she smooshed his cheeks with her tiny hands. "What about the last goddess you immortalized?"

Crazy-bananas all right, but she made him laugh with her randomness. Gently pulling her hands away, he answered, "She's dead. I can't immortalize them if they're still alive."

"Duh! But didn't she live around here?"

"Yes, but she ain't here no more."

"Her house still has trophies, right?"

Being bat-shit nuts didn't make her stupid. "Heh! You're absolutely right."

"And she has parents, right?"

"Her dad's in jail, because of me."

Trina sat up, her pupils swirling. "What if we go visit her mommy-mom now. You said you saw her. You said you hated her. You said I could play with her. How about now? Right now, now? You can get more trophies, and I can make balloon animals."

"That's a great fuckin' idea!" Little Lily's mother had intervened in the woods and kept Keith from getting revenge on Calista, so he owed her payback. Collin's master plan wasn't until tomorrow, so Keith had plenty of time to kill.

Trina hopped off the bed and bounced around the bedroom a few times, giggling, and humming before opening the door. "I'm going to reapply my face." She ran her hands over her cheeks and chin. Even though her body glistened from sweat, big patches of paint flecked away to expose the red and raw skin underneath. "My fake face keeps trying to come through. Your fake face wants to come through, too, Keithy, so you better fix that."

Keith laughed as she bounded out of the room and down the hall toward the garage where the spray paint was kept. There was plenty of face paint in Judith's closet. Any color he needed. He stuck with the traditional white base, blue eyes, and red mouth. However, the blue over his eyes angled inward and his red smile was sharp with the corners coming to points. No wig, so he spread the white all over his recently shaved head. Little Lily's mother would not forget this face. Of course, she wouldn't be seeing it for too long, knowing Trina's intentions. He dressed differently from his usual clown attire – black pants and suit jacket, but no shirt, because Trina would like that.

He thought of excuses and stories to give Collin as to where he and Trina were going. But as he walked down the hall, he realized he didn't need an excuse. The only other two people in the house were Delvin and Judith. A nuclear bomb could go off and those two wouldn't notice, too busy tying tiny bows to the matted fur of their purses. Were Collin and the others at Trina's house? Or out somewhere? Half of him was angry that he didn't know, thanks to Collin's shitty communication. The other half didn't care, too excited about going back to Little Lily's to get trophies. Extra excited, actually, because with Trina along, he didn't have to be sneaky about it. He decided that it didn't matter what Collin was doing right now. All that mattered was tomorrow. In the meantime, Keith and Trina were going to have some fun!

Trina put on her green girl's uniform, then sprayed the finishing touches on her true face.

"Lookin good! All ready, you little hotrod?"

Trina dropped the spray paint, the can clattering on the cement floor, and sauntered toward Keith. "Vroom, vroom, Keithy. Vroom, vroom."

July 1, 2002

Cali picked the lock to the backdoor of the Monticello Theatre, the evening dark enough for nearby streetlights to pop on. Cali didn't need the light; picking locks was natural, easy as choosing a dress from the closet or selecting the right shade of lipstick. *The new normal.* She chose this life. Yes, terrible things happened that pushed her in this direction, but she made a conscious decision to pursue this crusade, to forsake the old normal.

But, God, the morning had been nice.

She had woken up with her head on Chism's chest, his arms around her. At first, she thought she was in a parallel, alternate universe where men liked to cuddle. But as her sleepy-time fog lifted, she realized Chism was the lone guy who liked to cuddle. Any time she tried to snuggle with Tanner at night, it'd always be something lame like, "Babe, you know I have sensitive skin. I don't want a rash in the morning." That from the same douchebag who, whenever he forgot to shave, chafed the insides of her thighs from the rare moments of reciprocation. Chism was no Tanner. In a good way!

Tanner focused on being as buff as possible, or on stupid side hustles, and then had the gall to say it was all for her. Yes, she'd sometimes go cross-eyed whenever she got a good look at him naked, but that didn't justify him blaming her for his need to hit the gym. He had more skincare products than she did, haircare products as well. She practically needed clearance from the NSA to get into his closet or drawers, lest she screw up his system.

Chism wasn't like that at all. Super chill. Though, this morning, he got a little sensitive about his bonsai trees.

Groomed like potted poodles, they sat along the windowsill of his kitchen. While cooking eggs, Cali accidentally spilled the salt. As superstition dictates, she threw salt over her shoulder, and some accidentally hit the trees. Much to her surprise, Chism said, "Whoa!

She thought he was joking, because it was just salt, but he took the potted plants and dusted stray grains off the leaves. Cali squinted and asked, "Ummmm…?"

Chism played it off with a chuckle. "I know I overreacted, but I use these little guys as relaxation therapy. I'm sure that amount of salt wouldn't have done any harm."

"Why would *any* amount of salt do *any* harm?"

"Plants and trees don't like salt. Kind of kills them. That's how ancient armies fucked with the territory they invaded. Ever hear the term, 'salt the earth?' They'd salt the earth to destroy the crops and farmland."

"Hunh. I thought the phrase, 'salt of the earth,' was a good thing."

"It is. That came from the Bible. Back then, salt was valuable. Today, not so much. Next time you're on the internet, check out salt flats around the world. Massive, evaporated areas that used to be bodies of water. Now, nothing grows in them. Big ones are in Bolivia, Botswana, Pakistan."

"Ever been to any of those places?"

"No."

She felt a tad disappointed in his "no." It was stupid to feel that way. And unfair, because she was suddenly comparing him to Linda. She compared Chism to Tanner, and that was unfair to Tanner. He was no longer alive, so he couldn't defend himself or grow as a person. Comparing Chism to Linda? Cali had known Linda for only two days, but she was pretty confident that she had fallen in love with her. Or could have fallen in love with her. Linda was intelligent, wise, adventurous, and empathetic. Without a doubt, if Linda was still alive, she'd jump on the first flight to Bolivia, Botswana, or Pakistan to go see salt flats. Life with Linda was a perfect snapshot without flaws because Cali never had a chance to see them. And that wasn't fair to Chism.

"Everything okay?" Mother's voice entered Cali's ear and bounced around her brain, bringing herself back to the here and now, back to the Monticello Theatre door. "I thought I heard the latch click, but nothing else. Have you gone inside yet?"

The Killer of Devils

Cali shook her head. "Sorry. Just thinking. And being careful. Probably too careful. Entering now."

The back door opened to the end of a hallway, the word "EXIT," in glowing red letters above it. She walked past the dressing rooms and storage rooms. This was a recon mission to get a better understanding of the environment for tomorrow's meeting and to setup a possible ambush. She doubted the senators would need anything back here, so it'd do her no good to stake out these rooms. They'd be out front, in the audience seats.

The hallway led backstage. In school, she had never taken an interest in participating in plays or scripted drama. As a popular rich girl, she lived through plenty of unscripted drama. Thanks to her father insisting she be cultured, she had enjoyed live shows ranging from local theater to Broadway and everywhere in between. But she'd never been backstage. A weird sense of rebellion tickled her as she walked by the props and costumes. Fake walls, simple with brown, wooden doors and racks of peasant clothing in drab colors. It looked like a play she didn't want to see.

She walked past the rigging ropes tied to sandbags and examined the temporary scaffolding and permanent catwalks overhead. A few good areas to perch up there, but the metal beams could be problematic. Close to the stage was a workbench on wheels with various tools on top, at the ready should something go wrong with the set. She ran a finger over the ball-peen hammer.

On stage, she looked out to the empty seats.

The curtains were open, giving Cali an unobstructed view of the auditorium. There were almost a thousand seats among the three levels and side balconies. The auditorium walls were done in a gold and blue motif, a few fake windows and doorways giving the illusion of being in an Italian plaza. She felt exposed. She never liked the spotlight, the notion of being famous. The idea of people sitting in front of her and watching her every move sent slime down her spine. "You took care of the cameras?"

"Yep," her mother replied. "Right before you got to the building."

"Standing on stage gives me the creeps. But the theater is nice."

A podium and a few folding chairs were on stage, ready for tomorrow. Cali stood behind the podium, calculating which balconies would give her the best tactical access to the stage.

"Helmet!" she heard from a deep voice, stage left.

She turned just as the helmet-wearing clown slammed into her and drove her to the ground. *Right in the fucking ribs!*

A second clown in a black overcoat sprang from within the curtain folds. He, too, flung himself at her. All she saw were two red handprints over his eyes on a milk-white face when he landed on top of the helmet-head clown.

"Get her to her feet." A man's voice, but not Keith's. "And take her guns away from her."

Cali didn't struggle. She wanted to see what she was dealing with first as Helmet and Red Hands grabbed her arms. They tossed her guns and magazines across the stage, and yanked her to her feet, their grip unyielding.

An overweight man stood about a foot away from her, his furry belly button peeking out from under an ill-fitting and half-unbuttoned work shirt. Face painted yellow, a line of black streaked over his mouth. Drips of red ran from the circles around his eyes. At first, she thought he was the one who gave the command, but his smile was a landscape of broken teeth, and his eyes were windows to an empty room. He stepped forward and Cali winced as he dragged his tongue from her shoulder to her cheek. "She tastes like pain." His laugh sounded like a drowning man's gurgles.

"I'm sure she does." This voice belonged a tall, muscular man done up as a more traditional clown with his brown wig, white face paint, blue eye circles, and red mouth. He was the one in command. "She's been a pain in my ass for weeks."

The clowns broke out into exaggerated laughter, including the man and woman on either side of the leader. The woman's long green hair didn't look like a wig. Her yellow and jagged painted-on smile made her real, gleeful smile crooked. The purple around her eyes, a square over her left and a triangle over her right, made her look like a lunatic.

White paint also covered the other man's face. Two orange upside-down chevrons covered each eye while a large orange "V" was drawn down his cheeks to his mouth, with the point finishing on his chin.

"Where's your boss?" Cali asked. "Where's Keith?"

The muscular clown's cackle sounded fake. "I answer to no one other than Master Poppie. We *all* answer to him." His voice also sounded fake. But... familiar?

"Master Poppie? Is that the name of the sock you jerk off into? And that's your master?"

The leader frowned. He clenched his fists and stepped forward. "Master Poppie is a god! He will be your new god, *everyone's god*, soon enough!" His affected voice was nowhere near as jovial.

Besides his voice, something seemed familiar. His jawline. His cheekbones. His nose. No, not seemed – definitely familiar. The face paint threw off his smile and expressions, but Cali knew that face.

A lump bulged in the back of her throat.

It was Tanner's face.

But Tanner was dead. She had seen his decapitated head on a hook hanging from a ceiling. Zebadiah Seeley, an unkillable killer, had mutilated and half-eaten him. It was beyond impossible that this leader of the clowns was Tanner.

But there were two other men who looked like Tanner.

Chism.

Dallas.

Thanks to a recent epiphany regarding her decision-making process when it came to dating, she had "a type." The last three men she dated looked alike. They looked like this clown. But the blue makeup over his eyes and massive red mouth... She couldn't tell exactly who this was. "So, mysterious captor, care to tell me your name?"

He laughed, a poorly acted cackle of craziness. "And I thought I was the funny one."

Cali focused on his words, strained to hear the resemblance to Chism or Dallas. Nothing, no familiar accent or dialect. She then turned to the yellow-faced slob, his tongue dangling from his mouth like a caught fish. "Hey, Licky, what's his name?"

"Collin," he mumbled.

"Sally!" The female clown snapped at Licky. "Don't talk to her."

"Pssst, Sally," Cali said with an exaggerated whisper. Once she got his attention, she nodded toward the clown with the "V" on his face. "How about him? What's his name?"

"Sally, no!" Collin snapped.

Sally looked from Cali to Collin, then back again. Insanity was prevalent, but his eye flickered with a spark. Sally knew the clown's name and wanted to share it.

As much as it turned her guts, Cali flicked her hair behind her shoulder and tilted her head to expose her neck. Fighting to keep the squirming worms in her stomach, she said, "Free lick if you tell me his name."

Sally leered at her, then dragged his twitching raw oyster of a tongue along her neck, chin, and cheek. He stepped back, and the snail juice slid over her ear. To her surprise, though, he honored his end of the deal and said, "That's Manchester Albright."

"All I needed to hear," Mother said.

The rifle's silencer muffled the shot. Manchester winced and grabbed his shoulder, the "V" on his face extra pointed from twisting in pain. Another shot. Clutching his chest, he dropped to the ground. One more shot and he curled up into a fetal position. No blood. Not a drop. Mother had loaded her gun with rubber bullets. They wanted at least one of these weirdos alive to interrogate.

A rubber bullet bounced off Helmet's helmet. He loosened his grip and teetered. Arm free, Cali jabbed her fingertips into Red Hands' throat. They had taken away her guns, but left her knife.

Time to make them regret that oversight.

Collin and the woman tried to get to Manchester, who was still curled in the fetal position, but Mother kept them at bay with well-placed shots. One hit the woman in the leg, taking her down.

Cali swung a quick knife stab to Sally's gut, and he bent forward. She grabbed the back of his head and kneed his chin. After what sounded like

The Killer of Devils

a wet branch snapping, Sally bit his tongue and severed it. The fat pink slug tumbled through the air. A blubbering cry and the clown dropped to the floor, blood pooling around his face.

"Helmet!" Helmet screamed, announcing himself as he charged Cali. She spun out of the way and swept her knife across his ribs as he passed by. The reward of painting the stage floor red was instant.

"Helmet!" Another charge, another miss, and another slash.

These attacks were easily dodged and counterattacked, but they gave Red Hands enough time to recuperate. He rushed Cali as she dodged Helmet for the third time. A right hook connected with her cheek, and a bloom of stars burst into her view. Instinct took over and she timed his next punch to roll with it and over Helmet's back. Using Helmet as a shield, she kept behind him. Red Hands jumped out of the way, right into the elbow Cali threw. The hit was solid, but he spun and crouched down, throwing a punch to her gut. *Right in the fucking ribs! Again!*

Her forearm blocked his next punch, and she lunged, the tip of her knife outward. Thrusting his hips aside, Red Hands dodged the attack. Cali spun to backhand him in the ribs.

Red Hands blocked low, exposing his smiling, cackling face. She threw a punch and a knife swipe. Red Hands raised his arms to block her attacks, triggering noises of releasing springs and metal sliding against metal. Guns popped out from the sleeves of his overcoat, now in his hands.

Well, shit!

"Helmet!" Helmet was not stealthy, and his heavy footfalls reverberated through the wood of the stage floor. Spin, duck, pop up, and Cali continued to use him as a shield. That didn't stop Red Hands from unloading the clips of both guns.

The human body wasn't the best form of defense against bullets, but it was better than nothing, and Helmet carried more girth than the average human. Cali fought the urge to scream as bullets sunk with a splat into Helmet's body and whizzed by her. Two punched her right leg. Her tactical micro-mesh was designed to fend off knife attacks, not bullets, but it – and Helmet's body – had stopped them from piercing her leg. But they still hurt like a motherfucker!

A rubber bullet struck Collin's shoulder, knocking him back a few feet. "Ahh! Fuck! Brin! Red! We have to go!" he shouted.

"What flows from the cracked Earth will bathe the world red," Red Hands yelled, chasing after Collin and the green-haired woman as they ran off the stage. Cali started after them, but her right leg gave out, the pain too shocking. *Up. Up. Get up!* She stood and limped in their direction, hoping the pain would subside as she worked herself into a gimpy run. A gun was in her path, and she grabbed it as she shuffled by. She gimped through the backstage area toward the hallway and the dressing rooms up ahead.

Flames erupted in a bright flash. "Fuck!"

Hands over her face, Cali rushed through the fire just as her phone buzzed. *Double fuck.*

"Cali? What's wrong?" Her mother asked.

Ready to shoot the slightest movement, Cali continued toward the exit door.

"Fire. Do you need assistance apprehending Manchester?"

"Negative. He's still curled up onstage. Continue your pursuit."

Head on a swivel, gun pointing at everything, Cali continued to the door. She kicked it open and crouched. Nothing. Empty parking lot. Streetlights. Decorative hedges lining the perimeter. Glancing at every shadow, she stepped outside. *Control breathing. Focus. Be ready for anything.* She listened for crazed clown laughter, keeping her back to the building. *If one of those fuckers tries to jump me…*

Cali was ready for anything, except for nothing.

Frustrated, she almost threw her phone when it buzzed again. Bethany. She'd left a message. Still training her gun on shadows, Cali pushed play.

"Hi, Cali. Sorry to bother you. I… I feel stupid. I'm probably being nervous and paranoid and silly." She took an audible breath and exhaled slowly. "My flood lights keeping coming on, but when I look outside, I don't see anything, other than the neighborhood cat."

The Killer of Devils

Cali heard the sound of breaking glass, and right after that, Bethany screamed.

Sirens grew closer as the fire raged behind Cali, hot flames licking toward her. "Mom? Are you and the senator out of the building."

"Affirmative. I'm going to tie him up and interrogate him."

"I just got a message from Bethany. She's in trouble."

"Understood. Go check on her."

Cali crouched and shuffled to her rental, checking underneath it and in the backseats, visualizing a Jack-in-the-Box popping out and shooting the shit out of her. "Where'd you fuckers go?" she asked aloud, eyes sweeping the parking lot. Then she hopped in the SUV and sped toward Bethany's.

July 1, 2002

Bethany Pennington stood in the doorway of her daughter's room as she had done a hundred times before. She'd never get used to seeing it empty. Quiet. Lifeless. She had sobbed so hard her ribs cracked at the thought of Lily never coming back, never filling the room, never adding laughter to it, never bringing life to the stuffed animals and toys. She wanted to throw everything away and repaint the room. She also wanted to turn it into a shrine leaving everything completely untouched. The answer was somewhere in the middle, she knew. It'd feel good to drop the boulder she'd been carrying on her shoulders these past couple of weeks. *Why did I dump all my wine? The whiskey and vodka, sure, but the wine?*

Turning away from the room, Bethany massaged her temples. Thoughts like that no longer belonged in her head. She'd leave Lily's room as is, for now. It wouldn't be fair to make any decision without her husband. An image of Justin hit her hard – she paused in the hallway to collect herself. The lawyer was filing the paperwork to get him home. Soon.

A warmth with her chest carried Bethany to the refrigerator for a bottle of sparkling water. Yes, there'd be awful emotions to work through, but she'd help Justin work through them, then they'd figure out what to do with Lily's room, together. Hell, they might not want to stay in this house anymore. Especially when she tells him that murder clowns might be their neighbors.

Bethany peeked through the slats of her blinds at the house across the street. What did she *really* know about the Millers? They were an older couple who kept to themselves, but they liked her. She'd been inside their house plenty of times, shared many conversations. They were two of the few people who supported Justin from the very beginning. Probably not murder clowns. But her other neighbors?

Bethany's porch light flicked on. Motion sensors. Clutching the sparkling water bottle close to her chest, she peeked through the blind slats

The Killer of Devils

again. From this angle, she could see her front door well enough to know no one was there. Probably an animal got too close. Cats and foxes and deer were often the cause.

Feeling silly for being so paranoid, Bethany aimed for the couch. Remote in hand, she was ready to find something mindless to help her forget her fears, until she heard a thump from outside. She held the remote like a knife in her shaking hand.

Animals sometimes messed with the trash cans. The raccoons were her nemesis, and her cans were full. *Yeah, that's it. Just a raccoon or something.*

The floodlights over the glass patio doors popped on and Bethany jumped. No more fake knife; time for a real one. *Could be an animal, but assumptions make an ass out of u and my corpse.* She hurried through the kitchen to grab the butcher's knife. The floodlights turned off.

She drew the patio door blinds. Slowly exposing the darkness outside one inch at a time, knife tapping against the glass, her eyes strained as she searched the blackness of her backyard. She only saw the outline of her patio furniture. She opened the blinds farther.

The lights snapped on and Bethany jumped back, thrusting the knife forward. The tip bounced off the glass door. The neighborhood stray cat was perched on her patio table. Bethany stifled a scream. "Son of a bitch!" She slapped the glass.

The cat meowed, jumped off the table, and scampered away.

The lights turned off.

Heart racing, gripping a fistful of her own shirt, Bethany stepped away from the glass doors. Stupid cat! But something inside her tingled, a primal sense of unease. She pulled her cellphone out of her pocket and dialed.

Cali didn't answer. She called again, then decided to leave a message. "Hi, Cali. Sorry to bother you. I... I feel stupid. I'm probably being nervous and paranoid and silly. My flood lights keeping coming on, but when I look outside, I don't see anything, other than the neighborhood cat."

The patio light snapped on again. This time it wasn't the cat.

It was a clown.

With a brick in his hand.

Bethany screamed.

One hit was all it took to break the glass door.

Bethany jerked, dropping the phone. Her thoughts barely registered that a man with a clown face had broken her patio door and had stepped into her house, let alone to use the knife in her hand. *Run*, was the only thought in her head. *Run!*

When she turned, another clown, a woman at least half a foot shorter than her, stood in her way. Her face was painted silver and gold, including her teeth exposed by her pernicious smile. She was dressed like a child in a green scouting uniform. She snatched the knife from Bethany's hand. "I'll take that!"

A second word exploded into Bethany's mind – *push!* As the gold and silver clown reeled her arm back to stab, Bethany pushed. With a solid shove to the clown's chest, she flew backward, slamming into the dining room table.

"Trina!" the other clown called out.

Run, returned to the forefront of Bethany's mind. Bedroom. Pushing the clown bought her enough time to make it to the stairs, no other option since the clowns were blocking her exit. Top of the stairs, she turned into her bedroom, shut the door, and pushed her dresser in front of it. *Phone!* No dial tone to the landline; undoubtedly the clowns cut the wires. *Closet!* Bethany ripped handfuls of clothes and hangers out of her way. She squeezed in and looked up to the attic access panel, a three-foot square. Recently, Justin had installed a floor safe in the closet. Bethany stood on it to reach the access panel. After two hits, the panel moved free.

"Where are you, bitch!" the male clown yelled, his voice muffled. Wouldn't be long before they figured it out.

Bethany's mind raced faster than her heart, sweat pouring over her face and stinging her eyes. Using the hanger pole, the wall, the shelving, she pulled herself up. Her foot slipped, and she yelped.

SLAM! The clown slammed into her bedroom door.

"No, no, no, no, nonononono," Bethany mumbled to herself, shoulders burning, one arm in the attic. She grabbed the ledge with her other hand, her foot slipping off the wall.

SLAM! SLAM!

Bethany grimaced as lightning bolts of pain struck every muscle from her chest to her hips, tightening as she pushed and pulled herself into the attic. After fighting her way through, she returned the access panel. Hardly enough to stop the clowns.

SLAM! SLAM!

No way the man could fit through the hole. But the woman? Easily, and probably more deftly than Bethany.

SLAM! SLAM!

It had been over a year since she had been up here, but she remembered where everything was, including the chest holding old trinkets bequeathed to her by her grandmother. It was ten feet away and heavy.

SLAM! SLAM!

Bent at the waist, she stood over it and lifted it by the handles, a fire in her lower back as she pulled. Random sheets of plywood were scattered about to act as ersatz flooring for the dusty treasures, but exposed rafters threatened her balance. With a grunt, she twisted and swung the chest a couple feet and dropped it back onto the rafters. She shuffled closer to the access panel and repeated the process. Six feet to go.

CRASH!

"Where are you, bitch!" the man yelled. The woman's laughter flitted into the attic like discontent bats. Eyes stinging from sweat, tears, pain, fear, Bethany lifted and swung the chest again. Four feet to go.

Sounds of furniture being overturned. "Where is she, Keithy?" the woman asked.

Keith? Bethany froze. *As in Keith the Clown? The man who took my Lily from me is in my house? In my bedroom?*

More slamming noises. Keith sounded closer when he said, "She's gotta be in here."

Move! Move faster. Lift. Swing. Drop. Two feet to go.

"Why are there messy clothes on the messy bed, Keithy?" Trina asked.

"Clothes... Closet!" Bifold doors crashed open. Hangers smacked into each other. "She's not here. How could she not be... Ah ha! I'm coming to get ya!"

The rustling of more hangers and the clatter of him climbing onto the safe. Bethany called forth one last burst of energy and dropped the chest on the access panel just as it lifted.

"Ow!" he yelled. "Fuck!"

Bethany draped herself over the chest, flexing every muscle as if it would make her heavier. She twitched every time Keith yelled an obscenity, and her bladder almost gave out when he punched at the chest's bottom. She guessed that about two hundred pounds was keeping him out of the attic, but the chest moved each time he pounded against it. *SLAM! SLAM!*

Trina's shrill laughter shredded Bethany's nerves, minute after interminable minute.

Finally, Keith's pounding stopped.

"You think you're safe?" Keith yelled. "You think we can't get you? We got time. We got all the time in the world!"

Bethany knew he was right. He had broken through her patio door. Did any of her neighbors hear? Doubtful. She and Justin bought the house because of the healthy separation between homes. Even if someone heard, would they even call the police? After Justin got arrested, most of her friends and family disappeared as they assumed the worst. No chance of someone dropping by. She wouldn't last all night in the attic. She needed to think of something.

Silence. Other than the beat of her heart thumping through her head. No shouting from Keith, no cackling from Trina. No sounds of scuffling in her bedroom. Did they leave? Impossible. Listening closely, she *thought* she heard movement in a different part of the house. Where? What were they doing?

Bethany waited a few minutes. Her breathing had slowed, and she decided it'd be safe to slide off the chest. Careful to use only the rafters – she didn't want to fall through the drywall ceiling.

Lying down and bracing herself on the rafters, she leaned closer to a bare section of drywall and listened. Hearing nothing, she leaned closer. Holding her breath and trying desperately not to make a sound, her leg cramped and spasmed. The rafter creaked.

A butcher knife pierced the drywall.

Bethany froze, the blade close enough for her to see her reflection.

"You dropped this!" Keith shouted from directly below. The blade twisted, then was pulled out, gauging out a hole. His fist punched through, his arm all the way up.

Fingers tangled in her hair. Shrieking, Bethany reared backward, but he yanked her forward. Smacking her head against the joist, starbursts of color exploded along her vision. Fighting through the pain, she thrust backward, lightning striking every spot where he'd ripped hair from her scalp.

Keith punched another hole through. Bethany sat on her haunches, frozen with panic and nausea, watching beefy hands tear away drywall, creating a space wide enough to crawl up through.

A silver and gold face emerged, wide-eyed and smiling maniacally. "Balloon animal time!"

Bethany kicked her heel into Trina's face. A satisfying bone-crack resounded, blood pouring from her nose.

"Bitch!" Trina yelled.

Bethany crouch-ran away as fast as she could.

Trina growled and drywall cracked as she climbed up into the attic.

Bethany wasn't an expert on spatial awareness or estimated distances, but she had a good idea where she was. Praying that she did, she crawled to where she thought the hallway met the staircase and positioned herself between studs. She hopped. The drywall cracked and split.

Trina scampered toward Bethany on all fours, snarling, her chest close to the rafters, a gold and silver spider with her tongue hanging from her mouth.

After another hop, Bethany fell through the ceiling – arms, back, and chest scraping against the jagged drywall – and crash-landed on the carpeted hallway floor. Flesh torn and bleeding, feet and ankles burning from impact, Bethany sprinted for the stairs.

Tripping would mean certain death, but she hit the stairs fast.

The staircase shook with Keith's every stomp right behind her.

Trina dropped from the ceiling and followed Keith, dragging the knife blade along the railing, singing, "Balloons! I want your balloons."

As soon as Bethany's feet hit the bottom landing, she ran toward the closest exit – the front door. The knob slipped from her grasp as Keith grabbed the back of her shirt and yanked her away.

"Bitch!" he yelled as he threw her back into the living room.

Garage. The only chance she had to get out of this was the garage. She'd hit the garage door opener and run, grabbing any of Justin's tools to use as a weapon. The first tool that came to mind was Justin's last purchase, an oversized screwdriver. She thought the footlong monstrosity was a joke, but Justin had insisted that he needed it. It had never been used, but she knew exactly where he had placed it – his workbench right by the door.

She burst into the garage and slammed the door shut behind her; it did nothing as Keith barreled through and smashed into her. Twisting, stumbling, fighting to stay on her feet, she careened off the hood of her car. Keith lunged forward and grabbed her shoulder, pulling her. She fell and he fell with her. Bethany rolled away, thrashing her feet, but he grabbed hold of her pant leg. Screaming her lungs raw, she kicked his nose, face, mouth, and cheek. Harder! Faster! Kick harder!

Keith wouldn't let go.

"Get her, Keithy!" Trina screamed from somewhere behind him. "Get me her balloons!"

Crying and wheezing, Bethany reached up for the garage door button, even though it was a mile from her fingers. She squirmed as Keith crawled on top of her, his body pinning her legs. Crawling over her, face hovering, he smiled. The stink of old cheese and rotten eggs weighed just as much as he did. She punched and hit and slapped, but he laughed from a bloodied face and grabbed her wrists, pinning her to the concrete floor. Sweat and drool and snot and blood rained upon her face.

She stopped fighting. Tears flowed faster as she thought that her Lily might have succumbed the same way, suffered the same struggle, and lost in the end. All she could do was cry and pray for a quick death, and hope she'd be reunited with her daughter soon.

The garage's side door crashed open, a black boot kicking it in.

Cali strode inside, a gun in her hands.

July 1, 2002

Cali brought the Explorer to a screeching halt in front of Bethany's house. Fifteen minutes to get anywhere in Philly was a minor miracle – blowing through stop signs twenty miles an hour over the speed limit helped – but had she been fast enough?

Gun drawn, Cali heard sounds of a struggle inside the garage. Crying. Screaming. No outside button to open the garage door. But there was a side door. Anger revved her heart, pumping adrenaline through her system, as she smashed her boot against the door.

Keith.

Trina.

"Bethany!"

The half second it took for her to register was all the time Keith needed. Jumping to his feet, he used Bethany as a shield and Trina tossed a butcher's knife to him. Crouching to best hide himself behind her, half his face was obscured by Bethany's head while the knife tip played under her chin. Trina scurried behind Keith. "Not so fast, Blondie," Keith said.

"Fast is all I know." It was a stupid response, but Cali needed to stall and get a read on her surroundings. One Lexus in the middle of the sprawling space. A workbench extended along the wall to her right, larger tools and outdoor maintenance equipment hung on the opposite wall like trophies.

Cali stepped farther into the garage, trying to aim at Keith's disgusting head or Trina's retched face, desperately attempting to keep Bethany out of her sight. Trina peeked out from behind Keith. After a maniacal giggle, she quickly ducked behind him again. Cali willed one of them to screw up and move to become a better target.

Cali took another step forward.

"How about you stop right there," Keith said.

Bethany stood on her toes as the knife summoned a stream of blood.

"How about you drop the knife, Keith, and we'll settle this like men. Well, I'll settle it like a man, and you'll be settled like a bitch."

Bethany squeaked; more blood. Keith growled. "How about you drop your gun and kick it to me?"

Fuck. Cali couldn't shoot; neither the piece of shit nor the silver and gold psycho gave her an opportunity. She couldn't chance hitting Bethany, so she lowered her gun, skimmed it behind her along the cement floor, and out the door.

"I said kick it to me!" Keith shouted.

Cali shrugged. "Whoops. Do you want me to go get it? I can try it again."

"Shut up, bitch!"

"I wanna make a teddy bear with her balloon animals," Trina said, swiping the air with her curled fingers. "Rrrrrrawwrrr!"

"You got it, sweety. Right after I take these two bitches' heads off, you can make any balloon animals you want."

Trina clapped.

Cali thought she'd seen some loose tools on the bench, a screwdriver or wrench, but her eyes were locked onto Keith's and she couldn't look away for even a second. Christ, she was close enough to grab something, but doubted she'd be fast enough. Keith had the knife digging into Bethany's jaw. Even if Cali went for her own knife strapped to her thigh, she'd still be too slow. Damn it, she wished she could get closer to the bench.

Keith's frown morphed into a smile, made sicker by the blood-red halo around it. Cali tensed, ready to dive to the workbench and throw the first thing she grabbed, even though his fingers were tightening around the knife handle.

To Cali's surprise, Bethany grabbed Keith's knife hand and pushed it far enough away to sink her teeth into his wrist. Keith screamed and Bethany launched herself forward, diving to the ground.

Perfect! Cali snatched the handle of the closest tool and threw it at Keith. The head of a hammer careened off his skull, dropping him.

"Noooo!" Trina screamed. She grabbed a chainsaw from the wall behind her. Holding it in front of her, she rushed toward Cali. "Vroom, vroom! Vroom, vroom!"

"It's not even turned on, dipshit."

Trina stopped in her tracks and cocked her head, looking at the machine as if she had never seen one before. Cali snatched the chainsaw from the tiny wreck of a clown and smashed the blade against her face. The chain gouged her forehead, making a bloody gash.

Time to end this!

Cali tossed the chainsaw, grabbed two fistfuls of green uniform, and lifted Trina. Not even ninety pounds soaking wet, Cali wondered how so much batshit crazy could fit into such a small package. She rammed Trina as hard as she could into the tool-clustered wall. The wall shook and tools rattled as a few empty hooks skewered Trina's back.

The clown released an ear-piercing howl, and Cali slapped a hand over her mouth. Trina squirmed, flailing her arms, kicking her feet. Pushing her weight into her forearm, pinning the clown deeper into the hooks, Cali unsheathed her knife and stopped the ruckus by sliding it between Trina's ribs. Eyes unfocused, the clown's angry face shifted from confusion to pain. Cali yanked out her weapon, then stabbed again, never taking her eyes off Trina's face. It didn't matter if some plant pollen made her this way or not. That twisted, painted face had laughed and smiled among dead bodies. This creature devastated entire families, mutilated people, and took pride in her accomplishments. She had enjoyed herself. There was no coming back from that, no making right what she did. Cali stared into Trina's eyes until she was certain no life remained in them, until she was certain this monster could harm no one else.

Ribs! flashed through Cali's mind as pain exploded through the entire left side of her body.

Keith had tackled her, and her knife skipped across the cement floor.

Stumbling, she planted her foot and twisted just enough so they both slammed into the work bench. With middle finger knuckles raised from her fists, she repeatedly punched the sides of Keith's temples. He pushed her away, his fists up. Both of them screaming like rabid beasts, Cali and Keith exchanged blows. His punches to her gut knocked the wind out of her. Even though she painted everything around her with streaks of blood from his nose, he was too big for attrition.

The Killer of Devils

After a perfect connection to his right eye, Cali hurriedly took two steps backward. Hands planted on the hood of the Lexus, she smashed the heel of her boot into his jaw. It didn't drop him, but his reciprocating lunge toward her was slow and sloppy. Hands as pivot points, she jumped and slid across the hood, landing behind him. Not that much shorter, Cali wrapped her arm around his throat, and then grabbed her elbow with her other hand to tighten the grip.

Keith was bigger and hidden beneath his layers of fat was a surprising amount of muscle. With a twist, he planted his foot against the workbench and pushed, slamming Cali against the Lexus' hood.

Absorbing his full weight against her chest, Cali let go of the last little grip she had on him and released the barking cough of a clubbed seal. Dazed, she didn't realize what was happening until Keith lifted her off the car. Her vision blurred as he slammed her on top of the work bench, and she thanked God no tools had torn through her.

A waterfall of crimson flowed from his nose, over his chin, and poured onto her face. As his meaty hands tightened around her neck, she chopped at his elbows, but couldn't generate enough power to be effective. Throat feeling like she had just gargled broken glass, head filling up with gray cotton, she prayed. God wasn't listening, though, because He was too busy answering someone else's prayer.

The sound of a stone hitting mud resounded with a wet thump. Keith suddenly loosened his grip. Cali heard the wet thump again, and again, each time bringing more relief from his stranglehold. At the fourth thump, Keith released her and turned around to face his attacker.

Cali wanted to take a quick nap on the workbench. No! A miracle presented itself in its full divine glory, and she wasn't about to waste it. The scraping pain in all her joints be damned, she slid off the work bench and gawped at the gift from Heaven that had saved her.

Bethany. With the largest screwdriver Cali had ever seen.

Both hands gripping the handle, Bethany lunged forward and drove the tip of the tool through Keith's heart. Time stood still. The slush between Cali's ears and Keith's blood dripping against the floor were the only noises in the garage.

Then Keith wound the clock, mumbling, "She looked just like you."

Bethany pulled out the screwdriver in a gurgling slurp, and screamed, releasing a sound that hadn't existed since the Earth cracked canyons and created volcanoes. "Don't look at her!" She yelled. "Don't you dare look at her!"

Releasing a primal fury that had been stored for billions of years, Bethany plunged the screwdriver into Keith's eye with enough force to puncture the back of his skull. The bloodied metal tip poked through his head with bits of gray pulp.

Keith dropped to his knees, slumped against the Lexus, and slid to the floor.

Of all things to enter her mind, the thought of giving birth entered Cali's. She had been on the fence about having children, leaning toward, "No." She didn't want to cause abandonment issues or make the same mistakes as her mother. Now, witnessing what Bethany was going through, Cali knew she would remain childless, never wanting to bring this much potential pain upon herself.

Despite every bone and organ from her neck to her hips burning her alive from the inside, Cali rushed to Bethany and hugged her. Bethany squeezed back, and she released a torrent of gulping howls into Cali's shoulder. No matter how tightly the wounds inside of her twisted, Cali didn't move, didn't shift, didn't let go.

After hours, or minutes, Bethany's screams turned into sobs and eventually subsided. She loosened her grip. Cali guided her toward the door leading into her house.

But Bethany stopped and looked back, even though Cali tried to keep her moving.

"Wait," she said and walked toward Trina.

Cali expected Bethany to spit on the dead body, or punch it or scream at it, so she readied herself to tussle with a cyclone. Instead, Bethany got uncomfortably close to the corpse hanging on the wall and studied it. "I know her."

"Wait, what?"

The Killer of Devils

"Her name is Trina. He called her Trina. I don't know her last name, but I've met her twice before."

"Really?"

"Yeah. Her sister, Brin, is a photographer. Black and whites, nature pics, sells her originals for four figures. She got a book deal last year and had a release party at a local bookstore. Trina was there and we chatted. A week later, Justin and I were at a random party, and we saw Trina again. We thought it was pretty funny. She lives close by, I'm pretty sure."

Cali put her arm around Bethany's shoulder again and guided her away from the gruesome scene. No resistance this time as they entered the house. "You didn't happen to catch an address from her at the party, did you?"

"No, but I think between the internet and the phone book, we can figure it out."

"Okay, let's call the police and—"

"Not yet. I want to get you the address first."

Cali didn't want Bethany to become more involved than she already was, and she knew the poor woman was going to need therapy. But she wasn't going to say no to her offer.

July 1, 2002

Who is Collin?

Cali tried to focus on the directions to Trina's house, hurrying the Explorer along the residential streets while obeying traffic laws. She had called the police for Bethany and left shortly before their arrival. She felt blessed that *she* hadn't drawn the attention of any police... yet. The Monticello Theatre wasn't that far away, so it undoubtedly occupied their time, but the mysterious fire could have them on high alert. If that didn't do the trick, then receiving a call that the corpse of Keith the Clown could be found in a suburban garage would certainly raise their hackles. It only took five minutes to find Trina's address, and Cali waited a few minutes before she left, wanting to make sure Bethany spent no more time alone with the dead bodies of the people who ruined her life than she had to.

But her mind kept drifting back to the question: *Who is Collin?*

It was either Dallas or Chism and maggots toiled in her guts every time she thought about one of them betraying her. How could she have been such an idiot? Worse – she had been victimized. She hadn't known either man for long, but she had spent hours talking with each of them, including the wee hours past midnight when emotions lay bare within the meandering conversations. And there was, after hours of sexing each other's brains out, a level of intimacy that brought the truth closer to the surface. Her intensity with each man had amped her time spent with them, and it could only be measured in romance dog years; one hour together was like seven for regular people. Two days, a fortnight. She knew both men, knew that one of them was Collin.

Nope, her heart said as it twisted behind her chest, *you truly don't know either man.* How could she have been dating the leader of a twisted clown cult and not even realized it? How did she miss the signs? As much as she hated to admit it, she wanted one of her mother's stupid introspection cards, because she didn't know which emotion to feel. *Fuck emotions, work the problem.* The problem was the original question: *Who is Collin?*

The Killer of Devils

Both men had a son, but Dallas didn't share much about him. Never talked about his kid. Of course, it was rare when Cali and Dallas weren't naked, and no parent in the world wanted to talk about their children while post-coital sweat was drying from their skin. When they were together, they chatted about topics, hypotheticals, what they knew about the world around them. Nothing emotional, and opinions were scarce. Dallas hid in plain sight.

Chism, on the other hand, was an open book. His son lived on the opposite side of the country, yet Cali knew more about his kid than Dallas'. Being a murder clown would be an impossible secret to keep with that level of openness. Or would it? Didn't he say he was an actor at one point in his life? And he was right there when Cali took the call from Bethany about the Monticello Theatre. Chism knew where she'd be and when. Cali and her mother assumed there'd be an ambush, but thanks to Cali's carelessness, she might have made it inevitable.

Cali took the last turn hard, careful not to screech her tires, but hard enough for her throbbing ribs to tell her to slow down. People who lived in upper-middle-class neighborhoods by the woods didn't appreciate squealing tires at night. She was pretty sure they didn't like murder clowns either, so she needed to get out of her own head and focus.

The houses were large, but not obscene. More panache than the ones from Bethany's cookie cutter neighborhood: stonework on the facades, plentiful fencing, curved driveways, pathways lined with knee-high lights, and banister balconies. The trees between properties were thick enough to offer privacy, but thin enough should the desire to be neighborly arise. The lack of streetlights lining the main road was good news, and that provided a lazy stretch of blemish-free asphalt. The bad news was that the shoulder of the road was not inviting for vehicles. Cali parked off road as best she could and hoped passersby wouldn't get too suspicious.

Darkness enveloped Trina's house. No lights inside and no exterior lights other than the dim glow offered by the ones lining the driveway, on by default. Cali put on her night vision goggles and took another look.

No movement in the house. The murder clowns were psychotic, but they still needed light to move around a semi-mansion.

Thoughts of traps and other potential surprises raced through Cali's mind as she grabbed a filter mask from the passenger seat, a simple cup that covered the lower half of her face from nose to chin with filters sensitive enough to stop viruses. It should be more than enough to stop whatever the hell plant toxins were in Collin's powdery concoction. Glock – down to one with no spare magazines thanks to the theater altercation – strapped to her thigh, small pockets of her belt filled with useful accessories, and a good friend sheathed against her hip – her nine-inch Bowie knife with a spine so serrated it could saw through a tree. She locked the Explorer and aimed for Trina's house, but stopped when she noticed something odd.

The lawn was high enough for her to tell that it hadn't been mowed in quite a while.

Same with the next-door neighbor.

The other houses' grass was as tight and uniform as a Marine's buzzcut. But these two lawns were on the verge of being hippies. Trina's house was dark, but the neighbors had a light on. In the garage.

Expecting a situation similar to Bethany's, Cali drew her gun and hurried to the garage. She removed her night vision goggles and looked through the window of the door. No cars, one golf cart, a few maintenance tools, and all kinds of graffiti on the walls. Lawn ornaments broken and scattered, opened and unopened bags of fertilizer and ice-melt salt. A man sat in the center of the garage tied to a chair.

Chism. Zip ties bound his wrists together and strapped his ankles to the chair legs. Duct tape adhered his waist and hips to the chair. Random strips of tape fluttered from his shoulders and forearms as he moved. A strip covered his mouth, and a small piece stuck to his ear.

Cali tried the doorknob and it turned. *I guess murder clowns aren't concerned about crime in this neighborhood.* Gun pointed at Chism's head, she padded into the garage.

His eyes widened when he saw her, and he reeled back as best as the duct tape would allow.

After a quick scan of the garage, Cali removed her mask.

"Kummophf?" Chism asked.

Cali leaned in and ripped the duct tape from his mouth.

"Ooooow! Fuck!"

She quickly stepped back, targeting Chism between his eyes.

After a few seconds of stretching and pursing his lips, Chism shook his head. "Cali? What are you doing here? Why are you dressed like a black-ops video game character? Why are you pointing a gun at my head?"

"Because I've been taken by surprise twice tonight, and I'm not looking for a third."

"Surprise…? Oh my God! You're her. You're the one they were talking about."

"Who's *they*, Chism?" Cali knew who, but she wanted to watch him as he answered, see the look in his eyes, study his facial expressions.

"Are you asking for names? Or are you speaking in generalizations? If generalizations, then clowns. A few of them broke into my apartment, jumped me, and brought me here. They tied me up! So why you are you pointing a gun at me?"

"I'm thinking you're the leader and you're setting me up."

"The leader? You mean Collin? Well, that's what they called him. They were babbling about some bitch ruining Master Poppie's plans and that they weren't going to 'turn me' yet – whatever that means – because they wanted to make her, who I'm assuming is you, watch. One said something to the leader, Collin, about dating her – you? You're dating someone else?"

Cali lowered her weapon. "That's your takeaway?"

"Well, not my only one. I'm also beginning to think that you're the mystery blonde involved with the King of Prussia massacre. I'm also no longer surprised that you thoroughly kicked my ass. I'm suddenly suspecting that you were holding back, and if you were, I'm now thankful for—"

He wasn't Collin. "Chism! Stop babbling." His eyes widened as he chattered, his fingertips trembling. This was not an act. "Yes, to all of the above, but first, I need to know how many—?"

The door to the garage flung open, the knob hitting the wall, and a clown stood screeching in the doorway, holding up a dead cat in front of her as if the carcass were making the horrific noise. Cali raised her gun and squeezed the trigger three times. The cracks of thunder and the sulfurous metallic smell would have been worth it had the clown not disappeared back into the house.

Cali ran after her, Chism's words chasing. "Two! There are two clowns in the house!"

Gunpoint leading the way, Cali crossed the garage's threshold into a short hallway leading into the house.

Layer upon layer of colors coated the walls, ceiling, and hardwood floor. Random streaks and big splashes, various swirls, and the repeated words, "Meow," and "Woof." Disoriented, Cali kept her back to a wall and advanced.

The living room wall colors weren't as oppressive, but just as chaotic. Television, tables, vases, knickknacks, lay broken in small piles. A couch, a loveseat, and a lit torchiere were the only unbroken pieces of furniture. A dining room large enough to seat eight sprouted from one side of the living room, and on the other side was a set of glass doors to the backyard – unbroken and free from paint. They were also closed, and no outside lights were on. Cali assumed that the flood lights were still working since they had kept the patio doors clean. These fuckers were clever enough to keep up appearances.

The crazy clown lady hadn't run out the back door. And she had an accomplice, according to Chism. This would be the ultimate test; if there were more than two clowns, Cali might have to shoot him.

She heard water dripping.

Chills raced up and down her spine, arms, fingers as she moved farther into the living room. From the center, she saw the entire dining room and the start of the spacious kitchen. She approached the couch from behind and peeked over the back. White fluffs of stuffing poked from random holes and rips, but no surprises.

On toward the loveseat in front of the wall with the bay window, curtains closed. Cushions sat in the same state of disarray, but the love seat was far enough away from the wall for the crazy clown woman to hide behind while gearing up for a pounce. One steady step after another, Cali made as little noise as possible; her heart beating into her throbbing ribs and her pulse sloshing between her ears threatened to give away her position. Standing in front of the loveseat, she trained her gun about a foot above its back. After a slow deep inhale to calm herself, she held her breath, then placed her boot on the front edge of the loveseat's arm. And pushed.

The back corner of the loveseat shook the curtains and rattled the window.

No clown popped out.

Cali heard a shuffle behind her and whipped around, finger ready to squeeze, but spun right into a cooking pan. A metal gong, followed by sudden pain ripping through her left hand. Her gun toppled through the air along with couch cushions. Leaping from the hollowed-out couch, a tall clown with blue hair, blue Xs over his eyes, and fishhooks holding his smile into place advanced and swung his other weapon at Cali – a dead dog.

The dog's back legs slapped Cali's face, a surprising amount of heft to the hit, but the stench of rot and was far more painful. Rolling with the hit, Cali spun and crouched, unsheathing her knife in the process. The clown jumped backward, but she managed to slice his waist. Red bloomed along his already dirty shirt. The slice didn't slow him down, though, as he followed through with a kick. Avoiding his attack, Cali leapt back to her feet just as he swung both weapons at her. Arms up, she blocked his forearms. She stopped the pan, but the flopping dog-body smacked her on the head again.

"Disgusting!" she yelled as she sliced her knife downward, missing as he leapt away.

"Aaaaaaarggh!" he replied as he rushed her, his attacks fast and frenetic. He swiped with the dog carcass and jabbed with the pan, her face the target. Cali blocked and retreated from the swipes and stabs.

He was corralling her toward the kitchen, and she knew very well what awaited her there. Like the other rooms, it was a post-apocalyptic nightmare with busted cabinet doors and broken appliances. Shattered dishes and glasses weren't limited to the sink.

As Cali predicted, the woman clown jumped out. She'd been hiding behind the island. She came out screaming and swinging a butcher's knife and a dead cat.

Before Fishhook Face could drive her into the woman's range of attack, Cali ducked his frying pan and drove her knife upward. It slid into his forearm and burst through the other side in a splash of red. He screamed and let go of the dog, which Cali caught and threw at the woman. It hit her face and exploded with quarters, nickels, dimes, and pennies, knocking her down. The sick fuck had been using a dead dog as a change purse. God only knew what was stored in the cat, and Cali didn't want to find out.

Cali yanked her blade from the clown's arm. He brought his forearm to his face and dragged his tongue over the gash. Streaks of blood dripped from his chin, from his freakish smile. Cali yanked the pan from his other hand and hit him right in the smile. Then across the right side of his forehead. Then his left.

But the hooked smile remained.

And he started to laugh.

"Oh, that has got to stop!" She needed Collin and Master Poppie and Keith the Clown to stop using human bodies as barricades and decorations. Needed the children to stop going missing, and the families to stop breaking. Needed the laughter and the smiling to stop!

The woman stood back up behind the smiling fish-hooked nightmare. Cali rocketed the pan at the woman's head, and it connected with a satisfying crack.

"Stop it!" Cali yelled at the smiling freak.

He responded with bubbling laughter.

Grabbing his hair, she kneed him in the groin. "Stop it!"

He laughed.

Knife to his throat, she drove him back until he slammed into the island. She jammed the heel of her boot against his ankles repeatedly until his feet turned and bones shattered beyond the point of being useful. "Stop it!"

With the back of his head pinned to the marble-patterned slate of the island, the clown laughed.

She dragged her knife across his throat. Blood flowed, but not the gush she was expecting. As he continued to laugh, she realized she had the serrated side to his neck. And continued to saw.

"Stop it! Stop it! Stop it!" she shouted over and over as she dragged her knife faster and harder across his throat. She got the geyser, the gush coating her from elbow to fingers. She gripped his hair and kept sawing until her knife met cartilage and bone, then she put her weight into the action and stopped only when her knife ground against the counter. His decapitated body flopped to the floor.

Cali held his severed head by a clump of blue strands; it was smiling, but not laughing.

She turned to his woman-partner – stunned, but still standing – and said, "He wouldn't stop laughing."

Eyes bulging, the woman's mouth stretched into a distended scream. She dropped the cat and gripped her knife with both hands. Raising it over her head, she locked eyes with Cali and…

Plunged it into her own gut.

The pain from her self-inflicted wound added to her scream's intensity as she withdrew the knife and stabbed herself again, this time in the chest. Then again and again and again. Shoulder. Ribs. Shoulder. Finally, her warbling shrieks stopped after she thrusted the knife into her neck, below her ear. A gurgle of blood came from her mouth, and she collapsed.

"Fucking meant for each other," Cali mumbled as she tossed the severed head onto the dead woman's body.

"Cali?" Chism called from the garage. He'd obviously heard the commotion, but it'd do him no good to see her like this. She went to the sink and washed the blood from her knife and hands. After a quick stop in the living room to retrieve her Glock, Cali headed to the garage.

"Cali?" Chism's call to her got louder as she approached. Eyes wide, lips trembling, Chism was the personification of worry and relief. "Cali? Are you okay? What happened? Are you okay?"

"I'm okay." She tried to keep her tone as even as possible, pushing down the disgust of what she just experienced twisting in her gut. "Those two won't be bothering us anymore."

"What do you mea—? Oh. They're dead. You killed them."

A slight tremble rippled through Chism's body, not enough to shake the chair, but enough to solidify Cali's feeling that he wasn't involved with this nightmare. Cali crouched down and started to cut the zip tie around his left ankle. "After they brought you here, did they talk about anything else other than me ruining their plans?"

"The leader said he needed to talk to their master. And... I still can't believe you thought I was the leader."

Cali pointed her knife at Chism as if it were her index finger. "Look, you're an eccentric dude, all right? You're somehow hot and into recreational fighting, yet sensitive and smart, yet into cartoons and general goofiness. And don't get me started about your weird romance with trees and... and... and...." Cali couldn't get the word out of her mouth; it lodged in her mind with a sudden realization.

She stood and paced in circles while piecing together a mental puzzle, its pieces an avalanche of information that should have been obvious from the start. No matter how impossible it sounded, she knew she was right. "Master Poppie is a plant."

"That's... Wait, what?"

"The toxin... It's a plant-based toxin that is making people lose their minds, become clowns, and kill people."

Chism squirmed in his chair. "How?"

"I was told that it's like opium, and opium comes from... oh, Jesus... from a poppy. Right in front of me! But this toxin is stronger, more aggressive, more fucks-your-head-up."

"But why clowns of all things? And why is everyone who's been affected suddenly thinking the same way?"

"I don't know. Maybe the toxin links their minds together? Maybe it links their minds to the master plant? There are meat eating plants out there that wait for prey to come to them, so maybe this plant uses other creatures… uses people… to bring food to it?"

Chism's eyebrows folded together as he looked away, deep in contemplation. After a few seconds, his face softened. He turned back to Cali. "It's crazy, but it's certainly possible. We as a society know shockingly little about how our own brains work, and we know even less about Mother Nature."

"Okay, so it's possible. If Collin and the others have been here this whole time, and have been going to see it, yet it's hidden, then that means it's in the woods somewhere."

"If what you're thinking is correct, if Master Poppie is only one plant, and it's large enough to produce enough toxin to affect dozens of people at once, then it's a *big* plant."

Cali looked around the space and smiled. Calling upon something she had learned from Chism, everything she needed was in the garage. A golf cart and four bags of industrial salt for melting ice on the driveway, forty pounds each. Other than scribbles of paint, the golf cart looked in great shape. Nothing in it other than two spouted plastic water bottles and an unopened sleeve of golf balls. "Well, I have a big solution."

"Okay, cool. Now, cut me free so I can help."

Cali stared open-mouthed at Chism. "What did you say?"

Chism wiggled his bound hands, the zip ties digging into his wrists. "You need help. Cut me loose and we can find Master Poppie together."

"No."

"I thought we established that we can trust me?"

"We did," Cali lied. "But it's too dangerous and I don't want your death on my conscience." That was the truth. "I've been doing this for half my life." A lie. "And I only have one gas mask." The only truth that mattered at the moment.

Cali ignored Chism's pleas as she finished loading the salt onto the golf cart. As much as it pained her to leave him strapped to a chair, she started the cart, a blast of gasoline fumes filling the air, and drove away.

July 1, 2002

Cali had a decent sense of direction, though the darkness was currently ruining that. The headlights barely illuminated her path, the salt bags shifting in the back as she kept her gaze focused ahead.

The forest was thick but offered plenty of space among the trees to allow the golf cart. There were also plenty of close calls with tree trunks and branches whipping the thin, plexiglass windshield, but the headlights – *why the fuck does a golf cart need headlights?* – gave her some light. Enough, anyway. Bethany's neighborhood was on the other side of the woods and Cali had a general idea of how to get there. The night Bethany had saved her, she was close to the tree where Keith had buried Lily, which was the direction the clowns had run when she gave chase.

Mother had taught her tracking skills, but they were much harder to employ while chugging along in a golf cart at night. Still, she looked for signs of a path – broken branches, displaced ground detritus, any obvious disruptions. Like the golf cart tracks she just crossed over.

Damn it!

Pissed off that she had driven in a circle, she slowed to a crawl. The trees had started to look the same. She checked the compass attached to her belt and did her best to aim westward. *Get out and check for signs of people passing through*, her mother would say.

No. Driving or walking was a shot in the dark, but at least driving covered the ground faster.

Cali added a little more pressure to the accelerator. Then braked when something crashed onto the hood of the cart. Not something – someone. A savage face smiled at her through the windshield, white with two bloody handprints over the eyes. "I am the vomit of darkness!"

She jumped out of the cart. "You're vomit, all right, you sick fuck!"

Laughing, the clown launched himself at her, but the lava pumping through her veins burned too hot. She caught him by the neck and slammed him back down on the hood, his overcoat fluttering. She unholstered her Glock, but as she brought it up, a pointed memory hit between her eyes like a dart – he had nastiness hidden up his sleeves.

She lunged to the side as a knife sprung from his sleeve and into his hand. Her outfit's protective material helped, but pain ran in jagged paths along her arm as the knife sliced her left shoulder.

BLAM!

She could still hold the gun, but she couldn't aim for shit now, destroying the golfcart's windshield as Red Eyes rolled from the hood to the ground.

BLAM! BLAM!

Even though he was mere feet from her, he moved too fast, his overcoat distracting as he twirled and spun. Cali jumped back to avoid his attack, close enough to feel the wind of the knife slice.

BLAM!

Another spin and the bottom of his overcoat brushed her face. As it left her field of vision, it was replaced by two knives arcing downward.

Cali dropped her gun to catch his wrists, her left shoulder ablaze from the wound.

"The mother of birth is death!" he screamed.

Ape-shit crazy. She preferred the ones who just screamed or licked things.

Bad leverage, she twisted to the left and threw herself to the right to get away from his knives and ended up on the ground. Before she had a chance to get up, he threw himself at her.

Hands tucked close to her chest, Cali rolled out of the way. Red Eyes hit the ground with a thud, and pursued. Cali kept rolling as he continued to stab with his knives.

"Blood quenches all of the Earth!"

All she needed was one second to get to her feet and then she could end this, but he scabbled like a crab, stabbing the ground with every step. With no other tactic available, she kept rolling out of the way until she slammed into a tree. She sat up, much to the disagreement of her ribs, and tried to focus on how to avoid her impending demise.

Getting to his knees, the clown raised both knives over his head, the red handprints glowing with rapture as if the devil himself had reached up from Hell to bless his favorite demon.

Cali raised her forearms, calculating the variables of his attack.

BLAM!

A glob of red from the clown's shoulder splashed Cali's face. He fell toward her, and she threw her weight into a punch to his cheek, knocking him to the side.

Cali hopped to her feet and hurried away from the clown toward... Chism!

Eyes as wide as the full moon above the forest canopy, he held the Glock with both hands and trembled. "I've... I've... I've never shot anyone before."

"Chism? Chism, look at me." When she got close enough, she placed a hand on his forearm. "Hey. Chism, look right here. Look at me."

Even in the filtered moonlight, Cali saw his eyes, slick with tears. *He's not going to react well to what comes next.* She forced a soft smile and used both hands to lower his arms. The way she'd talk to a puppy, she said, "You saved my life. It's all good."

"Is he dead?"

Stroking his arm with one hand, she gently reached for the gun. "Nope, he's not dead. He'll be fine."

Chism nodded and relinquished the weapon. "Okay."

"Okay," Cali repeated. As soon as she had full control of the Glock, she strode over to Red Eyes and unloaded the clip into his head, coating the tree trunk with chunky waves of crimson paint.

The expression on Chism's face was exactly how Cali pictured it'd be – jaw tight, eyes wide, brows smashed together. If he'd never shot anyone before, then it was fair to assume he'd never seen anyone get their brains blown out by the woman he was dating. "Chism? I need you to listen to me. He was one of the sick fucks who—"

A streak of green flashed from behind a nearby tree and collided with Chism.

Brin.

Chism outweighed her and was a good half foot taller, but the element of surprise was a great weapon. Throwing the entire weight of her body into her hit, Brin connected shoulder-to-shoulder and slammed him against the golf cart, his head snapping back as his chin hit the roof. A kick to his knee and she suddenly became taller than him. There was no cracking noise, but his face was now in a direct line with her fists, thrusting back and forth like pistons.

Click. Click. Click.

Glock empty, Cali searched along her belt for another magazine. None. *Fuck!*

Cali covered the distance quickly and threw herself at Brin, driving the clown bitch to the ground. A twist, a push, a kick, and Brin squirmed free. Both women got to their feet at the same time. Cali snatched her knife from its sheath, ready for anything Brin threw at her. However, the clown relaxed her stance and strolled toward the front of the golf cart. Where Collin waited.

"Dallas," Cali growled.

Collin gave a huge open-mouthed smile, outlined in red, and it somehow made the blue circles over his eyes larger. After a quick jig that ended with jazz-hands, he sang, "Surrrrrpriiiiise!"

"You dated this guy?" Chism asked, his words tight with pain. Weight against the golf cart, he climbed to his feet. Blood flowed from his nose and the corner of his mouth, his left leg injured.

Collin repeated his dance. He then poked his index finger in and out, in and out, of the "o" hole formed with his other hand. "Ooooooh, you better believe we did, buddy boy! We dated in every room of my apartment and on every surface of her hotel room. Sloppy, sloppy dating!"

"Real classy," Cali moaned. "Collin, huh? I'm guessing the 'C' of D.C.?"

Collin dropped his arms and slouched, his jaw falling open in surprise. "It took you this long to crack that code? Good golly, murder Molly, you ain't the fastest crayon in the picnic shed, are you?"

"Didn't have much time to think about it because I was too busy acting like you were a good lay."

Collin grabbed his stomach and bent over cackling. Laughing louder, he flopped to the ground and rolled around while kicking his feet. Brin stepped over Collin on her way to Red Hands' splattered remains. She grabbed his knives, never once taking her eyes off Cali. "He'll be at this for a while. How about we play a game?"

"Is the game 'you be a cuckold while I fuck your man better than you?' If it is, I don't wanna play, because it's boring."

Her jagged yellow smile wrinkled into a horrific jack-o-lantern maw of rage.

"Oh, I struck a nerve!"

Screaming, Brin ran toward Cali with both knives over her head. Cali backed up and smirked. No matter which way she could dive, Brin would adjust and drive the two blades into unwanted places, so Cali went the best direction available. Down.

At the last second, Cali ducked and rolled toward Brin. Feet knocked out from under her, the smack of her face off the golf cart was a satisfying sound. However, being a fucking nutjob seemed to numb pain better than morphine, because Brin pushed off the hood and spun, slashing with both knives as Cali sprung to her feet. One knife slid impotently across Cali's tactical fabric, but the other managed to sever through the material, leaving a cut in her side. It burned like hell, but with no time to fuss, Cali quickly threw a punch. Brin jerked to the side, but Cali was ready, twisting to smash her elbow against the side of Brin's head.

Howling, the clown stabbed wildly. The uncoordinated thrusts were easy enough to parry. A slice across Brin's left wrist with the Bowie yielded an arc of red, and she dropped a knife. "Whore!"

"Yeah, yeah, yeah," Cali said as she stabbed Brin's other forearm, forcing the clown to drop the second knife. "I've been called worse by better."

No humanity left in her eyes, Brin looked like a beast attempting, and failing, to be human. Different parts of her face twitched randomly, as if a terrible creature beneath her skin desperately wanted to escape. Uttering a shriek that no animal could make, Brin rushed at Cali with her mouth open and fingers curled into claws.

The Killer of Devils

As if fending off a raging dog, Cali held her left forearm out to absorb Brin's attack. The material kept the mad woman's teeth from piercing skin, but Cali still felt the grip of her jaw.

"Ow! Fucking rabies!" Cali yelled as she headbutted Brin in the nose and then jammed the Bowie into her gut. While the clown was dazed, Cali spun her around and drove the Bowie into her back. Her spine offered resistance, but Cali pushed harder until the hilt pressed against flesh. She withdrew her knife and let her opponent fall to the ground.

Brin released a pained exhale. On her back, she reached for Cali, her fingers curled and ready to rend. After a high-pitched screech, she changed position and swatted her own legs. "Collin! Collin? I can't... I can't feel my legs."

Cali heard surprise in Brin's voice, but not fear. No worries upon her face. No panic. Like a toddler not understanding why a deflated balloon wouldn't float. She reached for Collin and repeated, "I can't feel my legs."

Hands behind his back, Collin stared at Cali through the big blue circles. The red around his mouth barely moved. "That's a shame, Brin."

Deep in the forest behind Collin, the trees started to blur, distorted by a film. No, a haze. A thick white cloud rolled closer.

"No!" Brin yelled. "No! I've been faithful! I've followed you and Master Poppie! I've been faithful!"

"But you know what comes next. Waste not, want not, and all."

The creamy mist flowed closer. When it got within a few trees, a massive vine snapped from within the cloud and wrapped around Brin's feet. Clawing impotently, she howled like a wounded cat as the vine pulled her into the mist. Cali would never forget those screams. If she lived past tonight.

The mist continued to flow, spilling past Collin's feet.

"Cali?" Chism said, voice shaking. "We should get in the golf cart and go."

Chism clutched his knee. Cali doubted he'd be able to outrun the mist, thanks to Brin's nasty kick. Cali had left him tied to the chair to keep him safe, but he had managed to get free and interjected himself. That meant he had to carry the torch after it fell from her hands. She yanked the mask from her face and put it over his.

"Cali? What—?"

"The 'what' is pretty fucking obvious, Chism. After I kill Collin, you find Master Poppie and salt the fuck out of it."

Cali pushed him into the driver seat, and then strode toward Collin.

Her mother trained her for this. Doing nothing, she could hold her breath almost five minutes; while active, a hint over three. She thought her training would come in handy for underwater scenarios, but this was similar enough.

The wall of white enveloped Collin as Cali took a deep breath and held it. So thick and chalky, she expected the cloud to offer resistance, but it was only a fog, parting as she strode through.

Cali swung with all her might, knife in hand, aiming for Collin's face. As casual as a dance, he stepped to his left. She planned for the miss, and thrust her hand back, holding her knife, pointed down. Collin growled as the tip sliced across his chest.

Not deep, but Cali was satisfied by the expanding streak of red across his shirt.

Collin's growl turned into a laugh. "It's no use, Cali. You can't hold your breath long enough to kill me and resist breathing in Master Poppie's mist at the same time. You might as well breathe it in now because you'll be one of us soon enough."

Fuck I will, she thought as she lunged forward, leading with her knife's tip.

He swatted her hand away and threw a quick punch at her face. She jerked out of the way and then spun into a crouch, another slice toward his waist. A miss as he jumped back.

"You have no chance at getting out of this. You *will* become one of us. Accept it now, and we can do great things. We'll both see Master Poppie's dream come to fruition."

She assumed Master Poppie's dream was really Collin's, and that Collin wanted to use Senator Albright to expand his influence within the government. But to what extent? What was the ultimate goal?

Cali jumped and kicked, but Collin blocked it. She landed on her shoulder, exhaling but still holding, and rolled backward, forest debris crunching underneath her. Collin hurried closer, and Cali sprang to her feet. After a solid connection of her knuckles to his cheek, she stabbed again. Collin accepted her punch to dodge the knife. This time, he Karate chopped the sweet spot on her wrist, sending a spiral of pain through her arm. The knife twirled through the air and landed a few paces away.

Feeling returned to her hand as she shook it. Fists raised; they circled each other. It was agony to hold up her left fist; her arm shook from the knife wound in her shoulder. A pulsing flare of jagged fire blasted through her waist from the other knife wound with every other step. Burning lungs told her she was running out of time.

Cali went in for a few left jabs.

He dodged, but that put him in the path of her right hook. Nice contact, but he countered.

Arms up in time to protect her face from his punches. A knee to his side and he grunted. That one must have hurt, so Cali threw a few punches to his ribs. She ducked to avoid a hook and snapped up to smash the heel of her hand into his jaw.

Collin stepped back, the two of them still circling each other. Smiling, he rubbed his jaw. "You got a few good moves. I know you can fight, but you seem to have forgotten that I used to be semi-pro."

With a brain-piercing cackle, he launched forward with his left fist rocketing toward her head. Cali raised both arms to block. But the left-fisted hit never arrived. Instead, his right knuckles drilled into the soft spot below her sternum.

Cali's residual breath blew out and she desperately needed to recapture it. She doubled over, stumbling a few steps away from him. Collin let her flail as he continued laughing that high-pitched maniacal madness. Cali swayed, then fell to her knees.

She couldn't hold her breath any longer. After his last punch, her stomach cramped and a trail of electricity crackled from her pelvis to the base of her neck. *What the hell do I do now?* She had to breathe. Hands cupped over her mouth, she dropped her forehead to the ground, hoping the mist was like smoke.

Don't change. Stay as me. Be me. Don't change.

Cali inhaled.

July 1, 2002

The sweet smell of cotton candy overwhelmed Cali, cloying and sticky. She coughed, unable to resist a deep inhale.

Collin leaned over her, gloating, faces inches from hers. "This is the white mist, baby! The one that taps into your deepest, hidden, most fucked-up self you're trying to hide. You're going to be all kinds of wild and feral. Heh... I know you're wild and feral in bed. Ooooh, after you change and adjust to your new thinking, I'm sure it'll be you and me non-stop, wild and feral fucking."

Cali's breathing regulated; her coughing subsided. Her thoughts hadn't gone bizarre, and she had zero desire to dress like a clown. Violence was at the forefront of her mind, but there was only one person she wanted to violate. And less than a foot away was her Bowie knife.

Collin started to laugh again, his timbre increasing in speed and pitch. Cali snatched her knife from the ground and spun, driving half the blade through his temple. His right eye crossed inward. The left side of his lip curled upward while his jaw snapped to the right. His tongue dangled from his mouth and his laugh held one unwavering note.

Cali released the knife's grip and stood as Collin backed away, his movements spastic and jerky. Both hands trembled with palsy as he tried to reach for the knife, but he continually gripped and pulled at the air in front of his face. He dropped to his knees, his hands grabbing for the knife in the same constant pattern.

Cali yanked her knife from his head. Blood pulsed, rhythmically flowing from the newly formed hole in his head, and the whine of laughter stopped. His eye remained crossed, but he regained control of his tongue and jaw. Wobbling, he looked up to Cali with his crossed eye, working hard to move his lips. Cali expected a laugh or more insane sycophantic praise of Master Poppie. Instead, with red tears in his eyes, he said, "My... my... son..."

Dallas crumpled and fell face first to the ground.

After calling herself every synonym for "stupid" she could think of for not realizing that she was dating the leader of the cult she'd been hunting, she checked his pulse. Nothing.

"So, it's over?" Chism asked, mask bobbing on his face as he limped closer.

The mist rippled and swirled; a whoosh cut through the air.

Cali tackled Chism and drove him to the ground right as a green vine snapped like a whip over their heads. As it retracted, the tip wrapped around her ankle.

"Fuck no!" she yelled and sliced the vine. Dark green liquid spurted from the gash. It released her ankle and twitched as it receded into the mist. A second vine shot out, but this one had a different target – Dallas.

As with Brin, the vine dragged Dallas's body away.

Cali scrambled to her feet and ran to the golf cart. She had to follow Dallas to Master Poppie. Right as she hit the gas, Chism jumped in on the passenger side. He grimaced, the pain in his knee evident on his face. He hadn't given her a chance to argue about not coming along, and he probably wouldn't have listened.

"I see movement ahead," Chism said, his voice muffled.

The headlights reflected off the white mist, and Chism acted as a spotter, pointing just in time for Cali to dodge a tree while they bounced along the uneven forest floor.

"I lost him," he said, leaning forward.

"Me, too." Cali slowed down, guiding the cart through the trees. After a few beats, she said, "How'd you free yourself from the zip ties?"

"Survival trick. Tied my shoelaces together and rapidly ran the zip ties across them while pulling to create tension. And then pop."

"Nice trick."

"Told you I'm not useless."

"Never said you were."

Chism side-eyed her. He tapped on his gas mask. "You don't need one with the mist?"

She shrugged. "Maybe I knew what to expect, so I was able to fight off its effects? Maybe I'm naturally immune?"

"Maybe."

Chism kept a solid, white-knuckled grip on the cart's oh-shit handle while scoping the terrain, like a bush hunter looking for a wild beast. Cali had never seen him so intense. Though she hadn't known him that long, she didn't know he was capable of such earnestness. *Was* he focused? Or was he pissed at her? On the one hand, this was a life-or-death situation. On the other hand, they were hunting a plant worshiped by the other guy she had been dating. And she had accused Chism of being that guy. Maybe this wasn't the right time for a discussion, but she felt the urge to fill the heavy silence. "So. About Dallas—"

"There!" he yelled, pointing. "What's that?"

Cali hit the brakes.

The rib-rattling beat of her heart played in time to the soft chug of the golf cart's motor. Hardly twenty feet away, the mist swirled as if caught in a breeze passing through the trees. In its center stood a clown.

Cali eased herself from the golf cart, quick to unsheathe her Bowie. "Master Poppie."

Chism put a foot on the ground, but Cali held up her hand motioning for him to stop. Eyes on the clown, she whispered, "Do not leave this cart. Be ready to drive and be ready to unleash the salt."

"Okay," Chism whispered back, sliding to the driver's side.

Cali crept through the mist, closer to the clown, not knowing what to expect. Was she wrong about Master Poppie being a plant? The clown stood beside a tree, his gray clothes billowy. Red circling his eyes and a red gash for a mouth were the only features she made from his round, white face, topped by a wild shock of blood-red hair. Who was this guy? Was he living in the forest? How did he gain so much influence over people? Wait...

The closer she crept, the clearer it became that this was a mimicry of a human being.

The gray clothes were flimsy leaves, curled and folded to resemble the rudimentary shape of a human body. The hair was thin, wavy petals, similar to those found on a chrysanthemum. The face was round like a daisy head with white filaments; red-tipped filaments made an approximation of eyes and mouth. The mimicry was good enough to twist that uneasy spot at the base of her spine, warning of danger.

She tried to sneak up to it from the side, but as she changed her course, its visage shifted. She had to remind herself that what followed her motion weren't truly eyes. No idea how the plant sensed her, but it wasn't from the two red dots on the white daisy head.

Now standing within ten feet, she saw the vinelike stem attached to the bottom of the thing. This was a flower, a single Master Poppie clown flower. Didn't matter. She had a plan, a simple one – run back to the golf cart and return with a bag of salt. "I'm gonna fucking kill you."

"Cali!" came Chism's urgent, muffled scream from the gas mask. She turned.

Through the mist, two snakelike vines whipped about the golf cart. Chism leaned away and swatted at the tips.

Cali tried to raise her foot to run to his aid, but collapsed – a vine had her by the ankle. Grip tightening on her knife, she went to slash, but another vine had wrapped around her forearm, rendering it immobile. Two more vines slithered along the mist-covered forest floor, heading toward her.

Cali never thought she'd hate a plant, but this thing went beyond leaves and stems and stalks. It possessed sentience. This thing... this *monster*... made people perform inhuman things to other people. It was a predator that reduced humans to food.

Roaring like a bear caught in a trap, Cali focused her strength on bringing her knife-wielding hand closer to her face. Fire burned from shoulder to shoulder as she flexed her arm, fighting against the vine. Closer. More. Closer. Finally within reach, she sunk her teeth into the vine.

Dank earthiness consumed her senses, liquid mildew sluiced into her mouth. Gagging and coughing, she spat out the chunk of vine she had torn away. She chomped into its flesh again, biting away another chunk. Another. And another until she had weakened it enough to release her arm. The two vines that had been creeping closer suddenly shot toward her, but she severed them with one slice each. Two hacks and she freed her ankle.

Chism! No! A vine had wrapped around his waist while another spiraled around his left leg, both pulling. His right leg was hooked around the support between the golf cart's base and roof. Both hands as well. He was no longer wearing his mask.

Cali pushed herself to her feet and ran to the cart.

The vines around Chism were thick, but not enough to stop the Bowie from hacking away flesh with her every swing. Green mucus streamed. After five, six, seven swings Cali severed the vine attached to his leg. His eyes bulged, and the ligaments of his neck tightened, signaling that he was holding his breath but couldn't for much longer.

"Hold out, Chism!" Cali ordered as her knife cut through the vine around his waist, painting the golf cart with vine fluid. Released, Chism fell, bouncing off the seat and onto the ground. Arms shaking, he held his hands over his mouth, eyes squeezed tightly shut.

Near panic, Cali searched the golf cart for the mask, praying that it was undamaged. There! On the cart's floor! She grabbed it and dropped to her knees next to Chism. She slid it over his head and ran her fingers around the edges, making sure it was secure and sealed. "Okay! Breathe."

He took a gulping inhale.

Cali's fingers played along the Bowie's hilt as she watched his breathing normalize. His body relaxed and his head rested against the ground. After a few more deep breaths, he said, "I'm good. All good. Just fucking peachy."

"Wanna wear clown makeup and kill people?" she asked.

"Nope, but I have a hankering to dump a bunch of salt on a weird fucking plant."

"That will not happen," said a voice within the mist.

Collin.

July 1, 2002

"I fucking killed you," Cali whispered. Was the mist starting to affect her? Or was she really seeing a ghost?

Collin approached, his feet not touching the ground, his arms dangling limp at his sides. His head was cocked as if his neck no longer supported it. A thick green vine ran up his back, holding him up like a hand-puppet.

"You killed the human pod. But you didn't kill me." The words possessed the slow slur of a drunk person speaking a foreign language.

Chism got to his feet. "I guess your ex can't take a hint?"

As the Collin-puppet hovered closer, Master Poppie's flower-clown moved out from behind the closest tree. Then a second one appeared from behind the next closest tree. *Oh, fuck me!* Two more appeared. Three more. Five more.

"More clowns?" Chism asked.

Keeping her voice low, Cali said, "No. They're flowers. I'm assuming all parts of the same plant. I'll kill this Collin-fucker again, then I'll start in on the flowers. We can follow the stems back to Master Poppie."

Chism nodded. "God, I know plants can mimic, but... Clowns? Why clowns?"

"This was the first human pod I found," said the drunken voice, "and it held clowns in its thoughts."

Cali raised her knife and sidestepped away from the golfcart. "What do you want?"

"What all life wants," the Collin-puppet replied. "I want to live."

"Bullshit. You want to kill. You want to wreak havoc on humanity. You want to annihilate."

"That's what humans do."

"You're an expert on humans, huh?"

"The more I consume, the more I learn."

"And mind control," Cali said.

"Mind control to protect me. To feed me."

"You're a monster."

"So are humans. So are you, Calista."

Cali advanced with her knife extended. "I'll show you a fucking monster!"

She aimed for the Collin-puppet's throat but missed as it jerked backward. It then rose in the air. As did the clown-flowers.

"No," Cali whispered.

The flowers rose higher, out of her reach. At about ten feet in the air, they billowed like dresses caught in an updraft. The petals unfurled to expose puckered pink bulbs. Each one reeled back and blew a stream of white mist from a hole in the bulb's center.

"What the fuck?" Chism said.

Couldn't have said it better myself. Suspended like a hanged man, the Collin-puppet laughed as a dozen mist-spraying flowers danced among the trees behind him like an arboreal gorgon. Cali no longer faced off against a monster, rather a god, one primed to reign down fire and brimstone in the form of mind-shattering mist.

Cali ran back to the golf cart and grabbed the two discarded water bottles. Soft plastic with adjustable squirt tops. *Perfect!* "Unscrew the lids," she said as she handed them to Chism. She crouched down and jammed the tip of her knife into the gas tank. It took ten seconds to fill up one bottle. She tightened the lid and left Chism to take care of the other bottle.

The distance made it difficult, but she was able to spray three of the flowers before she needed to toss the empty bottle back to Chism. He tossed her a full bottle and she sprayed two more. They exchanged bottles one more time, and then she doused the Collin-puppet.

Still hovering ten feet off the ground, his dead eyes locked onto hers. "Your efforts are useless."

Cali shrugged and adjusted the water bottle's spout, closing it almost completely. "That's never stopped me before." She then smiled and winked at the Collin-puppet as she pulled a lighter out from one of her belt's pouches.

Flaming on the first flick, she held up the lighter and squeezed the bottle. A finer mist sprayed from the tip, igniting on its way to the gas coated flowers.

The Collin-puppet released the dry, scratchy scream of a corpse, then yanked away, into the white mist. The flaming flowers twitched and twisted, retreating into the mist as well. Even the unharmed flowers followed.

"We need to chase after it," Cali said. She tossed the water bottle to Chism, and he filled it up with gasoline. He then ripped off his shirtsleeve and used the material to plug the tank's hole.

Chunks of flowers glowed orange in the haze, lighting the way. They sped through the forest, heads bobbing against the roof, jostled by the irregular terrain. Tree roots scraped under the golf cart as they followed wispy orange embers floating in the air.

Master Poppie is going to die tonight.

As they drove closer, they saw the last remains of one of the flowers, its petals curled like melted plastic, smoke flowing from the charred and blistered bulb. Seconds later, they drove past another one. After passing two more, the white mist swirled ahead, disturbed by something coming at them.

"Brake!" Chism screamed.

Cali crushed the brake pedal with both feet, back wheels lifting just as Collin slammed onto the hood. The puppet's body slid across the hood onto the dashboard. The plexiglass windshield was gone, and Collin's lifeless arms draped over the steering wheel.

For a few heartbeats, nothing moved in the forest. Cali stared at the limp body in front of her, a thick green vine still attached to the base of his spine.

The vine twitched and then Collin slowly moved. Open eyes stared at her. Then blinked.

"Do it!" Cali yelled.

Chism squirted gasoline from the water bottle. Cali sparked her lighter and they both dove from the golf cart as a conflagration engulfed Collin's corpse.

Master Poppie slammed Collin's body against the ground, beating the flames. Cali jumped to her feet and squirted more gasoline from her water bottle. Master Poppie lifted the flaming carcass once more, then let it collapse, as the vine detached itself and slithered away. It didn't have far to go.

"Ooooh, I think we found Master Poppie," Chism said.

Yes. Yes, we did.

It was a pitcher plant. Thick leaves curled together to resemble a drinking pitcher, a prey-trapping mechanism forming a deep cavity filled with digestive fluids. This pitcher was about five feet tall, and held both Red Hands and Brin, their armpits caught on the edge. A massive stalk supported the pitcher, growing upward about twenty feet and then curving downward, the end a tuft of thin leaves. Fleshy sacks dangled from the stalk at the intersection of each stem holding a clown-flower, expelling purple mist in rhythmic puffs. More than a dozen vines wriggled like angry snakes from the base.

Cali wondered how long this thing had existed in this world. Hundreds of years? Thousands? It was a hydra. A dragon. A chimera. Every terrifying beastly tale early man wrote about could have originated from those who witnessed this thing.

One of the flowered stems snapped toward Cali.

The flower was open, exposing the pink bulb, but Cali dove out of the way as the flower snapped shut. A somersault and she was back on her feet, taking care of the flower with gasoline and flame.

"Cali! The salt!" Chism yelled as he rushed to the golf cart. He tore at the thick plastic of the bag on top of the pile with no success. Cali's Bowie ran a slit down the middle and she then grabbed two corners of the bag while Chism grabbed the other two. With a steady rhythm, they swung the bag back and forth, and Cali gestured with her chin. "See that big rock a few feet in front of Master Poppie? We need to aim for that, getting as much air as possible. Ready?"

"Three."

"Two."

"One!"

The bag flew high in the air, arcing a trail of salt behind it, and landed exactly where they had aimed. The explosion of salt created a cloud thicker than the mist, coating the pitcher and most of the stalk. When settled, a thick white layer circled the stalk on the ground. Cali sliced a second bag, and they repeated the process. Another direct hit to the rock, another explosion of salt coating the plant.

The vines and stems wriggled spastically, silently, pulling closer to the stalk. It certainly seemed like it was in pain, but Cali expected it to shrivel like a slug. Another bag? Maybe, but first she wanted a closer look at the salt's effect to better place the next bag. Knife in her hand, she strode toward it. *Fuck it. I'll just kill it now.*

The pitcher walls rippled and rumbled, then released its contents.

"What the fuck?" Cali shouted as Chism tackled her out of the way.

He pointed to the smoking path of corrosive liquid dissolving the forest leaves and twigs it washed over. On the ground, Red Hands and Brin bubbled in various states of decomposition; pink pulp oozed from their chests to their hips and then tapered to clean bones from their knees down. "Just returning the favor."

"Thanks," she grunted as she started to get to her feet.

Chism pulled her back down to a crouch. "We need to wait.

"It's wounded. I can kill it!"

"Trust me. Look at what it's doing."

Using most of its vines, the plant pushed against the ground. A root burst from the dirt and then another root popped free. Both roots pushed against the ground, as if trying to free itself from the earth.

"Is it trying to run away?" Cali asked.

"Sort of. The salt is probably just a mild irritant on its leaves and stems. It's the ground that's important. I can't believe this, but apparently it can pull up its own root system and move."

Master Poppie pulled another of its roots out of the ground, the dirt falling away in clumps.

"We gotta hack this fucking thing to pieces before it gets too far," Cali said, rising.

Chism stopped her again. "Not yet. It uprooting itself is a good thing. Most plants have taproots. If you hack off the stalk, no matter how close to the ground you get, if there's still a taproot, it could come back. Even if we dump the rest of the salt, I don't know if it will kill it, or just make it go dormant. Hell, since it moves under its own power, it might 'play dead' until we leave and then move when no one is looking."

A semicircle worth of roots had freed themselves from the dirt while more sprung free.

Cali snarled and her knuckles cracked from gripping her knife so tightly. "Well, we can still hack away at the stems and stalk, right?"

"I don't think so. If we attack it now, it might shift back to 'fight' of the 'fight or flight' response. No matter how much we want to attack it now, we have to wait for the tap root to come out to be— AAAAH!"

Chism flopped to the ground. A vine pulled his ankle, dragging him away. Cali dove, their hands clasped, but the vine yanked him out of her grip. A second vine spiraled around him and lifted him off the ground toward the stalk.

"Not yet," Chism yelled down to Cali. "Not yet!"

"Come on, you fucker," Cali mumbled, grabbing both water bottles. She consolidated the gasoline into one and kept the top off. Bottle in one hand, knife in the other, lighter between her teeth, she approached the squirming plant. Sweat poured over her face and her throat itched.

Three quarters of a circle of roots had risen above ground and were pushing off. A clown flower arced downward, but Cali slashed and cut enough of the opened petals to make it withdraw.

A third vine wrapped around Chism, this one pinning his arms to his sides. And squeezed. Cali rushed closer to the stalk, but Chism squeaked out, "Not yet! Wait!"

Another root, then another. A few more to go before the taproot.

Cali's muscles were primed to react, waiting for the next root, her head on a swivel. A second clown flower dove at her, but she dodged it and sliced the stem, causing it to retract.

Come on, come on, come on, the only thought in her mind as one more root unearthed itself. The vines squeezed Chism tighter, and they might as well have been wrapped around Cali's heart. Guilt, anger, guilt, sadness, guilt. Tears stung her eyes as Chism's face twisted in pain.

One more root. One more squeeze. His eyes bulged and his mask stretched from his mouth opening. More flowers and vines snapped at Cali, her knife fending them off.

Then the biggest root right under the stalk lifted from the ground, the tap root. The other roots worked like centipede legs and propelled the plant along the ground.

Cali wasn't going to let it get far.

Screaming, she ran to its reformed pitcher and splashed gasoline all over where it connected to the stalk. She threw the water bottle into the pitcher – the lit lighter followed. The woosh of flame knocked her back, knocked her into her past.

Maybe Master Poppie's pollen finally caught up with her. Maybe exhaustion turned her brain inside out. Maybe her emotions substituted one monster for another. For the briefest of moments, Cali saw Zebadiah Seeley in the flames – the unstoppable killer who wore a bear-head and murdered Tanner. Linda. Dakota. Her father.

The fire flickered out, but the image remained.

Her knife expressed her feelings as she slashed Zebadiah across the chest, hacked at his head, and stabbed his eyes. Screaming, she repeated the process, faster. And again, harder. He kept reaching for her, but she kept pushing herself to gash and cut more, more, more, past the broken glass feeling in her joints, past the ripping of her muscles, past the aches clawing every part of her insides. Nothing was going to stop her from stabbing Zebadiah to death. Nothing!

"Cali!"

Her heart was the motor of revenge, pumping pure hatred into her arm, the piston of death. Even when it didn't feel like the knife was cutting through skin. Even when the globs of blood coating her face were greenish brown. Even when the world smelled like mold and loam. Zebadiah still didn't fall.

"Cali!"

The voice sounded familiar. Chism? *Why was Chism here?* That didn't seem right. *No, wait.* Chism was trapped, wrapped up in vines from Master Poppie.

One blink of her eyes and Zebadiah Seeley was gone, a phantom that never existed.

"Cali?"

Panting, she saw Chism, mask still on his face. Favoring his right leg and covered in small cuts and bruises, he stood in front of her. He limped a step closer and said, "You did it. You saved me. And possibly the whole fucking world. You killed Master Poppie."

Master Poppie? Right. Master Poppie. Not Zebadiah Seeley, even though Cali kept looking for a man in overalls wearing a bear's head. No Zebadiah. "Awesome," came out as a raspy grunt. "You helped."

Chism smiled behind his mask, Cali could see it in his eyes. He took another step forward. She took one step back, her boot sloshing as if in a mud puddle. Not mud. A pool of malachite sap that had flowed within Master Poppie.

What was once a monstrous plant was now a small field of fibers and sludge, as if a truck carrying celery and moss had overturned. Relief gave way to a flutter in her stomach.

Did I do this? she asked herself as she took in the enormity of the devastation. Nothing was definable. She couldn't tell which shreds had been the pitcher, which mounds had been the flowers, which piles had been the stalk. The only part that remained was the tuft of long, thin leaves at the downward tip of the stalk. And it was moving. "Chism?"

"Shit! I think it might be a seed pod!"

They ran toward the twists of leaves on the ground. The leaves rippled, pushing out whatever was inside. Cali hacked at the stalk while Chism tore away the leaves to expose the plant's final secret. A football-sized nut. Cali pulled it out of the ground with ease.

"Holy shit," Chism said. "God, if we didn't catch that, we'd have to do this all over again. Now all we have to do is destroy the seed and it's all over."

Cali held the seed against her hip and started back toward the golf cart, taking one last look at the monster's remains. "Yep. It's all over."

July 2, 2002

Melody's phone buzzed in her pocket. As subtly as the forest floor would allow, she snuck away from the other six people and leaned against a tree trunk wide enough to hide her. A text from Cali: `Im glad we ran into each other. Still sorry I hid and lied.`

A bloom of warmth tickled behind Melody's chest. She typed, `Me too!!! I understand. Where r u?`

Phone buzzed. `Upstate NY in one of my dads houses. Mine now I guess. He had four more that im gonna check out. Been putting it off but now feels like time is right.`

Melody typed, `Good for you for moving forward. Max has stuff to finish in Philly then who knows where we go next. But we must meet up soon!!`

Phone buzzed. `Yes plz!!`

Melody smiled. She placed her phone back in her pocket and joined the others.

Maxwell stood beside Harold with his hands in his pockets, wearing the CSI windbreaker. He said he wore it in case they were caught by prying eyes, but she knew he thought it made him look special. Even though the early evening felt cool, it was still summer, and Harold looked out of place in his black overcoat and fedora in the middle of the woods.

Dr. Laura Covington from Zeus Chemical was questioning Maxwell. "Why are we here? This is very unorthodox."

Maxwell could be charming when he wanted to, one of the many reasons Melody loved him. Now, that charm was a necessity. Like a friend, he put his arm around Dr. Covington's shoulders and turned her toward why they were there: a twenty-foot radius of charred and salted ground, covered by blackened and shriveled plant parts. "I understand your reservations, I really do. But this is a unique opportunity. We all know that the recent outbreak of people on murder sprees while dressed like clowns was caused by a toxin in plant pollen. Hell, *you* were the one who discovered that. When Missy called to say she found what seemed like an unusual plant specimen, I thought this might be *the* plant."

"Seems like a heck of a coincidence," Dr. Covington mumbled as she crossed her arms and glared at Missy. The young woman in spandex and a sports top, Missy, blushed and then moved closer to the two lab technicians collecting samples, their gloved hands putting charred green mush into clear plastic bags. It wasn't a coincidence that Missy happened to be jogging through this part of the woods – Melody had paid her.

Earlier today, Cali had called Melody to let her know the threat was over. Cali had killed the plant called Master Poppie and then returned to the scene – gas to burn its remains, salt to keep it dead. Melody slyly asked enough questions to pinpoint the location and then searched the Zeus Chemical database for employees who lived close by. Missy Keskin, entry-level Zeus Chemical employee fresh out of college. It helped that Missy had a secret website as a foot fetish model, a secret she wanted to keep from her employer. Melody offered her ten thousand dollars cash to take the credit for finding the plant remains.

"We should be calling the police," Dr. Covington said.

"The police? What are they going to do? Call the EPA? There'd be an army of red tapers here messing up everything. If it's just a weird plant, then we'll be wasting their time. If this is *the* plant, then they'll find some bureaucratic way to fuck it up."

"It doesn't bother you that there was a fire here with the aid of some form of human involvement as well a metric ton of salt?"

"Another mystery we're poised to solve."

With an eye roll hard enough to bruise Maxwell's face had he been any closer, Dr. Covington huffed, "Be that as it may, discovering and investigating botanical organisms isn't what Zeus Chemical does."

"We can't continue to think within such limited parameters, Dr. Covington. No business venture can be successful without the ability and desire to pivot and see opportunities beyond the horizon." Arm clutching her around her shoulders, Maxwell made a sweeping gesture with his other hand as if an open horizon loomed right in front of them instead of endless trees.

Arms crossed, Dr. Covington pulled away from Maxwell and walked toward the charred plant mass to join the technicians collecting samples. Not far enough away to be unheard, she mumbled, "I liked your father better."

*

I'm sure plenty of people do, Maxwell thought after he overheard Dr. Covington's snide remark. *But I'm going to use his resources in ways he'd never imagine.*

Stern face holding the slightest of smirks, Harold looked very fatherly. "Don't worry, kid, you're doing a great job. I liked him better, too, but you got potential."

"Harold!" Melody said, her tone a fake scolding.

The older man's smile widened by a fraction. Good. He was getting comfortable.

"It's okay, Melody." Maxwell returned her smile. "I understand what he means."

Harold nodded. "So, now what?"

"We figure out who did this."

Both Harold and Melody frowned. Harold asked, "Whatdoya mean?"

Maxwell grinned; he couldn't stop himself. "Come on, Harold. Does this look natural at all? Clearly this was a very controlled burn. Not a single singe on any of the surrounding trees. Someone scorched this plant but contained it to this area. I'm curious who that someone is. Aren't you?"

Hands still in his pockets, Harold looked around. Eyebrows raised and lips pursed, he nodded, clearly impressed. "Yeah. Yeah, I kinda am."

"In the meantime, I'll have my scientists study the plant. Figure out what it is. Not sure if there's any practical use for a toxin that makes people go insane, but I want to learn more about it."

Melody shrugged. "You could use it to find a cure for the toxin's effects."

Maxwell frowned; that thought hadn't crossed his mind. "A cure?"

"Yes. Authorities found two houses in a nearby neighborhood with clowns living in them. And the house where Keith the Clown was killed is around here, too. There could be more. You're already a secret hero for turning in Keith's hard drive to the police. Here's an opportunity to be a public hero. Plus, rumor has it that Senator Manchester Albright is in police custody. He was dressed like a clown when he was mysteriously delivered to them in connection with the Monticello Theatre fire. Maybe he needs to be cured? If so, he'd be undoubtedly in your debt."

Harold nodded. "Couldn't hurt to have a state senator in your back pocket."

"Well, then that's what I'll do. Great thinking, sweety." Maxwell kissed Melody on the cheek. She was smart. He needed to let her know that more often and praise the other hundred amazing qualities she possessed. He'd take the day off tomorrow and spend it doing whatever she wanted. "Plus, developing a cure might put Dr. Covington in better spirits."

Melody chuckled. "Some people just don't like change."

"I can attest to that. Give me a second, and I'll go let her know the plan."

Maxwell walked into the twenty-foot circle of plant gunk that Dr. Covington referred to as the "hot zone," glad that he chose to wear sensible boots. The field of burnt asparagus threatened to cover his foot with every step. He marveled at the large area and wondered about the size of the plant. He paused. How did they know it was one plant? It could have been multiple plants. Were there more? That thought terrified him. So many lives were lost, as well as the community panic and paranoia, from this one plant. How many more plants were there? A question he'd pose to Dr. Covington. But when he took a step in her direction, a glint of silver close to his foot caught his eye. He had kicked something. Metal. Small. He picked up a flip-top lighter and thumbed away the muck to expose an inscription on the side.

C.L.

For the first time in two days, his brain tickled.

July 3, 2002

Cali's fist shook, rebelling. *I don't want to do this.* After a cleansing breath, she regained control of her fist and knocked on the door.

In less than a minute, it opened.

Chism.

He smiled, and Cali's heart sank. She didn't know how he'd react to seeing her. It had been thirty-six hours. They had returned the golf cart and limped back to her rental, then drove back to his apartment in post-survival silence. Her thirty-six hours had been busy, starting with a debriefing. Apparently, her earpiece had fallen out during her fight with Keith, so Mother had no idea what was happening. But she and Cali returned to the forest with "cleaners" Mother had worked with to dispose of the clown bodies and burn the remains of Master Poppie. Then twelve hours of restless sleep. She hoped Chism had spent the last thirty-six hours resting and resenting her. Instead, he gave her that damn irresistible smile and said, "Hey, partner. Come on in."

Oh, Cali didn't like the sound of that. He limped to the kitchenette and retrieved a bottle of water for her. Half of his bottom lip looked like a tiny balloon past its recommended point of inflation. Both of his nostrils were bright red with busted capillaries. The bruises didn't stop at his black eye.

"How's your leg? And face?"

He chuckled. "This? I can think of three bouts that I finished worse than this."

Cali doubted that. His too-tight, white tee shirt displaying a smiling Speed Racer in no way concealed the blooms of purple along his torso. He cracked open a bottle of water for himself. "Soooo—"

"I'm leaving Philadelphia," Cali blurted, needing to get the words out before he said anything else.

After a few gulps, he nodded and said, "Okay, cool. Hitting home base for a bit to figure out the next assignment and—"

"I'm not coming back." Hints of tears tested the boundaries of her eyes as she prayed to every god she could think of that he'd get the damn hint.

His knitting brows let her know that he was putting two and two together. "Not coming back? But... But we have a good thing going."

Cali looked away, unable to handle that look of betrayal in his eyes. She wondered which "thing" he was talking about – their relationship or her unique lifestyle. "Chism, it should be pretty obvious why I can't do this."

"Actually, it's not. You were able to handle dating me and another guy, all while working on your monster hunting. Sorry, not trying to be dick, but clearly, you can muti-task. You can hunt monsters *and* be with me. There's no need to stop either."

"You want to be a part of that?"

"Oh, hell yeah! You're all but a superhero and I'm happy you came into my life. I want to be a part of your life, Cali. Your world."

Cali wished she had her mother's "Fortitude" card right now. She needed to break up with him and leave, but the only word she could muster was, "No."

"Okay, answer me this, honestly – Are you leaving because of your monster hunting?"

The correct answer was "No." If she had said that immediately, then they would have ended, and she'd have been on her way. But damn her "wants" for trying to supersede her "needs." She wanted a relationship, to be a partner with this man, to see what the future held.

But she had hesitated too long with her answer, and Chism said, "See? It's a non-issue. Now that you have this secret off your chest, isn't it liberating?"

"Liberating? Are you kidding me? This adds more weight to the burden on my back."

Chism looked away, as if looking over a cheat sheet outside the window. He frowned and looked back. "Wait... Are you implying that I'm a burden?"

"How could you not be?" The moment those words left her mouth, they hurt Cali's heart, so she could only imagine what they did to Chism's.

The kicked puppy expression lasted only a few seconds, then he shook it off. "I helped you the other night. I helped you kill the monster, and I can help you kill more."

"Chism, I've been doing this for years."

"How many?"

"Too many."

"I have skills," Chism said. "And knowledge. Without my weird plant romance, you might not have figured out what Master Poppie truly was and how to stop it."

"Chism, you've been on organized sports teams, right? You know how it is when you get new teammates. The whole team's hindered, no matter how skilled the new people are, until they get coached up."

"Then coach me up! I'm used to that. I've trained, I've been coached. You and your mom could mold me how you see fit."

"If you fuck up in this field, you don't get benched, Chism! You get dead. I'd be worried about you nonstop. No matter how good you get, even if you end up better than me, I'd still be worried. Even if we're not hunting something, then I'd be worried something would be hunting us. Hunting you. I can't have that distraction."

"Jesus, Cali, you just called me a burden, a hindrance, and a distraction. I'm literally none of those things. I want to be an asset. I want to be supportive. I want to help. I mean, think about how your mom feels about you, yet the two of you work together."

Her mother hadn't always been around for her due to that very reason. Two years ago, Cali found her boyfriend's head on a meat hook and now Chism wanted to hang his right next to it. Talking. Smiling. Being a perfect ideal that she so desperately wanted but couldn't have. The tears flowed in unstoppable waves, but she still couldn't say the words, still not strong enough to do what she needed to do. Chin quivering, all she could do was squeak out, "Chism, please."

"Cali, I—" He stopped and looked at her, *really* looked at her. A sigh. A look to the heavens. Another sigh and he brought his eyes back to hers. With a hollow tone, he said, "I thought it over, and I can't deal with my girlfriend putting herself in constant danger. I feel I have no other choice than to make an ultimatum. Either you give up monster hunting, or you... you leave out that door and never come back."

The tears didn't stop, but they changed from self-hating anguish to bitter-sweet relief. Cali placed the unopened bottle of water on the nearest table and headed toward the door. She paused and wanted to let him know it wasn't his fault, that he would have made a great boyfriend. That he made her laugh, feel valued, comfortable, excited to try new things. "Thank you," she said, and walked out the door.

*

Cali walked in the door, her fourth time in this house over the last two years, ever since taking full ownership. She had five houses now. When she was younger, she only knew of two. The one about twenty miles closer to NYC and this one – the one tucked away in the Appalachian forests of upstate New York. The other house was homier, where she had grown up. Just as huge as this 5,000-square-foot-getaway of glass with a white, gray, and black arrangement in a post-modern configuration. The other house held a metric shit ton of happy memories, but she always liked this house better. It was a treat coming here, like a secret dessert.

The walls held all kinds of minimalist artwork, with no knickknacks on tables, counters, or shelves. A nice fireplace and an open floor plan blended living room with kitchen. The house was hidden from the rest of the world and very few people knew about it. She felt like her father was showing his true self to her whenever he had brought her here. *Hunh. I guess that's some form of epiphany, right?*

Before her epiphany established its footing, her phone buzzed. A text from Bethany. `Justins coming home today!!!! THANK YOU!!!!` God damn it, more tears.

A long hallway from the garage followed along the exterior walls, floor-to-ceiling glass on the left, crazy expensive paintings on the right. At the corner, a quaint sitting area gave access to the rest of the house.

Mother greeted her in the sitting area.

Setting her Beaujolais on the table, she stood and hurried to her daughter. "Cali? Are you okay?"

"I did what I needed to with Chism and then cried for the entire five hours from Philly to here."

Mother hugged her. It still felt weird, a hug from a woman who had been absent from her life for two decades. But it felt good, needed. "I'm sorry, Cali. I should have never pushed you to meet him."

"It's okay. You just wanted me to connect. I'm the dumbass who fell for him."

"I'm happy you admitted that I am completely blameless."

Cali snapped back, frowning. Whimsy played on her mother's face as she gently placed both hands on Cali's cheeks. "Sorry. Too soon?"

Cali shook her head and chuckled. "No... Yeah, maybe. I don't know. Anyway, how is our guest?"

Mother led Cali into the living room. On the couch sat a kid. He was playing a Gameboy. "Jacob? This is Cali."

Dallas's son. Dallas, aka Collin. Cali couldn't let Jacob know the truth, that his father was a monster. Technically, his father had been killed by a monster, so she staged a scene to match that truth. She washed what makeup she could from his face and placed his burned and broken body in Trina's garage. Just another victim of Master Poppie. Well, a victim of Keith the Clown and his cult, as the police would believe. It was easy enough for the police to connect that sicko to what was found in Trina's house and her neighbor's house.

Cali crouched in front of Jacob. "Hey."

He was just a little boy, but life had aged a certain part of him. A monster took his father away and something in his eyes told Cali that he now felt a kinship with her.

"Hi. Did you know my daddy?"

"I did. I liked him."

"Your mom said you caught who hurt him."

"I did."

He lunged off the couch and wrapped his arms around her.

Instinct told her to shove, punch, fight, but luckily her heart took control and let her know that it was a hug. So did the soft sobbing in her ear. Fighting hard to contain her tears – *how do I even have any left?* – she hugged him back.

After a couple minutes, he unwrapped his arms from her and ground the heels of his hands into his tear-reddened eyes. "Thank you."

Mother put her hand on Jacob's back and guided him away. "Okay, time to go. Let's get you to your Aunt Shirley's."

Sniffling, he glanced back to Cali and said, "I'm going to live with my aunt now. Bye."

"Bye, kid," Cali whispered back.

On her way out, Mother winked at Cali.

Once the door closed, Cali tapped away at the open laptop on the coffee table. Monitors displayed the images of the security cameras, and she watched Mother's car pulled out of the garage and down the driveway. Perfect.

Heart racing, Cali hurried to the Explorer, popped the back hatch, and grabbed a duffle bag. Still surprised by the weight, it was heavier than it looked. Unless, of course, she was just sore from getting her ass kicked all over the place.

Back through the house to the basement door. Palm scanner. Retinal scanner. The thunk thunk, thunk of titanium cylinders shifting in the wall, unlocking the door. As she descended the metal stairs, motion sensors detected her, and the lights popped on.

Her trophy room.

Dozens of pedestals set haphazardly about, each with a cube of two-inch-thick Plexiglas. All of them were empty – except for one.

Right in the middle of the room, a bear's head occupied a cube. Its human eyes followed Cali when she walked into its view. Lips snarling, it snapped its teeth.

The Killer of Devils

Cali walked up to it and leaned down to look it right in its eyes. "Good afternoon, Zebadiah. Enjoying your stay?"

More teeth gnashing. If it still had its vocal cords there'd be a roar or two, a growl at the least.

"Guess what?" Cali asked with a girlish lilt to her voice. "I finally found another monster." She unzipped the duffle bag and pulled out the football sized seed. "I *killed* another monster."

Whistling a lively tune, she sauntered over to the closest container and dropped the seed inside. Lid shut and locked, she stepped back to admire it, since it was a trophy after all.

"Looks great, don't you think? Its name used to be Master Poppie. I'll leave you two to get acquainted."

Cali started to walk away, but abruptly stopped. She snapped her fingers, suddenly remembering something, and addressed the bear-head eye-to-eye again. "Almost forgot. I decided that I'm going to start living in this house. The good news is, we can have more quality time together and I can tell you how my monster hunting is going and how I'm killing all you fuckers. One. At. A. Time."

Zebadiah responded with another gnash of his teeth, leering forward, bumping its nose against the case wall.

Cali laughed and tapped the case with her index finger. "Boop!"

She ascended the stairs. Two monsters down, and she was just getting started.

"If I'm the child of a monster, does that make me a monster?"

The Progeny of Devils series, book 1

The Truth in Their Blood

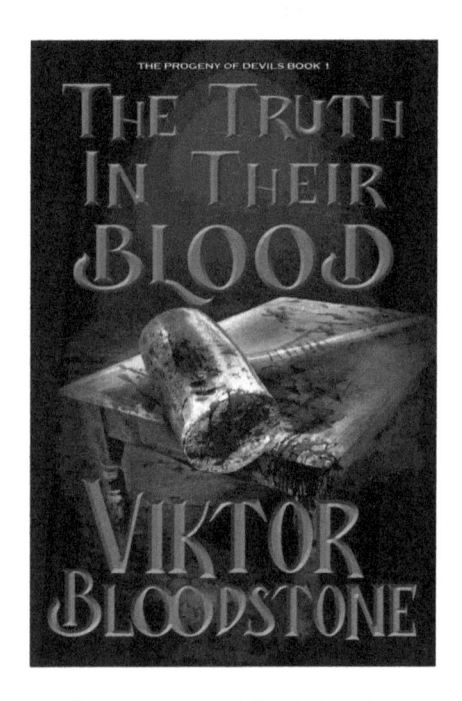

www.fortresspublishinginc.com

Want to learn about Cali's origin story?

Hammer and Blood

www.fortresspublishinginc.com

More from the *Legacy of Devils* series:

The Dream Eaters

www.fortresspublishinginc.com

Viktor Bloodstone

is

Brian Koscienski

Chris Pisano

Jeff Young

www.novelguys.com